FLAMING PASSION

"Put me down this minute!" Victoria demanded.

"I'll put you down when I'm damn good and ready," Cord retorted.

"I'm warning you, you can't treat me like this."

"What you need more than anything else, Chaps, is a good taming," he said, smiling.

"My name is not Chaps, and you're not man enough to do it."

"No?" He tossed her on the bed and leaned over her.

"No," she said, trying to get away from him, as he clasped her wrist. "Let me go!"

"I'm beginning to wonder if I can ever let you go," he replied, slowly drawing her to him, then slowly lowering his head until his warm lips touched hers.

Finally he raised his head and stared at her. "Don't ever play with me like that again, Chaps. I might take it from some women, but not from you." He kissed her again. "Never you."

BOOK SWAP
of Carrollwood
The Cascades   Tampa, Fla.

ZEBRA'S GOT THE ROMANCE
TO SET YOUR HEART AFIRE!

RAGING DESIRE   (2242, $3.75)
by Colleen Faulkner

A wealthy gentleman and officer in General Washington's army, Devon Marsh wasn't meant for the likes of Cassie O'Flynn, an immigrant bond servant. But from the moment their lips first met, Cassie knew she could love no other . . . even if it meant marching into the flames of war to make him hers!

TEXAS TWILIGHT   (2241, $3.75)
by Vivian Vaughan

When handsome Trace Garrett stepped onto the porch of the Santa Clara ranch, he wove a rapturous spell around Clara Ehler's heart. Though Clara planned to sell the spread and move back East, Trace was determined to keep her on the wild Western frontier where she belonged — to share with him the glory and the splendor of the passion-filled TEXAS TWILIGHT.

RENEGADE HEART   (2244, $3.75)
by Marjorie Price

Strong-willed Hannah Hatch resented her imprisonment by Captain Jake Farnsworth, even after the daring Yankee had rescued her from bloodthirsty marauders. And though Jake's rock-hard physique made Hannah tremble with desire, the spirited beauty was nevertheless resolved to exploit her femininity to the fullest and gain her independence from the virile bluecoat.

LOVING CHALLENGE   (2243, $3.75)
by Carol King

When the notorious Captain Dominic Warbrooke burst into Laurette Harker's eighteenth birthday ball, the accomplished beauty challenged the arrogant scoundrel to a duel. But when the captain named her innocence as his stakes, Laurette was terrified she'd not only lose the fight, but her heart as well!

Available wherever paperbacks are sold, or order direct from the Publisher. Send cover price plus 50¢ per copy for mailing and handling to Zebra Books, Dept. 2612, 475 Park Avenue South, New York, N.Y. 10016. Residents of New York, New Jersey and Pennsylvania must include sales tax. DO NOT SEND CASH.

Captive Desire

JANE ARCHER

ZEBRA BOOKS
KENSINGTON PUBLISHING CORP.

ZEBRA BOOKS

are published by

Kensington Publishing Corp.
475 Park Avenue South
New York, NY 10016

Copyright © 1989 by Nina Romberg Andersson

All rights reserved. No part of this book may be repro-
duced in any form or by any means without the prior
written consent of the Publisher, excepting brief quotes
used in reviews.

First printing: March, 1989

Printed in the United States of America

For the men of my family:
Gibson, Bryan, Jason,
J.E., Joe, James, and Dean

Part One

Victoria shook her head, still surprised, and annoyed

Chapter 1

"Your money or your life," a masked bandit commanded from astride a huge black stallion as three male passengers filed out of the El Paso to Tucson stagecoach.

"Make that your virtue," he added as Victoria Malone stepped down, her stawberry-blond hair windswept from the ride, her simple gray serge traveling suit dusty and damp, clinging to her curves. She locked pale green eyes with the man's arrogant blue stare, and he nodded in appreciation.

She looked away, glad she wasn't wearing any jewelry to attract his attention, although he seemed to have noticed her anyway, and she couldn't help noticing what a handsome desperado he was in black leather, riding a black horse. She hoped he wouldn't take the small valise she carried, for it held only writing material, a dime novel, and some personal items . . . nothing of great value to anyone but her.

Determined not to give the outlaw leader or the five masked men with him any satisfaction by showing fear or emotion, she calmly glanced around. They had been stopped by a rockslide in a narrow pass several miles west of El Paso, Texas, and were surrounded by rocky land and scrub pines. It was hot. The sun beat down on them, and she knew if she had to stand in the fierce sunlight very long her pale skin would burn. The day was quiet except for the sound of horses and buzzing insects.

Too quiet. There couldn't be much chance of being rescued by the law, for the bandits were smart enough to have chosen an isolated spot for the holdup.

"Get the strongbox," the outlaw leader commanded, cocking the rifle he had aimed at the stage-coach driver.

"That's the Silver Flame Mine's payroll," the driver protested. "They'll hang you when they catch you."

"If they catch me," the leader replied, laughing. "Get the box."

As the stage driver obeyed, the outlaw leader nodded at his companions. They quickly dismounted and began looting the stage, then took jewelry and valuables from the passengers. Since Victoria wore no jewelry, they took the small valise she held, and she didn't protest, deciding her life was worth more than the contents of the bag.

Finally, an outlaw shot the lock off the strongbox, and the masked men eagerly collected the money and stuffed it in their saddlebags.

"Okay men, mount up," the bandit leader commanded, then looked at the stage driver. "Thank the Silver Flame Mine for me, and don't move till sundown."

As the outlaws started to ride away, the leader suddenly swept Victoria into his arms, then led his band into the rocky hills nearby. Out of sight of the stagecoach, he stopped and looked into her wide green eyes.

"You must let me go!" she exclaimed, very much aware of the man's muscular arms around her, and

10

fearful of provoking him to violence. He was tall, heavily muscled, and his shirt was open just enough to reveal thick, red chest hair. Even though he wore a black hat and a black bandanna over his nose and mouth, she knew he must be handsome and, with his red hair, a fiery man.

"You're right," he agreed. "I want to keep you, but I can't. I've got to get out of here, and you'll only slow us down. If the law catches me, it won't matter that I rob from the rich to give to the poor 'cause they'll hang me anyway."

"Then you must hurry," Victoria replied, hoping he would leave as quickly as possible and not change his mind about releasing her.

"I'm called Red Duke, and I've got a hideout in the Black Range mountains in southern New Mexico. Come to me there, and I'll give you all the pleasures a woman could want . . . gold and silk and love."

"But I couldn't —"

"Here." He jerked a silver concho off his leather vest and pressed it into her palm. "This has a special design, and any of my men will recognize it. Use it to get into the hideout." He lowered his head to hers, quickly lifted his bandanna, and placed a firm, warm kiss against her lips. She shivered. Then he let her slide to the ground, took her valise from one of his men and handed it to her. "Come to me soon," he commanded loudly, his blue eyes hot, then quickly rode away with his outlaw band.

Victoria stood still, one hand to her lips, the other clutching her valise as she watched the bandits disappear over the rocks. She had never had anything so exciting or terrifying happen before in her entire twenty-one years. Red Duke. Imagine, she had just met an outlaw who claimed to be like Robin Hood. It would be fascinating to go to his hideout, to re-

11

search this bandit for one of her novels, but of course, she couldn't. It was too dangerous. Still, it was an exciting idea.

Coming to her senses, she realized she had better return to the stagecoach and let them know she was all right. She turned to go back, but suddenly a hand clamped over her mouth, an arm encircled her waist, and she was jerked backward into scrub pines and bushes. Shocked, she dropped her valise and struggled to get free, but was thrown to the ground and covered by a hard body.

Angry and frightened, she looked up into the narrowed, dark brown eyes of a man wearing a leather headband to hold back his thick, black hair. He was darkly tanned, with a lean, high-cheekboned face, a strong nose, and full sensual lips. He was wearing buckskin clothes.

A savage Indian! She had never been so frightened in her life. He was surely going to scalp her and leave her body for the buzzards. She struggled, but he was strong, holding her firmly under him.

She had to do something, but what? Suddenly she bit the savage's hand, determined to scream for help the minute he eased the pressure on her mouth. But he didn't do that. Instead, he covered her nose so she couldn't breathe, much less call for help. She struggled, trying to get free, to throw off his hand, but nothing worked. Finally, when her lungs were burning, he uncovered her nose, and she inhaled deeply.

Tears stung her eyes. She was losing hope, and yet she couldn't do that. She had to get free. If she didn't get away soon, the stagecoach might leave without her.

She lay still, renewing her strength, and noticed again how quiet it was. And how hot. A crow cawed overhead. Voices and noises drifted to them from the stagecoach. As the man's weight pressed into her, she could feel his hard muscles and his heat down the length of her. Suddenly she grew hot, feeling as if their bodies were somehow seeping together, making them irrevocably one. She caught his scent, tobacco and leather. She grew hotter yet and suddenly renewed her struggle, desperate to get away from him. But still she couldn't move.

She thought of Red Duke, wondering if he would have treated her like this. He had frightened her, but she had not felt hot and strange like she did now. Anger flashed through her at both men for abducting her. She moaned and shook her head, trying to get rid of his hand, but he held her firm, his dark brown eyes determined.

Were all her plans and dreams going to die here, now, at the whim of this wild man? Where was the stagecoach driver? Anyone?

Suddenly she heard the stagecoach roll forward as the driver called to the horses, then the coach thundered away down the rough road. She groaned, struggled valiantly, and was let up. Panting, she started to run after the stagecoach, but her captor caught her hand and jerked her back.

"Let me go, you savage!" she screamed, turning to glare at him as she tried to pull away. They were about the same height, for she was tall, about five eight, and he was of medium height for a man. But their similarity ended there, for her strawberry-blond hair and creamy skin were in sharp contrast to his dark hair and bronze skin. She quickly realized her slenderness was little match for his solid muscular body.

"You've no place to go," he replied, dropping her hand.

She rubbed her palm against her skirt to get rid of

13

the feel of him, grabbed her fallen valise and hugged it to her chest. "I'll just walk back to El Paso."

"It'll be dark soon. You don't have food or water. You wouldn't get far, even if I let you go."

"It's better than dying at your hands."

"I'm not going to kill you . . . at least, not if you do what I want."

"What do you want?" she asked cautiously, relieved he wasn't planning to kill her outright.

"You're Red Duke's woman."

"No, I —"

"Don't deny it. I saw him kiss you. I heard him tell you to meet him."

"But —"

"Red Duke's hideout is the best kept secret in New Mexico. It's kept him and his Comancheros alive. And the ones who boasted they knew where it was and went after him never came back. But you know all that."

"No, I don't. You've made a mistake."

"No mistake. You're Red Duke's woman, and you're going to take me to his hideout."

"Ridiculous!" she exclaimed, growing angry. "I never saw the man before today, and I know nothing about his hideout."

"There's no point in lying. You helped on that stage robbery, and you're one of his Comancheros. So it stands to reason you can get me into his hideout."

"For your information, Mr. —"

"Cord. No mister."

"All right, Cord. You may not have an intelligence much above that of a rattlesnake, but I believe you can understand English. Hear me. I am a dime novelist from New York City. I do not know anyone in the West. It is my first trip out here. I am doing

14

research. I do not know the location of Red Duke's hideout."

"Rattlers are smart. Thanks. You sound like you're from back East, but you're the one who's stupid if you expect me to believe you're a dime novelist. Red Duke must want you for something beside's what's under your brassy red hair."

"Brassy!" she exclaimed, indignant.

"You'd fit right into a whorehouse."

"If you're trying to anger me, it won't work."

"Did Red Duke find you in a brothel?"

"I'm not having this conversation. I'm going to El Paso." She turned away.

He jerked her back, keeping a hard hand wrapped around her forearm. She tried to pull away, but he simply dug his fingers in deeper. "You're going nowhere, Delilah. I captured you and I'm keeping you. Besides, I need you."

"My name is not Delilah. It's Victoria."

"Like the queen?"

"How interesting. Someone must have waved a book in front of your face once."

"Something like that. Well, Vicky—"

"Victoria!"

"Okay, Miss Victoria . . . it is miss, isn't it?"

"Yes, not that it will ever matter to you." She tried to wrench from his grip, but couldn't, so she kicked out at him. He easily evaded her foot.

"Be good," he said, shaking her. "You're going to take me into Red Duke's camp and help me rescue my sister."

"Your sister! A likely story. It's more believable you want to get in there to kill Red Duke and take over his territory. That's it, isn't it? You want it all for yourself."

"Are you just plain stupid?"

15

"For your information, I am a—"

"Dime novelist. Sure. Okay, lady writer, see if you can figure out this plot. Either you take me to Red Duke's hideout, or I take you to Mexico and sell you."

"Sell me?" she choked. "I am a United States citizen, an independent woman with responsibilities and rights. You can't treat me like a slave."

"A whorehouse down south should suit you. You wouldn't have to use your brain again."

"This has to be a nightmare. Outlaws. Indians. Whorehouses. It can't be real," she murmured.

"This is the West, if you hadn't noticed."

"You aren't serious about selling me, are you?"

"Damn right. Look around. You can't make it without me, and to keep me happy you're going to have to take me to Red Duke."

"And if I refuse?"

"I already told you. Mexico. Maybe I'll take you there anyway."

"Perhaps killing me right now would be kinder."

"I'm not inclined to be kind, especially not to Red Duke's woman."

"I am not his woman. I'm a—"

"Skip it. I need you, I caught you, and you're mine. I've been following Red Duke and his gang, hoping they'd lead me to their hideout, but it was only a matter of time before they spotted me. I was lucky, seeing the robbery and getting you. But Red Duke was a fool to use you in that holdup."

"He didn't use me, but if you think I'm a Comanchero you—"

"I know who you are. Now, let's get going. I've only got one horse. It's a long way to New Mexico, so we'll need to get some clothes and another horse for you."

16

"If you'll return me to El Paso, my publisher will reward you."

"I don't want money. I want Red Duke."

"But I can't help you."

"We're heading for New Mexico as soon as we get you outfitted. Now, you want to give me your word you won't try to escape and you'll ride easy, or do I tie you and throw you over the saddle?"

"You don't need to tie me. I will have to assume there is honor among thieves, so you have my word . . . for now."

"Okay, Miss Victoria. Give me your bag. Wait here while I get my horse."

As he walked into the scrub pines, she took a step toward the road. This might be the best chance she would have to escape. Then she heard the click of a gun's hammer being cocked, and hesitated.

"So your word's not worth much," Cord said from behind her. "You plan to ride tied?"

She turned around. He had a .45 aimed at her chest. "I was just . . . looking around."

"Sure." He grinned, showing even white teeth, then slid his Colt easily into the leather holster riding low on his right hip.

Victoria inhaled sharply. Where he had looked menacing before, now he looked feral, and for some reason she suddenly wondered how his teeth would feel against her skin. Shocked at herself, she pushed the thought aside. The man was an animal, nothing more.

"Come on over here, Miss Victoria."

She hesitated, realizing he was enjoying his power over her. She glanced around. It would be dark soon. If she could get away, she might get back to El Paso. But he had a pistol, he was strong, and she knew nothing about surviving in a wild land. Unfortu-

17

nately, her captor was also her savior. She must do as he said . . . for a while. Walking over to him, she stopped just short of his arm length.

"Come along," he instructed.

They walked into the scrub pines. A paint pony waited patiently and flicked its ears as Cord tied Victoria's valise to one of the saddlebags on the horse's back. He unwrapped the reins from a tree, took her arm in a tight grip, and started across the rocks toward the road.

At the edge of the dusty road, he hesitated, looking in all directions, then back at her. "Okay, get in the saddle."

"I'm not accustomed to riding."

"Does Red Duke have you drawn around in a surrey?"

"I don't know Red Duke."

"He kissed you like he knew you real well."

"It was a romantic impulse, I'm sure," she said sarcastically.

"Red Duke romantic! You say the damndest things. If I didn't know better, I could almost believe your story. Now, mount up."

"I'm not wearing a split skirt, and this isn't a side saddle."

"Damn!" Cord jerked up Victoria's skirt, showing a wide expanse of leg and petticoat, lifted her to the back of his horse, then threw himself into the saddle behind her. Pulling her against his hard chest, he headed his horse south.

"That was totally unnecessary," Victoria complained, trying to pull down her skirt to cover the absolutely unacceptable amount of leg showing and to put more room between Cord and her.

"We don't have all day to mess around, Miss Victoria, and you might as well give up trying to cover your legs. That skirt's going to be hiked up all the way to Mexico."

"Mexico! But I thought you said—"

"I'm not going to sell you. At least, not yet. I'm going to get you some gear and a horse."

"I see no need to go all the way there."

"You wouldn't, but I've got friends in Juárez. It's right across the border from El Paso. My friends will outfit us and give me information."

"I see now. You don't dare show your outlaw face in any law-abiding establishment this side of the border, do you?"

"You've got a vivid imagination, I'll say that for you."

"Look, it's not too late. If you can't go into El Paso, just leave me on the outskirts. I'll see you get money. It can be wired anywhere."

"I don't want your money. I want you, and I've got you. Now be quiet. I've got to think."

"But—"

He tighted his arms around her waist, almost cutting off her breath, then he released the pressure, still embracing her firmly. "Remember who's boss here."

She didn't say anything else, but shivered, much too aware of his muscled thighs around her hips, his corded arms around her waist, and his warm breath against her neck. Suddenly she felt hot again, much too hot. Of course, it was late May in the desert so it was natural to be hot. She just wished he wouldn't hold her so closely.

How could she ever have imagined that the reality of the West would be so harsh, so ungiving, so dangerous? Her dreams, her fantasies, everything she had read had painted a picture of romantic adventure, but she had never thought to be out of control, to be at the mercy of a savage man . . . a man so unschooled as to not even be able to understand or recognize a writer when he met one.

Not that she had published under her own name yet, but she had grown up on books and dreams and ideas, for her father had been a writer, earning a living with magazine articles then later dime novels after their introduction in 1860. Anne Stephens had made history that year when her novel *MALAESKA: THE INDIAN WIFE OF THE WHITE HUNTER* had sold three hundred thousand copies. Her father had explained that publishers had rushed to give their readers more of that type of book, and dime novels had been popular ever since.

She was sorry her mother had not lived to see her father's success as a novelist. Her mother had died in childbirth, and Victoria had been raised on milk and books. She had easily followed in her father's footsteps, learning to read and write early and then helping him with his assignments. When he had developed consumption, and his health gradually worsened, she had completed more and more of his work, not caring that she had few friends and fewer beaus, for reality could never live up to the wonderful fantasy she created in her head and read in her books.

Just after the new year of 1885, her father's doctor had recommended he move to the Southwest for the hot dry air, and since they had never been able to save much money, they had devised a plan to pay for the trip. They had created a concept for a series of novels set in the American West. Since such writers as Col. Mayne Reid, Col. Prentiss Ingraham, W.F. Cody, and Ned Buntline were having great success writing about their own experiences, this series would be based on the author traveling to the West and hearing tales and seeing sights firsthand.

Her father had insisted that her name be listed on the copyright when the series was printed, since he had explained that she needed to start establishing writing credentials of her own. His publisher had bought the series, but her father had died shortly thereafter.

She was left alone and distraught. To get over her loss and to honor her father's name, plus pay the bills, she had decided to complete the series. She had convinced the publisher to give her a chance to write the series on her own, and planned to mail in the manuscripts as she completed them.

Although she had worried about traveling alone in the West, she had not been able to imagine it being that much harder than surviving in New York City. Besides, she'd had the fantasy of herself as a great adventurer and chronicler, and the one to complete her father's dream.

She had paid off their debts by selling most of what they had, and with a small publisher's advance had bought serviceable clothes, a sturdy trunk, a small valise to carry writing material and what she thought suitable, such as medicinal ointment, to survive in the West, then had taken a ship to Galveston, Texas. From there she had made her way to San Antonio, listening to people, making notes, asking questions. And it had all been relatively uneventful, almost routine . . . until now.

She shivered, despite the heat, more aware than ever of Cord's hard body against her, of his leather and tobacco scent, of his strong, bronzed hands holding the reins in front of her. No, she could never have imagined this type of reality back in New York City.

21

Chapter 2

By the time they entered Ciudad Juárez, Victoria didn't know if she would be able to walk once she got off the horse. And the thought of ever riding again was a nightmare. She was stiff, sore, and the inside of her thighs felt rubbed raw. She ached all over, but she didn't mention her aches and pains to Cord. She didn't want him to think she was weak, for then he would only try to take further advantage of her.

As they wound their way through the dark, narrow, twisting streets of the Mexican city, she could smell rotting garbage, refuse and dead animals. Cord obviously hadn't brought her to the best part of town, but then she hadn't expected he would. Being a criminal, his contacts would naturally be in the lowest places.

During the long ride, she had thought a lot about Cord's story of a sister being kidnapped by Red Duke. Could it possibly be true? Red Duke had claimed he robbed from the rich to give to the poor. Was that true? Both men were obviously outlaws, and she had decided that only time would separate the truth from the lies. In the meantime, she would play a waiting game.

Victoria wondered how he could ever have thought she was an outlaw, too. And how could he possibly still believe she was Red Duke's woman? She didn't know how she was going to get out of her terrible situation, for now she was in a foreign country and completely lost — and at Cord's mercy. She could only hope there would soon be an opportunity to flee Cord and find her way back across the border. Once in El Paso, she would go straight to the law and report him. Then he would wish he had never kidnapped her.

But right now what worried her most, just in case she didn't escape Cord, was the fact that she truly didn't know the exact location of Red Duke's hideout. She had the concho he had given her, but other than the fact that the place was somewhere in the Black Range mountains of New Mexico, she had no better idea than Cord of its location. Would he sell her if she couldn't take him to the hideout?

Maybe. At least she had the concho, she assured herself, and she would use it if necessary for her survival. But first she would try to find a way to escape, for even though she had given her word that she wouldn't run away, she had given it under duress and didn't feel bound by it. Cord had forced her, and he deserved whatever he got.

They continued riding through Juárez. At least it was cooler now, for it was well past midnight. But she was so sore and tired she could hardly think straight, struggling with the fear and anger that constantly threatened to overwhelm her. How could Cord think he could get away with this? He must be arrogant beyond belief.

"We're almost there," he said, his voice tired. He caressed her shoulder gently with a warm hand.

"Good . . . I suppose," she replied, surprised that

23

he could sound tired or be gentle. But it was probably some outlaw trick, and she mustn't allow herself to be fooled by him.

"I want you to be nice to my friends, Victoria. They're going to do us a favor, so don't insult them."

"Why would you think I'd—"

"When we get there, either say something nice or don't say anything at all. And don't try to escape. I'm going to be watching you, and so will the other people who'll be there, and they won't be gentle if you try to run out on me."

"Guards! What kind of place is it?"

"You'll see." Cord chuckled.

It sounded ominous, and she didn't like that at all. He was probably taking her to some city hideout. No telling what kind of people lived there, or used the place to escape the law. She shivered. How could she survive? She was no match for this sort of thing. Or maybe she was overreacting to the whole situation. Perhaps this sort of thing happened frequently to women in the West, and they learned to handle guns and fight early in life so that it wasn't a problem; or they dealt with the violence and made money, or contacts, or gained experience.

Perhaps that was the way to look at it. Experience. And better than that . . . notes for her first novel. Just think how fascinated her publisher and readers would be at the description of even a single day like the one she had just experienced. There. That was the way to view the entire episode. Elements of a novel. Then it wouldn't be quite so real, or so dangerous, or so frightening. She would make some notes as soon as she was settled and rested. Taking a deep breath, she felt a little better.

Cord guided his horse down a dark street, turned down an even darker alley, then stopped near a dim light at the back of a two-storied adobe building. He got off, then lifted his arms for Victoria. She leaned down, resting her palms against his shoulders, and felt his muscles harden under her touch. For some reason the feeling caused an excited sensation to run through her, ending in the very depths of her being. But she shrugged the response away as he lifted her, then let her gently to the ground.

Pain shot upward from her feet, and her legs gave way. She sagged against him, embarrassed.

"Sorry," he said against her hair as he quickly lifted her, cradling her against his chest.

"It's not necessary to carry me," she protested as he walked toward the back door of the house.

"You really aren't used to riding astride a horse, are you?"

"No, but if you'll give me time to adjust, I'm sure I can walk."

"I should have given you a chance to rest on the way, but I was too afraid of losing you."

"Well, I'm not up to much running right now," she replied, surprised at her own humor.

"No, I guess not." He chuckled. "But I am sorry." He rapped three times on the back door.

Victoria was shocked Cord had apologized, and she wondered what new scheme had prompted him to do it . . . something to make her more vulnerable to him, no doubt. She reminded herself that she must not trust him, above all things, no matter what he said, or did. And he shouldn't trust her, either.

Cord rapped on the door again and shifted her so she was nestled more closely against his chest. She sighed, wishing she could just relax and let him take care of everything until she felt better. It would be so good to be able to trust him, to . . . what was she thinking?

As he started to knock again, the back door opened. A short, plump form stood silhouetted against the light inside.

"Cord, *mi amigo!*" a woman's sultry voiced exclaimed.

"*Buenas noches*, Teresa," Cord replied, bending down to kiss the woman's upturned face.

They spoke to each other in rapid Spanish, and Victoria could only listen like an eavesdropper to the cadence of the words which held no meaning for her. She was surprised to learn Cord spoke another language. Was he Mexican? And who was this woman? She hated not knowing what was going on and moved uneasily in his arms.

"Sorry, Victoria," Cord said, interrupting his conversation to glance down at her, "but Spanish is quicker and easier for Teresa, although she understands English." Looking back at Teresa, he added, "This is Victoria. She's going to help me find Alicia."

"*Bueno*," Teresa replied. "It is good to meet you, Victoria. Please come inside."

"Thank you," Victoria answered. "I think you can set me down now, Cord."

He stepped across the threshold and lowered her gently, watching her closely as she tested her legs. She nodded, and he let her go. She was still sore, but she could walk now. Glancing around, she saw that they were in a large, immaculate kitchen, and several Mexican women were busily cooking, washing and cleaning.

Victoria looked more closely at their hostess. Teresa was in her thirties, her hair was shiny black with a single silver streak running through the right side, and her black gaze was clearly curious. She was elegant, beautiful and cool. She was also dressed in the most sensual costume Victoria had ever seen, for the gown was of deep purple satin and fitted Teresa's high, rounded breasts like a second skin, while the skirt was tucked up on one side to reveal lacy white petticoats and a plump leg in black mesh stockings.

When Teresa noticed Victoria staring at her leg, she smiled and dropped the skirt, winking at Cord. "Are you sure you brought your prim miss to the right place, *mi amigo*?"

Cord laughed. "I wouldn't trust her with anybody but you, Teresa. She's Red Duke's woman, and it's all an act."

"I am not Red Duke's woman," Victoria insisted. "Perhaps you can make him see reason. I'm a dime novelist from New York City. I'm doing research, and I just happened to be on that stage Red Duke robbed, and—"

Teresa laughed. "She is good, Cord. I would almost believe her except she is much too pretty to be anything so dull as a writer. With that color of hair and skin, she could make her fortune fast in this city."

"Or with Red Duke," Cord added.

"I have heard he is a handsome man," Teresa replied.

"You've heard?" Cord chuckled. "I'd say you've more than heard, Teresa."

She smiled mysteriously. "I never talk about my patrons. You know that."

"Do you run a restaurant or something?" Victoria asked, looking about the kitchen.

Teresa glanced at Cord. "She does not know?"

"No. But don't worry. She's not new to this game."

"Do you want her in one of the upstairs rooms?"

"Yes. And give her some hot food and a bath."

"Do you want your regular room or—"

"My regular."

"*Bueno*. The ladies will be very glad to see you again. It has been too long."

"It always is."

"Then, I will take Victoria to her room now."

"Cord," Victoria interrupted, "could I have my valise?"

"I'll get it when I pick up my saddlebags."

"Thank you."

"And, Victoria," Cord added, "remember, don't give them any trouble. You wouldn't get far."

"I'll remember, Cord."

"Come along, *mi dulce*," Teresa said, picking up an oil lamp and starting toward a narrow staircase leading upstairs from the kitchen.

Victoria followed, feeling uneasy. There was something not quite right about the place, but then that was probably because it was a boardinghouse for outlaws. She would just pretend that everything was all right until she could get some food, a bath and some rest. Then she would see about escape.

Upstairs, Victoria followed Teresa down a long, dark hall. Passing door after door, she could hear murmurings, sighs and an occasional cry from behind the closed doors. Outlaws obviously had nightmares when they slept, she decided, and well they should. Finally, Teresa opened a door and indicated Victoria should precede her.

Stepping inside, Victoria glanced around while Teresa lit a lamp by the bed. An imported carpet in a rose and vine pattern covered much of the highly polished wood floor. Heavy velvet, rose-colored drapes covered the window, and two original oils in gilded frames hung on one wall. A huge mirror, framed in gold, had been placed on the wall opposite the bed, while a dressing table with its own mirror

28

held crystal bottles of perfume, face powders and oils. But what dominated the area was the huge tester bed with draperies of rose, pink and beige.

Victoria was astonished by the luxury and decided that outlaws must make a lot more money than she had ever imagined, especially if they could afford a boardinghouse like this. When she thought of Red Duke, she wondered if he was living in the same luxury, robbing the rich to feather his own nest instead of the poor he claimed to champion.

"Is the room satisfactory?" Teresa asked.

"Certainly," Victoria replied, still looking around, hardly knowing what to say or think. One of the paintings caught her attention, and she walked over to it. She had thought the picture was of roses and vines entwined, but now that she looked closer, it was clear that a woman's nude body was the real theme of the painting. The roses and vines were simply twined in the hair and around the limbs of the reclining figure. Somewhat shocked, she glanced hastily away.

"Do you like the painting?" Teresa asked.

"I've never seen anything quite like it before."

"I know. You must be as tired as I am of the familiar portraits of naked women lying on velvet or satin. I cannot tell you how many of those I have seen in the West."

"They must be popular."

"But no style, no class."

"I guess not," Victoria agreed, deciding not to look closely at the other painting just yet.

"You are obviously a woman of class, so I knew you would appreciate this room," Teresa continued, motioning toward the bed.

"As tired and sore as I am from riding, I have to admit this luxury looks good, although it's not quite

29

what I'm used to."

"I have heard Red Duke's hideout has all the comforts of home, or a place like this."

"I'm not Red Duke's woman."

"A smart woman to keep her tongue still. Red Duke must value you highly."

Victoria gave up. "To tell you the truth, I'm starving and I'd really love a hot bath."

"Oh, forgive me, *mi dulce*. You are so interesting I forget everything. *Un momento*, and you will have everything you desire." Teresa smiled conspiratorially, then quickly left.

Victoria went straight to the other painting and caught her breath. Where the first picture had been of a nude woman, this one was of a completely undressed man twined in thorns and roses so red they looked black. She had never seen a naked male before, and her eyes were drawn to the part of him that she had heard whispered about, the part that was supposed to bring a woman pain or pleasure. It was so large she couldn't imagine . . . no, she couldn't imagine at all.

And then she thought of Cord's face, of his sinewy arms around her, his powerful thighs, and a hardness against her that she had not understood before. She blushed. Had he wanted her?

She spun away from the painting and walked briskly across the room. She was in even more trouble than she had thought. What if Cord decided to force his attentions on her? It was just like a lurid novel she had read once, only she had always been a little confused, for nothing had been described, only alluded to. But the gentleman in the book had definitely been lusty and unable to control his needs. Was Cord like that?

For the first time in her life, Victoria wished she

knew more about men, that she had gossiped more with girlfriends, or had spent more time with beaus. Instead, she had immersed herself in books, ideas and dreams, and they didn't seem to be of any help to her now.

What was she going to do?

She paced the room, thinking. Then she stopped, glancing at one painting, then the other. She blushed and sat down on the bed. How naive of her! She wasn't in an outlaw boardinghouse. She was in a bordello, a brothel, a very high-class whorehouse. And Cord had brought her here!

But then, that's what he thought she was . . . Red Duke's woman and a lady of the evening. How dare he! She didn't know what to think to say, to do. What if he came in here expecting to take his pleasure with her? No, there were plenty of other women here, if this was indeed a bordello, and those women would be willing. She wasn't

Certainly not. And yet, she thought of his hands, of his heat, of his hard, compact body, and of his lithe movements. She could suddenly imagine him with a woman, like a sleek panther, ready to please, ready to pleasure, ready to—

There was a knock at the door. Victoria jumped up and smoothed her skirt as if afraid someone could read her thoughts. She didn't know what was happening to her mind, but she couldn't continue to think this way. It wasn't right.

"Come in," she finally managed to say.

The door opened, and a tall woman, big boned and blond, stepped inside, smiled, then gestured behind her. Several Mexican women hurried inside, carrying a hip tub and buckets of hot and cold water. As they set up the bath, the woman in charge looked closely at Victoria.

31

"My name's Bethanne. Miss Teresa sent me in as how I can speak English. I'm American," she finished proudly.

"Hello, Bethanne. I'm Victoria."

"You're sure pretty."

"Thank you. So are you."

"Back home I was nothing but a girl with a hungry mouth, and plain. But here I'm special."

"You look very healthy, too," Victoria added, trying to be friendly, since she didn't know who might be persuaded to help her later. Besides, Bethanne did look healthy, for she was pink-cheeked, with blond hair and blue eyes, large breasts squeezed into a low-cut, blue cotton dress, and large, square, capable-looking hands. She also looked like she had worked hard all her life.

"I am that, now I eat regular. I don't mind the work, not even on my back. It's better'n what I ever had back home."

"I'm glad to hear it," Victoria replied, thinking that if Bethanne thought she had come up in the world, she hated to think what her life must have been like before, for the young woman could not have been more than eighteen.

"Thanks." Bethanne turned her attention back to her crew and, with a few quick movements of her capable hands, had them finished and out the door. Going over to the dressing table, she selected a fragrant oil and poured a generous amount into the bath water, then stacked several fluffy white towels, a washcloth and scented soap near the tub. "There you go, all done." She smiled.

"Thank you," Victoria replied, waiting for her to go, but she didn't.

"You look tired, ma'am," Bethanne said, walking over to Victoria.

"I am."

"You don't have to fret about nothing now. Leave it all to me."

"Leave what to you?"

"Why, I'm to be your maid long as you're here."

Victoria took a step backward. She knew it was common for ladies to have maids who undressed them, bathed them and did their hair, but she had never had one. And she wasn't sure she wanted one now. "Thank you, but that's not necessary."

Bethanne's lower lip trembled. "You don't like me."

"Oh, no. It's not that. I just don't need any help. I'm capable of taking care of myself."

"Miss Teresa'll be mad, and I'll get beat if you send me away."

Victoria hesitated. Could that be true? Yes, she could believe it. "Well, why don't you help me undress."

Bethanne's eyes brightened. "Oh, thank you, ma'am. I'll be ever so gentle."

And she was, carefully unbuttoning Victoria's dusty, stained, gray traveling suit, removing her black boots, then her petticoats. But when Bethanne started on the chemise, Victoria held up a hand.

Confused, Bethanne stopped. "Did I hurt you?"

"No. But that's enough, I think."

"Let me get this corset off you, then you can breathe right again." She quickly had it off, and before Victoria quite realized what had happened, she stood nude in the bedroom. Bethanne looked her over like a prize racehorse. "I can see why that Cord was so all fired to get you here and get you cleaned up. With a body like yours, I wouldn't never have to work hard again."

Victoria quickly stepped into the tub, sat down

33

and was relieved to be covered by water.

But Bethanne wasn't done. She stepped closer, eyes narrowed. "I heard you're Red Duke's woman. You must sure know some tricks to keep that man happy. Would you show me some later? I'm doing my best to work my way up to be one man's special lady."

"I'm sorry, but —"

"Sure. You'd be a fool to give away your tricks of the trade, but you can't blame me for asking."

"I'd be glad to help you, Bethanne, but the only thing I know about is writing . . . you know, describing things."

"Oh, talking! Is that it? Hey, would you learn me some fancy words men like?"

Victoria once more gave up. "If I have time, I'd be happy to teach you some words, Bethane."

"Oh, thank you, ma'am. You don't know how much this means to me 'cause I never got much schooling."

"I'm sorry you didn't. I'll do what I can. But, for now, I'd just like to be alone and soak awhile."

"Right. Thinking up some fancy words for that Cord. You're a smart one. I'll get some food up here after a while and help you dress."

"Thank you."

As Bethanne quietly shut the door behind her, Victoria closed her eyes, then snapped them open. She'd better lock the door to her room fast, if she could.

Chapter 3

Awakened from a sound sleep, Victoria quickly burrowed under the covers away from a hand that was shaking her. "No," she murmured sleepily. "Let me alone." She heard a husky chuckle, and the hand pursued her. She tried to wiggle away, but the cover was suddenly jerked off her.

"Wake up, Victoria. It's time to—damn! Red Duke's a lucky man," Cord finished gruffly.

She opened her eyes to see Cord leaning over the bed, his brown eyes dark with hunger as he looked at her body. She quickly tried to cover herself, but he was quicker, tossing the covers off the bed.

"No point in acting shy, Victoria. Men have seen more than I'm seeing."

She glanced down, terribly embarrassed as she realized what she was wearing, where she was, and why Cord was staring at her. Her own clothes were in the trunk whisked away on the stagecoach, and Bethanne had dressed her in a sheer silk negligee, which was very different from the cotton nightgown Victoria was used to wearing. The negligee was full-length and cut low, with lace around the bodice and hem, but the pale green silk revealed almost more than it concealed.

35

"You should be gentleman enough to turn your back," she finally said sharply.

"But I'm no gentleman, and this is just whetting my appetite."

"Will you stop insulting me and get out so I can dress?"

"If you think what I'm doing is an insult, then you're not the Victoria I thought you were." He finally looked at her face and was surprised to see the anger and embarrassment. "You put on a damn good show, but I know better."

"Just get out, will you?"

"There's some breakfast on the dressing table, and your gray clothes have been cleaned. Hurry up and dress 'cause I'm going to buy you something new to wear."

"I can hardly wait if what I'm wearing is any example."

"No, much as I'd like to cart you all over the country wearing that, your skin wouldn't last long in the sun."

Victoria sat up and folded her arms across her breasts, determined that Cord see as little as possible. She was surprised to notice that she felt a strange excitement deep inside, and she was growing more flushed the longer he looked at her. She glanced at the paintings, thinking of Cord's body and how it would appear nude, then hurriedly glanced away. What was wrong with her? She had never had thoughts like these before. No other man had ever affected her this way. Cord was bad for her, and she wished desperately that she was with Red Duke, for he seemed to be more of a gentleman.

"Well, are you going?" she finally asked, feeling chills run up and down her spine.

"I thought you might invite me to eat with you."

36

"Go ask Teresa or somebody else in this house. I'm sure they'd be glad to oblige."

He grinned. "So, you finally admit to knowing we're in a brothel."

"After a while, it's hard to miss."

"You don't have to be cold, Victoria," he said, striding across the room and sitting down beside her. His thigh pressed against hers, and his heat began to penetrate her flimsy gown. She moved away, and he put an arm around her shoulders, drawing her against his solid chest. "I admit I want you, even if you are Red Duke's woman. I can pay, if that's what you want."

"I don't want to be paid."

"No? What do you want, then?" He ran a hand through her long, tossled hair. "I've been wondering what your hair would look like unbound since the first moment I saw you. A man could lose himself in it." He buried his face in the long tresses, then looked at her. "You smell like roses."

She jerked away and stood up, her heart racing. He was enticing her to stay with him, to know just what it would feel like to have his hands on her, his lips against her, his hardness—she stopped the thoughts. "I think you'd better leave."

"I suppose I'd better, 'cause if we finish what we start, we'll never get done what we need to do today. Meet me downstairs as soon as you're dressed."

After Cord was gone, she sat down on the bed, her heart racing. He was a dangerous man, and she had better be more careful around him. It was now obvious he wanted her, even in a house full of beautiful, desirable, willing women. She had to admit it was flattering in an odd way, but at the same time frightening. She couldn't depend on him to control himself, since he was no gentleman. Would it have been different with Red Duke?

She would have liked to simply go back to bed and forget everything that was happening to her; but she knew Cord would be back for her, and this time he wouldn't be in such a good mood. Walking over to the tray, she was pleased to see fresh orange juice and coffee, but a little dismayed to see several tamales. She had been introduced to them in San Antonio, but she couldn't imagine eating them for breakfast.

Nevertheless, she had to fill her stomach. After drinking the orange juice, she took the corn husk off a tamale, then cut off a small bite with her fork. It was still warm, surprisingly sweet, and delicious. She greedily ate the rest, then drank her coffee. She was beginning to feel human again, after her wonderful bath, long night's sleep and breakfast. She even felt like she could face Cord and whatever he had planned for her, if she just didn't have to ride a horse.

She would simply have to be firm with him. Of course, since she was the one kidnapped, she was not sure just how much power she had over him. On the other hand, he obviously wanted to touch her body, and maybe that would give her a power all its own. She might have to use that power to come out of this alive and free.

Of course, this could have been a problem with Red Duke too. As much as he claimed to be a gentleman, he might not have wooed her and might have treated her as a common trollop available to any man. But then Red Duke hadn't taken her, so she didn't really know how he would have behaved. But Cord had, and she had to live with the consequences.

She didn't ring for Bethanne when she was ready

to dress, even though she knew the maid would be disappointed. But she had been dressing herself all her life, and she could do it more quickly and easily. Besides, she could almost feel Cord's impatience, and she didn't want to anger him.

After dressing in her gray serge traveling suit, she was surprised to feel almost overdressed and shook her head in wonderment at her reflection in the mirror over the dressing table. Being with Cord was changing her, and faster than she could have imagined. She brushed her hair with a silverbacked brush, then pulled her long, thick strawberry-blond hair back into a neat chignon.

Satisfied that she was as well armored against Cord as she could be, she left her room, closing the door solidly behind her, but knowing it wouldn't lock. She had found that out the night before, much to her dismay.

She started down the hall in the direction she had come from the night before, noticing that it was now silent in the house, nothing like it had been. She blushed at her innocence of the previous night. How could she have been so naive? But then books were her forte, not fancy ladies.

"Miss Victoria!" Bethanne called, hurrying from the other end of the hall. "You're dressed!"

"I didn't want to bother you. I knew you'd be busy, and Cord's waiting."

Bethanne stopped beside Victoria, looked her up and down, then said, "You did okay. I'd have done your hair fancier."

"Another time, all right?"

"Really?"

"Of course."

"Thanks. Tonight. Be sure and wait for me." She grinned, then hurried into one of the bedrooms.

Victoria shook her head, still surprised Bethanne was so anxious to be her maid, then continued down the hall, carefully retracing her steps of the night before. When she came to the staircase, she was quite pleased with herself for remembering her way around after being so tired.

She walked down the stairs and into the kitchen. Once more it was busy, with several Mexican women cooking, washing and cleaning. Cord was sitting at a heavy, wooden table, drinking coffee and talking in low tones with Teresa. As if feeling Victoria's presence, he suddenly glanced up, and his eyes darkened with what she was beginning to realize was his passion for her.

"Good morning," she said, smiling at Teresa.

"*Buenas tardes,*" Teresa replied, laughing.

"It's afternoon," Cord explained.

"I slept that long?" Victoria asked.

"You needed it," Teresa replied. "You look much more rested today."

"Thank you. It was a long, grueling ride," Victoria said, looking accusingly at Cord.

"All my fault," he agreed, and stood up. "We're going to get Victoria some riding clothes, but we'll be back by this evening."

"*Bueno,*" Teresa agreed. "I will look for you then."

When they stepped outside, Victoria was surprised and pleased to note that this area of town was not nearly as disreputable as she had imagined on her first trip through. Nevertheless, it was not an area where ladies would stroll, and not a place where she would want to walk alone.

Cord led her to a small surrey, helped her up, then drove down the alley until they came to a wide, dusty street. As he turned onto the road, she was careful to watch, mentally mapping the street and buildings as

40

he drove past establishments with signs advertising different types of merchandise for sale. Not far away, he stopped in front of a dry goods store.

Helping her from the surrey, he let her body slide down the length of his, and when she glanced into his brown eyes, they had darkened with passion. Experiencing a sudden heat deep within, Victoria quickly turned away, determined not to let him affect her.

They walked silently into the dry goods store, which was large and stuffed with a variety of merchandise, much of it with a distinctive Mexican flavor, but some of it obviously American, Spanish, or European. While Victoria glanced around, amazed at the diversity of items, Cord talked rapidly in Spanish to a plump woman with iron-black hair and wearing a severe black dress with a white apron. A man, equally severely dressed, watched from behind a counter.

A short time later, Cord walked over to Victoria and said, "I want you to pick out some comfortable, protective riding clothes, boots and a hat. And, remember, you're going to be riding astride, so a split skirt or even pants would be best. I've told them to give you whatever you want, and I'll be back soon to pay for it."

"Where are you going?" She was surprised to feel a little afraid and uncomfortable at the idea of being left alone in the unusual store with people who didn't speak her language.

"I'm going down the street to buy you a horse. And, Victoria, don't try to run away. I've told them you're a nervous bride, and if you try to leave to stop you."

"You didn't! They wouldn't!" But she started doubting her own words the moment she spoke them

41

and glanced at the woman, then the man. The proprietor laid a Colt .45 on the counter with narrowed eyes. Her gaze returned to Cord. "This is shocking! How can they do such a thing?" she demanded.

"This is Mexico, Victoria, and here you're my woman. I'll be back in a minute."

She watched him walk out of the store in stunned amazement, then glanced back at the couple. They watched her closely. She supposed he had bribed them, or threatened them with horrible consequences if she wasn't there when he got back. In fact, if the truth were known, they probably recognized him as Cord the vicious outlaw and were terrified not to do as he said.

Well, she might as well get some clothes out of the deal. If she escaped, she would need something more serviceable than what she was wearing, which was suitable for stage travel but not any wild riding.

She glanced around. Cord had said to get a hat. She would probably be better off with the biggest one she could find, since it would offer her the most protection. And gloves. She began to rummage around in the store. High leather boots would be best. A long-sleeved shirt, a split skirt. And chaps. She had read about the leather gear called chaps that was worn to protect a cowboy's legs from being cut by brush while chasing Longhorns. She could certainly use a pair of those. And maybe she should even get a pistol, if they would let her have one.

She discovered that she liked the colorful, patterned clothes of Mexican style, and began to select those for a costume which she could just imagine a heroine in her book wearing. Of course, her choice of clothing would appear outrageous in New York City, but here it seemed delightfully free from the constraints she suddenly realized she usually wore.

When she had picked out what she wanted, she went behind a screen and tried it on. Satisfied, she walked out to view herself in a mirror. Cord was just walking into the store and stopped, then stared, as if he couldn't believe what he was seeing. Finally, he started laughing, so long and hard that she became furious.

Turning around, she looked at herself in the mirror. She was dressed all in black, with white swirls embroidered over the shirt and skirt. A huge sombrero, again black with white swirls decorating its rim, hid most of her head, and she had to admit it was a little big. The black, leather boots were comfortable, but the black chaps, studded with silver conchos and dangling leather strips, were hot and heavy and didn't seem to fit over the split skirt.

She turned around and looked at herself from the back, becoming more irritated by Cord's laughter all the time, especially when the Mexican couple joined him. But she had to admit, she did look a trifle overdone. Perhaps she hadn't made the best of choices, but she wasn't going to admit it.

"Victoria," Cord choked, his laughter finally beginning to subside. "I don't know when I've seen anything so outlandish. Damn, but you're funny. You did that on purpose to get back at me, didn't you?"

"No."

"No?" He started laughing again.

"Okay. You don't like what I picked out, then you do better."

"It's just that you're all dressed up for a Mexican fiesta, but it's totally wrong for the desert."

"How was I to know? I like this."

"All right. I'll buy it for you, but not the chaps. Those you're never going to need. Chaps. That's a good name for you. I was getting tired of saying Victoria. It's too long. So from now on, you're Chaps."

"Think again," she said coldly, and hurried behind the screen to remove the offending clothes.

Still chuckling, Cord, quickly picked out a split skirt in soft natural-colored leather, a red cotton shirt, a pair of brown leather boots, silver spurs and a tan hat. "Hey, Chaps, try these on," he called, and tossed them in to her.

"Thanks," she replied dryly, "but it's Victoria."

When she came out dressed in Cord's selection, he nodded in approval, and she had to admit the clothes were much more comfortable and looked more appropriate for riding in the desert or in the mountains. Still, she was glad she was getting the Mexican fiesta clothes, too.

"Do those fit okay?" he asked, looking at her critically.

"Yes, but the skirt is too short."

"Teresa'll see that it's let out. By the way, I bought you a horse, but I don't know if anything can compare to your Mexican finery."

"Only if it's black and white," she retorted, and his laughter followed her as she walked back behind the screen.

While Cord paid for her new wardrobe, she redressed in her own clothing, glad to be back in something she understood. Her mistake had been terribly embarrassing, and Cord had only made it worse by laughing. She was angry with him, and she desperately wanted to be far away from him, but, so far, he hadn't given her any opportunity to escape. However, maybe now that she had suitable clothes and a horse, she could find a way to return to El Paso.

Cord was holding several brown-paper wrapped

packages when she came out, and he smiled. She ignored the smile, instead handing the second set of riding clothes to the Mexican woman, who wrapped them. Picking up the packages, she gave Cord a frosty glare, and he chuckled as they left the store. Outside, he threw the packages into the surrey, helped her up, then clicked to the horse.

"Where is the pony you bought?" Victoria inquired.

"They'll deliver it to Teresa's place."

"That's convenient." Secretly, she figured he had stolen it, or bought a stolen mount. She just hoped she wouldn't be labeled a horse thief on the American side of the border. Life with Cord was getting more dangerous by the moment.

"I'm going to drive you around and show you some of Juárez. We can eat at one of my favorite restaurants. Then we'll retire for the night. I'd like to leave tomorrow at first light. The longer my sister is in Red Duke's clutches, the harder it'll be for her."

"Do you really expect me to believe that kidnapped sister story?"

"Yes. It's true."

"Maybe it is, and then again, maybe Red Duke doesn't have her at all."

"Chaps, when you've been in the West long enough, you'll know how to size up a person."

"And I suppose you're an expert on the subject?"

"Let's say I've dealt with Red Duke's kind before, and I know what he's capable of."

"No doubt you tried to steal their money, too."

"Damn it, Chaps! I'm trying to be reasonable with you, but you're so all-fired stuck on that man you can't see what's as plain as the nose on your face."

"You can believe what you want to believe, and nothing I say is going to change your mind."

"Damn! I'm taking you back. You can forget doing any sightseeing."

"Good. The less time I spend in your company, the better."

A cold silence settled between them, and Cord drove them quickly back to Teresa's house. Victoria flounced inside, and Cord carried in her packages. He handed them to Teresa, gave Victoria a long, angry look, then left.

"You had a fight?" Teresa asked.

"He's impossible."

"So much man, yes?"

"Too much man, yes!" Victoria agreed. "And a man I don't want."

Teresa chuckled. "You are blinded by Red Duke. Cord is a better man, not as showy or flashy, I admit, but a much better man."

"Hardly!

"If I am not mistaken, you are upset because you are attracted to Cord."

"I'm not."

"He wants you, and I have known Cord many years. He always gets what he wants. Why fight what you both desire?"

"But Cord wants to destroy Red Duke," she said, trying to get information from Teresa.

"That is a matter for men. For the moment, let us think of happier things."

"What things?"

"Would you like to make Cord regret his anger with you today?"

"Yes."

"Then, why not let Bethanne dress you tonight. You could come downstairs to the parlor. There will be men. Oh, such men. And their eyes will be all for you. Cord will burn with jealousy. He will be able to

46

think of nothing but besting all the others to gain you."

"Would it make him hurt?"

"If you deny him, certainly."

"Good." Victoria grinned wickedly, her eyes glinting with satisfaction. "He laughed at me today. But I'll have the last laugh. Tonight."

Watching Victoria's expression, Teresa chuckled softly.

"Please tell Bethanne to do her best, or, in this case, her worst," Victoria said.

"I will. In the meantime, why do you not take a hot bath, then a nap. I will send up a delicious supper. When Cord returns, hot and tired, you will be waiting."

"Only, I'll be smiling at other men."

"*Sí*. And they'll be smiling at you."

Chapter 4

Several hours later, Victoria was standing down-stairs in the parlor, a glass of champagne in one hand, a crimson rose in the other, with five gentlemen grouped around her. Teresa nodded at her from across the room, and she smiled in response, glancing around at the exquisitely appointed room and the richly gowned women who graced it, each on the arm of a well-dressed man.

Earlier she had been oiled, massaged, bathed, perfumed and dressed in the sheerest of silk underwear, the tighest of corsets, then squeezed into a red satin gown with a plunging neckline and a skirt that was pulled into a bustle in back, creating a drapery effect in front. Red silk roses were nestled into the bustle and at the plunging point of the neckline, and fresh ones were tucked into her strawberry-blond hair, now piled high on her head, with three curls left dangling to one shoulder.

When Bethanne had led her to a mirror after dressing and coiffing her, Victoria had been absolutely amazed at the difference in herself. She had never imagined she could look so pretty, so elegant, or so sensual, for she had always considered herself a bookworm, relying on intelligence and dreams

48

rather than on physical charms.

She knew the outer transformation in her appearance should have shocked her, or at least have made her feel uncomfortable, but instead she had been pleased, especially since she wanted to make Cord jealous and angry. Teresa had insisted that Cord would do whatever Victoria wanted, looking as she now did, but she wasn't so sure. Cord was a tough, mean outlaw, and he was probably used to having or taking any woman he wanted.

She could hardly wait to make notes once she got back to her room. Cord had brought up her valise containing her writing material, and before she went to sleep, she intended to fill several pages with images and impressions of the West since Cord had kidnapped her. She had never dreamed reality could be so fascinating. And all would be well, if she could just escape when she wanted. But that was another matter, and one she didn't want to examine too closely at the moment.

Nodding to the men around her, she listened to soft piano music, smelled expensive perfume, and saw cigarette smoke spiraling upward. The beautiful women in the room laughed in sultry tones and were responded to by the deep voices of men speaking Spanish. If she hadn't known better, it would have been easy to imagine herself at some exotic party in the home of an upper-class Mexican family.

Of course, the parlor had more mirrors than might be normal, and it definitely had a great deal of plush, velvet furniture in a deep crimson color. There was also an overabundance of crystal glasses on mirror trays which were constantly being carried back and forth from the kitchen as they were emptied and refilled. And there certainly was a lot going on upstairs that probably didn't occur nearly so frequently in family homes.

She smiled to herself, thinking how much her attitudes were changing. At one time she would have been shocked to be dressed as a lady of the evening, standing in a bordello's parlor, and drinking champagne with customers. And, come to think of it, she was pretty shocked, but also intrigued. Being with Cord was definitely altering her, but whether for better or worse, she had yet to decide.

"More champagne, señorita?" one of the dark-haired, dark-eyed men asked, his eyes straying to the smooth, creamy skin exposed by the décolletage of Victoria's gown.

"Yes, thank you," she replied, feeling a bubbling warmth spreading throughout her. She liked the sparking wine, and laughed, a low, tinkling sound which delighted her admirers.

As her glass was exchanged for a full one, another man asked, "Which of us will you choose for the night?"

Victoria smiled seductively at them, looking from one to the other, as if trying to make a decision, then pouted slightly, absolutely amazed at her simulated coquettishness. "How could I possibly make such a decision? You are all equally handsome."

"She's already made her decision," a stern male voice interrupted.

Victoria looked up to see Cord striding toward them. He no longer wore buckskins, but instead had put on a black suit, white shirt and black string tie. Gone, too, was the leather headband. Instead of Indian, he now looked like the Spanish grandees around him, and it was quite a surprise. But she had also never seen him so angry. His dark brows were pulled together in a straight line across the bridge of his nose, his mouth was tight, and his brown eyes were a blazing black.

He stopped by the group, narrowed his eyes at the men, then wrapped a strong, tanned hand around the bare flesh of Victoria's upper arm. "And she's coming with me now."

"Cord, really," she complained, trying to pull away from him.

He simply tightened his grip and pulled her toward him. "What are you drinking?"

"It's none of your business!" she replied, starting to become angry herself. He didn't own her!

"If I'm not buying it, you're not drinking it." He jerked the crystal glass out of her hand and sent it flying across the room. It shattered in the fireplace, and for a moment all sound stopped in the room. Everyone looked at Cord and Victoria, smiled knowingly, then went back to their conversations.

"That was quite unnecessary, Cord," she said stiffly. "And I've had enough of your uncivilized behavior. Now leave me alone while I talk to these gentlemen." She turned her back on him and smiled disarmingly at the men, who had taken several steps back and were looking uncertainly at Cord.

"These gentlemen have better things to do. Don't you, men?" Cord turned steely eyes on them and flipped back the front of his black coat, exposing a Colt .45 tucked into his belt.

The men nodded, and one said, "We will talk with you later, Victoria, when you are available."

"But—" she began, as the men melted away. She turned furious eyes on Cord. "How dare you do that to me?"

"That's not all I'm going to do." He swept her into his arms, knocking the rose from her hand, threw her over a shoulder, and calmly marched up the front stairs, amid chuckling and laughter.

Victoria had never been so embarrassed in her life, but she didn't struggle at all, determined not to be even further humiliated by showing how ineffectual she was in dealing with Cord, or by showing any more of her legs than was already being exposed by her most undignified position. And she hated to admit it, but she had asked for it. She had set out to anger Cord, and she had. However, she had never dreamed he would react so strongly, making her angry, too.

As soon as they were on the second floor, she hissed, "Put me down this minute!"

"I'll put you down when I'm damn good and ready."

"I'm warning you, you can't treat me like this."

"What you need more than anything else in your life, Chaps, is a good taming."

"My name is not Chaps, and you're not man enough to do it."

"No?" He stopped in front of a room, turned the door knob, and carried her in, slamming the door behind them. He tossed her on the bed. Her carefully coiffed hair came tumbling down to fall in swirls around her face and arms, her skirt was pulled up to reveal pale, creamy flesh in black net stockings, and the narrow straps of her gown slid down to expose even more of her full breasts.

"I am not impressed with your ungentlemanly behavior," she said, quickly pulling down her skirt to cover herself. She started to scramble off the bed, then stopped, fascinated to see Cord jerking off his string tie, pulling off his jacket and shirt, then throwing them to one side. His chest was as bronzed as the rest of him, with thick black hair in the center, tappering downward into his trousers. He set the .45 aside and walked toward her.

52

"No," she said, suddenly realizing he was coming for her. She started to jump off the edge of the bed, but he caught her, clamping a hard hand around her wrist. "Let me go!" she demanded, trying to pull free and realizing in horror that she was responding to the sight of his bare flesh.

"I'm beginning to wonder if I can ever let you go," he replied, slowly drawing her to him, obviously unable to get enough of the sight of her. She shivered and tried harder to pull away, but he was relentless. When only a fraction of an inch was separating them, he wrapped a strong arm around her waist and placed one hand at the back of her head, pressing her against the length of him, then slowly lowered his head until his heated lips touched hers.

Stunned at the sudden wave of feeling that rushed through her, Victoria struggled, trying to get free, especially as she felt his hot bare flesh against her own exposed skin. She felt on fire and desperately tried to get away. But Cord held her firm, the friction of her struggles inflaming them both all the more.

Finally, he raised his head, locked dark brown eyes with her green gaze, and said, "Don't ever play with me like that again, Chaps. I might take it from some women, but not from you." He kissed her again. "Never you."

"You don't own me!" She kicked him as hard as she could and, with satisfaction, saw him grimace. "Let me go!"

"That's not what you really want."

"Yes, it is. You kidnapped me. I—"

"Kiss me." He covered her lips with his again, nudging their softness, trying to part them, testing her, tasting her with his tongue, demanding entrance. He dug strong fingers into her riotous blond

53

hair and pulled slightly in frustration.

She moaned, feeling his heat, his need, his power throughout her, and began to want nothing more than to submit to him, glory in what he could give her, in what they could share. Then her desire stopped cold. This man was an outlaw, a ruthless man. She felt nothing for him, couldn't feel anything . . . ever.

"Do you hate me that much?" he asked, raising his head.

She shook her head, remaining mute, not knowing what to say. Somehow she couldn't hate him, but she couldn't give in to him, either.

"Damn!" He let her go and strode across the room, then turned back. "It's Red Duke, isn't it? You can't get him out of your mind, or his touch from your body. It's him you want, isn't it?"

"I don't condone the violence you mean to do him."

"And what about his violence? It doesn't matter to you that he hurts countless people, does it, as long as you get what you want from him? You're cold-hearted clear through, aren't you?"

"No, that's not it. I—"

"Go on. Get out. I don't want to look at you, not like that, with your hair down and your mouth red and swelling from my kisses. All I can think of is Red Duke and your wanting him. Go on. Leave." He turned his back to her.

Surprised and suddenly feeling bereft, but pleased with her victory, she quickly left the room. She hurried down the hall, slipped inside her own bedroom, and turned up the gas lamp. Shivering, she draped a shawl about her shoulders and sat down at the dressing table. How could everything have gone so wrong?

She looked at her face. Cord had been right. She did look well kissed. She touched her lips with a fingertip. Her mouth was sensitive. What had he wanted that she hadn't given him? She hadn't returned his kiss, of course, but he had wanted more from the kiss than she understood. She had only had a few quick pecks on her lips before, and they had been nothing like the feeling Cord had aroused in her. No, she couldn't let him affect her, or make her want to please him. He was her captor, and she mustn't give in to him

Anyway, what did it matter that he had wanted something from her? She had nothing to give him. He had kidnapped her, and he wanted to use her for his own devious ends. Somehow she had to stop him. And then she caught her breath. Cord wanted everything Red Duke had . . . including his woman. Her! He didn't want her for her own sake, but for what she represented, the possession of another man.

It was disgusting. And she had actually thought he wanted her. She was surprised it could make such a big difference to her, but it did. Looking into the mirror again, she combed her hair back with her fingers, noticing the unhappiness in her eyes. Why should she care why Cord wanted her? He would never have her. She would escape from him, and that would be that.

There was a heaviness in her heart and spirit when she thought of leaving him forever, and she took a deep breath, trying to dispel the sensation, but the feeling persisted. Leaning down, she pulled out her book of blank pages, her pen and a small bottle of ink. She might as well begin making some notes. It would be better than thinking about Cord, and now she didn't have the heart or need to go back downstairs. Although he probably would.

She gripped her pen hard. No, she wouldn't think about Cord slaking his passion with another woman, a willing woman who didn't care why he touched her, only that he did. Maybe that was the right way to think, to be; maybe that was the way of the West. Maybe.

But it wasn't for her. None of this was. She was a writer, a chronicler, and she had a job to do. She mustn't forget that, no matter what happened to her. Bending over her writing book, she got to work.

Later, she felt better and yawned and stretched. Standing up, she paced the room a few times. She noticed black ink between the first two fingers of her right hand, and smiled. Hazards of the trade. Her father's hands had been almost permanently stained. She stopped and thought of him, of his gentleness, of his intelligence, and of his love of fantasy and the written word. She missed him, and sometimes it was hard not to cry when she thought of her loss. But he would have been the first to tell her to go on, to fulfill her destiny, whatever it might be.

Suddenly, the door creaked open, and she whirled around. Cord stood in the doorway, his shirt back on, a carefully guarded look on his face.

"May I come in?" he asked.

She glanced around, noticed her open book, and walked over and shut it. "Do I have a choice?"

"Yes, but I wish you'd let me come in. I won't touch you."

"All right." She wanted to hear what he had to say, although she couldn't really believe he wouldn't try to touch her again. And maybe a part of her hoped he would.

He stepped inside and shut the door behind him. "I'm sorry. I don't normally try to force women, and

I don't usually make a fool of myself."

She simply watched him in amazement.

He paced across the rose-patterned carpet, then turned back. "My only excuse is that I'm on edge, worried out of my mind about my sister, and you're my best hope of saving her."

Still, she said nothing, but found herself almost believing him. But he was a trickster, an outlaw, a practiced storyteller, Victoria reminded herself. Of course, as a novelist she was a storyteller, too. Maybe they had something in common after all. However, she earned her living honestly, and he didn't.

"Well?" he finally asked.

"Well what?"

"Do you accept my apology?"

She didn't know what to say. This was so out of character for him that she didn't know what to think. Now he was acting like an intelligent gentleman, where before he had been a wild animal, protecting his woman at all costs, and then trying to lay claim to her in the most basic, physical way possible. "I don't think you need to apologize, Cord. You kidnapped me and threatened to sell me. I guess you can do whatever you can get away with."

"I don't want it to be this way. I want you to help me freely"

"No, I can't. You want to pursue your own selfish ends, and you're willing to use anybody who gets in your way. And, no, I won't accept your apology."

"Damn!" He strode over to her. "I could make you . . . I could make you do anything."

"Only at gun point."

He smiled grimly and stepped closer, within arms' reach of her now. She backed up slightly and hit the dressing table with the back of her thighs.

"Chaps, either I've got you all wrong and you're

the most innocent woman in the world, or Red Duke's a damn lucky man to have this kind of loyalty, because I know you want me. That's something you can't hide."

"No, I don't. You're mistaken."

He moved even closer. She could feel the heat radiating from his body as he trapped her between him and the table. She had to prove him wrong. Slipping on a personality she didn't know she possessed, she smiled seductively at him, half-closing her eyes. Then, leaning forward, she lightly brushed his lips with hers. Desire immediately leaped between them, and she realized how wrong she had been to try to prove he could not affect her. He did. There was no denying that. But before she could pull away, he wrapped his arms around her, one hand at her waist, the other at the back of her head.

He kissed her, slowly, agonizingly, sensually, as if he had all the time in the world and nothing he would rather do forever than touch her. Slowly she felt her inhibitions falling away, felt herself press against him, her hands pushing into his thick, black hair, reveling in the feel of him, the smell of him.

He lifted his head, smiled and fingered a strawberry-blond lock, then let it fall. "I could kiss you forever."

"But—"

She never finished her sentence, for he suddenly captured her lips with his again, and while her mouth was still parted to speak, he drove inside with his tongue. Shocked, she stood motionless for a long moment, as he explored her honeyed depths. Then she reacted, not in disgust as she would have guessed if anyone had ever told her a man would do this to her, but, instead, she shivered and felt liquid heat pour through her, melting her to him, making her crave more of him.

Following his example, she explored his mouth with her tongue, learning the taste of him, the feel of him, and still wanted more, as her body began to burn with its own wild desire. He was setting her aflame, claiming her, making her his captive as never before, as he never could have done by force. And when he finally ended the kiss, lifting his head, they were both breathing fast, their hearts racing, their bodies trembling.

"Let's go to bed," he said softly, nuzzling her neck.

Quickly, she put her hands against his chest, lowering her forehead to rest there. She breathed deeply, trying to get herself under control. He wanted her . . . completely, right this very moment. But she couldn't allow that, no matter how she felt, no matter what she wanted. What had he done to her?

"No," she finally said, and raised her head, looking into his passion-dark eyes.

"It's still Red Duke, isn't it?" He dropped his arms and stepped away. "But I proved something, didn't I?"

"Yes," she said quietly. "But it doesn't matter. It was just a kiss."

"Just a kiss! Damn, Chaps. That was more than a kiss. That was . . . but you aren't going to listen to me, are you? You've made up your mind. Well, I'll just have to change it. And I've got plenty of time on the way to Red Duke's hideout. When it's all said and done, I'm going to take you and my sister both away from him."

He strode over to her and pressed a hard kiss on her lips. "Be ready to ride at dawn." Then he left, shutting the door tightly behind him.

She sat down at the dressing table, feeling hot

tears sting her eyes. He had made her want him, but it was only to take her away from Red Duke, only to prove his superior male strength.

Well, she wouldn't let him use her to overtake Red Duke's gang, not if she could help it. Besides, what if Red Duke had been telling the truth, that he did rob the rich to give to the poor. Then, did he deserve to die at Cord's hand? There was only one way to view the two men. They were both outlaws — one claiming to help the less fortunate, the other out for power and money.

But all her rationalizations did not leave her feeling satisfied, because there were so many unanswered questions about Red Duke and Cord. She clenched her hand and hit the table with her fist. Her pen rolled to the floor, but she didn't notice. She looked up and stared at her face in the mirror. Her lips looked bruised, but so did her eyes. However, no matter what she told herself, Cord had touched her somewhere deep inside and hurt her, and she wouldn't have believed it possible.

But she would not be the only one hurt. He would feel pain, too, and soon.

Chapter 5

By the time Victoria had been riding several hours in the blazing southwestern sun, she was ready to do almost anything to get off the back of her horse. Although she had to admit she was a lot more comfortable in her new riding clothes and on her own mount, she was still hot, sore and desperate to find some way to escape.

But Cord was making sure she didn't run away. He kept all the food and water on his horse, and she was hopelessly lost without his guidance. Still, she wished she had been able to escape him in Mexico, but he had given her no chance there, either. She had tried to get Bethanne to help her; but the idea had terrified the young woman, and since Teresa was loyal to Cord, she had been unwilling to help. All in all, Cord was keeping her by his side.

Nevertheless, she hadn't given up escaping, for there would surely be an opportunity to run away from him somewhere along the way. And she had better escape soon, before he realized she didn't know the location of Red Duke's hideout, for she was afraid when he found out, he would sell her to a bordello in Mexico. He was a ruthless man, no matter that her body responded to him.

Glancing around, she was once more overwhelmed by the vastness of the land about them. It was so flat, with only the purple mountains rising high in the distance to break the landscape. Cacti grew here and there, with a few vivid blossoms in yellow, pink and violet. A gust of wind toyed with her hat now and again, bringing with it the fresh, clean scent of the desert. They had crossed a few dry washes and ridden past several strange rock formations where snakes sunned themselves. Otherwise, there seemed to be little movement or life except for Cord and her.

What she noticed most about the land, in direct contrast to what she had been accustomed to back East, was the lack of green, for there were no green trees, green grass, or green shrubs. Instead, there was a vast sea of beige, highlighted by the sun with pastel orange or muted purple in the shadows, and dotted here and there with dark green cacti. It was a land of sharp contrasts, and she was beginning to suspect it honed its people to sharp edges. Cord was certainly proof of that.

She glanced over at him. He was wearing buckskin once again, and a leather headband held back his thick, black hair. She could see tanned muscle and black hair between the laces of his leather shirt and couldn't help remembering back to the bordello when he had stripped down to his trousers. He held the reins of his mount with his left hand, while his right was kept near the Colt .45 worn low on his right hip. A stained beige cowboy hat was pulled low over his face, warding off the rays of the sun.

He noticed her watching him and looked back. "You want to stop awhile, Chaps? We could rest the horses and eat in the shade of that rock outcropping up ahead."

"My name isn't Chaps, and I wish you'd stop calling me that."

"In the West, a lot of people use something besides their given name."

"Why?"

"There're folks who want to leave their pasts behind, or a nickname gets hung on them early."

"Like Chaps?"

"Right. You have to admit Victoria is a mouthful."

"But it's my name, Cord, and I like it."

He didn't reply, but simply shook his head.

Frowning, she suddenly wondered if Cord was his real name. He could be anybody. And she thought of Red Duke. Of course, that wasn't his real name, either, now that she thought about it. She began to feel a little better about Chaps. Maybe it did suit her in the West, and it had been a funny incident now that she thought about it. Chaps Malone. She might even use it as a pen name, since it sounded so Western. Still, the fact that Cord had renamed her was irritating.

Thinking of names brought her back to Cord. He really could be anyone, and he had slipped easily into the Spanish grandee character, especially since he spoke the language so well. He did tend to have a very correct speech pattern on occasion. Perhaps there was much more to him than she had originally thought. Or maybe he was simply a good student of character. Being an outlaw, he probably needed to adopt different roles. But nothing changed the fact that he was a savage, ruthless kidnapper. And an outlaw determined to destroy Red Duke and his gang. She thought about the handsome bandit and wondered if he was truly the gentleman he claimed to be.

"What are you smiling about?" Cord asked, interrupting her thoughts.

She glanced back at him. "Red Duke," she said, hoping to provoke him.

"Damn! I should have known it."

"You know, Cord, if Red Duke is as mean as you say and if he has been terrorizing people in New Mexico so long, then why hasn't he been caught?"

"That's real simple. First of all, nobody can find his hideout, and his Comancheros are totally loyal."

"That tells you a lot about his character."

"It sure does. He's as ruthless as they come, and his people know it."

"Or he is benign."

"You're determined to see the best in that man, and I know why."

"Why?"

"You're in love with him."

"No, I'm just willing to give him the benefit of the doubt."

Cord laughed harshly. "Sure. Another thing that keeps him free is the fact that there isn't a lot of law in New Mexico Territory. The towns have sheriffs. The military patrols the rest of the land, but they have orders to control the Apache, and that keeps them plenty busy."

"Then the law doesn't pursue him?"

"Sure, they go after him when they can; but it's a big territory, and he always escapes into his hideout. I don't know why you're asking me all this, unless you're just plain dumb or you're trying to cover Red Duke's tracks."

"Look, Cord, I only met Red Duke one time, and—"

"I don't want to hear that story again."

"Then tell me why, if he has everything he wants and the law can't catch him, he would kidnap your sister?"

Cord looked at her for a long, hard moment. "He kidnapped my sister because he thinks she's the way to control a lot of land and get the power and prestige that goes with it. He's grown arrogant enough to think the law won't stop him, and maybe it can't. But he didn't count on me, and I'll get him. Nothing will stop me."

She shivered at the intensity of his words, for she suddenly realized that there was a lot more going on here than she had at first understood. It was almost as if Cord had a vendetta against Red Duke, and she had to fight the urge to help Cord, for she had no proof he was telling the truth about his sister.

"Your love for Red Duke is blinding you," Cord said quietly, then added, "but I don't want to talk about him. Let's stop. We can rest in the shade of that rock."

"All right." She didn't want to talk about Red Duke, either, and she wanted desperately to rest. She didn't wait for Cord to help her down; the less he touched her the better. She didn't know why she was so affected by him, except that it had to be a purely physical reaction to her unusual situation. And she had to admit Cord was a very sensual man — and good-looking, although she hated to acknowledge that, too.

As she touched a booted foot to the sand, she felt a searing pain stab up her leg. She quickly clutched the saddle horn for support, then swung her other leg down. Standing, she leaned against her horse for support while the feeling returned to both legs. Suddenly she felt a warm hand on her waist and glanced up.

"You could have waited for me," Cord said, looking straight into her eyes, his gaze as warm as his hand.

"I've got to get used to riding long distances some time."

"I'm beginning to think Red Duke did have you drawn around in a surrey."

The idea was so ludicrous that she smiled and shook her head. "I can ride. I just never rode so far or so long before."

"That doesn't make any sense. Anybody living out West rides and rides and rides."

She chuckled. "But, remember, I'm from back East."

He quirked a brow at her.

"You'd really hate to admit you make a mistake, wouldn't you?"

"No." He grinned. "Nothing would suit me better than to know you weren't Red Duke's woman." His brown eyes gleamed as his hand tightened on her waist.

She could feel his breath warm on her face and once more caught the scent of tobacco and leather, although she had never seen him smoke. "But what about your sister?"

His eyes narrowed. "You're right. She has to come first. You'd damn well better be Red Duke's woman." He turned away and pulled his saddlebag and a canteen of water from his horse. "Come on, let's rest while we can."

Following him, she was surprised to feel a tightening around her heart. Had she wanted to come first in his life, even before his sister? She shook her head at herself. Silly. Here she was almost believing him, and she couldn't do that. Still, he was a powerfully persuasive man, and she was drawn to him more than ever.

There wasn't a lot of room in the shade of the

mushroom-shaped rock, so she had to sit down closer to Cord than she would have liked. In fact, they were so close, she could feel his body heat, and she supposed, he could feel hers, for the desert was hot. She imagined it was probably around a hundred degrees, and even though it was dry heat, there was no way to keep cool, even in the shade.

She took off her hat, fanned her face a few times, then set it aside. Brushing back damp tendrils of strawberry-blond hair, she eagerly took the tamale Cord handed her. It was filled with chicken and beef and a delicious hot sauce, and she ate it quickly, amazed at how easily she had become accustomed to Mexican food. Cord ate with as much gusto as she did and soon handed her another tamale. This one was sweet, filled with raisins and apples. As she was finishing it, Cord leaned over and touched the corner of her mouth with his fingertip, wiping off a bit of apple.

Then he put his fingertip into his mouth, watching her all the while, and ate the sweet piece of fruit. She felt a sudden heat spread out from her center and vividly remembered all he had taught her about kissing in the bordello. Now her body craved more. But she must not give in to the desire, for Cord was the enemy. She looked away from him and finished eating her tamale.

Cord handed her the canteen, their hands touching as she took it from him. Fire leaped between them, and she jerked the canteen away. Letting warm water flow down her throat, she tried to quench her thirst, but Cord was suddenly imprinted on her mind, her emotions and her body, so that there was no satisfying her, not with food or drink.

She handed the canteen back, careful not to touch him again, and watched as he drank, rationing the precious water. Finished, he set the canteen aside and smiled at her. Then he took out a tobacco pouch, papers and matches. He rolled a smoke, expertly putting just enough tobacco on the thin paper, pulling the drawstring bag of tobacco closed with his teeth, licking the paper along one edge, then smoothing it shut with one hand. Finally, he lit the cigarette, took a long draw, then exhaled.

"Want one?" he asked.

"No, thank you. I don't know any women who smoke."

"Quite a few do in the West, especially Indian women. But tobacco is sacred to the Nations, and they smoke to give thanks or to make a treaty with another tribe."

"They smoke to make treaties?"

"Yes. They believe that writing on paper can be destroyed, but what is carried on smoke into the air goes to the Great Spirit where it lasts forever."

"But that would be hard to prove in a court of law, wouldn't it?"

"In the white world, yes, but in the Indian world, there is nothing worse than to lie. So if nobody lies, then a bond by smoke lasts forever, generation through generation."

"That is amazing."

"Yes, but it works, or at least it did until treaties were made with whites, then even words on paper were broken by white leaders."

"I understand there has been a lot of duplicity in dealings with Indians, but—"

"We won't sort that out here or now, Chaps. The Indian has lost. Now they cling to what little they have left." He hesitated and leaned toward her. "We have something else to work out here. You can try to run away, Chaps, or you can face what's between us."

"There's nothing between us."

"I've already proved there is."

"Oh, that. It's strictly physical and will go away. It's nothing like true love, or romance, or destiny."

"How do you know?"

She glanced at him, watching his eyes squint as he took another puff. He exhaled, and smoke spiraled upward. She didn't want to admit it, but being with him, alone in the desert, made her feel good deep inside, like she didn't need anything else in her life, not writing, not other people, not anything. Just Cord.

And that was a dangerous feeling. He was a vicious outlaw, without principle, a kidnapper, far from being a gentleman. Why did she feel happy with him?

As he smoked, he looked at her, waiting for her reply.

"You're not that kind of man," she finally replied. "You aren't romantic."

"And Red Duke is?"

"Maybe."

"He's really got you fooled, hasn't he?"

"No, but maybe there is some good in him."

"There isn't any, take my word for it." Cord stubbed out his cigarette against the rock, then tore it up and cast it into the wind.

"Why did you do that?"

"An offering, a gift to the land, to the rock for allowing us to rest here."

She was taken by surprise. Sometimes Cord could seem so sensitive, so aware that she wanted to get to know him better, but it had to be a trick, an act of some kind. "Do you think the land or rock notices?"

"Sure. Indians believe the land is alive. Earth

69

Mother she is called. And the Nations give thanks to her in many ways for giving everything that keeps them alive. Without her bounty, humans and animals would go homeless and hungry."

"I hadn't thought of it that way."

"Whites don't usually. They see the earth as something to use or abuse for their own benefit. Indians see all living creatures as existing in harmony with the Earth Mother and seek to worship and protect her."

"And do you?"

"Yes. I am Apache."

She shivered, even though it was such a hot day. Once more Cord had touched her deeply, in a place never before touched. She could understand what he was saying, even feel it. Running her hands through the sand near her skirt, its smoothness flowed easily through her fingers. "I can almost believe you, Cord, out here where the land still dominates and holds your life in its hands. Yes, I can almost believe your words."

"They're true, Chaps. I think you're bound to this land, more than you realize, bound like I am, for it will always be my duty to care for it, to help it produce, to nurture it."

She looked deeply into his eyes, wanting to know if he spoke truly, and his eyes were dark with an intensity she had only seen when he looked on her in passion. "You really love it out here, don't you?"

"Yes. It's my home and all that I am. I was born from this soil, and to it I'll return."

Shivering again, she looked away, down at his hands, tanned, slightly callused, and capable. She could imagine them working the soil, and yet he was an outlaw. "How did you become a robber, then?"

"A robber?" He laughed. "Maybe I am right now,

70

because I warn you, I'm going to steal you away from Red Duke and get my sister back, too."

"You can't take everything you want, Cord. Some things have to be given freely."

"Will you give me your heart?"

"No. You're an outlaw. You're bad. And I'm only here for research, not to stay."

He leaned closer and took her chin in his hand. "You're right. Some things have to be given. Will you give yourself to me?" he persisted.

"I told you—"

But she didn't finish her sentence, for he suddenly pulled her close, covering her mouth with his. As his tongue flicked teasingly, she could smell and taste tobacco, and somewhere deep inside a small part of her melted, welcoming him deeper than ever before.

She returned his kiss, pulling off his leather headband so she could push her fingers into his thick, dark hair. She loved the feel of him, the taste of him, the smell of him, and she gloried in his need of her, as he ravaged her mouth with his tongue, as hungry for her as he had been for food.

And when he could not slake his desire, he moved onward, kissing her face, her closed eyes, her earlobes, her throat, stopped only by the fabric of her shirt. Frustrated, he cupped her breasts with his palms, kneading gently until her nipples hardened under his touch.

She moaned, startled, shocked, and yet excited by his touch. At her sound, he moved back to her mouth and delved once more into her sweetness, his hands roaming over her back, then to her neckline once more, where he began to unbutton her shirt. Surprised, she tried to push his hands away, but he was not to be stopped, not until her soft, pale flesh was exposed to his hands. Once more he cupped her breasts, only this time his fingers stole under her chemise and captured her nipples.

Inhaling sharply, she forgot all about stopping him, for she was hot and filled with a desire she would not have thought possible. She wanted him to touch her, desperately, to satisfy the wild feelings that were coursing through her. And when he lowered his head and she felt his warm breath against her breasts, she moaned and clutched his shoulders. As his lips closed over the tip of one nipple, she shuddered, feeling him kiss and tug gently until she was weak with desire.

Then he raised his head, looked into her eyes, his own dark with passion, and nodded in satisfaction at what he saw, for her pale green eyes were dark and wistful and slightly confused. She pulled at the strings that bound his buckskin shirt until it was open, then ran fingers through his dark chest hair. Finally, she bent forward and kissed the tip of each nipple. He groaned and pulled her hard against his chest, so that his hair tickled her sensitive breasts.

"Make love to me, Chaps," he whispered against her hair, his breath warm on her face.

She shivered and drew him closer, wanting what he offered, although she wasn't exactly sure what it was, more than anything she could imagine.

"I'll make you forget all about Red Duke."

She grew cold. Red Duke. Suddenly she remembered Cord only wanted her because he thought she was Red Duke's woman, and not for herself.

"No," she said, forcing the words from her lips, although her body refused to obey. "No," she repeated more loudly, as much for herself as for him. Then she pushed away from him and stood up, trying to stop the longing that was pulsing through her.

Cord's face suddenly turned into a mask of indif-

72

ference, but he couldn't stop the burning in his eyes. "You won't always say no." Then he grabbed his saddlebag and canteen and started for the horses. "Let's go."

Chapter 6

Several days later, as the sun was setting in the
west, sending crimson and purple rays across the sky,
Cord stopped his horse and looked at Chaps. She
pulled on the reins of her mount, took off her hat,
and fanned her face. Sunlight glinted in her strawberry-blond hair and turned her skin a warm golden
hue. She glanced at him inquiringly.

"There's a spot not far from here where we can
spend the night," he said. "It'll be safe, and there's
water for the horses."

She nodded, remembering the past two nights
when they had hardly spoken, sleeping on opposite
sides of a campfire. The tension between them had
been palpable and had grown worse with each mile
they traveled. Maybe tonight it would ease, but she
didn't know how.

They were deep into southern New Mexico now,
and she knew Cord would start questioning her soon
about the exact location of Red Duke's hideout. He
would have to, for mountain ranges could be seen in
the distance, and they were the obvious location for
Red Duke's hideout, even if he hadn't told her about
the Black Range.

But what was she going to tell Cord? She didn't

want to get into an argument with him, for it could set off intense emotions, and she didn't know if she could handle them. She was also too much in his power. If he didn't get the information he wanted, he might just turn around and head for Mexico and the nearest bordello. Yet, somehow it was hard to believe he would do that to her, even though he had warned her that he would.

"Come on," Cord said, interrupting her thoughts. "You'll like this place. It's a secret Apache watering hole."

"You mean whites don't know about it?"

"Not unless they've been taken there like I'm taking you, or stumbled onto it themselves, and that's not likely."

He clicked to his horse and started forward. She put her hat back on her head and followed him. They had been leaving the desert the last several hours, moving slightly upward in elevation, passing more scrub pines, which clung tenaciously to rock and sand, more cacti, and even some sparse grass. She had seen lizards sunning themselves and a few more snakes. But of humans, she had seen nothing and was beginning to miss the contact, feeling more overwhelmed than ever by the power of the majestic land around them.

Cord led them around scrub pines, through dry washes, following a winding trail only he knew. Even when the sun dipped below the horizon and night began to fall, he continued unerringly on, as if guided by scent rather than sight. Her horse picked its way nimbly behind Cord, dislodging rocks and pine cones as they moved higher and deeper into sandy, rocky hills.

Just when she thought they were going to have to camp under a piñon tree, Cord led them into a slight canyon that quickly deepened; then, before it flattened out again, he suddenly disappeared into what looked like the face of a cliff. Before she could stop her horse, it followed, and she realized there was a break in the rock which looked like a shadow unless one had been through it before.

On the other side, she glanced around and was surprised to see a deep green pool of water nestled among fragrant piñon trees and protected by sheer rock cliffs on all sides. She couldn't help wondering if perhaps Red Duke had a hideout like this somewhere in the Black Range, and she realized that if he did, it would be hard to find without a guide. No wonder Cord was so set on keeping and using her. If she had truly been Red Duke's woman, she would have been invaluable in catching him.

She shivered, realizing how vulnerable she was in this play for power between two desperate outlaws.

"How do you like it here?" Cord asked, sliding off his horse and walking to her side.

"It's beautiful." She glanced around, breathing deeply of the pine-scented air.

"You can take a bath."

"If you were a gentleman, I might," she replied, thinking how wonderful it would be to wash off the trail dust, but not knowing if she should trust Cord.

He laughed. "You say the damndest things. What the hell do you care if a man sees you? I'm sure you've been paid for doing a lot more."

"No, I haven't, and I'm going to be very glad to hear you apologize when you realize I'm telling the truth."

"I'd be glad to apologize, if I didn't need you to be Red Duke's woman so bad."

He reached up and helped her down, letting her slide down the length of him. When she was standing firmly on the ground, she was eye level with him, and she couldn't ignore the sudden flare of heat in his eyes. She quickly looked away, feeling an answering flame within her.

"While I take care of the horses, why don't you bathe, Chaps. I'm going to, as soon as I get done here."

"I don't think it's such a good idea, Cord."

"Why not? You want to get cooled off just as much as me."

"Of course I do, but—"

"Damn! You're being loyal to Red Duke by not letting any other man see you, aren't you?"

"No. I'm just not accustomed to bathing naked with a man, any man."

"Okay, I'll turn my back and take care of the horses. You can get in the water while I'm not looking. Fair?"

She hesitated, looking at the water. It was terribly tempting, and she was feeling more hot and sticky by the moment. Maybe it would be all right, if he was busy with the horses. There were some bushes growing near the bank, and she could undress behind them and leave her clothes there. Besides, she could keep on her chemise and drawers, so she wouldn't be completely nude.

"Damn, Chaps, do you have to think that hard about it? If I haven't proved myself by now, I don't know how else I can. I could have had you a dozen times over if I'd wanted to force you."

Narrowing her eyes, she looked him over. "We're about the same size, and—"

"Height's one thing, Chaps, but I can guarantee you that blow for blow you're going to lose to me. I bet you don't know the first thing about fighting, or maybe Red Duke taught you to use a tickler."

77

"A tickler?"

"I'm getting tired of having to explain everything to you, when I know damn good and well you already know. An act to protect Red Duke is one thing, but—"

"A tickler?"

"Knife. I figured Red Duke taught you to use a knife."

"No, but I'd like to learn."

"Well, I'm sure as hell not going to teach you. I'd never know when you were going to decide to tuck one between my ribs just to help out poor, helpless Red Duke."

"Fine, don't teach me. Just take care of the horses. I'm going to bathe."

"Good." He smiled, a crooked movement that crinkled his brown eyes at the corners.

For a moment, her breath caught in her throat and an excitement rushed outward from her center, then she pushed the feeling down. Cord was simply a kidnapper and outlaw. Nothing more. Absolutely nothing more.

She turned and walked away from him, her head held high. No matter what, she must not let him think her weak, or he might try to take advantage. She was going to take a bath. He was going to take care of the horses. That was all.

Quickly walking behind the bushes, she began undressing, listening to Cord's movements all the while. When she heard the horses drinking, she knew he still had to take off the saddles and rub down the animals. That should keep him busy for a while.

She took off her boots and sighed in relief as the night air cooled her feet. Setting her hat aside, she removed her skirt and folded it neatly, then placed her shirt on top of it. She hadn't worn a corset on

78

the trip since Teresa had explained that it would restrict breathing and be too hot while riding through the desert. It was advice she was glad she had taken.

When she was wearing nothing but her pale green, silk chemise and drawers, she smiled in pleasure, having ridden and slept in all her clothes since leaving Juárez. She listened and heard Cord jingling bridles, then peeked from behind the bushes. He was busy, not looking her way, and she quickly slipped into the pool of water.

It felt wonderful, cooling and soothing her hot, tired body, and she leaned back, her head against the bank, her body gleaming white under the dark water. Glancing upward, she saw stars twinkling in the night sky and a full moon just rising over the piñon trees. A cool breeze ruffled her hair, and she sighed, completely at peace.

"You can use sand to bath with," Cord called from across the water, smiling at her.

She jerked up, brought harshly back to reality. "You weren't supposed to look."

"I can't see much. If you hadn't noticed, it's dark and you're in the water."

"But there's a full moon."

He laughed, shaking his head, and turned back to the horses.

Sighing, she relaxed again. Maybe she was being a little silly. After all, the circumstances were unusual, and what was normal elsewhere wasn't here. Besides, the water felt wonderful, and she deserved a bath.

She would just have to trust Cord, especially since he hadn't forced his attentions on her yet. But that didn't mean they both weren't aware of the tension that had been building between them since they left Juárez. Being with Cord, or keeping away from him, had been almost harder than the ride, for after a few

79

days she had gotten fairly used to long hours in the saddle, although she still grew easily hot and tired.

Cord was still the real problem. How was she going to escape him? And did she even want to anymore? Of course, she did. She had to get away, for she had research to do, books to write, and yet everything that had once seemed so vitally important paled when confronted with the vivid presence of Cord. She knew she mustn't let him overwhelm her senses, for it was strictly a physical attraction.

As she lay in the water, she remembered Cord's body as he moved, taking care of the horses, holding her, building a fire, handing her food. He was so compact, so sure, so graceful. And most of all she remembered his kisses hot on her face, her breasts, her—suddenly she didn't feel so cool anymore. Quickly, she began to scrub her body with sand from around the pool, determined to keep her mind off Cord.

But that didn't keep his mind off her. Naked, Cord suddenly dove into the water and resurfaced near her. Startled, she moved away, but he followed, wiping water from his face and grinning with pleasure.

"The horses didn't take as long as I thought they would," he explained, glancing down at her body.

"You tricked me!"

"No, I didn't. Your modesty is safe . . . for the moment." Then he began scrubbing himself down with sand.

She looked away from him, now not as concerned with him seeing her as with him touching her. Then she smiled, suddenly envisioning the pool of water bubbling hot from the heat they created. What was it that drew them together so strongly? It didn't make sense. She didn't even like him. He wasn't her dream man at all, and she could never use him as the hero in her novels.

"What are you smiling about?" Cord asked, as he finished cleaning, swirling water with his hands.

She laughed. "I was just thinking that you didn't make a good fantasy man."

"Should I be insulted?"

She laughed harder. "Yes. Now, Red Duke is perfect," she replied, teasing him.

"Damn! I don't want to hear about him again. I want him wiped from your eyes, your body, your mind." He pulled her against his chest, their bodies touching intimately, buoyed by the water around them.

She inhaled sharply, his body hot in contrast to the cool water around her. "Cord, you said—"

"I know. Kiss me."

"It'll just make us lose control."

He grinned, a feral movement of his lips. "I'll take the chance. Kiss me."

"It'll make us uncomfortable."

"I couldn't be any more uncomfortable." He ran hot hands down her back to her hips and pulled her against him. She could feel his hardness through her thin chemise and drawers, and tried to move away. But he held her steady, his heat invading her, making her want him all over again, making her want to explore what he was offering.

"Do you . . . hurt? she asked.

"I've been hurting since the first moment I saw you in Red Duke's arms."

"I meant—"

"There are lots of kinds of pain, and I think you're putting me through them all. Why don't you be kind to me?"

"You said you weren't kind. Why should I be?"

"I'll be kind to you now. We could stop this fever

between us. You know it. Kiss me."

"Just a kiss," she murmured, finally giving in to the emotions rushing through her. She brushed his lips with hers. He groaned low in his throat, and the sound excited her, making her feel powerful, in control and desperate for more. She kissed him again, this time lingering, toying with his lips, brushing them with her tongue, tickling him, teasing him, then nipping his lower lip.

"Damn, Chaps, what're you trying to do?"

"I'm trying to make you feel better."

"You're making it worse."

"Do you want me to stop?"

"No, but I'm going to give you some of your own medicine."

With his hands cupping her hips, he pulled her urgently into his hardness, his heat, his burning desire, and she whimpered against him, seeking his lips again. He kissed her hard, pushing deep into her mouth, as he pushed against her body, determined to fill her completely. She wove her arms around his shoulders, then caressed his thick hair with her fingers, unable to get enough of him, straining against him, desperate for him.

Suddenly, he pushed her back. "We've got to get those clothes off you." He quickly pulled the chemise up and over her head. Soft moonlight glited off her breasts, turning them silver. He inhaled sharply. "Give me the rest of your clothes, Chaps."

She hesitated, knowing they were going far, much too far, but she was unable to stop. Reaching into the water, she slipped off her drawers and handed them to him, as if handing him her life, knowing she shouldn't, knowing what it could lead to, but not caring as she realized that all she wanted was him, fulfilling her wildest fantasies, satisfying all he had

82

taught her to desire.

Tossing her silk underwear to the bank, he drew her against him again, this time pushing his hardness between her thighs. She inhaled sharply as she felt the long, hard heat of him so intimately touching her. Strong hands brushed down her back, pulling her against him, so that her breasts were pressed to the hard muscles of his chest.

"I've never wanted a woman like I want you, Chaps," he granted, "and I've never waited as long, either. Tell me you want me."

"Yes."

"Say it."

"I want you."

He kissed her, biting her lips gently, then delving into her mouth while he pushed between her thighs, his hands roaming her body as if memorizing the feel of her. She strained against him, her hands molding the hard muscles of his shoulders, then feeling of the strong beat of his pulse in his throat. She was on fire, and only Cord could help cool her. Only Cord. She moaned.

Raising his head, he looked deep into her eyes. "Now, Chaps."

She opened her lips to speak.

"No. Say nothing. Just feel."

He lifted her to the bank, so that she sat on the edge, her feet trailing in the water. He kissed the tip of each breast, then sucked, teasing them taut. Once more she moaned, holding his shoulders, as if to let go would send her plunging over the abyss into total darkness. Only he could keep her safe.

Then he was out of the water and pushing her back into the soft sand, covering her with his hot body, trailing kisses and bites down the length of her, his hands following, soothing, exciting, worshiping.

When he came to her secret place between her thighs, he stopped, then gently touched there with his fingertips. She groaned and arched toward him. He massaged her harder, bringing more moans from her, and when he felt her ready, he raised her legs and positioned himself between her thighs.

Looking into her eyes, his own dark with hunger, he trembled with desire, then pressed the tip of his passion against her entrance. She arched once more, ready to accept him, anxious, weak in her need. He pushed inside, then stopped, a puzzled frown on his face as he looked at her questioningly.

"Cord, please," she moaned, her body bathed in a light sheen of moisture, heat and desire radiating from her center. "I need you."

He plunged into her depths, and she cried out in pain. But the sound was forgotten as he began to move rhythmically, the cadence growing ever faster and harder as she clung to him, digging her nails into his shoulders, accepting his thrusts with her own wild movements, determined to reach a peak that she didn't understand and had never experienced before. Her body knew the way, and when they finally climaxed together, she shuddered, moaned and clasped him to her breasts as he collapsed against her, his own body wet with sweat.

They clung together for a long moment, then he stirred, raising himself on an elbow. Pushing damp hair back from her forehead, he gently kissed her lips. "I'll never let you go now, Chaps. You're mine, really mine."

"Cord, I—"

"You're not Red Duke's woman. You're not any man's woman, except mine. And what's mine, I keep."

She didn't argue with him, for she wasn't thinking

about his words, only about what they had shared. That had been real, wonderfully real, no fantasy at all. She began to realize that she had lived with too many words, too much fantasy all her life. Reality was exciting her in a way she could never have imagined before.

She snuggled against him, unbelievably happy, hardly able to understand what had just happened. She had never dreamed sharing her body could bring her so much pleasure, and to have shared such a wild abandon of herself with Cord was almost too much to be believed. Yet it had happened, and she was glad, so very glad.

"Did you hear me?"

"Yes. Is this the point where you say you were wrong and you're sorry?"

Chuckling, he nipped her lips with his teeth. "Yes. I was wrong, and I'm glad. You can't know how glad. Except that . . ."

"What?"

"If you're not Red Duke's woman, then I don't know how I'm going to rescue Alicia. I've got to find his hideout, and soon, or I don't want to think what he may do to her."

He sounded so sincere and so worried that for the first time she almost believed him. What if Red Duke had kidnapped Cord's sister? What if Alicia were in terrible danger? What if she had been wrong about Cord? She shivered and nestled closer to him. Could that be possible?

"I apologize, Chaps. I must look like a damn fool to you. Kidnapping you, and all. But it looked like — what was he doing kissing you, anyway?"

She took a deep breath. If Cord was telling the truth, then she had to help him find his sister. If he wasn't, and she had been right in the first place, then she would warn Red Duke as soon as they found him—if they did. She would not be party to the killing and violence that would certainly occur. Either way, she had been drawn into this triangle, and she had no choice but to see it through. Cord might not be her fantasy man, but he wasn't all bad, either . . . she hoped, because she didn't think she could control her desire for him ever again.

"Chaps? Are you mad because of what I did? I honestly didn't know you were a virgin, not until the very end, and by that time I don't think I could have stopped. And you didn't want me to, anyway."

"No, I'm not mad. It was very, very good. I'm trying to think how to answer you. Red Duke kissed me because he wanted me, I guess."

"I can sure understand that, but he'd better not try it again. Fact is, I've got to take you to the nearest town, leave you there, and get on with finding him. I don't want to leave you, but—"

"I can help you."

"What?"

"Red Duke didn't just kiss me." She pushed back the damp hair that had fallen across his forehead. "He told me to meet him in the Black Range mountains in southern New Mexico."

"Black Range. That narrows the search, but only a bit."

"There's more. He gave me a concho off his vest and said it was special and any of his men would recognize it and take me to his hideout."

Cord whistled softly. "That's the best break I've had, Chaps. Thanks."

"But who do we show it to?"

"We'll take it to the biggest town hear the Black Range and start showing it and asking questions."

"What town is that?"

"Silver City. There's plenty of mining and plenty of money there. It stands to reason Red Duke would have Comancheros nosing around there."

"But what if nobody recognizes the concho?"

"No. Don't think that way, Chaps. That concho is going to take us straight to Red Duke, and Alicia. I'm not going to think anything else." He pulled her tight and pressed a soft kiss to her lips. "I don't know what I'd do without you. I knew you were my lucky break the minute I saw you."

"I hate to mention this, Cord, but Red Duke might not really have meant for me to come to his hideout. It might have just been—"

"You're gorgeous, especially with that hair, so he'd be a fool not to want you. But, you're right, he may have told you all that so you would go back to the stagecoach and tell them and it would spread that he had robbed again. He has a mystique to keep up, a power that grows each time he robs and doesn't get caught."

"In that case, the concho could mean nothing."

"Yes, but the hand I'm betting on says he wanted you to meet him there, and that's the hand that will get my sister back."

"I hope you're right, but—"

"No buts!"

"All right. At the very least, I should get a good story out of all this."

"Are you really a dime novelist?"

"Yes. Well, actually I'm working on my first novel, but I have a publisher."

"I'm impressed. Am I going to be your hero?"

"I had been thinking about Red Duke, but—"

Cord growled, bit her neck, then nuzzled her.

"However, you're looming larger in my mind all the time," she amended.

"I'd better be, and if I'm not enough hero for you now, maybe I'd better try again."

"Oh, I don't know if I could stand any more of your heroism."

"We've got all night."

"But what about sleep?"

"Who can sleep around your body?" He began to press soft kisses over her face, then slowly moved lower.

"You're my hero now," she moaned, and pulled him closer.

Part Two

Chapter 7

A wild wind sprang up as Cord and Chaps rode into Silver City the next night. Dirt whirled around them, tumbleweeds careened down the dusty street, and lightning split the sky, followed by rumbling thunder. But the weather didn't keep people off the boardwalks, or out of saloons where bright light and laughter spilled from open windows and swinging doors.

Chaps was glad to get back into civilization, such as it was, and looked eagerly around her. Dark mountains rose to the north, dominating the area, making the town seem tiny and insignificant compared to the towering peaks.

She shivered, once more affected by the wild land, wondering if she would ever come to be as comfortable with it as Cord was. But then he had lived with it all his life. Suddenly she realized just how little she knew about the man with whom her life had become so entwined. She didn't even know where he had spent his life, but she was going to make it a point to find out.

"How do you like Silver City?" Cord asked, moving his horse closer to hers.

"If it's got a soft bed and a hot bath, I'm going to love it."

He laughed. "It's got that, but a lot more, too."

"Someone to take us to Red Duke's hideout, I hope."

"Count on it."

"Do you think it'll rain?" She glanced up at the sky.

"No. It's probably a dry storm. Pretty, isn't it?"

"Yes, and wild."

Cord nodded at her, grinning.

She smiled, then looked back at the street, the boardwalks, and the people walking down them, dressed from black-suited gamblers to cowboys and miners in faded denims to satin-clad saloon women. Chaps felt a thrill, imagining describing the scene in her novel for her publisher and readers. Suddenly she was anxious to get settled in a hotel room and make some notes. She knew her father would have been very proud of the books she was going to write, because she planned to be very accurate in describing the West and its people.

They continued down the main street, and while a few people saw them and nodded, for the most part they fit in so well they were hardly noticed. Chaps saw that many of the businesses were closed and dark, and she smiled to herself at how naive she had been when she had shopped in Juárez. Now she understood just how inappropriate the Mexican fiesta outfit she had chosen was for riding across southern New Mexico.

Silver City reminded her a little of El Paso, for the main streets of both were comprised of wooden buildings with flat roofs, connected by wooden boardwalks and sporting storefronts with glass windows advertising products and services. Many of the residences were Victorian in style, with intricate woodwork and pastel-colored paint.

"That's the Pinos Altos range of the Mogollon Mountains," Cord explained, pointing to the dark peaks north of them. "There's a lot of pure silver up there, and it's what brought miners and mining companies to this area." He looked at her. "Silver City used to be an Apache camp, now it's a shipping point for miners, with Fort Bayard in the Mimbres Mountains to protect the area."

"Where are the Mimbres?"

"To the east of here, and north of them is the Black Range." He pointed out the general direction.

"I didn't realize the Black Range was so far away."

"Harder to get to than far away, Chaps. Red Duke picked a good place for a hideout. From there he can prey on the cattle ranchers in the valleys as well as the miners in the mountains."

"Are there a lot of ranches around here?"

"Yes," he explained. "Spanish families were deeded large grants of land here, in Arizona and California, and they've run successful cattle ranches for some time. But now Americans are moving in and taking more and more of the land, just like they've taken most of the Apache land."

"Can nothing be done?"

"The land is part of the United States now, and Spanish and Apache descendents are called Americans, although they aren't treated the same."

"But isn't there enough land for everybody?"

"Yes, but most people have a different way of wanting to use the land. Like Red Duke."

"What does he want to do with it?"

"Power. But, come on, I don't want to talk about him right now. Let's get a room."

"Two rooms." She gave him a hard stare.

"I thought we'd settled that last night."

"It wouldn't be proper for—"

"You'll be safer sharing a room with me."

"Or you don't trust me."

"Both."

She didn't reply. It would be easy to break the truce they had enjoyed since the night before, but she didn't want to argue with him, not over this. Besides, if the truth were known, she would prefer to stay in the same room with him, no matter how improper it was.

They rode on in silence, until they came to a place near the end of town called the Sagebrush Hotel. Cord stopped his horse in front of it, got off, tied the reins to the hitching post, then helped her down.

"You know I can get down alone."

"I know, but I'd rather help you."

She smiled at him, understanding his desire to touch her whenever possible, for she felt the same way about him. He caressed a straying lock of her strawberry-blond hair, his brown eyes suddenly dark with passion.

"I'd better get the saddlebags," he said, and stepped away.

A secret smile hovered on her lips, for she knew how she affected him and what he was thinking of doing when they got in the room. She realized she should have been shocked with herself for wanting him, for accepting the situation, and yet she wasn't. Here in the West, life seemed to move at a different pace, and if one didn't grab on to what it offered, life might be lost completely. Or maybe she was just rationalizing her desire for Cord. In either case, he had brought a joy to her life that had been lacking since the loss of the companionship of her father.

Not that she expected to be with Cord forever. She was still very much afraid he was a desperate outlaw, and his story about his sister was nothing more than a clever ploy to get her help. She didn't plan to let him hurt her or anyone else in any way, for if he turned out to be a desperado, she would simply warn Red Duke, then use the experience to help write a novel.

"Come on," Cord said, throwing the saddlebags and her valise over his shoulder, then putting a hand around her waist. "This looks like the kind of place Red Duke's Comancheros might like. Maybe we'll get a lead early on."

They walked into the Sagebrush, and a bell jingled as Cord shut the door behind them. Chaps was immediately struck by the austerity of the room, especially after the luxury of Teresa's brothel. The parlor had a wooden floor, wooden walls, a large wooden desk across from the door, and in one corner, two settees covered with worn dark green velvet. An open door led to a small dining room filled with round, wooden tables covered by dingy, white tableclothes. A narrow staircase led upstairs.

"What'd you want?" a man with long, graying hair and a large, white mustache asked as he walked from the dining room. He stopped behind the desk and looked at them with narrowed eyes.

"We need a room for a couple of nights," Cord replied, walking over to the desk.

Chaps remained behind, deciding to let Cord take care of it all. But she couldn't help noticing that the proprietor watched her with steely eyes, and she began to feel uneasy.

"That the missus?" the proprietor asked.

"Yes," Cord replied brusquely.

The man still didn't look convinced, but took Cord's money anyway. "Third door on your right." He handed Cord a key, but kept watching Chaps as he turned the registration book around.

Cord scrawled something in the ledger, then nodded at the proprietor, who still watched Chaps.

Finally, she glared at the man and walked over to Cord. Taking his arm, she smiled sweetly at him. "Come on upstairs, darling. I'm tired but not too tired."

Cord looked at her in surprise, then grinned, pressing her hand with his. He glanced back at the proprietor. "Send up some bath water."

The proprietor nodded, his eyes narrowed as he watched them climb the staircase.

When they turned down the hall at the top of the stairs, Chaps hissed, "What was wrong with that man?"

"Another red-blooded male who wants you."

"Cord! No, there was something strange about him."

"Think he's a Comanchero?"

"Is that possible?"

"Sure."

"What are we going to do about it?"

"Nothing, yet."

He stopped outside room number three, smiled at her, then opened the door. She stepped quickly inside, and he followed, shutting the door quietly behind them. Then he carefully locked it. Tossing the saddlebags and the valise on the double bed, he

96

took her in his arms, pressed her close, and simply stood there for a long moment. Then he stepped back and smiled.

"I've been wanting to do that all day," he said, looking her up and down.

"What took you so long, stranger?" she quipped.

"Had a damn horse under me."

She laughed and glanced around the room. It was as austere as the parlor, with a washstand that had a plain white pitcher and bowl and two white hand towels on it, and a single ladderback chair in one corner. On a table by the bed stood a glass lamp with matches.

"It's not quite like Teresa's place, is it?" she said, sitting down on the bed. "But this feather mattress feels good anyway."

"So, you took a liking to living like a—"

"Luxury. I liked the luxury."

Cord chuckled and sat down beside her, taking one of her hands in his. "Damn, I'm glad you aren't Red Duke's woman."

"Wait until we find your sister to be glad."

He kissed her forehead gently. "No matter what, I'm glad."

"Cord, did you grow up around here?"

Suddenly he grew still, cautious. "Why?"

"I was just wondering, since you seem to know the area so well."

"I grew up in a lot of places, New Mexico, Arizona, Mexico. That's why I know the land."

"It has a beauty all its own."

"Yes, it does." He stood up and walked to the door. "Look, I think I'll go out and have a look around. Go ahead and take your bath. We can have dinner when I get back."

"But Cord—"

The door shut behind him.

Shocked, she simply sat on the bed, looking at the closed door for a long moment. What had happened? She had simply asked him about his past, and . . . did he not believe her any more than she believed him? Did he think she really was a Comanchero, just not Red Duke's woman? Or was his past some deep, dark secret?

She stood up and paced the room. She had told him about her past, how her father had been a novelist and so was she. Maybe he didn't believe her. But after all they had shared, how could he suddenly turn so cold? Anger began to build in her. The nerve of him! She had given him one of the most precious gifts she had, and he had walked out just because she had asked how he knew the land so well!

She didn't have to put up with that. She didn't even have to help him find Red Duke. She could find Red Duke on her own and determine the truth of Cord's story for herself.

That settled it. She would find somebody to take her to Red Duke, and she would simply leave Cord to stew in his own petty, little schemes. That would show him, the conniving ingrate. The low-life savage. And she'd finally put an end to all the questions that had been nagging at her from the moment she had met Red Duke and Cord.

She glanced around the room and grabbed up her valise and saddlebag. She had some money of her own, and she had connections . . . the concho. She even had her own horse, and it was still out front, if Cord hadn't moved it.

Storming out of the room, she closed the door

tight, then walked downstairs. The proprietor looked up in surprise, but she simply turned her nose up and walked outside, for it was certainly none of his business. Besides, there had to be a better place to stay in town anyway.

Fortunately, her horse was still tied to the hitching post, and Cord was nowhere in sight. It might be dark, it might be a strange town; but she had learned a lot since coming West, and she figured she could take care of herself. In fact, the next day she would just go out and buy herself a tickler, maybe even a Colt .45. It was time she started fending for herself. She couldn't just let any man who wanted to come along and kidnap her. At least, not anymore.

She threw the saddlebag over the back of her horse, tied on her valise, then put a foot in the stirrup and threw a leg over the saddle. Sitting tall, she felt quite pleased with herself and started down the street, looking at all the buildings. She wanted a nice place to stay, something worthy of a Western writer.

Pausing, she looked toward the sky where lightning still flashed, followed by thunder. Wind tugged at her hair and tossed tumbleweeds across the street. But still no rain. Good. Maybe she could find a place to stay without getting wet, or perhaps Cord had been right and it wouldn't rain at all.

She continued riding down the street, not seeing anything she liked, but not seeing Cord's horse, either. However, she didn't give up and turned down a side street. She immediately saw a very nice Victorian style house, with a porch lamp highlighting a sign that read, "A Day, A Week, A Year, Trust Smilin' Sam to Board You Right."

There, that was just the kind of place she wanted. She slipped off her horse, looped the reins over the hitching post, picked up her saddlebag and valise, then went up to the front door. Taking a deep breath, she opened the door and stepped inside.

"My dear, you look positively exhausted," said a short, plump man with a mass of curly blond hair and a large waxed mustache. He was wearing an immaculate white suit and a frilly white shirt, with a gold watch on a heavy gold chain across a white satin vest. As he hurried toward Chaps, she simply stood there, stunned at the sight.

He stopped in front of her and clasped pink hands with glinting gold rings. "I know, you expected some uncouth Westerner, didn't you? Well, you've come to the wrong place if that's what you want."

"Are you Smilin' Sam?"

"Certainly not. I bought the place from him about a year ago and kept the name. Didn't want to lose customers, you know. But do come in. Sit down. Would you like sherry? I think I could use a glass. Are you from back East? I do hope so."

"New York City."

"Wonderful. We'll have so much to discuss. I'm originally from Philadelphia, but I love New York."

"Do you have a room?"

"Yes, but only the little one in back. Really, I stay full. I'm sure it's because I have the cleanest rooms and best food in town, and I wouldn't mislead you about that."

"I'll take it."

"Of course, but do sit down so we can talk."

"My horse is outside."

"Don't worry about a thing. My man will take care of it all. Just a minute, let me alert him. You'll be wanting dinner, too, and a bath, no doubt."

"Yes, that would be wonderful."

"Essential. Here, let me have your bags. My man'll have everything in your room, your horse stabled, and a nice meal ready in no time. Now, have a seat, relax, and I'll be right back. Oh, yes, what is your name?"

"Oh—Victoria Malone."

"Lovely. I'm Philip Justine. Just call me Phil. It'll be my pleasure to serve you while you're in town." He took her valise and saddlebag, then hurried from the room.

She shook her head in amazement. A fancy gentleman from back East was the last thing she had expected to find in Smilin' Sam's, and for a moment she almost wished it had been Smilin' Sam who had met her at the door. She would have told him her name was Chaps, but that name wouldn't have done for Phil. Yet, strangely enough, she almost felt like a fraud using the name Victoria. But that was silly.

Glancing around, she marveled at the decor of the room, for it was exquisite. A Queen Anne desk in gleaming cherry wood with a matching chair occupied one corner. Deep green velvet drapes were tied back by gold tassels at each window, with white lace curtains over the lower windowpanes. A grouping of chairs and a velvet, rose and green covered settee had been placed on a forest green rug before a marble fireplace. On a small cherry sideboard, crystal decanters with amber liquid and crystal glasses had been placed on a silver tray.

"My dear, how do you like my little room?" Phil

101

asked, hurrying back into the parlor.

"It's lovely, and quite unexpected."

"I know what you mean. What this town lacks is taste, but I do my part. But here, let me get you a drink."

After carefully pouring two glasses of sherry, he handed her one, then motioned toward the fireplace. When they were seated, he leaned back, took a sip, then sighed. Chaps also took a drink and smiled at the remembered pleasure of good sherry.

"This is delicious," she said.

"Thank you. I have it brought in special. I wouldn't dream of serving that rotgut stuff they serve in those awful saloons on the main street."

"I don't blame you."

"Of course, this sherry would cost me dearly . . . if I didn't have friends in the right places." He gestured around the room with a plump hand. "You must wonder how I can afford furnishings like these. Frankly, I can't, but these miners are boom or bust, and when they're riding high, they will buy the most amazing things, then have to sell cheap when they go broke."

"So you're cashing in on the mining boom," she surmised.

"Yes, partly, but the East got too hot for me. I was an actor. Oh, maybe not the best in the world, but adequate. Still, actors attract people, and that can make others jealous. And it can get very difficult, let me tell you. So, sometimes, it pays to let things cool off somewhat."

"Then that's what you're doing here."

"Well, that, and making money. You may not realize how much in demand a well-run establishment like this is."

"I hadn't really thought about it."

"You should. I'm saving a pretty penny all the time, plus . . . oh, well, I do run on. Now, tell me about yourself."

"I'm a dime novelist, doing research on the West."

"Do tell!" He twirled his sherry glass. "That is terribly exciting. You must sign my register. You're my first celebrity."

"I'm not a celebrity. These will be my first novels under my own name."

"All the better for me. I'll be able to say I knew you when you were just a struggling writer. So, how is the research coming?"

"Actually, a lot better, or a lot worse, than I could have imagined, depending on how you look at it."

"Oh, what kind of exciting things have been happening to you?"

"Well, for instance, my stagecoach was robbed, I was kidnapped by an Apache, taken to a bordello in Mexico . . . and that's just the beginning."

"My, I'm impressed. You must tell me all the sordid details, or are you going to make me wait to read them?"

Chaps laughed. "Actually, right now I just want some food and a bath. Later, maybe we can talk."

"Of course, how insensitive of me. It's just that you're a fascinating rarity. But, I'll control myself and just lead you upstairs where your food and bath await. However, I must warn you that I'm going to ply you with questions tomorrow."

"Then I may be able to answer, but tonight—"

"I understand. Just leave everything to me. Perhaps we can get you some publicity. I know the

103

man who runs the local newspaper. You know, a little advance promotion couldn't hurt."

"I hadn't thought about it, but I suppose not."

"Certainly not. It's the best thing in the world for a beginning writer, or actor, and I should know. But for tonight, it's upstairs with you, and tomorrow we'll talk."

Chaps finished her sherry, feeling a little like she had just been run over by a herd of buffalo, and followed Phil from the parlor.

Chapter 8

An hour later, Chaps was back on the streets of Silver City, only this time she was bathed, refreshed and full of a delicious meal. She had changed to her gray serge traveling suit and carried her reticule, a small drawstring bag containing her room key, money and a lace handkerchief. Thus armed, she was determined to find somebody who would take her to Red Duke's hideout.

She glanced up at the sky, noticing that the brilliant display of lightning and rumbling thunder continued. Back East she would have been concerned about getting wet, but storms here seemed to come without rain. At the moment, she was glad of that, since she had no desire to fight a rainstorm while she was on the trail of Red Duke.

There was a chance she might run into Cord while she was asking questions, but she would just have to deal with that if it happened. In the meantime, she would concentrate on showing the silver concho around, and she supposed the best place to do that was in the saloons on main street. She had never been in a saloon before, but she figured it couldn't be much different than a restaurant.

As she walked down the side street, she realized it

was not nearly as well lighted as what she was accustomed to in New York City, and she began to glance over her shoulder in concern. After all, she had already been kidnapped twice since coming West, so it could happen again. And she hadn't had time yet to buy a pistol. She walked faster and faster until she finally came to the main street, then quickly stepped onto the boardwalk.

Stopping, she caught her breath and glanced around. The saloons still looked busy, and there was enough light spilling out of them to make her feel safe. She started walking again, determined to try every single barroom until she had some answers that would lead her to Red Duke.

Pushing open the swinging doors to the first saloon on the boardwalk, she stepped inside and was surprised to see it was simply a long, narrow room, with a high, wooden bar along one side, and a few round tables in back. A lot of men, mostly in faded cotton shirts and denims, stood, leaning against the bar, while talking and drinking whiskey.

When she walked farther into the saloon, heads turned, and slowly speech died until there was no sound and everybody was staring at her. She didn't know when she had ever felt so uncomfortable, but she wasn't about to let anyone know; so she simply lifted her chin and stepped up to the end of the bar and looked at the bartender.

He finished polishing a glass, then slowly walked over to her. "What can I do for you, ma'am?"

"I'd like a whiskey, and some answers."

Shrugging, he poured a drink and slid the glass to her. She paid for it, and before he could step away, she held up the concho, and asked, "Do you recog-

106

nize this?"

"It's a concho. Plenty of those around."

"This one has a special design," she pushed.

"So? Look, lady, I've got a business to run. You drink or—"

"All right." As he turned away, she took a quick sip and nearly gagged on the strong, raw liquor. It was in total contrast to the smooth sherry she had enjoyed earlier.

Glancing around, she noticed that the men had gone back to their conversations, but they kept an eye on her, as if she were an outlaw or unwelcome. Then she realized there weren't any other women in the room and decided that her being there was unusual. But she couldn't let that stop her, not if she wanted to get to Red Duke.

She turned to the man next to her. "Pardon me, sir, but do you recognize the special design on this concho?"

He looked at her as if she had been in the sun too long and shook his head, but not before he had given her body an appreciative stare. Questioning these men was obviously not going to be easy. Maybe she needed Cord more than she had realized. But she wasn't giving up and continued on down the line. Each man treated her the same, until she didn't know if she was more angry or embarrassed by the situation. Finally, she gave up and left.

Outside, she took a deep breath. Western men were either obtuse or impolite, or Red Duke owned the whole town and nobody was talking. Still, she wasn't going to let Cord think a few men in a small, dusty town had gotten the best of her. She squared her shoulders and started walking toward the next

107

saloon. Immediately, she heard footsteps following her.

She stopped and glanced around. One of the men from the saloon was behind her. Her heart began to beat fast as fear built in her. Why hadn't she waited until she had bought a pistol before she started questioning these mean-eyed men? She stood a little straighter, glad of her height, gave the man a hard stare, then continued down the boardwalk.

The streets were almost deserted now, making her feel vulnerable, but she couldn't let that stop her. Besides, the fact that the man was behind her could just be a coincidence. She would simply hurry to the nearest saloon and get inside around other people. But as she passed the next dark alley, a hand suddenly clamped around her arm and jerked her into the shadows.

She didn't get a chance to scream because a hard, smelly hand clamped over her mouth and a smellier body in rough clothes slammed her up against a wall. She started to struggle, then stopped. Maybe this man had recognized the concho and just wanted to make sure nobody overheard them.

"I figur' you're wantin' a man." He fumbled at her breasts, trying to get inside to her bare flesh.

She moaned in denial and mounting frustration, and tried to twist away from him. But he simply pulled her slightly forward and slammed her back against the building, knocking the breath from her. While she gasped, trying to breathe, he jerked up her skirt. Horrified, she tried to get away, but he hardly noticed, having gotten a hand under her petticoats to grasp her thighs.

Finally, gasping in air, she kicked out and struck

his shin, making him curse and stumble. It was the chance she needed. She kicked him again and, while he was vulnerable, pushed him away. She ran out of the dark alley, but suddenly collided with the hard chest of another man. Without looking up, she instinctively jerked back and tried to get away, but he stopped her.

"Chaps!" Cord exclaimed, holding her by the shoulders as he looked at her in relief. Then he saw the man come out of the alley, and a look of understanding crossed his face. Cursing, he set her aside and went after the stranger.

Events were moving so fast she hardly had time to take them all in as she watched Cord hit the man squarely on the jaw, dropping him to the ground. Then he bent over the stranger, pulled him up by the shirtfront, and hissed several low words to him. When he turned and walked back to her, she saw his face, and she wished she had run as hard from him as she had from the stranger.

"What the hell are you trying to do?" he asked, stopping beside her, his expression furious. "I've been turning this town upside down trying to find you, and when I do, you've snuck off in the alley with some woman-starved miner. I wasn't enough for you, is that it?"

"As usual, you have completely misinterpreted the entire incident. The man followed me and attacked me, but I got away. Without any help, I might add. Now, if you will excuse me, I'm going on about my business."

"Damned if you are. You're coming with me." He took her arm and began pulling her down the street.

"Unhand me, Cord, or I'll start screaming."

"Go ahead. I'll shoot dead any man who tries to come between us."

Shocked, she glanced at his face. As far as she could tell, he meant it. "I think you're overreacting, Cord. As I told you when I first met you, I'm a free and independent woman."

"Not until I get my sister back. You're mine until then, and you'd better start acting like it before a lot of men get killed."

"That's ridiculous."

He stopped and shook her slightly. "I'm serious, Chaps, and you'd better start believing me. Now, I'm going to take you to a cafe. We'll have a cup of coffee and get this straightened out. You want to do it the easy way or the hard way?"

Narrowing her eyes, she glanced around. She probably couldn't expect much help, unless she could get to the sheriff, and so far she hadn't had much luck escaping Cord. Maybe if she screamed long enough and loud enough, she could get the sheriff's attention, but then she probably wouldn't get to Red Duke, for surely none of his Comancheros would be willing to help her if she were involved with the law.

"Did you make up your mind yet?" he asked sarcastically.

"Look, Cord, it's late, I'm tired. You must be, too. Why don't we just leave this until tomorrow morning?"

"You seem to think I'm some kind of fool just because I wasn't raised back East, and I'm getting tired of it. If I let you go off tonight, you'll be gone tomorrow, and I'll have to hunt you down again. I don't have that kind of time to waste. Why'd you run off anyway? I thought we were in this together."

"You never told me your last name."

"My what? You mean you pulled this stunt just because . . . Cordova. Cord Cordova."

"How could I trust someone who never told me his last name and wouldn't discuss his past?"

Cord looked at her a long while, then nodded, as if understanding. "You're the damndest thing, Chaps. You never told me your last name, either, but that didn't make any difference to me."

"That's because you renamed me."

"Yes, and maybe I'm not through yet."

"It's Malone. Victoria Malone."

"Pretty name."

"Thanks. Does that mean I get to keep it?" she quipped, trying to calm her herself.

"No."

"Really!" Her anger began to boil again.

"Come on, Chaps, I'll take you home. Where are you staying?"

"If I'd wanted you to know, I'd have told you."

"It's not that big a town. I can find you, and sooner than you think."

She hesitated, not having thought of that before. The town was small, and the hotels and boarding-houses had to be limited. Was there any point in fighting him? "Smilin' Sam's."

"Good choice, but I don't think we'll find any answers there."

"I don't care right now. I just want to go back and sleep." She couldn't quite keep the hurt from her voice. She had been mad and scared and lonely, and she didn't want Cord to know it. But if he realized just how vulnerable she was, he was sure to take more advantage of her.

He rubbed her shoulder with a strong hand. "All right, Chaps, I'll take you home, but I'm not leaving you alone."

"Cord, I've got my own room."

"You're going to share the room, 'cause I'm not letting you out of my sight again."

Taking her hand, he started walking toward Smilin' Sam's boardinghouse. She didn't know how to stop him, didn't even know if she really wanted to anymore. He was warm and safe, and she felt her body starting to crave him once more. But she couldn't trust Cord yet until she discovered the truth. She had to get to Red Duke.

It was surprising how much safer she felt walking beside Cord, and she hated to admit that, even though it was true. But it wasn't her fault she hadn't been raised to defend herself. There had never been a need before. And when she thought about the difference between fantasy and reality, she was amazed at how much she had yet to learn.

But Cord didn't give her much time for thinking through what had just happened, for he hurried her to Smilin' Sam's front door, then into the parlor. Before they had a chance to go upstairs, Phil came out of the back room.

"My dear, whom have you brought? I was under the impression you were alone."

"I was, but—"

"I'm her guide," Cord explained curtly, "but she keeps thinking she can do a better job of it than me. Tonight, I'm sleeping with my boots across her doorway to make sure she doesn't go exploring on her own again."

112

Phil raised a brow and smiled knowingly. "And you're?"

"Cord."

"I'm Phil. You aren't by chance a celebrity, too, perhaps with a Wild West show?"

"No. I'm just trying to make sure she doesn't die doing her research."

"With a strong man like you around, I think she'll make out fine. Isn't that right, Victoria?" Phil questioned, waiting for her to confirm what Cord had just said.

Cord gripped her elbow hard.

"Yes. He's helping me with my research," she replied, her voice tight with repressed anger.

"I understand the need. When I first moved out here, I had a lot to learn. Well, if you're both in for the night, I'll just get off to bed."

"Good night," Chaps said, and as Phil walked away, she started up the stairs, with Cord close behind.

At the top of the staircase, she turned right and hurried down the hall to the back of the building. Inserting her key in the lock on the bedroom door, she quickly opened the door and stepped inside, noticing that the lamp beside the bed was still lit just like she had left it. After Cord stepped inside, she locked the door, tossed the key on top of the dressing table, then turned and glared at him.

"I hope you're glad," she said, "because you just made me look like a fool in front of Phil."

"Who cares about him? Unless you do. Maybe you like pretty, Eastern boys. Is that it?"

"No."

"He was damned protective."

113

"That seems to be his way."

"He'd better watch it around you from now on."

"Really, Cord! Let's just get some sleep. And you'll have to sleep on the floor because I only have that one narrow bed." She pointed at the bed covered by a deep blue comforter.

"That'll suit me fine."

"It isn't big enough for two."

"Sure it is, if we sleep real close."

"I don't want to sleep close."

"You're just being stubborn. I don't know what you're so mad about anyway."

"I don't like your high-handed ways."

He walked across the room to her and looked into her pale green eyes. "I'm trying to save what's mine, and I'll do whatever it takes."

"I'm not yours."

"Since last night you are."

She turned away, took a few steps, then looked back. "No."

"I'm beginning to think you care about Red Duke, 'cause you're being damned loyal to him."

"Loyal to myself, that's all."

He followed her and put his hands on her shoulders. "Kiss me."

"Cord! I don't even want you here, why should I —" Her protest was cut short by a brief touch of his lips, and she felt the heat run through her. She shivered and turned her head away.

"You can't deny that, can you?"

"It's got nothing to do with anything."

"It has everything to do with us." He kissed her again, this time lingering, letting their heat blend, their feelings flow through the single touch.

114

"You can sleep on the floor," she repeated, but already feeling herself weaken.

"Then you'll sleep there, too." A third time, he kissed her, and they both trembled. "I can't stay away from you, Chaps. Help me."

"Oh, Cord," she murmured, reaching up to run long fingers through his thick hair, then pulling off his headband and tossing it aside. "I don't want to want you."

"But you do." He pulled her close, running his hands up and down her back, then cupping her hips to pull her against his growing hardness.

"Yes."

Then his lips were hard on hers, and she opened her mouth to him. He invaded her honeyed depths, driving deep with his tongue, questing, conquering, and in turn giving way as she kissed him, glorying in their passion, in their growing need for each other.

They moaned, struggling to get closer to each other, needing absolute union to slake the driving desire that was building in them. Cord tore his mouth away and pressed fevered kisses to her eyelids, her earlobes, her throat.

He began urgently freeing the buttons of her blouse, and she helped him, suddenly wild to have no constraints, nothing that stood in the way of their joining. He pulled off her jacket, then her shirt, and she helped him with the skirt and petticoats. When she stood only in her sheer chemise, corset, drawers and stockings, he stopped and gazed at her.

"Cord, hurry," she entreated.

But still he didn't move. Finally, he said, "You're so beautiful. So perfect. I can hardly believe you're mine."

"Oh, Cord." She began removing his buckskin clothes, anxious to feel his skin, anxious to feel him against her, wanting what only he could give her.

When his shirt was thrown to one side, he pulled her against him, his body straining, his muscles taut as his hands roamed over her, stroking all her curves. She groaned, digging her fingernails into the sleek skin of his back, feeling the muscles harden under her touch, and lightly bit his earlobes, inhaling his leather and tobacco scent.

"Chaps," he groaned, then removed her chemise, so that her breasts were bare, pushed up by the corset to peaks. Unable to resist, he molded her breasts with his hands, then kneaded them until their tips were hard and she was panting. Then he kissed each pink nipple until she moaned with pleasure.

Unable to wait longer, she undid his trousers, and they slid to the floor, revealing his powerful arousal. Now it was his time to hurry, and he pulled off her drawers, leaving her naked except for her corset and stockings. Enflamed, he could wait no longer and lifted her to the bed, then covered her with his hot body.

They twined together, their meshing, molding, then separating as they stroked, petted, cajoled and heightened their desire until it was a blazing fire between them. They both panted with the mounting tension, while outside the wind howled, tree limbs scraped against a window, and lightning lit the room.

Cord knifed his fingers into her thick hair, feeling its silky softness, then buried his face in it, smelling the rose scent as he felt her hands move lower and lower on his body. She clasped his buttocks and massaged, exciting him until he rolled to one side, exposing the center of his desire. She touched his long, hot shaft gently, then more boldly as he groaned with passion, and when he could take no more, he stilled her hands. Parting her legs, he knelt between her thighs, rubbing his hands up and down the smooth, silk stockings that perfectly fitted her long, slim legs.

Raising her hips, he fitted himself to her soft entrance, then glanced at her face, his eyes dark with a wild, unbridled passion. Seeing that her pale green eyes mirrored the same urgent need he felt, he plunged inside.

She gasped as she felt him slide deep into her, then moved with him as he began to rhythmically stroke her depths, bringing them closer and closer to total oneness. As the fever between them grew, she called his name and stroked the hard muscles of his back, then dug in her nails as the wildness caught them, plunging them together into a fury of passion that peaked in flaming bliss. Then they returned, sated and still.

He pulled her close and stroked her damp hair, his breathing hard and fast. She clung to him, as if he were the only safe haven in a world full of wild emotions. He gently kissed her forehead, then glanced up. And frowned.

"Chaps, there's something I've got to tell you."

"Not now," she murmured, too sleepy and contented to deal with anything except snuggling close to him.

"There's a man's shadow outside our window."

"What!" She sat up and jerked the comforter over her. Staring at the window, she could see nothing except tree limb shapes through the lace curtain covering the lower windowpane. "I don't see a man."

117

"He's gone now."

"Are you sure that's what you saw?"

"Yes. But the worst of it is, I haven't got my Colt with me. Damn city ordinances says a man can't carry his gun in town. I left it in my room at the Sagebrush."

"Do you suppose this has something to do with my showing the concho tonight?"

"Maybe. I'm going out there."

"Cord, no!"

"We have to know what's going on." He slipped off the bed and started pulling on his clothes.

"I don't want you going out there. It's not safe."

"If somebody can get in through your window from that tree, I want to know it."

"Well, so do I, but why would someone come snooping around?"

"That's what I'd like to know." He finished dressing and pulled on his boots.

"I'm getting dressed, too."

"Just put on your chemise and wait for me. I'm going outside, and if I can I'll come to the window and knock. You let me in if I've gotten that far."

"Cord, I don't like this."

"Wait here." He picked up the key to her room and quietly slipped out the door.

She put on her chemise, then got under the covers. She hated waiting. Maybe she should have insisted on going with him, but she would probably have slowed him down. Shivering, she stared at the window. But all was quiet, and she could see nothing unusual. Light from the bed would have cast their bodies in shadow, but could anybody watching from the second floor window have seen enough to know

118

what they were doing?

She shivered again and glanced around the room to keep her mind off Cord. The bedroom was as beautifully decorated as the downstairs parlor, with an expensive blue flowered rug, blue velvet drapes held back by rose-colored tassels, a blue print wallpaper, and a bed, dressing table, washstand and chair in the Queen Anne style.

But she didn't care for the room so much if somebody could climb a tree and peek inside, or even get into the room. The idea was outrageous, and she hated to think what might have happened if Cord hadn't been with her. She did seem to need him, and once more she was glad he had been with her.

She anxiously looked at the window and waited impatiently. Where was he? Had he been hurt? Would someone else try to get inside? She shivered again, wishing she could feel safe like she had by the secret Apache pool, when it was just the two of them totally isolated.

Suddenly there was a tapping at the window. She hurried to it and cautiously pulled back the lace curtain, not knowing what face to expect. Cord nodded back at her, and she raised the window. He stepped inside, then closed and locked the window.

"It wasn't even locked," he said, turning and taking her in his arms.

"Are you all right?" she asked, stroking his hair.

"Yes. Somebody left us a message." He held out his fist, then opened his hand. In his palm lay a silver concho.

She took it and hurried to the lamp. Holding it under the light, she could see that the concho was exactly like the one Red Duke had given her. She

119

turned to Cord. "It's just like—"

"I know."

"But what does it mean, and did they see anything?"

"Whoever it was couldn't get high enough to see above the lace curtain, and I couldn't see anything distinctly through it, so don't worry about that."

She sighed in relief.

"But that man knew we'd seen him, and he left the concho on the windowsill for us to find."

"What kind of message is it?"

"I don't know, but whatever you did tonight worked. Somebody in this town knows you want Red Duke, and I guess we'll be contacted again, and soon."

"Do you think they'll take us to him?"

"Either that, or try to kill us."

"Kill us?"

"They might think we're getting too close."

"But, he told me—"

"I know, but it doesn't mean we'll get taken straight into the hideout. If they don't try to kill us outright, we might have to prove ourselves in some way."

"But we've got the concho. This is strange, Cord, and I don't like it."

"It's the first step in the game. I suggest we get a good night's sleep and see what happens tomorrow."

"I don't know how I can sleep now."

"Maybe you need some help." He grinned and began taking off his clothes.

She couldn't help watching, marveling again at his compact strength, his sleekly muscled body and darkly tanned skin. She wanted him all over again.

When he came to her, she held out her arms, and they embraced, their feelings more powerful for the fear they had just experienced.

"Come on, Chaps, I'll see what I can do to make you tired enough to sleep."

She smiled and let him lead her to the narrow bed.

Chapter 9

Chaps awoke late the next morning, feeling rested and happy. Warm, yellow light streamed in through the window, and for a moment it was hard to believe the storm of the night before, or that someone had looked in at them. In the light of day, it was even hard to believe the wild passion she and Cord had shared, but the slight soreness of her body proved that.

She glanced at Cord and smiled. He looked younger asleep, his face peaceful, the worry and tension gone. Could he really simply be Cord Cordova, out to rescue his sister, or was he, indeed, Cord the outlaw? At moments like this she wanted very much for him to be simply a man doing the right thing. But there was no way to know, not without going to Red Duke's lair.

And what of Red Duke? Well, he had entranced her with his handsomeness and his claim to be a champion to the poor, and she still wasn't sure she believed Cord. However, at the moment, it wasn't a man who concerned her, it was food and a bath and then information. She was also going to stop by the stagecoach office and let them know she was all right and find out what had happened to her trunk. She could certainly use more clothing, although Phil had taken her riding outfit to clean and that would help.

She eased out of bed, trying not to wake Cord, but as she stood up, he rolled over, groaned and threw out an arm as if to catch her and bring her back. She smiled, thinking how much she liked his body, and started to touch him. Then she stopped herself. It was time for business, not pleasure.

Turning her thoughts away from him, she looked at her clothes. Without her trunk, and since her riding clothes were being cleaned, she had a choice of her gray serge traveling suit or the Mexican fiesta outfit. She chuckled silently at the idea of walking around Silver City in the fiesta clothes, but maybe they wouldn't be so unusual here after all.

Really, she had no choice and began picking up her discarded clothing from the night before. It was sadly wrinkled, and she tried to smooth out the creases with her hands, but it didn't help much. She would just have to look like she had slept in her clothes until she could get her trunk or the cleaned riding outfit back.

She walked over to the washstand and poured water from the pitcher into the bowl, then lightly washed her entire body with rose-scented soap. Feeling refreshed, she sat down at the dressing table and glanced at herself in the mirror. She looked well loved and was a little surprised at the rosy glow to her skin and the gleam in her eyes. Maybe Cord was good for her, after all.

Picking up the hairbrush Phil had provided her, she began brushing her long hair. When it was sleek and gleaming, she nodded in satisfaction and set the brush down. As she did so, she noticed a concho on the dresser. Puzzled, she picked up the piece of silver and examined it.

She didn't remember leaving either of the two conchos on the dressing table the night before, but she must have because this one had the same special design. Glancing around in concern, she decided to check her reticule, where she thought she had left the conchos. She picked up her drawstring bag, then knelt down and emptied its contents on the rug. Along with several other items, two silver conchos rolled out. She clasped the new one in her hand until it bit into her palm.

Then she looked at Cord. She would have to wake him and tell him the news, but she didn't want to because he was going to be angry. Somebody had been in their room while they were sleeping and left another concho. What kind of game was this? Did the man want to prove just how vulnerable she and Cord were?

They had slept heavily, exhausted from their long ride, as well as from their lovemaking. They would have to be much more cautious in the future, for obviously someone was after them.

Pushing everything back into her reticule, except the two conchos, she set the bag aside and walked over to the bed. Sitting down on the edge, she stroked Cord's dark hair. He awoke with a start and grabbed her, forcing her down with his hands around her throat.

"Cord! It's me. Cord!"

He focused on her slowly, then eased the pressure on her neck and sat up. Shaking his head, he pushed back his hair. "Sorry, Chaps, but you startled me."

"Do you always react like that?"

"I'm not used to sleeping with anybody, and I slept sound, which isn't usual, either. You must have relaxed me."

He smiled at her then, his eyes traveling down her

124

nude body. "Are you trying to tempt me again?"

Smiling softly, she stroked his face, then shook her head. "I wanted you to sleep as long as you could, but I found something in the room."

Immediately, he was alert. "What is it?"

"Another concho."

"Damn!" He stood up, paced across the room, then returned. "Let's see it."

She handed him the three conchos.

He looked them over, then glanced back at her. "They're all alike, aren't they?"

"Yes."

"And that means somebody was in here last night. Damn! Wait till I get my hands on that Phil, 'cause somebody has got another key to this room, and if he's playing games with us, he's going to wish he wasn't."

"I can't imagine Phil doing this, or being involved with Red Duke."

"Red Duke. Conchos. I don't have time for these games. I've got to get to Alicia before she's hurt." He paused and glanced around. "Where are my damn clothes?"

She smiled, thinking of the way they had hurriedly undressed the night before. "Maybe under the bed, or—"

"Here they are." He pulled them out from under the discarded comforter and began dressing.

"I'm going with you," she said, quickly starting to throw on her clothes, too.

"No. I'll get more information alone."

"If that little display this morning when you woke up, or last night on the street, is an indication of how you intend to question Phil, then I'm definitely going along."

"I'll give him the chance to answer on his own, but

if he needs roughing up to talk, then I'll be happy to oblige."

"That's why I'm going along."

"I told you—"

"We're in this together. Besides, it's my room."

"What does that have to do with anything?"

"It's my room. It's my problem."

"If that's supposed to be logic, then how can I refuse your help?" he replied sarcastically, glancing at her in frustration.

"Thanks." She got a stocking twisted and had to start over.

"But if you're not ready when I am, I'm leaving without you."

"That's not fair. You're almost dressed." She glanced at him. "Don't forget to comb your hair."

He frowned, but picked up the brush and ran it through his thick, black hair a few times. "Okay, am I presentable?"

"You're in a nasty mood," she replied. "Here, help me."

As he buttoned up her blouse, his hands suddenly slowed. He sighed and pulled her close, hugging her against his warm body. Then he set her back and finished the job. "I didn't mean to be so grumpy, but all I wanted was a good night's sleep, then to wake up and make love to you again."

She smiled and kissed the corner of his mouth. "Thanks. But duty calls."

"It sure does."

"Maybe we should eat breakfast first, then question Phil."

He laughed. "You can be damn practical when you need to be. Good idea. Are you as hungry as me?"

"Starving."

126

"Let's go raid the kitchen and find Phil when we're done."

"Okay," she agreed, grabbing her reticule and putting the three conchos in it.

They left the room, carefully locking the door behind them, then walked down the stairs together. A few people were sitting in the parlor talking, but they didn't recognize any of them and continued into the back.

"Good morning," Phil greeted them from the dining room, where he was putting the finishing touches on a table setting. He looked them over. "Looks like you rested well. I'm sorry, but you've missed breakfast. Would you like some coffee, perhaps some bread and jam?"

"Yes," Cord agreed gruffly and sat down at the table.

"Is he always this cheerful in the morning?" Phil asked, glancing at Chaps.

"He's hungry," she replied.

"Then, I'll be right back."

She sat down beside Cord and clasped his hand. "Don't be so hard on Phil. He may not be involved."

"Involved in what?" Phil asked, stepping into the dining room with a tray laden with food.

"Somebody came into our room last night."

"Oh, dear," Phil said, looking contrite as he set the heavy tray on the table, "and you think I'm to blame." He poured hot coffee into thin china cups, then sat down. "It's that Smilin' Sam. I don't know how many keys I've taken away from that man, but he seems to have an endless supply. And, of course, putting you in that room was a mistake, but it was all I had."

"What's wrong with that room?" Chaps asked, while Cord began eating, having lavished huge amounts of butter and strawberry jam on a hunk of bread.

"Well, it was Smilin' Sam's room when he owned the place, and he shared it with his wife. They were very happy, I might add, until that day."

"What day?" Chaps inquired.

"I thought everybody knew. They went out for a picnic east of here. However, they just happened to run into an Apache renegade war party retaliating for army atrocities against their nation."

"And what happened?" Chaps asked, completely involved in the story, and thinking that it was something she must make notes about later.

"They killed his wife and thought they had killed him, but they hadn't. They had shot him all right, right through the face, but he lived."

"How?"

"The bullet went through the left side of his face, and while it didn't really hurt him, other than making him a little strange, it tore through the muscles. That's why they call him Smilin' Sam."

"You mean?"

"He's always smiling now."

"But how awful."

"Dreadful. Just be glad you didn't wake up to see him standing over your bed."

"If I had, he'd be dead now," Cord said, downing the bread with a cup of coffee, then starting on another piece.

"No doubt," Phil agreed, nodding at Cord, "but I do apologize. After he sold this place to me, Smilin' Sam just started wandering the area. I never know when he'll show up."

"But how does he live?" Chaps asked, taking a sip of coffee and buttering a slice of bread.

"Off the land, and then I'm rather generous, I

128

must admit. Plus, on occasion, he'll turn up with the most amazing things to sell me, like jewelry, or clothing, or sherry, and at very good prices. I suspect he gets them from miners that have gone bust, or, perhaps, outlaws. But I'm not particular, and if he didn't sell to me, he'd sell to somebody else."

"How do we meet Smilin' Sam?" Cord asked, then finished a second hunk of bread.

"I can't help you there. He comes and goes at will. However, if he stops in again, I'll tell him you'd like to meet him and, of course, to stay out of your room until you leave. But you'd better put a chair under the door to be on the safe side. I don't think he'd harm you, but he does like to play little tricks. He's almost childlike in some ways, but I believe he could be dangerous, too."

Cord finished his coffee, stared hard at Phil, then said, "I hope you're being straight with us, because I don't want to have to get rough with you later."

"Oh, dear!" Phil exclaimed, looking hastily at Chaps. "He really can be fierce, can't he?"

Chaps nodded, eating a piece of honey-coated bread.

"I'm just warning you," Cord repeated and stood up. "We've got some business in town, then we'll be back."

Quickly finishing her coffee, Chaps stood up, too, and smiled at Phil.

"Your clothes will be ready for you when you get back, my dear," Phil said, "and maybe your bear will be in a better mood by then."

Chaps couldn't help laughing, and took Cord's arm and led him from the room. They nodded at the people in the parlor, then walked outside. It was a beautiful day, with a clear blue sky and the heat not yet overwhelming. They walked down the street, her hand tucked in the crook of his arm.

"I don't think Phil has anything to do with the conchos, Cord."

"Didn't you tell me he was an actor?"

"Yes."

"A little pain will loosen his tongue."

"Violence isn't the answer to everything."

"Maybe not, but it sure works good sometimes."

"Phil is just trying to make money. He doesn't necessarily have anything to do with Red Duke."

"It'd be a cozy setup if he did, wouldn't it?"

"Maybe." She stopped and looked at him to make her point. "But I think he's telling the truth, and the man we need to talk to is Smilin' Sam."

"It shouldn't be hard to spot him if we ever see his face."

"No, it won't. Wasn't that a grisly tale?"

"Yes, but I could quote you a dozen more about what whites have done to the Apache." He started forward again, and she walked with him.

"I suppose it's been bad on both sides," she admitted.

"Right. But that's not what concerns me right now. We need somebody to take us to Red Duke, and if Phil can do it, he's going to."

"I can't imagine him going back into the mountains. He might buy merchandise, but he'd never dirty his hands. You know that, Cord."

"No, I don't, but I'll give him a little slack while I look for Smilin' Sam."

"All right. I want to go to the stagecoach office and let them know I'm alive and well, and try to get back my trunk."

"You need me to help you?"

"No thanks."

"Then, while you do that, why don't I ask around

130

about Smilin' Sam?"

"Good idea. And we can meet back at the board-inghouse?"

"Yes, but first thing I'm going to do is pick up my things at the Sagebrush. I want my .45, and I want to change clothes."

"All right. I'll see you later."

They parted on the main street, and Chaps crossed to the other side, for the stagecoach office was at the end of town and away from the other businesses. As she walked, she passed people going about their daily chores, but she didn't really notice them, for she was thinking about Phil.

He was probably telling the truth and simply buying things from Red Duke through Smilin' Sam or somebody else. Or, at least, that's what she thought he was doing. If she listened to Cord, she would think the worst of everybody, and she wasn't going to start doing that . . . at least not yet.

She arrived at the stagecoach office and stepped inside the wooden building. The attendant was napping, and she cleared her throat. He jerked awake and smiled sheepishly.

"Sorry, ma'am, but I've got to sleep when I can. Those stages are late or early or lost or something. Seems like I'm down here most all the time."

"That's quite all right. I'm Victoria Malone, and—"

"Ma'am, I'm sure glad to see you. Got a telegram about how you were kidnapped. Red Duke, they thought. Did he hurt you?"

"No. Red Duke was a perfect gentleman."

"Brave woman. That man's plenty mean."

"Could I get my trunk?"

He scratched his head. "Don't rightly know where it is. Best bet is Las Cruces. Tell you what, I'll cable

131

in and have your trunk sent here, no matter where it is. Okay?"

"That'll be fine, but how long do you think it will take?"

"No telling. You going to be here long?"

"I don't know. Probably not. But go ahead and send it here, and if I move on, it'll be sent to me, won't it?"

"Yes, ma'am. We're mightily sorry about your trouble. You sure you weren't hurt?"

"No. He let me go right away. It just took a while for me to get here."

"I'm glad to hear it, but I never heard of Red Duke not hurting someone. The stage company said as how you were to get back ticket money, and if you'll sign this form I'll give it to you now."

"That's wonderful. I can use it." She quickly signed the form.

He handed her the money, carefully counting it out into her palm.

"I'll check back about my trunk. And thanks."

She left, thinking about what the clerk had said. Red Duke certainly wouldn't be popular with the stage coach company. Yet she couldn't dismiss the clerk's comment about Red Duke's harming his victims.

Walking back down the boardwalk, she inhaled deeply, smelling the clean pine fragrance that permeated the area from the local piñon trees. She wondered if her trunk would ever catch up with her. But even if it did, it would be a while, so she decided to try shopping in a dry goods store once more.

When she came to the shop, she stopped and peered in the window. It looked full of merchandise, so she entered. Smiling at the woman behind the counter, she said, "I'd like to buy a shirt, not red, maybe green, and a cotton camisole and drawers."

"I haven't got green, but I believe I have a nice blue plaid that should fit you." She rummaged through several shelves of clothes, pulled out a shirt, then continued looking. "Don't know if I've got a camisole in your size, but I could get one made."

"I don't think I'll have that much time."

"Let's see, here's something. You're a tall woman, but this should fit. And these drawers ought to do, too." She set the clothes on the countertop.

"Thanks," Chaps replied, and held the camisole up to her. "I think this will do, as well as the shirt and drawers. Please wrap them up for me." She hesitated and glanced around. "Do you also sell guns, maybe little ones?"

"I have guns, but do you know how to use one?"

"No, but I figure I can learn."

"It takes practice. Did you say little? A Colt .45 would serve you best." She pulled a heavy gun and box of bullets off a shelf and laid them on the counter.

"Oh, no." Chaps shook her head. "I couldn't carry that around. It'd be too big and heavy."

"I've got a two-shot derringer. That's a lady's or a gambler's gun, but you've got to be close and shoot straight." She laid the pearl-handled gun on the counter.

Chaps picked it up, stroked the smooth metal barrel and smiled. She could handle this, especially at close range, but where would she carry it? In her reticule, probably, but it might be hard to get to. "How do women usually carry these?"

"I probably shouldn't mention this to a lady, but I've heard of them stuck in garters, or down the front of gowns, or in reticules."

"But none of those are very good places."

"You want it on your hip?"

"No, but —"

"I just remembered another small gun I have." She reached under the counter, pulled out a small black box and opened it. Inside was a large silver dome nestled in blue velvet, with six silver studs near it. "My man bought this off a gambler a long time ago. Men don't think it's powerful enough, and ladies don't seem to need it; so it has never sold."

"What is it?"

"Look." She pulled out the large silver dome, which turned out to be a ring. "This was special made, I can tell you, and it'll stop somebody close up."

"That's a gun?"

"Yes, ma'am." She pulled out one of the studs which was actually a long, thin bullet, then inserted it in the ring. "Just point with your hand, make sure you're stable, and press here. You may not kill them, but you'll stop them."

"That's amazing."

"Sure is, and look at the band. See what's engraved on it?"

Turning the ring over, Chaps read, " 'Little Stinger.' Well, it's certainly that. I'll take it." She slipped the ring on the first finger of her right hand, and fortunately the gun fit, for it was her largest finger. Although Little Stinger was heavy, there was a comfort to it, and she felt safe for the first time since meeting Red Duke.

"That gun ring don't come cheap."

"Just tell me the total, and I'll pay you."

"All right, but you be careful with that ring. Don't shoot yourself, and don't wash your hands with it on."

"I'll be careful," she agreed, and pushed all the

money she had with her toward the woman. She got back only a small amount of change, but for once didn't mind, especially since she had gotten the refund back from the stage company.

"Do you want to wear the ring?" the proprietor asked, wrapping up the new clothes in brown paper packages.

"Yes, and I want one of the licorice sticks, too."

"No charge for that, ma'am, and I'll wrap up the box with the bullets in with your clothes."

"That's fine, and thanks."

"You just be careful, and don't get yourself into trouble."

"I'll try," Chaps replied, then stepped outside.

Soon she was happily walking down the street, the gun ring on her finger and black licorice staining her lips. As she headed for Smilin' Sam's, she decided she wouldn't tell Cord about the ring. She would just let him think it was a piece of jewelry she had brought with her. After all, he might turn out to be the worst enemy of all, but somehow she couldn't imagine that, not anymore.

As she neared the front of the boardinghouse, she noticed something glinting on the walk. Looking down, she realized it was a concho. She picked it up and recognized the now familiar design. She glanced around and noticed another one, then she looked farther ahead and saw another, until she realized they formed a trail, leading around the house.

She hesitated, wondering if she should wait for Cord, then remembered her gun ring. No, she didn't have to wait; now she could take care of herself. Besides, she was anxious to find out just what was going on. She finished off the licorice stick, licked her fingers clean, then started picking up the conchos. For something supposedly special, there sure seemed to be a lot of the conchos around. It would be a joke on her if they turned out not to be special at all.

She followed the concho trail until it ended by the tree under her bedroom window, and although she looked all around the ground, she couldn't pick up another trail. Deciding it was all some kind of joke, she turned around and started for the front of the house. Suddenly, there was a thud behind her, as if someone had jumped from the tree.

Whirling around, she was face to face with Smilin' Sam. She had no doubt he was the man Phil had described, for the left side of his face was twisted into a constant grin, showing blackened teeth. He did not look nearly as happy or friendly as the name suggested, and she decided he must have a grisly sense of humor.

"You been wantin' Smilin' Sam?" he asked, spraying spit from the side of his mouth as he spoke.

Chaps involuntarily stepped back, but steeled herself not to reveal her revulsion, thinking that as soon as she got used to Smilin' Sam's unusual facial structure she probably wouldn't be bothered at all. "Actually, I'm looking for Red Duke. He gave me a special concho off his leather vest and said one of his Comancheros would recognize it and lead me to his hideout."

"You gonna pay me?"

"How much?"

"I been needing a woman. Hard to get one 'cause of my face."

"You mean—"

"If you make me happy, we'll go to Red Duke."

"I . . . I don't think Red Duke would like that. I believe he wants me to save myself for him."

"What about that damned Apache in your room?"

136

"Oh, he's not really so Apache. I believe there is possibly a strong English ancestry in his background, but it doesn't show . . . as I'm sure you've noticed."

"I hate Apaches."

"Yes. I heard the terrible story about what happened to you, but the fact is that I needed a guide and—"

"I'll kill that Apache and take his place."

"No. I have an agreement. The Apache, that is, Cord, is to deliver me to Red Duke."

"I'll deliver you."

"You guide."

"Then you pay."

"Red Duke will reward you."

He spit, fortunately using the good side of his mouth, and then she was horrified to notice that he chewed tobacco. She backed up another step and noticed a gleam in his eyes. He was teasing her, playing with her, trying to make her uncomfortable, not knowing what he might do next. She had played right into his hands. He was also using his face as a very potent weapon. Clever man.

"See here, Smilin' Sam. Red Duke gave me that concho, and I'm sure he would be very pleased with the man who brought me in. And I'm sure he would reward him in one way or another. Do you want to be that man or not?"

"Yes, but no Apache."

"I'm not going without Cord. We've got a deal. I've paid him. And I'm going to get my money's worth."

Smilin' Sam spit tobacco dangerously close to her skirt, but she didn't move back this time, finally understanding his power game. "Okay. I'll take you both in blindfolded and unarmed."

"Oh, no, I—"

"Only way. Be here, packed, tomorrow at dawn." Then he turned and walked away, quickly disappearing behind a building.

Chaps was left standing under the tree, holding a handful of conchos.

Chapter 10

Two days out of Silver City, Chaps began to think it might have been a good idea if Smilin' Sam had left her blindfolded the entire trip, for as they had traveled north into the Black Range, the terrain had gotten more and more wild.

She glanced at Cord, noticing that he wore the same tight-lipped expression he had worn since she had told him about Smilin' Sam and their plans. He had hated the idea of going in without a weapon, and she hadn't told him the ring she wore was really a gun. The blindfold hadn't suited him any better. When Smilin' Sam had decided to let them remove the bandannas because not seeing was slowing them down so much, Cord had been glad, and so had she, but at that time she hadn't known they were going to ride into such wild country.

For the last few hours, they had been climbing up rocky, slippery paths, higher and higher, until any mistake by her horse would have sent them careening over a ledge into the valley below. And neither of them would have walked away. She alternated between looking down and being dizzy and looking up and feeling sick. If it got any worse, she was about ready to give up and go home, except that she didn't

139

think she would be able to find her way back. The other choice was to be blindfolded and led into the hideout, but she surely couldn't find her way out in that case.

Cord had certainly been surly the entire trip from Silver City, but then she didn't know if she could blame him. Smilin' Sam had been less than polite, and everybody in the group, including the horses, sported tobacco stains. Just as she had originally thought, the man's spit was dangerous, and intentionally so.

She glanced to the west, noticing the sun was low on the horizon. They would have to stop for the night soon, and she hoped it wouldn't be necessary to camp on the narrow ledge, for the least little movement in her sleep and she would go over the edge. Not that she was able to sleep very soundly in Smilin' Sam's company anyway, because he snored loudly enough to frighten off any wild animal. How he slept through his own noise, she didn't know. And she knew Cord hadn't slept deeply since the boardinghouse, because he didn't trust Smilin' Sam at all.

But she supposed it was wasted energy to be worrying about sleep, since they would camp wherever Smilin' Sam decided to bed down. It was just that there had been a lot of time to think on the long ride, since Cord and Smilin' Sam were stonily silent. So she was left to her own mind's meanderings, and she had drifted into thinking a lot about the book she would write. Maybe there would be time to make some notes at the hideout, and perhaps even start the novel.

When the sun finally disappeared behind the horizon, turning the sky beautiful shades of red and orange and magenta, she decided they were, indeed, going to have to camp on the ledge, and she nervously began watching Smilin' Sam. Cord didn't seem to be concerned about where they slept, for his face was set in grim lines, totally engrossed in reaching Red Duke's hideout.

Prepared for a night on the ledge, she was shocked when Smilin' Sam suddenly turned to them, and said, "Get your blindfolds back on."

"Are we almost there?" she asked excitedly, then looked down and felt slightly dizzy.

"I ain't saying. Get your eyes covered."

"But it's too dangerous here, and aren't we about to camp for the night?" she objected.

"Either get your eyes covered, or forget our deal," Smilin' Sam commanded, spraying spit in exasperation.

"Chaps, do as he says," Cord insisted, giving her a warning look with his dark eyes.

Reluctantly, she untied her bandanna from about her neck and carefully retied it over her eyes. Unable to see, she clutched the reins and saddle horn.

"Give the horses their head, and you won't have no trouble," Smilin' Sam informed them, nodding in approval as Cord tied his bandanna over his eyes. "Okay, let's go."

Blind, Chaps felt more vulnerable than ever, especially on the rocky ledge. Her horse started forward, and she swayed in the saddle, clutching desperately at the saddle horn. It would be terrible to have come this far, only to end up at the bottom of a cliff.

She heard rocks tumbling over the side of the steep cliff as they rode on, Smilin' Sam in front and Cord in back. Suddenly, she feared hearing Cord's horse stumble, rocks fall, and then his cry as he went over the edge. She shivered, hardly able to stand the thought of losing Cord, and suddenly wondered if he meant more to her than she realized.

141

Then she scoffed at the idea. Of course, she didn't want anyone to die, and that included Cord. They continued on, the silence broken only by falling dirt, debris and rocks. Then after taking twist after turn after stumbling climb, they suddenly stopped, and Smilin' Sam said, "Take off your blindfolds."

Chaps quickly untied her bandanna and glanced around, blinking as her eyes adjusted to the light. Focusing on the scene before them, she could hardly believe her eyes. They were at the entrance of a huge cavern lit by numerous lanterns revealing tents, mostly of Indian design, some of white canvas, and in the very center, a huge one of royal blue silk, with shiny gold tassels at each corner.

Glancing upward into the cavern, she could see only darkness, for the lantern light did not reach that high. She couldn't help wondering just how big the cavern was, how high it loomed above them, and if there were any smaller caves and crevices and passageways honeycombing the mountain. It was a formidable hideout, and she could understand why Red Duke had chosen it. She noticed the obvious luxury and thought that if he was giving to the poor then why was he living so extravagantly.

Then, again, perhaps he simply lived with what he was able to steal, and since he robbed from the rich to give to the poor, he had to use whatever the rich had. That would certainly explain the luxury.

Then she noticed the armed guards, two on each side of the cavern's entrance, and probably several more outside to give advance warning. The Comancheros were wearing dark denims and dark shirts crossed by black leather ammunition belts, with a pistol slung low on one hip, and each holding a rifle.

For the first time she wondered just how far Red Duke's empire extended. With this type of central operation, and possibly smaller hideouts in other areas, he must be robbing a lot more than southern New Mexico. She glanced at Cord, wondering if he was thinking the same thing. He nodded at her in encouragement, then went back to examining the cavern, no doubt making mental notes of how he was either going to take over, or escape with his sister. Whatever he did, she would have to be ready when he decided to make his move.

Then she saw Red Duke walking toward her, looking just as magnificent as she remembered, maybe more so. Again he was dressed in black leather. A pistol hugged each hip in a black leather holster, and he was carrying a coiled, black leather whip in his left hand. She felt a chill run up her spine. Red Duke looked terribly dangerous, even mean. All she had heard about him was beginning to ring true.

As he reached her, Red Duke smiled, and she wondered at the transformation in his face. He held up his arms to help her down from her horse, and she slipped into his embrace, feeling muscles harden as he gently lowered her to the cavern floor. Then he held her at arm's length, looked her over, and smiled again.

"Welcome to my humble abode," he said, then dropped his arms and stepped back. "I'm glad you accepted my invitation, Miss . . ."

"Malone. Victoria Malone. But please call me Victoria," she said, slipping into a compliant role until she figured out what was going on.

"A lovely name for a lovely lady. I'd be honored to call you Victoria, and please call me Duke."

"Oh, thank you, Duke."

Then he glanced at Cord. "Who's this?"

"My guide, Cord," she replied. "I'm afraid I didn't quite trust Smilin' Sam."

143

Red Duke laughed, a loud, hearty sound. "I don't blame you, and a lady must always be careful, especially in the wild West, right?"

"Yes, that's true," she agreed, casting a quick glance at Cord.

He nodded in agreement, but kept silent, obviously figuring it was the best way to keep Red Duke from killing him on the spot or throwing him over a cliff later.

"But Smilin' Sam is a man I trust," Red Duke added, "and I'll reward him for bringing you here, Victoria."

"I'd hoped you would."

"It's the only way to inspire true loyalty in followers, I've discovered. But you must be tired after your long ride. You'll want a bath, fresh clothes, and then will you join me for dinner?"

"I'd like that." She hesitated. "And Cord?"

"I suppose he has come in hopes of joining my Comancheros," Red Duke said, casting an experienced eye over Cord. "I've always got room for a good man, if that's what he wants."

"I can shoot straight and fast," Cord replied quickly, looking mean.

"Good," Red Duke responded. "We'll see about that later." He glanced at Smilin' Sam. "In the meantime, Sam, take care of the horses and show Cord where he can throw his saddlebags and blanket roll. Then take Miss Victoria's things to my tent."

"But—" Chaps objected.

"Don't worry, Victoria," Red Duke interrupted. "Your reputation is safe with me. My tent is large, and the safest place for you in the cavern."

"Well, if you think so," she reluctantly agreed.

"I do, and now I'll take you to your bath and leave you to relax," Red Duke added, letting his eyes

144

quickly scan her body, then glanced at Cord. "I'll talk with you later."

Red Duke extended his arm for Chaps, and she put a hand on his heavily muscled forearm. As they started to walk away, she glanced back at Cord. His face was set in determination, and his eyes were dangerous and threatening as he glared at Red Duke's back. Then he glanced at her and nodded, his dark eyes promising or commanding, she didn't know which.

Red Duke led her into the vast cavern, and she walked on a stone floor, noticing how cool the air was compared to the heat outside. Having never walked beside Red Duke before, she hadn't realized how tall he was, well over six feet, and he made her feel short, even at her five foot eight height. She couldn't help comparing him with Cord and realized she had come to prefer Cord's height, for it complemented her own so well.

But she wasn't here to think about Cord, at least not at present, although she planned to keep a sharp eye on him in case he turned out to be a desperado. For now, she wanted to concentrate on Red Duke, and she smiled up at him. When he looked down at her, his blue eyes bright, she decided his height was just right, for he was simply a naturally big man.

"How do you like my home?" Red Duke asked, gesturing around the cavern.

"It's impressive."

"Thanks. I don't always plan to be here, you know. One day I'm going to settle down, maybe own a ranch."

"I think that'd be nice, Duke," she replied, smiling at him, wondering how he planned to get it.

"But you haven't told me about yourself," Red Duke insisted. "We didn't get much of a chance to talk before."

"I'm a dime novelist, doing research in the West," she said, playing along with him and trying to gain more information.

"Really! I'm impressed." He squeezed her hand. "Then, not only are you beautiful, but you're smart as well. And you have the coloring I like best in a woman."

"Perhaps because it matches your own?" she said coyly.

He laughed. "Partly, but your hair is much more unusual, and very beautiful. But I take it you like red, too, or you wouldn't be here."

"Yes, I'm partial to red." She smiled, hardly able to believe she could carry on a conversation with him so easily when her stomach was in knots. "And thanks for the flattery, but—"

"It's the truth, and I dare anyone to disagree."

Laughing, she blushed uncomfortably.

"I'd like to see you blush more often. It's especially charming on your pale skin."

"If you keep flattering me, I may blush forever," she said teasingly.

He grinned, showing perfectly even, white teeth, and stopped outside the royal blue tent. "I could talk to you this way all night, but I know you must be tired. Wait out here while I get something from my tent."

While she waited, she glanced around, noticing small centers of activity all around the floor of the cavern, and from somewhere came the neighing of horses, which meant there must even be room to hide the horses within the cavern, as well as keep them out of bad weather. She was more impressed with the hideout the more she saw of it.

Continuing to wait, she looked around. Against

one wall was what appeared to be the cooking center, for supplies were piled up in an orderly fashion, next to what looked like a stone oven. A black stew pot hung over a fire, while nearby a roasting animal was being turned on a spit over an open flame by a young man.

It was to this cooking area that Cord had been taken. She watched as he was handed a tin plate with food laddled onto it, then he hunkered down near one of the fires and quickly ate. When he was done, he accepted a tin cup of coffee, then began rolling a cigarette. Finally, he glanced up and saw her watching him. His eyes narrowed, but it was the only expression he allowed to cross his face. She felt a chill run up her spine, for this was the Cord she had first met, the man who had convinced her he was a wild savage, a vicious outlaw, and he was in sharp contrast to the gentle lover she had come to know. Which was he, concerned brother and tender lover, or desperado?

"Sorry to keep you so long," Red Duke said, stepping from the tent.

"I didn't mind waiting," she replied, quickly looking away from Cord, hoping Red Duke had not noticed.

Red Duke was carrying a pair of pale yellow satin slippers and a matching yellow satin robe in one hand and a lantern in the other. As he stopped beside her, she raised an eyebrow, quite leery of accepting anything so personal from him.

"Allow me to make your stay here more comfortable," he explained, extending the clothes to her. "I know you couldn't have brought much in your saddlebags, and my men tend to drag in all kinds of things I have no use for. I'd consider it an honor if you would wear some of the clothes that are just

147

gathering dust in my tent. And don't feel obliged by wearing them, that's not my intention."

She hesitated, warmed by his small speech and the lovely clothes. The robe would be wonderfully comfortable, and if he truly meant she shouldn't feel obligated, then perhaps there wouldn't be any harm in wearing them. "Thank you," she replied, taking the clothes from him. The satin was smooth and cool to her touch, and she knew the robe was very expensive.

Suddenly she felt a compulsion to look at Cord, and glanced his way. He was standing still, a cigarette dangling from his lips, his hands clinched at his sides, his attention totally concentrated on her. She quickly looked away, realizing how her accepting the clothes must appear to him. But she couldn't do anything about it, for she didn't want to offend Red Duke, and Cord would just have to understand.

"Don't worry, your honor won't be hurt," Red Duke added. "If my men stare, it's because you're the only woman here."

Her heart beat a little faster. But what of Cord's sister? Did this mean Cord had been lying to her all along, or was Duke not telling the truth? There was no way to know, not yet. She might as well enjoy the luxury while she could. "I won't take offense, if they won't."

"They're only too happy to have a beautiful woman here, even if they can only look. But come, I know you want that bath, then later we'll dine together."

He extended his arm, and she touched him again, feeling the softness of the expensive black fabric of his shirt against the hardness of his muscles. As they walked away from the tent, she could feel the men watching them, but most of all she could feel Cord's intense stare. She straightened her shoulders and determinedly didn't look back.

They wound their way around bedrolls, small tents, supplies and lounging men. It was a confusing sight, although she sensed an underlying order and an alert tension all around her. The smell of cooking food, hay, horses and a group of men combined to give the cavern its own distinct scent. When they arrived at the back of the cavern, she noticed several tunnels leading off into dark labyrinths.

"This way, Victoria," Red Duke said, holding up the lantern to light the way down one of the tunnels.

She hesitated, not wanting to enter the tunnel, for the single lantern's light did little to dispel the darkness, and she had no idea what might be hiding in its depths.

"It's all right," he encouraged, stepping into the tunnel and pulling her with him. "It's perfectly safe, I assure you. You wouldn't be afraid of the dark, would you?"

"No, of course not. It's just that I've never been in a place like this before." She couldn't let him think she was afraid or weak, but she felt more nervous the farther they walked down the tunnel, for if he decided to turn off the light and leave her there, she would be almost helpless. But she mustn't think that way.

"Good, I don't like weak women," he replied. "I know this place is a little confusing at first, but soon you'll know your away around as well as I do."

"I hope so. Is it far?"

"No, not far at all, and worth the walk."

She realized that as they walked she was clinging a little harder to his arm all the time, for she felt the stifling darkness begin to overwhelm her. And it didn't help that their shadows were cast huge and menacing on the tunnel's smooth wall by the lantern's light.

After they had walked awhile, he suddenly stopped and held up the lantern, casting light over the interior of a small cave. Water dripped constantly, rhythmically, and had obviously spent many years forming stalactites like icicles hanging from the ceiling, over stalagmites resembling large fangs rising from the floor. And in the center was a deep, dark pool of steaming water, with the scent of minerals permeating the air. It was completely quiet there, except for the sound of dripping water and the harsh rasp of their breath.

"Lovely, isn't it?" he said, smiling at her.

"Yes, I've never seen anything like it." She glanced all around, feeling as if some prehistoric animal was suddenly going to amble in for a drink or a meal, meaning her. Or that Red Duke having her alone might take advantage of her. But she couldn't let Red Duke know the way it affected her.

"I don't want you to feel hurried," he said, setting the lamp down near the pool of water. "Take your time. Let the water soothe your muscles. It's the best thing for you after a long ride."

"You mean, bathe here?"

"Certainly. That's a naturally hot, mineral spring. But, beware, as far as I know, it's bottomless. There's some rose soap in the pocket of your robe, and you'll find washcloths and towels by the pool." He turned to go.

"You aren't going to leave me here alone, are you?"

Looking back, he smiled. "Do you want me to stay and join you? I didn't mean to rush you, but—"

"Oh, no. I meant that . . . it's just that I'm not used to this place."

150

"Trust me, you'll like it, and I'll leave the lantern for you."

"Can you find your way out in the dark?"

"I know this cavern well. Don't fear for me. Take your time, then we'll have dinner and get to know each other better."

He smiled again, then turned and walked into the darkness of the tunnel, the sound of his footsteps bouncing off the walls creating the illusion that he was coming and going in all directions at once.

She covered her ears, squeezing her eyes shut, then took a deep breath, disgusted with her fear. She had to control her uneasiness. This was obviously used regularly as a bath, and she knew of famous mineral baths that were supposed to be very good for you. She just had never heard of one deep in a cavern in the Black Range mountains in New Mexico, although Fred Harvey's Montezuma Hotel in northern New Mexico had been famous for its mineral baths.

Nevertheless, she wasn't in a resort, and she didn't feel safe. It was going to be hard to relax. Maybe she wouldn't bathe at all; but Red Duke would know if she didn't, and she didn't want to upset him, not here, not now, because no matter how gentlemanly he was being, she was beginning to realize just how much power he had, especially deep in his own lair.

Had she been foolish, even naive to come this far? Even though it would be great to describe in a novel, she didn't need quite this much experience. But that was not why she had really come, and she knew it. There was Cord, and if what he had said about his sister was true, he would need her help. She was beginning to believe his story.

If only Cord was with her now, they could share the pleasure of the pool, like they had before. But that couldn't be, not here.

151

She sighed and walked over to the water, then ran a finger through it. The temperature was perfect, and she felt tempted to soak herself. She had no doubt it would feel wonderful, especially after the hard, grueling ride through the mountains. There was also no doubt she was dirty, and a bath and clean clothes would do wonders for her spirits.

Glancing around, she decided it would probably be quite safe to go ahead. Red Duke was certain to be very busy and wouldn't miss her for quite a while. Also, she would be able to hear if anyone was coming and see their lantern's light, if they used one, which surely they would. But, most likely, Red Duke wouldn't let anybody near the place until she was finished.

Well, she would just be adventurous. She took off Little Stinger, her gun ring, and carefully placed it in the pocket of her shirt. Unbuttoning her blue plaid shirt, she glanced around the cave, wondering if bats lived there and if one might suddenly swoop down and bite her. Then she shook her head and stilled that thought. No, she was safe, and that was that.

As she slowly undressed, the soft light of the lantern illuminated her creamy, white skin as more and more of it was exposed until she stood only in her cotton camisole and drawers. She took the pins from her hair and shook it out, the heavy, strawberry mass glinting golden and rosy in the light. Then she took off her camisole and set it aside. Her breasts turned to warm golden globes with dark pink tips in the soft light. Finally, she slipped down her drawers and stood completely nude.

She was surprised to feel so relaxed. The constant sound of water and the deep, muffled quiet was soothing her, making her feel completely at peace as she experienced a oneness with the earth around her.

She stretched, extending her arms upward toward the ceiling and rising high upon her toes, suddenly feeling like Aphrodite rising from the water in some artist's painting.

Smiling at her fancy, she took a step toward the water and heard a sound like scraping nearby. Shocked, she covered her breasts with her hands, then realized the futility of that gesture and called softly, "Who's there?"

No answer.

"Duke?"

Still no answer.

Perhaps it was a bat, or an animal, or—but she stopped that train of thought, for she was letting her imagination run away with her. There had to be many small sounds in a cavern this size, and sound was magnified and confused by the walls. She was all alone, and yet as she sat down at the edge of the pool, the hairs raised on the back of her neck, as if somebody was watching her. She looked behind her, but she could see nothing beyond the pool of lantern light except darkness.

Deciding not to be caught by surprise, she walked around the pool, so that she was facing the entrance to the cave, and sat down again, extending her legs into the water. It felt wonderful, hot and soothing. She slipped completely into the water, letting it come up to her chin, while leaving her arms over the edge, holding her up. She could swim but didn't like the idea of swimming in an isolated, bottomless pool of water.

She leaned her head back and shut her eyes, letting the water's heat penetrate deep into her muscles, relaxing her, soothing her, healing all her small aches and pains. And it was as if the quiet penetrated her, too, soothing, lulling, protecting. She smiled, feeling really good for the first time in a long while, at least since the death of her father.

Here, she could begin to accept his death, as she thought of the earth and how there was always an end to life, an end to a growing season, but always a new beginning, too. Out of her father's death had come his legacy to her. It was as if he had entrusted his love of literature and writing to her, and she was now to continue it, not in the same way he had, but in her own way, extending his talent and yet beginning with herself. Yes, she felt good, relieved, as if all would be well, if she just followed the pattern that was emerging in her life.

Smiling, she fell into a light sleep, her head tipping slightly backward, her body buoyed by the mineral water, her face slightly pink from the heat.

Suddenly Red Duke stepped out of the shadows.

Chapter 11

Red Duke ran long fingers down the smooth, damp skin of Victoria's arm, and she jerked awake, stifling a scream at the sight of the tall man bending over her. Then she recognized Red Duke and relaxed . . . but only slightly.

"You frightened me," she accused, stalling for time to try and draw her wits together to deal with the sudden intrusion.

"I thought you didn't want to be left alone. Are you sorry I came back?"

"It's not very proper," she replied, really wanting to tell him to go away, for she was shocked and worried at being in such a vulnerable position.

"But do we need to worry about propriety?" He sat down, continuing to run his hand up and down her arm.

She shivered.

"You like my touch?" It wasn't a question as much as a statement.

"I'm afraid I'm tired," she evaded.

"There are many ways to dispel tiredness." He lightly touched the back of her hand, tickling her

155

until it bordered on the painful.

"That's certainly distracting." She moved her hand away and dipped it into the water.

He chuckled. "You're so sensitive. I knew you would be. You had to be, with that color of hair. It's what first attracted me to you. And you have no idea how rare it is out here."

"Really?"

"Have you seen another man with red hair?"

"No, I can't remember one."

"And you won't. It's become my trademark."

"You mean in your name?"

"Yes. Red Duke." He lifted her hair and let it fall softly through his fingers. "I've become so tired of dark-haired, dark-eyed, dark-skinned women, and I've missed the Yankee spunk that was immediately evident in you. You're obviously a woman who won't easily be broken."

"Well, no, I guess not."

"But you haven't been tried to the breaking point, have you?

"I suppose not, however—"

"That excites me." He pushed his fingers into her hair at her forehead, then combed backward, hard enough to pull her head back. When she was looking up at him, he smiled, then let her go.

"You hurt me," she accused, frowning, trying to figure out what kind of game he was playing, and what he might do next.

"Only slightly. You've forgotten you were tired, haven't you?"

She hesitated. Actually, he had made her forget about being tired; but he was also beginning to frighten her, and perhaps he was even as dangerous as Cord had suggested. Although Red Duke had obviously been having fantasies about her, she didn't want to encourage him, because he might try to make his fantasies reality. She wished desperately she wasn't in such a vulnerable position.

"Your tiredness?" he insisted, stroking her hair.

"Yes, you made me forget about it," she reluctantly admitted, thinking there were a lot of better ways to get over being tired.

"Good. You're turning out to be everything I'd hoped you'd be. Beautiful, not just your face, but your body, too."

"You looked!"

"Of course I did. You weren't naive enough to think I wouldn't."

"I trusted you."

"But I didn't lie. I left and came back. And you're glad, aren't you?"

"You told me I could take my bath alone."

"You wanted me to stay, remember? But where was I, oh yes, listing your assets. Beautiful. Smart. Talented. Innocent, but not for long. You're tired of that innocence, aren't you? You want me to initiate you into all the pleasures a woman can experience, don't you?"

"I came because I'm researching my novel." She kicked out at the water in frustration, unable to figure out his game, but feeling his power over her more and more all the time. She hoped he believed what she'd said.

He chuckled. "Surely you don't expect me to believe that. You went to a lot of trouble to get here, and it can only mean one thing . . . you've thought of me as much as I've thought of you. Admit it." He tugged her hair, a little too hard.

"Yes, I've thought of you . . . as a gentleman," she

said, trying to make him behave like one.

"Oh, yes, I know the part of the gentleman well, but I also know other roles, and some I want to teach you. Do you learn well?"

"What kind of lessons?" she asked suspiciously.

"Perhaps exciting. Maybe painful. But very interesting. I think you'll make an apt student."

"Maybe, but perhaps I'll be gone—"

"Tomorrow? The next day? I think not." He stood up, picked up her clothing, leaving only the new green robe and slippers, and walked to the entrance. "Come to dinner soon. I'll be waiting for you." Then he walked away, his footsteps echoing and reechoing down the tunnel.

She exhaled slowly, unable to stop the chill that had invaded her body at his touch and his words. Nor could she ignore the fact that he had just taken her clothes, and her gun ring was in the pocket of her shirt. She was now quite defenseless, and it worried her.

She was ready to leave. But could she get out? Not very likely. She very much feared Red Duke wouldn't let her go, not until he had gotten what he wanted from her, and she was afraid of what that might be.

Cord. She took a deep breath and felt a little warmer just knowing he was nearby. But he wouldn't leave without his sister, if she existed, and she didn't think she could get safely back to Silver City or any other area of civilization without a guide, even if she could sneak away. But what if Cord was a desperado? If that was the case, she had the feeling she just might be in very big trouble.

For now, she would assume that Red Duke was not a man who robbed from the rich to give to the poor. He seemed to be power hungry and willing to do whatever was necessary to get what he wanted. She remembered his fingers on her skin, his voice smooth and caressing, yet dangerous, and she shivered again. Perhaps it was just a power game to control her, and she was overreacting to him. But she didn't know what to think, for she simply hadn't had enough experience with men or matters of the heart.

Perhaps it was best to play a waiting game. And for that, she would have to be smart, smarter than she had ever been before. And she would have to continue being a good actress, convincing enough to make Red Duke think she was going along with him, good enough to fit the image of the dream woman he had conjured after their first meeting. She had the feeling it might be the only thing to keep her free and to help her find out just what he had in mind.

Cord wasn't going to like what he saw, but she would have to find a way to talk with him in private and explain. It was a big place, so maybe they could plan a secret rendezvous. Also, if his sister was here, she was being kept in some secret cave or passage, somewhere away from the main activity, and she felt sorry for the young woman, for it was seeming like a more dangerous place all the time.

But she had no proof that Cord's sister existed yet, and no proof except her own feelings and what she had seen that Red Duke was a dangerous man. However, she was not going to be caught off guard again, if she could help it. She was going to keep watch and learn as much as she could as quickly as she could. It was the only way she knew to come out safe and alive, and her own woman.

So, she might as well get on with it. She looked around the cave again, realizing just how isolated and vulnerable she was. At least she had the gun ring, and if she could get her clothes back, nobody would ever suspect it was anything more than a pretty bauble.

But for now, she might as well finish her bath, for she was hungry and it was time to brave Red Duke in his own tent, then try to make some decent sleeping arrangement. Getting out of the water, she sat on the edge of the pool and rubbed rose-scented soap over her body, then lathered her hair. Finally, she rinsed off in the pool and felt more refreshed, although tense again. She stood up, completely nude, but no longer caring if Red Duke was lurking in the shadows, for he had already seen all he wanted, and she couldn't do anything about it anyway.

She rubbed dry with a fluffy towel, then slid on the satin robe over her clean body. Although the fabric felt delightful, so smooth and so soft, she felt very exposed in it. Even with it belted around her waist, it was very little clothing compared to what she usually wore. Putting on the matching slippers, she picked up the lantern.

Taking a deep breath and a last glance at the pool, she started down the tunnel, looking behind every few steps, sure she was being followed or watched or something. But she quickly reached the main cavern unharmed. Hesitating there, she tried to calm her confused emotions, knowing she would need all her wits to deal with Red Duke.

Smilin' Sam suddenly appeared, looked her up and down, then spit tobacco dangerously close to her pale green satin hem. "He's got you all dolled up, don't he?"

"I simply had a bath."

"In his special pool, right?"

"A mineral bath."

"Red Duke's favors don't come cheap."

"Well, neither do mine. And, if you'll excuse me, I have a dinner to attend."

Smilin' Sam chuckled and leered. "No, ma'am, I bet your favors don't come cheap, but if Red Duke don't want to pay the price, come to me. I'd 'bout put my life on the line to kiss you all over."

She shuddered and tried to walk around him.

He blocked her path. "Hold on, Miss Victoria. I'm to take you to Red Duke, seeing as how I got you here."

"Then please do so."

"All in good time, ma'am . . . just as soon as I get an eyeful." He grinned and spit in the direction of her hem again. "Come on." He started walking toward the royal blue tent in the center of the cavern.

Behind him, she quickly became aware of the curious and lecherous stares that followed her as she made her way to Red Duke. Work stopped, conversation lapsed, and men froze as they watched her walk, the yellow satin robe clinging to her curves, revealing the cleft between her breasts and her bare ankles as the skirt parted when she moved. She felt as if she had been stripped naked by the time Smilin' Sam stopped in front of Red Duke's tent and motioned her inside.

She hastily entered, relieved to be out from under the stares of the woman-hungry men. But Red Duke awaited her there, and she suddenly was not very relieved at all. He had removed all his clothes except a pair of very tight, black leather trousers, which revealed more than they concealed, and for the first time she realized just how powerfully muscular he was. But she also had the feeling he was trying to intimidate her with his powerful body, and that

161

didn't please her at all.

The second thing she noticed was that there was no furniture in the tent, except a trunk and a low table. The floor was covered with animal skins, from bear to buffalo to rabbit, and tossed on top of the furs were large stuffed pillows covered in brightly colored silk. Hanging from the center of the tent was an oil lamp, shedding soft yellow light.

Red Duke nodded at her, then walked gracefully to the low table and poured a deep Burgundy wine into two golden goblets. Handing one to her, he caressed her fingers as she took it, and smiled.

"You look lovely," he said, then lifted a lock of her hair and pressed it to his lips. "And you smell delightful, too. Did you enjoy your bath?"

"Yes." She smiled, determined to play the game well, and raised the goblet to her lips.

"Wait. A toast." He clinked the rim of his goblet with hers. "To us."

They drank, watching each other over the rims of their goblets, then he motioned for her to sit on a cushion near the low table of Chinese design, painted with black lacquer and exotic birds and flowers.

Sitting down, she tried to keep the robe closed and not expose any more of herself than she already had. After arranging the yellow satin as best she could, she glanced up.

He was smiling at her in amusement. "I've already seen you, Victoria. Although modesty is becoming, it's certainly not necessary."

She blushed lightly, saying, "It's a natural response."

"A conditioned response, not natural, and one day soon I hope to recondition you so that you will feel

162

comfortable to walk this cavern completely naked and watch my men twist in pain, seeing you, wanting you, but knowing they can never have you."

"I hardly think that's necessary." She was horrified.

"Not necessary, but amusing, and I do so like to be amused. Don't you?"

"It depends."

"I'll teach you how to be amused, and you'll like it. Wait and see."

"There may not be time."

"You have someplace to be? Family? I think not. You're on a trip, and your publisher won't expect to hear from you for some time. No, I believe we have plenty of time to make you exactly the woman I want."

She shivered and drank deeply of the wine to soothe her nerves. It was a good vintage, expensive, and she wasn't surprised. She was beginning to realize that Red Duke required the best for himself, and as for the needy he helped, that had all been a lie.

"But you must be hungry. I've had Cook prepare something special for us. Just a minute." He stood up, walked to the front of the tent and stepped outside.

She took a deep breath and tried to relax, knowing she needed to eat if she was going to keep up her strength. But at the moment, she didn't feel in the least hungry and was even feeling a little lightheaded from the wine and the tension. Still, she must remain calm and in control, and as Red Duke stepped back inside, she smiled and hoped it looked genuine.

Sitting down beside her, he rubbed her knee, his hand warm and strong and dangerous. She shivered.

163

"You're cold, or—" he asked.

"This isn't very proper."

He laughed. "Did you think coming to an outlaw's hideout would be?"

She shrugged, feeling foolish and very naive.

"Well, no matter. You'll make me happy. And that's what counts. Ah, here's Sam."

Smilin' Sam carried a heavy tray laden with food to the low table and set it down. Glancing at Red Duke, he stepped back, awaiting further orders.

"That'll be all, Sam," Red Duke said.

Looking at the food, she couldn't help thinking about what Smilin' Sam might have spit in it on the way over, for that would be just his kind of humor. But she said nothing and decided to keep that thought from her mind as she ate, if she could.

Smilin' Sam nodded, then quickly left the tent.

"Now, what have we here?" Red Duke asked, looking over the tray. "I think we have several morsels which might tempt you, Victoria."

"I'm sure I'll enjoy whatever it is."

He handed her a large, white linen napkin, then spread one over his lap, indicating that she should do the same. "I'm not set up for all the social graces, so we'll do this the fun way." He placed a small, roasted bird on a golden platter, then added a sizzling rabbit haunch, a slice of deer and a huge, boiled egg. Then he added two biscuits. Handing her the plate, he asked, "Look good?"

"Delicious," she replied, determinedly not thinking about Smilin' Sam.

"It's a lot better than what the men get. You'll notice them eating beans and beef and whatever wild animals they can trap. And, of course, there's always biscuits. But, go on, don't let me stop you." He

164

picked up the rabbit haunch and bit into it.

She didn't ask for silverware, knowing he would be insulted if she questioned his hospitality, and everything could be eaten with her fingers anyway. She started with the egg first, wondering what kind it was, imagining a huge eagle that would never fly, then stopped that line of thinking before she lost her appetite again. Next, she tried the rabbit and found it tasty if a little tough. As she worked her way through the meat, amazed she could eat so much, she watched Red Duke thoroughly enjoying his food, making it as much a sensual experience as a culinary one.

When she was finally full, she set the plate aside and began wiping her hands on the napkin.

"No, Victoria," he said, setting his plate down and taking her hands in his. Slowly, he began licking clean each finger, making it seem more intimate than even a kiss on her lips would have been, for he was obviously enjoying the texture of her skin as much as the flavor and scent of the food on her fingers.

Shivering, she wanted to pull her hands away, but she knew she must play the game, and play it well. But how far could she go? How far would he push her before she had to push back and risk her freedom, perhaps even more. She didn't know, but she didn't like what he was doing. Suddenly, she couldn't help thinking of Cord and how she loved his touch . . . so very different from the way Red Duke made her feel.

"Victoria, are you paying attention? I'll expect you to do likewise for me in a moment."

Her eyes widened in dismay. "Couldn't you just wash your hands?"

He laughed and sat back. "You can be so amusing. What would be the fun in that? Didn't you ever play slave before?"

"No."

Again, he chuckled. "You're going to be a delight to teach. Maybe we'll get somebody else to play slave. I don't particularly like that role, either."

She didn't know how she was doing it, but somehow she kept passing his tests. Maybe it was because he was misinterpreting her, or toying with her. But as long as he was relatively happy with her, she would have some freedom around the cavern, and she intended to use that to learn more about the place and its master.

Red Duke went back to eating, and when he was finished, he washed his hands in wine, then wiped them on his white napkin, leaving it stained red. He refilled their goblets, then lay down, putting his head in her lap.

She froze, not daring to move or to tell him to get up. "Are you comfortable?" she quipped, deciding she was learning things that she would never be able to put into one of her novels. She was also about to give up making notes until she was someplace safe and quite.

"Delightfully so," he replied, stroking her satin-covered thigh. "You're so soft and delectable I can hardly stay my hand; but I don't want to rush you, and I want to slowly savor your innocence."

"Perhaps I'm not as innocent as you think."

He looked up at her, his blue eyes narrowing slightly, then smiled, his sensual lips parting to reveal even white teeth. "You like to tease me, don't you? I like that in a woman. It shows courage and spunk. But don't go far."

"I might go too far, if I wasn't so sleepy and

166

tired." She yawned, hoping he would take the hint and suggest they go to sleep.

"Then you need something to wake you up." From behind a pillow, he pulled out a beautiful peacock feather.

"How lovely."

"Almost as lovely as you." He stroked her neck with the feather, and she shivered as he continued downward until he reached the cleavage of her breasts revealed by the robe. Tickling her breasts until tiny bumps raised on her flesh, he inserted the tip of the feather farther, caressing slowly, surely, until her nipple hardened against the fabric. Then he chuckled and removed the feather.

She was horrified that she had responded to his manipulation, thinking that only Cord had ever made her react before. But Red Duke was a very experienced man, and when she looked into his eyes, she realized that he wanted to see only himself reflected in her gaze, her eyes, her lips, her body telling him how handsome he was, how wonderful he was, how fulfilling he was. He was a man in love with himself, and his fantasy woman was someone who reflected that image. That was why he was so enamored with her strawberry-blond hair and pale skin, and ladylike background.

"You're very handsome, Duke," she said softly, realizing how to play the game and hopefully win, then ran a hand through the thick red hair on his chest. "So strong, so muscled, so sensual."

"You want me now?"

"No. I want to wait, to savor you, until I want you so badly I can't stand to be near you if you don't take me."

He grinned and nipped her fingers lightly, then

167

kissed the tips and finally sucked them. "I thought you were perfect for me, Victoria. Now I know for sure. You want the pain first, so that the pleasure is more intense, don't you."

"Yes," she whispered, hoping it didn't mean she would be hurt in some way.

He rolled over, so that he was looking straight at her. "When the sight of me sets you on fire, I'll dress you in the finest clothes a woman has ever worn. Your hair will be styled in the latest fashion. Then I will undress you so slowly that you will finally rip the clothes from your body and beg me to release you from the pain of wanting me."

"And will you?"

He chuckled. "Maybe, but then again, perhaps not. You will burn for me, never knowing when I will stop the pain."

Then he stood up and paced across the animal skins, letting her watch his body move, and she couldn't help noticing the hard bulge in the front of his trousers, tightly molded by black leather. As he strutted around the tent, she had to admit he was a magnificent example of a man, but she didn't want him. What she really wanted was to snuggle with Cord, who was so much more her size and so much more sensual to her.

Red Duke stopped before her. "Now, I leave you to your lonely bed, Victoria. Just pull any of the skins over you for cover. I'll see you in the morning." Then he stalked from the tent.

Amazed to be so quickly left alone, she took several sips of wine, set the goblet aside, then snuggled into the pillows and furs. Whatever happened, she was going to get a good night's sleep, for she didn't think she would see Red Duke again until morning since he was tormenting her by letting her sleep alone.

Yawning, she quickly fell into a deep sleep.

Chapter 12

Chaps awoke the next morning, her robe tangled around her body, revealing much more than it concealed. Hastily, she jerked a fur over herself, then glanced around.

A lantern burned on the low table near her, casting soft light over the inside of the tent. Nobody was in sight, and it was very quiet in the cavern. She was a little surprised at that, but not too concerned, for she felt much too relaxed and rested to worry about anything just yet. She yawned, stretched and sat up. She had really slept well and felt ready to take on Red Duke and his Comancheros, as well as find out the truth about Cord Cordova.

Standing, she pulled her robe into place, pushed back her thick hair, and looked around the tent some more. Nothing seemed to have changed from the night before, except that the tray of food and wine had been removed, making her realize just how tired she must have been not to have awakened when somebody took it away.

She wondered what time it was, but there was no way to know deep within the cavern. Perhaps she had slept very late, and it was so quiet, the men must all be out doing something. Had she missed an important robbery or some other crime? Feeling left out, and a little worried about being excluded, she decided she had better get dressed and find out what was going on.

Looking around for her clothes, she didn't see her saddlebags or the clothing she had taken off the night before. Instead, she found a forest-green silk gown, with matching soft, leather green shoes, and pale green silk underwear. None of it was hers, but she assumed she was supposed to wear it since there was nothing else around, unless she wanted to wear the revealing robe, which she certainly did not.

What concerned her most about her missing clothes was the fact that her gun ring had been in the pocket of the shirt Red Duke had taken away from the pool. What if he discovered what it really was, or had locked all her things away someplace where she couldn't get to them? Then she would be without any means of defense, and that scared her, because Red Duke already had too much power here and she too little.

As she began dressing, she decided that one of the first things she must do this morning, or afternoon, was get back her gun ring and saddlebags. Her second priority was food, for she suddenly felt ravenous and would have been quite willing to share the Comancheros' beans and beef just to relieve the ache in her stomach.

Pulling on the silk gown, she realized how expensive it was and how well it fit, almost as if it had been made especially for her. But how could that be? Shaking her head in perplexity, she buttoned up the front, very much aware that it was a lady's afternoon gown, meant for visiting, or shopping, or riding in a carriage. Also, it was in the latest Parisian style, with the rich fabric pulled into a bustle in back, creating a drapery effect in front with a narrow skirt.

It felt good to be dressed well again, actually better than she had been accustomed to in New York City. She just hoped she didn't suddenly need to ride a horse, or scale a cliff, or do any one of numerous other things that could make the gown uncomfortable at the least and possibly quite dangerous. But she wouldn't worry about that right now. She had to think about getting some food and her gun ring, and once she got her clothes back, she could change to something more appropriate and serviceable.

Taking a deep breath, she left the tent, expecting to see Smilin' Sam, or Red Duke, or Cord suddenly appear, but as she looked around the cavern, she saw no one. It made the place feel eerie, and she began walking quickly toward the cooking area to see if she could find any food.

Fortunately, there were still some biscuits, a beef stew and hot coffee left, so she filled a plate and began eating, continuing to glance around the cavern. She had no idea where to start looking for her own things, and if Red Duke had hidden them, they would be almost impossible to find. But why would he do that, unless he wanted complete control over how she dressed? She didn't like that thought at all and hurriedly finished the food.

Holding the tin mug of coffee, she walked toward the outside entrance of the cavern, deciding to question the guards, who should be on duty. As she got closer to the entrance, she began to hear voices outside. Quickly finishing her coffee, she set the mug aside and hurried to the front of the cavern.

The sounds were louder now, as if men were cheering one another, and she looked around in concern but could see nothing except a guard standing sentry on each side of the cavern entrance. They both looked at her, hands on rifles and stern looks on their faces, although those softened slightly at the sight of her.

"I need to see Red Duke, or Cord, or even Smilin' Sam. Where is everybody?" she asked, a sudden fear growing in her.

The guards looked at her for a moment, as if deciding if she should be told anything, then one said, "Follow that trail around back."

"Thank you."

Even though it was a cryptic answer, it was better than none at all. It also meant that she wasn't being kept a prisoner, and she wondered why.

Following the path, she pushed that question from her mind and was determined to find out what was going on. It was good to know she wasn't intentionally being kept out of Comanchero business, but what could they be doing, for she could hear the voices louder now, shouting, calling, encouraging, cussing.

She grew more and more confused as she followed the steep, winding path around the side of the mountain, holding up her skirt and trying to step on as few rocks as possible, for the soft leather shoes were not made for rough country. By the time she made her way downward, she was panting from the corset constricting her breath, and her feet hurt from the soft shoes. She decided she wasn't going to be put in this position again, so she would simply have to get her clothing back from Red Duke.

Following the path around a corner, she was suddenly looking down at a natural stone platform sticking out slightly from the mountainside, with a breathtaking view of the valley below. Tall pines and

173

gnarled piñons clung to the rocky soil, and the scent of evergreen filled the air.

On the platform, two men fought, their torsos bare and glistening with sweat. Ringed around them were Red Duke's Comancheros, hollering, encouraging, cursing, even betting. And back from them, standing on a higher dais of rock, stood Red Duke, sunlight turning his red hair into a golden halo.

Her eyes were drawn back to the combatants, and she looked at them more closely. One of them was the height and size of Cord, but she didn't dare believe it was him. Why would he be fighting? Shaking her head, she continued downward, realizing no one had noticed her because they were all so intent on the fight. And, naturally, they didn't expect to be surprised by outsiders, since they had constant sentries on guard.

She took a few more steps, and Red Duke looked up, saw her and smiled, motioning her toward him. She walked over to him, and he helped her up to the dais, then held her hand a long moment, taking the time to look her over completely, before nodding in satisfaction.

"You're truly beautiful, Victoria. That gown suits you perfectly."

"And it fits me perfectly, too. It could have been made especially for me."

"Perhaps it was." Then he added, "Have you come to watch the fight? Those men might interest you."

For the first time she had a good look, and she grew cold when she realized that one of the men fighting actually was Cord. She hadn't been mistaken, although she wished she had been. She glanced at Red Duke in concern and realized he was watching for her reaction. She quickly tried to appear less interested. "Why is Cord fighting?"

"He has to prove himself if he wants to join my Comancheros."

"But that man's much bigger than him. Cord might be hurt, then what good would he be?"

"I don't need men who can't take a pounding. Besides, Cord seems to be taking care of himself."

She looked back, dreading to see what might be happening to Cord, worrying that Red Duke might somehow suspect Cord's true motive for entering the hideout and have set up a fight that would get Cord killed. What if something happened to him? She would be left alone, but worse than that—suddenly her whole body tingled as she realized her concern was not for herself but for Cord. What if he died?

She couldn't stand to think about it and tried to turn her mind back to the fight, but her thoughts persisted, almost with a will of their own. Could Cord mean more to her than she had thought? Had their lovemaking bound her in some way to him?

As she watched Cord holding his own against the bigger man, using an incredible amount of cunning, instinct and skill, she grew more and more sure that he mattered a great deal to her. She was relieved to know he could take care of himself, even against a much larger opponent, for this obviously wasn't his first battle, by any means, and he was showing himself to be a formidable opponent. She exhaled softly in relief, then glanced at Red Duke.

He was scowling, the lines marring his perfectly chiseled face.

"Don't you want Cord to win?" she asked.

"I can always use a good man. And since it looks like he may join my Comancheros, I think I should warn you that I'll share you with none of my men." His blue eyes were steely.

175

"But I had no intention—"

"Just a warning, in case he thought you owed him something for bringing you here."

"Smilin' Sam came with us."

"Yes, but he knows his place, despite his desires. Cord strikes me as a man who doesn't take leadership well. He'd better learn quick, or he won't live long around here."

"I'm sure he wouldn't question you, Duke, since you've obviously proved your ability to lead men."

"That's right, I have, but there's always some cocksure newcomer wanting to knock me off. And it can't be done." He gave her a hard stare, then looked at the fighting ring again and called, "Okay, I've seen enough. It's an equal match."

But Chaps was watching, too, and it wasn't equal. Cord was definitely winning, because he had the other man down, with a knee on his chest. But when he heard Red Duke, he immediately stopped and stood up, blood dripping from the corner of his mouth, his chest heaving and sweat glistening over his chest and back.

She wanted him suddenly, feeling the heat begin in her center and spread outward. She wanted to take him away from here to some safe, quiet place in the mountains, maybe to a waterfall, then she would bathe him, patch up his wounds, and make love to him, slowly, wonderfully, and . . .

"Victoria, are you coming, or are you going to stare at my men all day?" Red Duke interrupted her thoughts, irritation in his voice.

"Yes, of course. I'm sorry, I was thinking about the beauty of the mountains, and wondering if there was a waterfall somewhere nearby."

Suddenly smiling, he took her hand and tucked it in the crook of his arm. "I should have known you wouldn't be interested in dirty, sweaty men. You hardly noticed them, did you?"

"No. I came looking for you, since I couldn't find my saddlebags or clothes or—"

"Silly woman." He chuckled indulgently. "I put all your things in the trunk in my tent."

"Oh." She smiled, trying to look embarrassed at her stupidity, but actually disliking his attitude. How could she have guessed what he had done with her things, but now she would be able to get her gun ring, if it was still there.

They stepped down from the dais, and the men filed by, nodding in appreciation at Chaps and deference to Red Duke. Then the Comanchero who had fought Cord stopped, and Cord walked up behind him.

"I want to congratulate both you men," Red Duke said, "and you will each get an extra cut on the next robbery."

"Thanks," the Comanchero said, then moved on.

Cord looked straight at Duke, his dark eyes narrowed and hard. "I'll fight them all, if that's what it takes to be one of your Comancheros."

"I've seen enough. You fight well. Now, I want to see you shoot. Come on."

Red Duke started forward, keeping Chaps' hand tucked in the crook of his arm, and Cord followed.

Chaps was suddenly concerned about Cord. He hadn't looked at her, hadn't acknowledged her in any way, and he now seemed so much like the man who had jumped her from the bushes after the stagecoach robbery that he was frightening. She had been terrified of him then, and she was beginning to be again, for he looked mean and sinister, like a man willing to do anything to get what he wanted.

She hated to admit it, but she still might have to

warn Red Duke about Cord, for until she had more information, she couldn't trust either man. Wanting to believe in Cord, yet not being able to, made her feel sick. Maybe she had been right to put her faith in dreams and books and ideas, rather than people. But then she remembered what she and Cord had shared and knew that nothing in her mind could ever have compared to the intensity of their physical passion.

Until she knew the truth about Red Duke and Cord, she had better depend completely on herself, for she was determined to deal with reality and come out of this alive.

As she walked up the path with Red Duke, she could feel Cord staring at her back. Was he thinking that he had gotten what he wanted from her, so he didn't need her anymore, since he was being accepted by Red Duke? Or was he wondering why she was wearing clothes Red Duke had given her and if she wanted the tall Comanchero leader rather than him now? Or maybe he was just concentrating on staying alive.

Maybe that was the best thing for both of them to be concentrating on, anyway. Just as soon as she could, she would change to her own clothing and put on her gun ring. Life was definitely a lot more dangerous than fantasy, and she was finally beginning to realize it. The blood on Cord's lip was real, he was probably in pain, and yet now he would still have to prove his skill with a gun.

When they got to the top of the trail, Smilin' Sam was waiting for them. He was wearing his Colt .45 and holding another pistol in a leather holster. When Red Duke nodded, he turned onto a narrow path which wound around the back of the mountain, and they followed.

178

Finally, they came to a clearing with a target of bottles set up at one end. The range looked extremely far to Chaps, and she was glad she wasn't going to have to shatter bottles with a .45. She glanced at Cord, but no expression crossed his face.

"Put on the holster, Cord. I want to see you draw and shoot," Red Duke commanded, motioning toward Smilin' Sam.

Smilin' Sam handed Cord the extra Colt. 45 and holster, and Chaps realized that it was the gun Smilin' Sam had taken from Cord before leaving Silver City.

Cord strapped on his holster quickly, expertly, as if he had done it repeatedly all his life, then turned toward the target. He hesitated, focusing his concentration, then drew, and one bottle went down. Repeatedly, he drew and fired, but although he hit more times than he missed, he did not have a perfect score. When the pistol was empty, he turned back to Red Duke.

Chaps suddenly wondered if Cord had intentionally not drawn or fired as fast or as accurately as he could have, underplaying his abilities so Red Duke would not feel threatened. But would Red Duke consider Cord's performance good enough or fast enough? She glanced at Red Duke, but his face was expressionless.

"Not bad," Red Duke finally said. "Just don't draw on a fast-gun, and you may live awhile. I assume you can handle a rifle."

"Yes," Cord agreed.

"Okay, you're good enough to join my Comancheros, but there's another little matter. Smilin' Sam brought you in so you're his responsibility. If you go bad, he'll kill you; if not here, then he'll hunt you down if it takes the rest of his life. Isn't that right,

Sam?

"Yes, sir," Smilin' Sam replied, a fanatical gleam in his eyes.

"When you sign on here," Red Duke continued, "you join a brotherhood. We don't cheat on each other, steal from each other, or run out on each other. We work together, no matter what happens, and we never, ever tell outsiders anything about the brotherhood. You understand?"

"Yes," Cord said, nodding.

"If you want to become a Red Duke Comanchero, you will swear an oath of fealty to me. It's a blood oath and binding for life."

"I'll take the oath," Cord agreed.

Chaps felt chilled. She didn't like this oath business, nor the fanatical gleam in Smilin' Sam's eyes.

"Good," Red Duke replied. "You should know that I am actually descended from royal stock, and I have proved my leadership abilities over and over. I do not take you into my Comanchero brotherhood lightly, for I also give an oath to protect and keep my men as well and as safely as possible."

"I'm glad to hear that," Cord said, his dark eyes unreadable.

"Then, we will begin. I, Red Duke, in taking on this man, Cord, swear to watch out for his welfare, cloth him, feed him, and house him as best befits his new station as a Red Duke Comanchero, and in turn he will swear an oath to me." He nodded at Smilin' Sam.

Smilin' Sam stepped forward, pulled out a bowie knife, picked up Cord's left hand, slashed it across the center, then did the same to Red Duke. Holding the two bleeding hands together, Smilin' Sam gave Cord a hard stare and said, "Repeat. I, Cord, swear undying fealty and unswerving loyalty to my duke,

Red Duke, and will support his causes unto my death."

Cord repeated the words, and Sam dropped their hands.

"Then, I pronounce you a Comanchero," Red Duke added, and smiled, a tight movement of his lips.

"I'm glad to be one," Cord replied.

Chaps was looking at the blood on their hands and feeling horrified. Surely there had been no need for that. She heard a slight ringing in her ears and glanced around, for suddenly it seemed unnaturally quiet, as if she could hear all the way to Silver City. But, of course, that couldn't be so.

Maybe she just desperately wanted to be out of this place where men played like boys in a clubhouse and women were not permitted. Only here, these were grown men with the power to make their fantasies real, and she shivered, wishing she was someplace safe, someplace where she had more control and clubhouse boys did not run free.

Red Duke put a heavy hand on Cord's left shoulder. "Take care to remember all we have sworn, and also remember that Smilin' Sam will be your shadow."

"I'm glad to be a Comanchero," Cord replied, "and I won't forget what we've sworn, for I have every intention of doing for you all that you've done for me."

Chaps shivered, wondering if Cord's last words had carried a double meaning, referring to his kidnapped sister, or maybe it was just her imagination playing tricks again.

"Good. Sam, see that he's assigned some tasks," Red Duke said, then took Chaps' hand and tucked it in the crook of his arm, possessively covering it with his own.

Cord didn't seem to notice. He simply nodded at Red Duke, then followed Smilin' Sam out of the clearing and toward the cavern.

"I think Cord will make a good Comanchero, don't you, Victoria?"

She forced herself to laugh lightly, knowing that Red Duke was testing her interest in Cord. "I have no idea what makes a good Comanchero."

He laughed, too, then squeezed her hand. Stepping away from her, he drew his .45 with almost blinding speed and shattered six jars with six bullets, making Cord's performance seem almost clumsy and slow. He turned back to her. "That makes a good Comanchero, but there's no man I've ever met who can beat me, and that makes me the best leader."

"And where does that place me?" she asked coquettishly, trying to get as much information from him as she could.

"The leader gets his pick of women, and his followers, because they aren't as good, get what's left. And I picked you."

"I think I should be honored."

"Yes, but I doubt if you realize it quite yet. You will in time though." He looked around. "This is just the beginning of my empire. Before it's all said and done, I intend to own the ranch lands of southern New Mexico and Arizona. There I will be king and you will be my queen, except in bed where I'll require you to be my whore."

"What!" She shuddered, realizing Red Duke was proving once more how power hungry he was.

He grinned. "Oh, you'll be glad to play that role. I have no doubt after last night. I'll teach you to be everything a woman can be, and you'll be glad."

182

"And what if I'm not?"

"Oh, you will be. Our children will rule this land, like my ancestors ruled their land. It is time for my family's power to return, and I will see that it does. Glory for us is not far away, Victoria." He took her hand and started up the trail toward the cavern.

She walked with him, furiously thinking. Whore? Children? Rule? Power? The more she learned about Red Duke the more frightening he became. How could he be taking so much for granted, especially about them? They barely knew each other, and here he was talking about children. Or maybe it wasn't taking everything so much for granted, as his totally arrogant notion that everything in his life must go as he wanted it, that there was no choice, that he ruled and ruled absolutely. Red Duke was a man who would do anything to achieve his own ends, viewing it as his natural right. Descended from royalty! Perhaps so, but that didn't give him the right to control and use others, she fumed.

The idea of Cord overthrowing Red Duke's empire was looking better all the time. But was that even possible? She shivered. What had Cord gotten himself into, especially if his sister was truly being held captive?

There was obviously a lot more to Red Duke than she had originally thought. But what really terrified her was the fact that he seemed determined to mold her into his fantasy woman, no matter her true personality, or desires, or goals, or talent.

Suddenly, she realized that he hadn't asked any more about her books or her publisher or her goals, but then he wouldn't be interested in her dreams if they didn't fit in with his.

Shaking her head in frustration, she realized she would have to get some answers soon, for Red Duke was moving fast, and Cord was there, armed and ready to put into effect his own scheme, whatever it was. And if she wasn't careful, she could get caught in the middle.

Chapter 13

Several days later, Chaps was no closer to knowing if Red Duke had Cord's sister, even though she had prowled around the cavern, watching the men, listening to conversations, and even walked outside, enjoying the beauty of early summer and learning the lay of the land.

But always in the back of her mind was the fact that she would have to do something soon, for she had to know if Cord was lying to her or if Red Duke was hiding his true intentions, and the best way to do that was to find Cord's sister Alicia, or prove she didn't exist.

And today was the day, or rather evening, because Red Duke had finally left the cavern, riding out with several of his Comancheros to check on the men standing guard down on the mountain. But he wouldn't be gone long, so her time was limited, and she had decided to start with what she knew best.

Walking down the tunnel toward her bath, she held up a lantern, watching for any signs of a break in the stone, or an entryway of some kind, anything to indicate that Alicia might be concealed in a small cave, or crevice, or behind large rocks. As she passed the cave with the mineral pool, she held up her lantern and glanced inside. It was as empty as she had expected, so she kept on going, determined to explore to the end of the tunnel.

As she walked, she stopped to check in slight depressions and behind small mounds of loose rock, always looking for something that would indicate a hidden cave, but she found nothing. Finally she came to the end of the dark tunnel. She had walked far, coming to a seldom used place. It was obviously just a dead end, she decided, so there would be no need to spend much time there.

Holding up the lantern, she glanced quickly around and was surprised to see something white sticking out of the rock. She stepped closer. It looked like white fabric. Curious, she set her lantern on the floor, then pulled at the material. It came loose, revealing a large, but solid hole in the rock face.

Bending down near the lantern, she unfolded the fabric and was shocked to realize she was holding a ripped skirt and a bloody blouse, both designed and embroidered in the style she had seen women wear in Mexico.

Shivering with sudden cold, she held the blouse closer to the light. The back was torn in strips and soaked in blood, looking very much like it had been done by a whip. Suddenly she vividly remembered seeing Red Duke holding a coiled whip the first day they had arrived. Of course, lots of his men could have whips; but little went on here without him knowing it, and he would have to be involved or at least have given his approval if someone had been whipped.

Maybe she was just letting her writer's imagination run away with her. Perhaps the clothing had simply been taken as part of a robbery and later used as rags to stop the bleeding of a wound. But what of the blouse's ripped back? Again, there could be a simple answer, for maybe a knife had been cleaned on it. But why was the clothing back here, stuffed out of sight? This time she had no ready answer.

Terribly concerned, she quickly examined the back wall and found two narrow holes higher than her head which could have been used to hold manacles. Her imagination really began to run wild. Had some Mexican woman, perhaps kidnapped, been brought here, manacled to the stone wall, then whipped? Or even hurt in some other way, perhaps taken by force? But why? Amusement for the Comancheros, or Red Duke?

She shuddered, hoping she was wrong, but if she was right, was the woman still alive? She had a terrible growing fear that she was correct and that it hadn't happened long ago. Then where was the woman? Had she been moved when they arrived? Suddenly her heart began beating fast. What if Cord was telling the truth and it was his sister Alicia who had been held here, questioned, tortured, forced against her will? And then killed, her body dumped somewhere outside to be disposed of by wild animals.

No. She didn't want to believe that, not of Red Duke, not of anybody. Feeling slightly ill, she leaned against the wall, unable to stop her whirling mind. What if Cord's sister wasn't the first woman brought here for Red Duke's pleasures? She suddenly remembered what he had said the first night she had arrived, the way he had crept back to watch her bathe, enjoying his power over her, telling her how he would teach her, make her into his woman. His slave.

She didn't know if Red Duke would go that far, especially after being with him the last few days. He had courted her, taking her for a ride in the countryside, to see some unusual animals and birds, on a picnic, and even to explore some of the smaller caves. Although he had kept his passions under control, he had let her know how much he wanted her, with words and touches, determined to make her burn for him.

Also, he had wanted her to know how good their life together would be, but he had never revealed anything about his organization or how he would obtain all the luxuries he had promised her.

But if she had believed him, and if she hadn't already experienced so much with Cord, he might have had a chance of succeeding in wooing her. During the past few days her thoughts had constantly turned to Cord, even though they weren't together. Now she desperately needed to know if she could trust him, and the key to that, as well as to Red Duke, lay in finding Alicia, if she existed, or a very good explanation for the clothes she held.

But even more than that, if a woman had been hurt or was being hurt, she had to find her fast and save her. But how? Her only answer was to continue her search; but she must hurry, for Red Duke would be back soon, and she didn't know when she would get another chance to get away from him and search the caves.

Picking up the lantern, she quickly glanced around the area again, then stuffed the skirt and blouse back in the rock crevice so no one would know she had found it. Satisfied, she hurried back down the tunnel, glancing at the walls a second time, then passed the cave with the mineral pool, knowing there was no need to examine it since she had been there several times before.

Continuing on down the tunnel, she came back to the main cavern, peered inside, but didn't see Red Duke, so took one of the other branches. She followed the tunnel, but it dead-ended, and she quickly retraced her steps. The next tunnel she tried was no better, and by the time she had examined several small caves, with nothing suspicious to show for her efforts, she knew she had to go back. Red Duke would surely get suspicious if he returned and she had been gone a long while.

However, if she used an excuse like wanting to bathe, she could at least go back to the first tunnel and examine it more closely, not that she expected to find anything the second time, but she felt she had to at least try again.

Walking into the main cavern, she glanced around. Everything seemed normal, with men standing around talking, drinking coffee, eating, working, or gambling, but her heart beat a little faster when she saw Red Duke was back and talking with Cord near the royal blue tent.

She certainly had to go into the main cavern now, but a plan began to form in her mind as she walked toward the two men, careful not to appear tired or worried or distressed. Stopping beside them, she smiled.

"Duke," she said, touching his arm as she interrupted the conversation.

"Yes, Victoria?" he replied, turning to look at her, and smiling. "Did you miss me?"

"Yes, of course, but I'm rather tired. I think I'll take a long, soothing bath in the pool and maybe muse about old times, like how much my sister would have liked it here. But before I do, I thought I'd ask if you needed me for any reason."

"Thanks for asking, and of course I need you, if for no other reason than to have you by my side making my day a little brighter. But for now go ahead and enjoy your bath."

"I'll see you later, then," she replied, smiling and squeezing his arm.

Turning away, she quickly walked into the tent, careful not to have looked at Cord, for fear of making Red Duke angry. But she hoped Cord had gotten her message and would meet her at the pool later, if he possibly could. Of course, it could be dangerous if Red Duke decided to check on her; but at this point she decided they had better chance it, for they hadn't had a moment alone since arriving, and they desperately needed to talk.

In the tent, she grabbed up her yellow robe, took off her boots and replaced them with the yellow slippers, then she stepped back out, carrying a lantern. Smiling again at Red Duke, she walked toward the back of the cavern as casually as possible, although she wanted to yell at Cord to hurry. He simply had to get away, even if it meant creating a diversion to keep Red Duke occupied while he came to her.

But she said nothing and casually entered the dark tunnel alone. Once there, she hurried, the lantern's light causing her shadow to dance on the walls, but revealing nothing new. Discouraged, she arrived at the cave and stepped inside.

Holding up her lantern, she looked at the stalactites and stalagmites, wishing they could speak and tell her what had been going on in the cavern. They must have been there for countless years, growing bigger and bigger with no one to see them, until Red Duke had found the cavern. Then, again, perhaps the local Indians had used this place before

190

being confined to a reservation.

As she walked by a stalactite, she was surprised to notice its tip had been broken off. Curious, she held the lantern up and saw that the break had left a sharp edge, not worn away at all, which was surprising, since it should have eroded away, not broken.

Holding the lantern lower, she looked for the tip of the stalactite, but saw nothing until she walked to the back wall. There a piece lay on the floor. She picked it up and held it up to the stalactite. A perfect fit. Carefully putting the piece back on the floor where she had found it, she glanced around, her mind whirling.

She supposed someone could have accidentally hit the stalactite when coming in or out of the cave; but she had thought only Red Duke used the pool, and he was always very careful, which she had thought was because he appreciated the natural beauty of the place.

But what if there was another reason? What if someone had been hurriedly carried through here, and the tip of the stalactite had been knocked off in the rush, or kicked off by a struggling person wanting to leave behind a message of what had happened.

Maybe her imagination was running away with her again, but she felt as if she was on the right track. With her heart beating fast, she began touching the back wall, holding up the lantern so she could see clearly, but nothing seemed out of the ordinary. Then she looked beyond the pool, and a chill ran up her spine; for even though it was dark and she could see little, something did not look quite right about the wall, now that she had noticed it.

Hurriedly, she checked the tunnel to see if anyone

was coming, then walked carefully around the narrow edge of the pool. Everything looked normal until she held the lantern at a certain angle, then she noticed the gap in the wall. Upon examining it, Chaps realized it was actually two walls overlapping. If she hadn't been searching, holding the lantern just right, she would never have seen it.

Glancing over her shoulder to check the entrance of the cave once more, she decided she was as safe as she would ever be in the hideout and slipped between the two walls. Extending the lantern, she saw another wall directly in front of her, then she turned and walked left. In the soft light, she could see that she was now in a long, narrow cave.

Taking a deep breath, she began to walk forward, holding the lantern high, but she could see little except darkness beyond the lamp's light. Then there was a glint in the darkness ahead. Her breath caught in her throat as she wondered if Red Duke had entered the cave from another entrance and was waiting for her.

No matter, it was too late to go back now. She would just have to brave whatever lay ahead. Walking slowly forward, the glint remained until she could see a large pale shape ahead. She shivered, causing the lantern to quiver, but she hurried forward, determined to see what she had found.

At the end of the long cave, a young woman stood, her arms raised high above her head and manacled to the stone wall. She wore only the tattered remains of a white cotton chemise and drawers, and a gag made of what appeared to be her stockings.

Chaps rushed to her and held the lamp high, revealing the woman's terrified brown eyes in a pale face surrounded by long, matted, black hair. She was short and very thin, as if she hadn't eaten much in a long time.

"I won't harm you. My name is Chaps Malone," Chaps said quickly, trying to think what to do, what to say. She started to remove the gag, then realized that if she was unable to get it exactly back like it had been, Red Duke or his men might notice. She couldn't take that chance.

"Listen," she continued, "I'm afraid to remove the gag, for fear Red Duke might notice, but I need your help. Nod your head forward for yes and sideways for no. All right?"

The young woman simply looked more frightened than ever, her dark eyes red from weeping. Chaps looked at her more closely and could see she had been whipped, mostly on her back. A terrible fury rose in her. If Red Duke had done this, and she didn't see how it could have happened without his knowledge, then he was going to pay. But first they had to get this young woman safely away.

"I'm here to help you. Please don't be frightened. I've got to hurry. Do you know a man named Cord Cordova?" Shutting her eyes, tears crept down the cheeks of the young woman, but she didn't shake her head one way or the other.

"You're protecting Cord, aren't you, in case he's been captured, too. But he's here and he's safe. Is your name Alicia?"

Again she refused to answer.

Frustrated, Chaps walked a few paces back, then returned. "Listen, you've got to help me. I'll get to Cord, and even if you aren't his sister, we'll help you."

The young woman's head snapped up, and her eyes were suddenly wild with joy as she nodded vigorously at Chaps.

"You mean . . . what are you answering to?" Chaps asked, thrilled she had somehow reached this woman, even if she didn't understand why. "Okay, let's start again. Do you know Cord Cordova?"

The young woman nodded.

"Is he your brother?"

Again, a positive response.

"And you're Alicia?"

The woman nodded vigorously in reply to the third question.

"Wonderful. I can't tell you how happy you've made me, and I guess that's mutual. Look, like I said, I can't stay long, but I'll find a way to tell Cord where you are. He'll be so relieved to know you're all right. And don't worry, we'll get you out of here someway, but it may take a while. I'm sorry, but I'm going to have to go now."

Alicia's large, brown eyes grew panicky, and she wildly shook her head no.

"One other thing, did Red Duke do this to you?"

Alicia vigorously nodded yes.

"All right, we'll deal with him. But I must go now. I'm sorry," Chaps replied and started to hug her, but realized that Alicia probably hurt all over. Instead, she leaned forward and gave her a light kiss on the cheek. "Trust me, I'll be back, and I'll bring Cord. I hate to leave you in the darkness, but if Red Duke suspects I've found you, none of us will get out alive."

Still, Alicia looked wild and shook her head desperately back and forth.

"I hate to do this. I really do," Chaps said, then touched Alicia's face gently. "Remember, we're not far away now, and we'll free you soon . . . very soon."

She quickly turned her back, knowing that if she

looked into Alicia's terrified eyes a moment longer she could never leave her alone, in the darkness, and in pain. But she had to do it if they were to free her. Steeling her heart, she quickly walked down the cave and didn't look back even when she came to the exit.

She stopped, hesitated and listened. When she heard nothing, she stepped back into the cave. Holding up the lantern, she glanced quickly around and, when she saw nothing, breathed a sigh of relief. Red Duke hadn't come for her, at least not yet.

She had to make coming for a bath look good and quickly began stripping off her clothes. Just as she tossed aside the last of her underwear, she saw a light coming down the tunnel. She quickly slipped into the pool, then glanced around, reassuring herself that nothing looked out of the ordinary. Pretending to be relaxing in the mineral water, her heart was racing and her breath was coming fast.

Expecting to see Red Duke, she was surprised when Cord stepped quietly into the room and set down his lantern. He hurried to her side and, kneeling, kissed her gently on the lips. For the first time she could believe him, realizing that not only had he mistaken her when they had first met, but she had been mistaken about him as well. She was so relieved she could have cried, and she wanted nothing so much as to melt into his arms and have him make love to her all night long. But they had someone else to think of first

"Cord," she whispered, afraid of being overheard, "I've found Alicia."

His face paled. "Is she . . . is she—"

"She's fine, except that she's alone and in the dark."

"Where is   What did she say? Take me to

her."

"Cord, wait. She's near here. But she couldn't speak because she was gagged, and I didn't want to disturb anything in case Red Duke noticed and suspected someone had found her."

"Can you take me to her?"

"Yes, but what about Red Duke?"

"He should be busy for a while."

"You distracted him?"

"Yes."

"All right, then,"

Stepping out of the pool, she reached for a towel, but Cord picked it up first and wrapped it around her, his hands lingering. He kissed her again, then nuzzled her neck.

"I've missed you," he said softly.

"You've been so cold I thought you didn't care."

"An act. I've been damn jealous of Duke. He hasn't touched you, has he?"

"No, but we're going to have to leave soon."

"We will, now that you've found Alicia. I've been listening, looking around the cavern, but they've kept me under such tight guard that I haven't been able to do much. I was getting damned discouraged until you gave me the message earlier."

"I'm so glad you came." She quickly dried off, then slipped on the robe and slippers. Picking up the lantern, she motioned him to her side. She held it up and pointed. "See that ledge. It looks solid, but it's double. She's on the other side of that and at the end of a long cave, manacled to the wall."

"Manacled!"

"Shhhh. Come on."

They started for the ledge but suddenly heard footsteps reverberating in the tunnel.

"Here," Chaps said, thrusting the lantern into

196

Cord's hands. "Get through there and blow out the light."

Not waiting to see if he got out of sight, she tore off her robe and kicked off her slippers, then eased herself back into the water, trying to make as few waves as possible. She had time for only a few calming breaths before Red Duke stepped into the cave.

"What took you so long?" she asked sweetly.

He grinned and set his lantern down before walking to her side. Kneeling, he stroked her arm as he said, "Just had to settle an argument between two men. They thought something had been stolen, but it hadn't. You haven't seen Cord, have you?"

"No. Isn't he with you?"

"He was, but I lost track of him."

"I'd offer to give him a message, but I don't think I'll be seeing him around here."

"You better not be," he replied, continuing to stroke her arm, long after he knew the tickling was bothering her. But it was a game he liked to play, and she endured it silently, knowing it made him feel powerful.

"I didn't think you allowed any of the men back here while I was bathing," she said, trying to keep Duke's mind occupied so he didn't notice anything unusual, but she was terrified he might find Cord.

"I don't, but with a little encouragement, they might — "

"No, Duke, they're much too loyal and you know it."

"Maybe you're right, but I don't want to talk about my men right now. I want to talk about us. You know I want to marry you, but I have to take care of a few things first."

"What things?"

"Nothing to worry your pretty little head about,

197

but I may have to go away for a while. I'd like for you to stay here where you'll be safe, but I don't want you to be bored or lonely."

"But how can I be anything but that with you gone." She marveled at how she could still speak to him at all, knowing what he had done to Alicia, much less pretend to care.

"That's what I like to hear; but I thought you could work on your book, and if you needed more paper or ink or whatever, I could have it brought up here for you. What do you think?"

"If I must be alone, then that's a good idea. I need to get to work on it anyway."

"Good, then that's settled."

"If you say so, Duke."

"It's for the best, and you know I won't be gone any longer than necessary."

"When will you be leaving?"

"Soon. I'm not sure just when."

"And how long am I to be left alone?" She tried to look dejected at the idea of him leaving, while desperately trying to come up with a plan to get him out of the cave.

"A few weeks, maybe more."

"That's a long time."

"It'll go fast if you're working, and I'll leave a few men here to guard the place and take care of you. Smilin' Sam has requested that job. Do you want him to stay?"

She pouted.

Laughing, he squeezed her hand, then pulled the pins from her hair and let it fall free. Running his fingers through it, he said, "I can never get enough of your hair. You'll make a wonderful wife and queen, and we'll have handsome, intelligent children, all with red hair."

"You're planning quite a future, Duke."

"Knowing you're in my future means I have to plan well because you deserve only the best. And that's what you'll get, the largest, greatest cattle ranches in the world, and we'll run them all ourselves, hiring only the best."

"And the Comancheros?"

"Of course, the Comancheros will work for us. We'll need the expertise to make sure nobody takes away anything we've worked so hard to get."

"And I'll feel very safe."

"Right. They'll guard you and our children just like they guard me." He tugged on her hair, tipping her head back, then he leaned over and placed a hot kiss on her cool lips. "I've got to go. I don't like not knowing where a new man is, and that Cord is crafty."

"Do you really have to go?"

"Don't tempt me. Besides, I want you to wear white on your wedding day. Everything must be done perfectly, including our marriage." He stood up. "I'll expect you in the tent soon. Cook has something special prepared for us."

"I'll look forward to it," she replied, trying to look languid but feeling as if she had been running a mile.

He nodded, picked up his lantern, and left the cave.

This time she did not make the mistake of assuming he had gone, even when she heard his footsteps gradually recede. Instead, she quietly lay in the pool, wondering what Cord was doing and if he had heard the conversation. She knew the best thing to do now was to pretend nothing had happened and give Cord a chance to see his sister.

She waited nervously, expecting either Red Duke

199

or Cord to step into the cave at any moment, but the seconds crept by like hours until finally Cord stepped inside the cave and walked over to her. His face was white, his mouth set in a straight line, and his dark eyes were furious.

Kneeling, he set the lantern down and took her hand. "Thanks, Chaps."

"How is she?"

"Better now, but we've got to get her out fast. She's weak and sick."

"Decide on a plan, and I'll help."

"Are you coming with us?"

"What! Of course I am." She glared at him, her green eyes sparkling with insult.

"But I thought you might prefer Red Duke's plans?"

"No, never, but there's no time to talk now. He's looking for you, and you'd better get far away from me."

"Okay, but I want to thank—"

"Cord, thank me later when we're all safely out of here. Okay?"

"Yes." He stood up. "I'll let you know the plan as soon as I can." Picking up his lantern, he walked to the entrance and disappeared into the dark tunnel.

She leaned back and sighed, but couldn't relax. Red Duke was waiting for her, and she didn't know how she was going to carry on the charade. But somehow, for Alicia's sake, she must.

Chapter 14

Chaps sat inside the royal blue tent, lounging against a pillow, trying to appear docile and happy as Red Duke fed her strips of beef. Keeping up the charade with him was getting harder and harder to do. It had been almost twenty-four hours since she had found Alicia, and in that time she and Cord had come up with an escape plan and put it into action.

That afternoon, she had lured Red Duke away from the hideout for a ride, giving Cord the chance to set up his plan. Since returning, she purposefully hadn't changed from her leather skirt and red shirt, plus her boots, so that she would be ready to ride when they made good their escape.

Now that it was dusk, it wouldn't be long before Cord set off the first series of events that would hopefully get them safely out of the hideout. But it wasn't going to be easy, and they both knew it.

Red Duke chose a tasty looking piece of deer meat and fed it to her with his fingers, then cleaned her mouth with a napkin, just ever so roughly, as if it could have been an accident. But now she knew better, for he liked to play pleasure and pain games with her, and she was finally realizing how rough they could get.

Even now, after thinking about Alicia for a day, she could still hardly believe Red Duke was capable of such a dastardly act. Watching him, so gallant, so handsome, so gentlemanly, it was still hard to accept that he had kidnapped Alicia and tortured her, and yet she knew it was true. Of course, knowing all that, it was obvious that he wasn't robbing the rich to give to the poor, and the way he lived and his grandiose ideas made his true reason for crime quite clear.

Smiling at Red Duke, she buttered a biscuit, then dribbled honey on it before feeding it to him. When he playfully nipped her fingers, she had to resist the impulse to jerk her hand away. Somehow she had to keep him convinced that everything was fine and that she loved all his plans. But it was becoming harder to do by the moment, especially with him courting her so diligently before he left.

Next he held a golden goblet of wine to her lips so she could drink, then he fed her sweetbread. When he began stroking her hair, she could hardly hold still, and when he nuzzled her neck, placing warm kisses up her throat, she shivered, almost unable to stand his touch. But he misinterpreted her reaction and pulled her close, stroking her hair again and murmuring endearments.

She didn't know if she would be able to remain in his arms a moment longer. She wanted to jump up, screaming, and run from the cavern. But she couldn't. She had to stay calm for Alicia's sake. Just a little longer. But when he began to caress her breast, his breath hot on her face, she almost reached the breaking point.

Suddenly there was a loud explosion, and Red Duke jumped up. "Stay here," he commanded, and rushed out of the tent.

Chaps waited a moment, then picked up a lantern and hurried out, too, but instead of going toward the front with everybody else, she turned and walked quickly to the rear of the cavern. Glancing behind to see if anybody was watching or had trailed her, she breathed a sigh of relief, for the Comancheros were following their leader.

She plunged down the tunnel toward the bath, listening all the time for sounds of somebody following, but all was quiet behind her. Arriving safely, she hurried into the cave, glanced around to make sure all looked normal, then walked around the pool, almost slipping on some spilled water. Stepping through the concealed opening, she hurried down the long narrow cave to Alicia.

"It's time to get you out of here, Alicia," she said, setting down the lantern.

She began twisting on the right manacle to free Alicia, trying to be gentle, but the metal was stubborn, and she couldn't get it loose. Cord was supposed to have loosened the manacles so they would appear normal yet come out easily, but it wasn't working. She jerked on the manacle in frustration, knowing their time was running out.

Alicia began to pull with her wrists, desperate to get free, and working together, the right bolt suddenly pulled loose. Encouraged, they started on the left manacle, and soon it pulled free, too. Alicia dropped her arms, then groaned in pain as circulation began to return. Trying to be gentle yet knowing they had to hurry, Chaps unwound the stockings from Alicia's head and pulled the gag out of her mouth.

"Can you speak?" she questioned, throwing down the stockings.

"Yes," Alicia responded hoarsely.

"Can you walk?"

"I'll try."

"Good. Then let's go We haven't much time."

Picking up the lantern, she took Alicia's arm, then started forward, walking quickly. But Alicia suddenly pulled back and stopped.

"What's wrong?" Chaps asked.

"I'm sorry . . . my legs are weak, and . . . the pain."

"Don't be sorry. We'll take it easier."

Putting an arm around Alicia's waist, unable to keep from pressing against her injured back, Chaps supported the much smaller woman down the long cave. She didn't say anything, but she grew more and more worried. They were simply moving too slowly. Cord's diversion wouldn't last forever, and at this rate they would probably be caught in the middle of the main cavern; and then they would all be killed. She couldn't let that happen. She wouldn't!

They finally made it to the bathing cave and began walking across the stone floor, Alicia becoming more of a burden with each step. Just as they rounded the mineral pool, Alicia stepped in the spilled water and slid. Chaps tried to stop her, but Alicia slipped into the water, splashing loudly and throwing water on Chaps.

As Alicia disappeared completely under the water, Chaps dropped the lantern in horror, then knelt by the pool, her hands outstretched. When Alicia came to the surface, fighting for air, Chaps pulled her to the side.

"You're all right," Chaps said soothingly, glancing behind her, hoping Cord's ruse was still working. . . . "Now, just relax a moment. This is mineral water. It's supposed to be healing, and maybe it'll help you feel better. Relax. Catch your breath before we go on."

"I'm . . . sorry."

"Don't be. It's not your fault. Just rest a minute. We have time. Cord is getting the horses. Shut your eyes, and relax."

While Alicia did as she bid, Chaps tried desperately to control her own growing fear of being caught by Red Duke and Smilin' Sam. She couldn't let Alicia rest much longer, for Red Duke might already be looking for them.

"Alicia, Cord has come up with a plan," she said. "Please don't question anything we tell you to do. Just react the minute we tell you to do something. It's the only way we stand a chance of getting out of here alive."

"Yes. I understand."

"I know you're in pain. I know you're weak. You're awfully thin, so I know they haven't been feeding you right. But you've got to draw the strength from somewhere to walk out of this cavern on your own two feet. Once we're free, you can rest. But for now—"

"Thank you. I am feeling . . . better now. I think the water helped."

"Good. All right, I'm going to help you out of the pool, then while I dry and dress you, and please don't be modest, you're going to have to eat as much as you can."

"Yes. I won't be modest."

"Okay."

Chaps helped Alicia out of the water and, with the wet chemise and drawers clinging to her, realized just how thin Alicia really was. She obviously had been Red Duke's captive for weeks, with little food or water to help sustain her. She was lucky to be alive.

But no matter how bad Alicia's condition was, they had to get her ready to move. She handed Alicia a hunk of beef and a biscuit, and as the young woman started eating, Chaps gently peeled off the last of her clothes, thankful that the water had loosened the dried blood that had attached the fabric to her skin. Even so, she could tell it hurt Alicia, although she only stiffened and stopped eating during the worst of it.

After that, Chaps quickly and gently dried her, hoping the mineral water had cleansed the terrible criss-crossed cuts scarring Alicia's back.

"Water, please," Alicia said.

"Don't drink too much," Chaps warned, handing her a canteen. Cord had explained earlier that he had given his sister food and water, taking a chance no one would notice, so she wasn't quite as weak as she would have been. And he had also left some clothes.

When Alicia finished drinking, Chaps took the canteen and what was left of the food from her and set them aside. Gently, she dressed Alicia in her own clean white camisole and drawers, then together, they got her into a small pair of men's denims and a small man's shirt, which Cord had stolen from the cavern. Even so, the clothes were still too large, and they had to roll up the pants and sleeves. Finally, they tied a bandanna around Alicia's neck, slipped a pair of large boots onto her small feet, and twisted her long, dark hair up under a hat.

"You look about as much like a man as I do," Chaps complained, holding the lantern up to look at Alicia better. "But you'll have to do. Maybe you'll fool them from a distance long enough for us to get away."

"I'll do whatever has to be done. And don't worry about me. I'm feeling stronger after the food."

"All right. If you're ready, let's go."

Chaps picked up the canteen and the lantern, then they left the cave. Walking down the tunnel, she held the lantern behind her, hoping no one would recognize them very quickly if the light wasn't good.

Moving fast, Chaps was relieved that Alicia was keeping up with her, not complaining, not hanging back, just silently doing whatever was necessary to escape. She was a lot like Cord in his single-minded determination to rescue his sister, no matter the cost. Chaps suddenly felt a great deal of respect for them and vowed again to get out of Red Duke's hands alive.

Chaps led Alicia toward the main cavern, knowing they would have to go out the way they came in, for she and Cord had been unable to find another exit. They hurried, but by the time they reached the cavern, Alicia was panting and leaning against Chaps.

They hesitated in the entryway, glad to see a lot of activity in the cavern, men running to and fro, leading wild-eyed, neighing horses out through the front. Dust billowed out of the cave used as the horse's stables, and men were coughing, despite the bandannas most wore over the lower half of their faces, as they led the horses out. Most of the mounts had only bridles, although a few were saddled, too.

Deciding that everything was going according to plan, and that the horses hadn't been hurt by the small dynamite explosion Cord had rigged with explosives he had found hidden in a storeroom, Chaps looked at Alicia and said, "Come on. We're to meet Cord near the front."

Setting down her lantern, Chaps began leading the way into the confusion, for it was obvious the Comancheros didn't know if the cavern was falling in, they had been attacked, or just what; but she knew Red Duke would have it sorted out soon, and she wanted to be far away by then.

Fortunately, she didn't look out of place, and no one gave Alicia a second glance because she was in cowboy gear. Stopping by the royal blue tent in the center of the cavern, Chaps pulled Alicia inside, then glanced around, her hand on her gun ring in case Red Duke might for some reason be there. But the tent was empty.

"Rest a moment," Chaps said, and watched Alicia crumple to a pillow, exhausted.

Setting down the lantern, she quickly pulled her saddlebags from the trunk, stuffed in some food she had saved, then threw the saddlebags and the canteen strap over one shoulder. Then she pulled Alicia to her feet and glanced out of the tent.

"All right," Chaps said. "We're going out now. Just stay close to me. If everything goes as planned, Cord should be bringing out three horses. Look for him and grab the reins of one of the horses the minute you can. Agreed?"

"Yes," Alicia replied, a determined look in her dark eyes. "We'll make it. We have to."

"Okay. Let's go."

They hurried out of the tent and made their way directly toward the line of horses that was being brought out of stables. They got as close as they could, then stopped. Men hurried horses past.

They waited. But no Cord. Chaps began to fidget. Where was he? Had he already gone? Had they missed him? There was no doubt they had taken longer getting to the front of the cavern that she and Cord had anticipated, so he might already be outside, waiting for them.

As they waited, the dust grew worse, and the number of horses being led out began to decrease. Something had to be done, and soon. Chaps looked at Alicia and hissed, "We must have missed him. We're going to have to come up with another plan to get outside."

"How?"

"I don't know. Oh, no! Here comes Duke. Alicia, get away. Try to hide over there in the kitchen area."

As Alicia darted in between horses, Chaps waved to get Red Duke's attention and make sure he didn't notice the small form scurrying away. It worked, for he led his huge black stallion out of the line and stopped near her, smiling tiredly.

"Are you all right? he asked.

"Yes. What happened?"

"I'm not sure. We thought we were being attacked, but it seems a section of the wall in the stables suddenly collapsed, or was blown by dynamite."

"Dynamite! But who?"

"That's what I'd like to know. Have you seen Cord?"

She tried not to tense and glanced around. "No. You don't suspect him, do you?"

"Yes. We've never had this happen before. But he won't get away with it."

"I feel so guilty because I brought him here."

"Don't. It wasn't your fault." Then he looked at

209

her shoulder, a frown forming between his eyebrows. "What are you doing with your saddlebags and that canteen?"

Shocked, she realized she was wearing the telltale evidence of escape, and her heart began to pound. Then she managed to blush, looked embarrassed, and did her best to lie convincingly. "I didn't know what was happening, and I was so afraid I'd lose everything I had, or suddenly be out on the mountain without food or water, that I just, well, brought what I could carry. I'm sorry if it was the wrong thing to do."

He laughed indulgently. "No. It was a good idea."

"Thanks, I'm glad you think so. Is there anything I can do to help?"

"Why don't you heat up some food? The men are going to need it after we get the horses calmed down and stabled outside, then get some of that mess cleared out."

"All right. And, Duke, be careful."

He nodded, then led his horse toward the entrance.

She hesitated, making sure Red Duke wasn't turning back, then hurried to the cooking area. Acting as naturally as possible, she looked for Alicia and found her crouched behind a huge bag of flour, looking terrified, but determined.

"We're safe so far," Chaps whispered, picking up a skillet of biscuits to look busy. "But we've got to get outside. I can do it, but you're the problem. You're just too short to be one of the men."

"Chaps, give me those rags over there. These boots I'm wearing are huge, and I'm going to stuff them with rags, then put my feet back inside and walk out of here. We can let down the pants and pull down the hat."

"But how can you balance?"

"You'll have to help me."

"All right, that's a good idea. We'll do it, but just don't dare fall over."

Chaps pretended to drop the rags next to Alicia, Alicia picked them up, then jerked off her boots and began stuffing them. Chaps watched her off and on, as she found a cloth and picked up a hot pot of coffee, then several tin mugs.

"I'm going out there to take tired men coffee," Chaps explained, "and you're going to be taking the time to help me. But keep your head down. In all the confusion, they hopefully won't notice you."

After Alicia had finished filling her boots with rags, she carefully got to her feet, gasped in pain at the strain on her ankles, then teetered precariously before clutching Chaps's arm. But it was worth it, for now she was about Chaps's height and passable as a Comanchero.

"Can you walk like that?" Chaps asked.

"I'm going to shuffle along, but don't make any sudden moves," Alicia replied, pulling her hat down low.

They started forward, Chaps trying to balance saddlebags and a canteen on one shoulder, with a coffee pot in one hand and tin mugs in the other, and Alicia clinging desperately to one arm. She knew they would have made a strange sight if the place hadn't already been in turmoil. As it was, she could only hope nobody would really look at them.

As they got close to the entrance, several men hurried outside, leading horses, and Alicia overbalanced, almost knocking Chaps over. They stumbled several steps, then managed to regain their balance. Sighing in relief, they started forward again, but

Chaps suddenly realized Alicia was getting shorter by the moment, for the rags were compressing as they walked.

Horrified, Chaps realized there was nothing to be done, except find Cord and get out of there as fast as possible. Walking onward, they neared the two guards who stood sentry on each side of the entrance. Now was the time to make or break the plan.

"Take the mugs, Alicia, and keep you head down," Chaps whispered, handing the tin mugs to Alicia, who stumbled, then clutched at Chaps desperately until she managed to steady herself. They continued onward, trying to look as natural as possible, despite Alicia's dwindling height.

"Hey, cowboys," Chaps called, stopping by the two guards on the left. "Duke thought you could use some hot coffee."

They glanced at her, nodded in appreciation, then quickly looked forward again. Chaps took the opportunity to look around, too, and saw that men and horses milled around everywhere, while Red Duke sat astride his stallion, giving commands. As far as she could tell, they were finding a temporary place for the horses farther down the mountain and meanwhile were trying to keep the horses from scattering or doing any damage.

Looking back, she nodded at Alicia, who held out two mugs. Chaps poured hot coffee into them, then handed a mug to one Comanchero, then the other. They looked appreciative, then went back to watching the chaotic scene before them.

"Wait for me here, partner," Chaps said to Alicia, as she poured two more mugs.

Making sure Alicia was leaning against the cavern wall, Chaps traded the full mugs of coffee

212

Alicia held for the pot of coffee, then walked across the front of the entrance and handed the other two Comanchero guards their coffee. While there, she took the opportunity to look intently for Cord.

She saw him standing near a clump of bushes on the far side of the cavern's entrance, and behind him were three horses, mostly concealed by the brush.

Nodding to him, she walked back over to Alicia and took her arm. "Okay, I've seen Cord. Just stay with me."

She took back the half-full pot of coffee, and they started forward, trying to avoid the milling horses and cursing Comancheros, but also hoping to get lost in the confusion. Out of the corner of her eye, Chaps saw Cord leading the horses forward. They were close now, really close. Nobody else was mounted, except Red Duke. Just a little longer, and they could ride like the wind.

Then suddenly Alicia stumbled, lost her balance, clutched at Chaps, and they both went down. Horses pranced around them, almost trampling them. Chaps jerked the boots off Alicia so they could get away from the horses and noticed that Alicia's hat had fallen off, leaving her long, black hair to stream free. She reached for the hat to cover up Alicia's hair again and heard her name being called.

Glancing up, she saw Red Duke holding out a hand to her from astride his huge black stallion, then his eyes traveled to Alicia. He looked puzzled a moment, before fury transformed his face.

"Comancheros!" Red Duke shouted, spooking his horse, who reared into the air.

Desperate, Chaps looked around. Something had

to be done, and fast. Cord was running toward them, leading three horses, but he wasn't going to get to them in time. She stood up, clutching the coffee pot, and as the stallion came down on all four feet, she threw hot coffee straight at Red Duke's face.

Not waiting to see the results, but knowing Red Duke had to be stunned, Chaps grabbed Alicia just as Cord rode up, and pushed her up on the back of a horse, then threw herself into the saddle of the other.

Cord cut a path through the horses and men, and Alicia followed, Chaps bringing up the rear. They pounded down the trail leading away from the hideout and heard Red Duke bellow, "After them, men. Don't let them get away! I'll double your usual cut if you catch them."

Chapter 15

If going up the mountain to Red Duke's hideout had been bad, then coming down was twice as bad, for night was descending and the twists and turns of the path that wound along the edge of the Black Range made Chaps hope to never be off flat land again. She was only glad that Cord seemed to know the way, for she would have been hopelessly lost without him to guide them.

The ride that night would have been difficult enough, but added to it was the constant worry about Red Duke and his Comancheros. They hadn't seen the outlaws since leaving the hideout, and the tension was building, for she knew Red Duke would not simply let them ride away, especially after the last words she had heard him say which kept ringing in her ears.

No, he wouldn't let them get away without a fight. For one thing, his pride and prestige before his men had been terribly wounded, and for another, if they escaped, they would surely bring back the law. His whole empire depended on catching them, so she expected a surprise attack at any moment, or surely before they got off the mountain.

They had at least one thing in their favor, a

slight head start. With the stables in such confusion, it would take the Comancheros longer than usual to saddle their horses, then pack provisions.

Of course, Red Duke might not have taken time for provisions, assuming he would catch them soon, and in that case the outlaws could be closer than she thought, maybe even traveling a secret trail that would gain them time. She shuddered, hating to bring up the rear, for she constantly felt as if somebody was going to grab her from behind, or jump down from a ledge above, or simply shoot her through the heart at a distance with a rifle.

Maybe she was overreacting, but she doubted it. She had been the only one to see the look on Red Duke's face when he had realized she was rescuing Alicia and escaping herself. It hadn't been a pretty sight, and it had promised the utmost in revenge. She felt chilled just thinking about it.

And that had been before she threw hot coffee in his face. She wondered if she had scarred his arrogant face for life, or if he was so charmed the coffee simply scalded him, disorienting him long enough for them to escape. Either way, he was going to want revenge, and she had no doubt he would use all the power and force at his command to exact it.

She shivered again and looked behind her. Still nothing. That worried her almost more than if she could have heard the whole hideout of Comancheros thundering after them. What was Red Duke doing? Could he be too hurt to lead? Then, wouldn't he send somebody else?

There was no way for her to know what Red Duke was planning, but one thing she was sure of, he was bound to have planned and replanned his strategy for responding to an attack or an escape from his hideout fortress. The only way she could see to escape him was to be smarter, or to use his blind arrogance against him, for he probably didn't really believe they could escape, not completely. Maybe that would save them.

In any case, they couldn't keep riding like this forever. The horses would have to be rested, but more than that was her concern for Cord's sister. Alicia seemed to be holding up, clinging to her horse, even though she had to be in terrible pain. She was also worried that Alicia had no boots to help ease the ride and control the horse, but the stirrups were hanging down too low for Alicia to use, so they wouldn't have helped much anyway.

She didn't know how long they could keep up the grueling pace before the mountain got them, or the horses became winded, or Alicia collapsed, but she knew they had to keep going, keep pushing, anything to stay out of Red Duke's hands. With luck, maybe they could make it.

Suddenly there was the sound of gunfire, and Cord jerked his horse off the trail, pushing into underbrush, slipping, sliding down a sharp incline, then disappearing behind some piñon trees. Alicia followed, and Chaps turned her horse, too, feeling it begin to slide, then catch its footing and continue downward, brush catching at her skirt, but unable to penetrate the leather.

A ripped skirt was the last thing Chaps was worried about as several bullets whizzed past her. She felt a sharp sting on her shoulder, then heard more gunfire. Alicia jerked, grabbing her arm just before

217

she disappeared behind the piñon trees. Chaps could only hope Alicia hadn't been hurt badly, for she had surely been shot.

As Chaps followed, bullets continued to harry her. She wanted to scream at the Comancheros to stop, demanding to know how they could cold bloodedly be trying to kill people. But she knew that was a foolish question, for this was no novel she was writing; this was reality, and she couldn't control the villains.

As she reached the piñon trees, she glanced back, but could see nothing except gathering darkness. Then a last volley of bullets was fired at her as she fled behind the trees. Glancing around, she was relieved to see Cord and Alicia in their saddles, still pushing their horses hard. But for the first time, she wondered if they really could escape, for Red Duke's Comancheros must know the land around them extremely well.

There would be no safety, except to keep moving, which was exactly what Cord was doing. He was cutting through trees and brush, winding his way downward with a sureness Chaps found amazing, but maybe he knew his way in these mountains, too. She hoped so, for that knowledge might save them.

Alicia was now slumped in the saddle, but they couldn't stop to help her. Chaps felt her own shoulder, which still burned, and discovered it was wet. She had been grazed, but they couldn't deal with that now, either.

They had to keep riding, no matter the noise they made, no matter the slower pace, because Red Duke and his men were on their trail, and close, unless they had been shooting with rifles. Hopefully, with the trees and brush for cover, they wouldn't be the targets they had been on the trail.

Cord kept them moving, always downhill, but never in a straight line. He kept zigzagging, trying to cover their tracks by making use of the natural terrain. Since they couldn't return to the trail, the going was slow and rough.

Chaps began to worry more and more about Alicia, for she was swaying badly in the saddle. If Alicia was losing blood, they needed desperately to stop and bind the wound, but Cord kept going, even though he repeatedly looked back to check on his sister.

Although she listened for sounds behind them, Chaps didn't hear the Comancheros and decided they must have been using rifles earlier since they hadn't caught up yet. Maybe Red Duke was taking the trail now because it was safer and faster, planning on cutting them off and ambushing them later.

She shivered, wishing her mind would be still instead of conjuring the worst possible scenarios to frighten her. But there was nothing else to do as she followed Cord's lead, knowing he was picking the safest path for them, at least to the best of his ability in the dark.

Alicia was now slumped over her horse's neck, the reins clutched in her right hand. It was a dangerous way to ride, especially going downhill over such rough terrain, and Chaps wished they could stop and help her. But she trusted Cord to know best and continued following, although frequently looking over her shoulder.

As they continued riding and the Comancheros didn't attack, she began to relax, only then noticing all the aches and pains from the escape and the long, rough ride. Her shoulder still burned from the bullet wound, and she wanted desperately to put some healing, soothing ointment on it.

Fortunately, she would be able to do that once they stopped, for along with the writing material she had brought from New York City, she had also tried to prepare for any emergency she might have in the West by bringing along some basic medicine, such as a healing ointment, headache powders that would also ease general pain, and a few small bandages.

Now she was very glad of her foresight and for keeping her valise with her at all times. She had stuffed the small, fabric bag into her saddlebags before leaving Silver City, and she would pull it out as soon as they stopped. Then she would treat Alicia, Cord and herself before allowing anybody to rest, and perhaps the medicine would ease their escape from Red Duke and his Comancheros.

As the night wore on, Chaps grew more and more tired, but hopeful they might have lost Red Duke. Finally, Cord held up his hand to stop, then motioned for them to be quiet. He edged his horse forward around a thicket of brush, and Chaps could see the glint of pond water ahead. Good. Cord was stopping to feed and water the horses, and check on Alicia. She could hardly wait to get down, hoping they could rest awhile.

Cord rode slowly toward the pond, his .45 unholstered and cocked. He looked in all directions, but everything was still and quiet, so he guided his horse into the clearing. Suddenly gunfire exploded from all directions, and his horse reared. He fired several times into the bushes, fighting to control his mount, then caught a bullet and plunged from the saddle, catching his foot in the stirrup. His horse panicked and ran, dragging Cord along the ground toward the pond, with bullets whizzing around them.

Chaps simply sat in stunned amazement, too exhausted and surprised to react instantly. Then Alicia began to moan, shaking her head in terror, and that ignited Chaps. She had to save Alicia from any more torment. Slapping the flank of Alicia's horse, she set it tearing into the clearing after Cord's mount, which was just disappearing into the brush on the other side of the pond. Gunfire followed Alicia, who lay slumped across her horse.

Leaning low over her saddle, Chaps kicked her mount into a gallop, thankful it was dark so she presented less of a target, and raced across the clearing, greeted by a hail of bullets. Ahead of her, Alicia's horse, with her small form clinging to its back, galloped across the pond and disappeared into the woods.

Feeling several sharp stings graze her body, Chaps never paused, never stopped, but raced across the shallow end of the pond into the darkness and undergrowth on the other side. More bullets followed, but she kept going, determined to catch up with Cord and Alicia. She heard the Comancheros calling to each other as she urged her mount onward. Red Duke had obviously never dreamed they would get away again, and it was taking him time to regroup, or send out parties to surround them.

But now she couldn't worry about the Comancheros, for she had to find Cord and Alicia, and help them if they needed it. Pushing her mount toward its limits, she finally saw a horse up ahead, standing still, its head down, its sides heaving. Beside it lay a still body.

Terrified Cord or Alicia was seriously wounded or killed, she hurried forward, then stopped and slipped off her horse, continuing to hold the reins. She knelt by the body and discovered it was Alicia. Gently taking the young woman in her arms, Chaps felt tears sting her eyes as she checked for a pulse. Yes, it was there, but faint. She hugged Alicia close.

"Alicia," she whispered. "Can you hear me?"

"Yes," Alicia responded weakly.

"We've got to go on."

"Cord?"

"I don't know. I'll find him, but I've got to get you somewhere safe first. Duke's right behind us."

Alicia nodded, tried to move, then slumped again.

"Remember Red Duke. You can't let him win, Alicia. Remember what he did to you, what he may have done to others. We have to get away and stop him. But first you've got to get up. Help me."

Alicia groaned and nodded. "I'll get up. I will. He'll never hurt anybody again, not if I can stop him."

"That's right. Just get up, and we'll stop him."

Chaps helped Alicia to a sitting position, then took the bandanna from around Alicia's neck and bound the bleeding gunshot wound on her shoul-

222

der. When Alicia nodded that she was ready to stand, Chaps helped her to her feet, then supported her as she walked to her horse.

"Do you want me to tie you on your horse?" Chaps asked, wondering how Alicia could be strong enough to ride.

"No. Just get me up there. I'll cling, one way or another, 'cause I've been riding all my life and I'll never let Duke take me again. But, Chaps, we've got to find Cord. He may need our help."

"I know, but we must get you someplace safe first, then I'll look for him. He can't have gone far. I just hope he's all right."

"He'd better be, or Duke's a dead man."

Chaps felt chills run up her back at Alicia's tone, and never doubted her for a moment. But Cord had to be safe. Wasn't he invincible? She helped Alicia into the saddle, handed her the reins, then remounted her own horse. She could hear the sounds of men and horses in the distance, probably regrouping at the pond.

They had to get out of there, and fast. Clicking to her mount, she rode around Alicia, then started forward in the general direction Cord had been taking them. She glanced back to see Alicia following, and smiled grimly in encouragement. Then she started looking for Cord, as well as a place to hide.

They hadn't gone far when they heard a sudden explosion behind them, sounding like it came from the pond. Chaps exchanged a worried glance with Alicia, then pressed her horse faster, not knowing what had happened behind them, or what to expect in front. But their mounts couldn't take much more, and Alicia's wounds had to be tended soon.

Desperately looking for a small cave, a protected clearing, or anything that would get them safely out of sight where they could rest, Chaps was beginning to give up when she saw a rider on horseback move out of the brush just ahead. She jerked back on the reins of her mount, signaling for Alicia to stop, and looked behind. Had Red Duke's men surrounded them? She didn't see anyone, but that didn't mean they weren't there.

Rubbing her gun ring, she decided that if she couldn't get away and she had time for only one shot, she would get in close enough to kill Red Duke. His Comancheros might murder her afterward, but she wasn't going to let him have Alicia, and she wasn't going to let him hurt anybody else ever again.

But first she would try to escape. Glancing around, she realized she couldn't get through the thick brush on either side. She would have to go forward, and at the last minute try to race by the person in front. Alicia would follow her, and maybe it would work. She started forward again.

Suddenly she realized the figure in front looked familiar, and her breath caught in her throat. "Cord?" she questioned softly, almost to herself. Then she moved closer. "Cord! Alicia, it's Cord."

She rushed the last distance to his side.

When their mounts were side by side, he took her in his arms and murmured, "Chaps, I was so afraid I'd lost you."

"No, I'm fine. That's what I thought about you, too." She hugged him tight, thrilled to feel his hard strength against her, but also feeling him wince.

"Are you sure you're okay?" she asked, looking at him intently, noticing the blood on his shirt sleeve.

"Except for a few bruises and scratches and where they skinned me, here, I'll survive. It's Alicia I'm worried about."

He glanced up just as his sister rode up, and leaning forward in the saddle, moved his horse forward. Silently, he took Alicia in his arms, then held her close. "I'm sorry I took so long to find you," he said, his voice hoarse.

"You came. I knew you would. And I'm safe now," Alicia replied, tears running down her cheeks. "We're all safe."

"For the moment," Cord said, reluctantly letting her go. "But we'd better get out of here. I threw all the dynamite I had at Red Duke's gang, and it should have slowed them down, but I don't know for how long."

"Maybe you got them all," Chaps added hopefully.

"I don't think so. I couldn't get in close enough."

"Then what are we going to do now?" Chaps asked, glancing around uneasily. "I was looking for a place to camp. We simply can't go on much longer."

"I was headed for a cave not too far away when they ambushed us. That's still where we'll go. It's an old Apache campsite, and I doubt if Red Duke knows anything about it. Come on, we can lose our tracks in a creek just ahead."

"I'm right behind you," Chaps replied in relief. "Alicia, can you make it that far?"

"Yes. I've already stood a lot worse."

225

"Damn that Red Duke!" Cord exclaimed. "He's going to pay, and soon. Come on, let's go."

They started through the brush again, with Alicia in the middle and Chaps bringing up the rear. This time Chaps kept glancing over her shoulder and all around, not planning to be surprised again. They arrived at the creek with no trouble and let the horses drink a little water before heading downstream, taking it easy to keep from bruising the horses' hooves on rocks or debris.

There was more moonlight here, and Chaps could see that Cord's clothes had been torn from being dragged by his horse and wondered about cuts and bruises that she couldn't see. They all had wounds that had to be tended before they could rest, and if they could sleep soundly with no fear of being surprised, it would be a great relief. But would she ever be able to sleep like that again? She didn't know. She feared Red Duke would haunt her dreams for the rest of her life.

They rode on, and it seemed forever before Cord finally turned his horse west and left the stream. Alicia followed, slumped in her saddle, hanging on to the saddle horn to keep from falling off. Chaps was so tired she was barely awake as she followed Cord through a stand of piñon trees, around a mound of cacti, then finally behind a hill. There, nestled among twisted trees and thick bushes, was the small opening to a dark cave.

Cord stopped, and they did, too. He looked at them for a moment, then said, "I know you're tired, but we've got to take care of the horses. If we build a small fire in the cave, I don't think anybody'll see the smoke."

"I can't build a fire," Chaps said, "but if you'll take the saddles off, I'll water the horses."

"All right," Cord agreed, "then I'll build a fire. But first let me check out the cave."

He dismounted, then lifted Alicia out of her saddle and carried her near the cave. While he gently set her down, Chaps got off her horse, then removed her saddlebags and carried them over to Alicia. Setting them down, she smiled wearily at Cord. He squeezed her shoulder, then went to get the saddles. When they were all piled near Alicia, she laid her head against one and went to sleep.

"She'll be all right, Cord," Chaps said softly. "She just needs to rest."

"I hope that's all," he replied, pulling her against his chest. "You don't know how much I've missed you and hated seeing Duke touch you. If it hadn't been for Alicia, I'd have killed him that first night."

Chaps kissed his lips gently. "He didn't hurt me."

"Good." He squeezed her tight, then stepped back. "I'm going to make a torch and look at the cave before we all fall asleep standing out here."

"I'll take care of the horses."

"Let me hobble them, so they can get the bits out of their mouths and eat and drink comfortably. They sure as hell deserve it after the way they've worked for us."

They walked back to the horses, and after Cord had hobbled them, Chaps led them down to the stream, not worried in the least about controlling the animals since she knew how tired they were. While they drank, she bathed her face and hands, and felt a little better. She also listened to the

227

night, now attuned to hear any unusual sound, fearing that Red Duke might somehow have found them again. But all was still, and soon she led the horses to a grassy area in back of the cave's entrance.

By then, Cord had a small fire started in the back of the cave, and she stepped inside to glance around. It was a small but cozy cave, and the fire shed soft light over the interior, but was banked so that little light shone outside. Cord had laid Alicia on a saddle blanket by the fire and was carrying the saddles and bridles inside.

Chaps picked up the saddlebags and lugged them into the cave, then pulled out her valise, picked up her canteen and some food, then sat down beside Alicia. Before long she heard Cord slapping the dust off himself outside, then he stepped in, pushing back his hair, now wet from rinsing his face and hands in the stream. He sat down beside Chaps, groaning in relief as he stretched out.

"If that's food, Chaps, I'm a lucky man."

"It is, and I imagine you weren't eating like this at the hideout."

She unwrapped a piece of silk, spreading it out to make a tablecloth, and exposed strips of venison, beef, rabbit, boiled eggs, biscuits and sweetbread. Then she set the canteen of water beside it.

Cord didn't hesitate, but picked up a piece of meat and started eating. Chaps smiled at him, then opened her valise and pulled out her medicine container. Cord looked interested, but didn't say anything as he kept eating, watching her closely. She touched Alicia's shoulder and gently shook her awake.

228

"You need to eat something, Alicia," Chaps said, "and I need to know where you hurt. I've got some ointment and cloth bandages to put on your wounds. And you, too, Cord."

"That's a relief," Cord said. "I thought I was going to have to go out and find some Apache medicine if any of us needed it."

"I think this will do fine," Chaps replied, smiling, as she tightly bound his injured arm and then tended Alicia's scrapes and cuts.

Alicia yawned, then smiled tiredly. "Am I really sitting down on firm ground?"

Cord smiled. "Yes, and we should be safe here for a while."

"I want to thank you both for rescuing me," Alicia said, her eyes filling with tears. "I don't think I could have lasted in that cave much longer."

"It's all right now," Chaps said, hugging her. "Don't think about it anymore. You've got to rest first. We'll talk about it later, if you want, all right?"

Alicia nodded, and picked up a biscuit, looking at the bandage around Cord's arm. She took a bite, then began chuckling. "That bandage reminds me of a rag I once had."

"I don't know what's funny about that," Cord said, eating a biscuit, too.

Looking at Alicia, Chaps started to laugh. "Rags!"

She and Alicia both laughed harder.

Cord just looked at them in complete amazement.

Finally taking a deep breath, Chaps said, "Alicia stuffed rags in those huge boots you found for her, so she'd be tall enough to look like an outlaw when she walked out of the hideout."

Cord simply looked from one of them to the other as if they had lost their reason. "But rags would—"

"I know." Alicia laughed. "They squashed down, and I got shorter . . ."

"And shorter," Chaps finished, laughing so hard tears were running down her eyes.

"That's why I fell," Alicia added. "Those rags!" Then she doubled over laughing, brushing at the tears streaming from her eyes.

"That stunt just about got us killed," Cord complained, then he began to chuckle, too. "But the idea of you using rags to make your escape from Red Duke's armed camp is such an affront to his dignity that I've got to laugh."

Chaps and Alicia nodded, their laughter finally beginning to dwindle to mere chuckles, now joined by Cord. Soon they all felt better, as if purged of the horror they had just been through.

"Damn," Cord said, "if you two don't lead a man a merry chase."

"I think Red Duke would have to agree," Chaps replied, her smile thinning.

"And we aren't done with him yet," Alicia added, a hard glint coming into her eyes.

Part Three

Chapter 16

Three days later, Cord, Chaps, and Alicia rode into Arizona Territory, then crossed the Gila River onto Vincente Rancho land. Chaps was amazed at the size of the huge ranch, which lay southwest of Silver City, nestled in the valley between the Gila River and the Peloncillo Mountains.

As they rode along the dirt road that led to the main house, Chaps saw huge herds of cattle in the distance, plus smaller herds of horses. The grassland was flat between the blue river and the purple mountains, with a few gnarled piñon trees, cacti and an abundance of buffalo grass. Along the river, cottonwood trees grew tall, shading the riverbanks. The sky was a clear, brilliant blue, and the day was hot and dry.

But Chaps didn't care how hot it got, as long as she was riding on flat ground, in the daylight, and able to see far into the distance, for she would not soon get over her wild ride out of the Black Range. She glanced over her shoulder, as had become her habit, but there was no sign of Red Duke and his Comancheros. Not yet, anyway.

Cord figured they were about a half-day's ride ahead of Red Duke, who had not given up the chase, but Cord also thought the Comancheros might have relay points throughout the area and so could change horses without slowing down. In that case, the Comancheros might be a lot closer. She wouldn't be surprised at that, but at least she would be able to see a group of riders coming and not be caught off guard again.

When they had come out of the Black Range, she had tried to persuade Cord to go to the military for help, but he had explained they couldn't take the time, even if they could get help, which he doubted. Since Red Duke hadn't caught them in the Black Range, he would head straight for the Vincente Rancho, knowing it was where they would go for help.

She had asked Cord why, and he had gone on to explain that Alicia was engaged to Miguel Vincente. Red Duke was bound to try and stop Alicia's marriage by killing everybody in the Vincente family, leaving her homeless and vulnerable, and then waiting patiently for them to arrive. But Cord was determined to get there first, warn Miguel, then try and lead Red Duke away, giving Miguel time to call in his vaqueros and get help from some of the other ranchos.

She had then tried to persuade Cord to go into Silver City and send a message from the telegraph office to the nearest town near the Vincente Rancho and have it taken to them. Again, he had said they couldn't chance going into any town, for Red Duke was sure to have Comancheros watching for them everywhere.

Easily believing that, she still thought the military could help, but Cord wanted nothing to do with the military since he was Apache and they

234

were more likely to arrest him than anything. Alicia didn't want to ask the military for help either, explaining that their family had always taken care of its own battles.

When she had suggested going in herself, Cord had told her that she would never get there alive, not so close to the Black Range. Besides, the military had been after Red Duke for years, and wasn't likely to send out a personal force, even if they had it available, at the request of three bedraggled travelers.

She had finally conceded to them, realizing that they and their families had been taking care of themselves for generations, not relying on strangers to protect them, so they weren't likely to change now, not when the danger was so great—and especially not if Red Duke was headed straight for the Vincente Rancho.

They were handling the situation the way Westerners did, and all she could do was hope they survived. What Chaps really wanted was to be in New York City, where she could rely on the police just around the corner to answer her summons of help. But this was a vastly different way of life, and she was realizing it more all the time.

Glancing around, she noticed that Alicia still rode slumped in her saddle, dozing most of the time, and Cord was lost in his own thoughts, constantly on guard, watching, expecting Red Duke and his Comancheros to materialize at any moment. All of them had been exhausted and wounded coming out of the Black Range and, after making the decision to ride straight to the Vincente Rancho, had spoken little to each other on the long ride.

But now that they were close, Chaps began to relax a little, thinking of a hot bath, a warm meal, and time to be with Cord. Although they had been riding together, their time had not been their own. Besides, now that Alicia had been rescued, Chaps didn't know how Cord felt about her, a writer from New York, and after her terrible experience with Red Duke, she wasn't sure how she felt about men in general, and Cord in particular.

She did know that when she looked at Cord, she felt a quick hot desire flood her, making her want to be alone with him to explore the sensuality he had awakened in her. But she didn't know if he still wanted her, or if what they had shared had all been part of the game of getting her to help him find Red Duke and rescue his sister.

There was just so much she didn't understand about men, about feelings, about life. Maybe she should have stayed safely back in New York City and written articles or books that didn't require a trip to a hostile land. But then she would never have met Cord, and she couldn't imagine having lived her life without that. He was special, and there was no doubt about it.

And as for fantasy men, she didn't even want to think about them. She had been burned badly, believing Red Duke's stories of good will, and didn't trust herself anymore. If Red Duke could have confused her, then maybe any man could, even Cord. She didn't want to think that about Cord, and yet she had come through too much to be able to take anyone at face value anymore. It was a shame, but maybe a lesson well learned.

What she now wanted was a lot of comfort and time to make notes about all she had experienced, but she didn't think that time was going to come just yet. There was still Red Duke to deal with. It had entered her mind to escape back to New York City, and leave Cord and Alicia and the Vincentes to deal with Red Duke.

But she had decided against that, for she figured Red Duke had Comancheros guarding stagecoach and train depots, and she couldn't ride out on her own, nor trust anyone to guide her, fearing they would turn out to work for Red Duke. Besides that, she simply couldn't abandon her friends, not until this was all said and done; for it was now her battle too, and she wanted to see justice done.

"There's the Vincente hacienda," Cord said, interrupting her thoughts as they rounded a curve in the road. He pointed to a house of Spanish design on a hill ahead of them.

"It still stands?" Alicia asked, coming fully awake.

"Yes," Cord replied, "but that doesn't mean Red Duke didn't get there ahead of us."

"Cord!" Alicia exclaimed. "You can't believe that."

"It's possible, but I think we're ahead of them."

"Then, maybe we should wait and ride up tonight," Chaps suggested. "I don't want to ride into an ambush."

"We'll know in a minute," Cord responded. "Vacqueros watch the road, and if Miguel's there, he'll know we're coming by now and send somebody out to greet us."

"Or come himself," Alicia added, straining to get

237

a good view of the hacienda. "Look! Somebody just rode out of the gate."

"Then, they're safe," Cord replied in relief.

Chaps watched as a man on horseback raced down the hill toward their weary group. He was riding a large bay horse and reined it in abruptly at Alicia's side. Lifting her into his arms, he set her across his lap, then raced back up to the hacienda.

Cord laughed. "That was Miguel Vincente, if you hadn't guessed." Then he picked up the reins of Alicia's horse, and they started forward once more.

"I don't suppose he's going to do that for you and me?" Chaps asked, chuckling.

"No, probably not."

"Then, I guess we'll arrive the slow way and in less style."

"But no less welcome."

"I hadn't thought of that. Are you sure they won't mind having me as a guest?"

"Mind! Chaps, for one thing, they're known for their hospitality, and for another, you saved Alicia."

"I couldn't have gotten her out of the hideout."

"But you found her."

"You set off the dynamite."

Cord laughed. "Okay, we both rescued her, satisfied?"

"Yes, but I didn't mean to argue. I'm just so confused, and now I don't feel like anybody needs me anymore. I guess I'm sounding childish, but—"

"You're tired, that's all." He guided his horse close to hers, and taking her hand, he squeezed it. "Don't ever think nobody needs you. Consider yourself part of the family. The Vincentes will.

238

And if I don't miss my guess, they'll try to get you to become their honored guest for life."

"Cord, they will not."

"I'm serious. But they'll have to get in line behind me."

He was still holding her hand, and she suddenly pulled away. She couldn't believe him, for his words had sounded like something Red Duke would have said. Cord was just trying to make her feel better, after she had complained. She felt silly and embarrassed, practically begging to be allowed to join the group, so she wouldn't have to feel like she was standing outside looking in at a warm, cozy family. "Thanks, but you know I've got some books to write."

Cord dropped his hand and hesitated, obviously thinking. "I don't suppose life on a ranch could compare much to fancy New York literary parties and things like that," he commented as he suddenly began galloping toward the hacienda.

"No, that's not what I meant," she said as she watched him ride away, knowing too late that she had said the wrong thing. Now she felt even more confused, hating to go into the Vincentes' home alone, so much the outsider.

However, as she rode up to the house, and noticed its stately beauty, subtle charm and warmth, she could easily imagine living happily in a place like it, sharing life with Cord. And then she stopped her thoughts, for they were dangerous and not to be trusted.

Instead, she concentrated on the house. It was Spanish in design, with two stories, and made of pale stone with a flat, red tile roof. A stone fence surrounded the house, with black wrought-iron grill work for a gate and over the windows. Not only was it a beautiful house, but it looked like it could be used as a fortress as well. Behind it were several more buildings, and to one side horses were fenced in a corral attached to a stable.

She couldn't help being impressed and realizing just how far she had come from what she had known in New York City. But she wouldn't let herself be intimidated. There would be people inside just like any others, plus there was sure to be a hot bath, soft bed and good food. She smiled, thinking how much she had come to prize what she had always taken for granted before.

Riding up to the gate, she saw that Cord had waited for her. She was glad. Stopping her horse near him, he helped her down, held her against him for a moment, then stepped back.

A Mexican man, wearing white cotton pants, shirt, and a large sombrero, took the horses and began leading them to the stables in back.

"I'm sorry I rode off on you," Cord said. "We're all tired and on edge, but that's no excuse."

"It's all right. I probably said the wrong thing. I'm sorry, too."

He put an arm around her shoulders and squeezed. "Come on inside. There're some people I want you to meet."

They stepped through the open wrought-iron gate, then followed a stone path surrounded by a wide variety of cactus in bloom to the front of the house. Huge oak doors, in an intricate leaf and vine design, with heavy brass handles, stood open.

Cord tucked Chaps' hand into the crook of his

arm, and they stepped through the open doorway. It was cool inside and dim in contrast to the bright afternoon sunlight outside. The foyer, with a red tiled floor, led to the center of the house which was an open courtyard, with brilliant sunlight shinning down on plants and vines.

Cord led her into the courtyard, and she looked around in amazement, for there was a running fountain in the center, with a cherublike child holding a fish with water constantly pouring out of its mouth. The sky was a brilliant blue overhead, but the harsh and hot sunlight was shaded by the trees and the vines growing overhead to form a canopy. Stone benches, tables and chairs were set here and there, in groups or seclusion.

The courtyard made Chaps want to stay forever, away from the noise and bustle she had known in New York City and the viciousness of outlaws like Red Duke. But she also knew the beautiful and peaceful courtyard was as much fantasy as reality, for she had been out in the real world enough now to know how harsh and cruel it could be.

"You want to sit, Chaps?" Cord asked, a note of concern in his voice. "I don't know where everybody is, but I'll go look. Usually, there're plenty of family members around to greet me."

"Maybe Alicia warned them about Red Duke."

"That could be, but—"

"Cord!" Miguel Vincente called, striding into the courtyard with his arms outstretched.

The two men, about the same height and coloring, embraced, then stepped back and looked at each other. Cord was more heavily muscled, while Miguel was slimmer, and Cord had more prominent cheekbones and a reddish tint to his skin than Miguel. Still, they had a similar look, and they treated each other like brothers, or old friends.

"*Mi amigo,*" Miguel said, "Alicia told me Red Duke was headed our way. I immediately sent the family to the nearest rancho. They were sorry they couldn't greet you, but—"

"I can see them later," Cord replied. "I'm glad they've gone to safety. And Alicia?"

"She wouldn't leave me."

"I'm not surprised."

"We have been separated so long, you know." Miguel clasped Cord's shoulder. "How can I thank you, Cord? She is my life, you know that."

"And my sister."

"I was beginning to fear I had lost you both, then one of my men hurried to tell me you were riding in. I can't tell you the joy in my heart at that moment."

"You don't have to tell me. I felt the same way when Chaps told me she had found Alicia." He hesitated and glanced at Chaps. "But we're being rude. Miguel, I want you to meet Victoria Malone, or Chaps. Without her, none of us would be here."

"Then, I owe you my life, señorita," Miguel said, "and my eternal gratitude. Anything of mine or my family's is yours to command, always."

"Thank you," Chaps replied, a little embarrassed. "But Cord got us out of there and safely here."

"We worked together," Cord insisted, then looked at Miguel. "Chaps is from New York City, and she's in the West doing research for some novels she's writing."

"A novelist! How delightful. The Vincentes are

242

all readers, and we will help you in any way possible to complete your books."

"Thank you," Chaps replied, "but right now more than anything, I'd like to have something to eat and drink."

"How unforgivable of me," Miguel responded, looking contrite. *"Un momento."* He snapped his fingers.

A slim, Mexican man stepped quietly into the courtyard. Miguel glanced at him, spoke rapidly in Spanish, then watched the man leave. Miguel looked back at Chaps and smiled.

"I have sent the women servants with the family," Miguel explained, "so the service may not be quite as good as usual; but plenty of prepared food was left, and we will see you are well taken care of. Alicia is upstairs bathing and changing, and if you would like to do that, too, a bath will be prepared for you immediately."

"That would be wonderful," Chaps replied, smiling happily. "But I think I'll eat first."

"A wise woman," Miguel agreed, then turned to Cord. "We need to discuss the situation, *mi amigo*. Do you want to go to my office while Señorita Malone has food here in the courtyard, or—"

"If you don't mind, I'd like to be part of the discussion," Chaps interrupted. "And, please, call me Chaps."

Miguel hesitated, glancing at Cord.

"She's been part of it from the beginning, and I'm not going to leave her out now," Cord said. "I'm hungry, too. I don't know how much time we've got, so why don't we eat out here and talk at the same time."

"Fine," Miguel agreed. "I was just trying to save Chaps the unpleasantness of the situation."

"She's already seen plenty," Cord explained as they walked to a round table and sat down on stone benches around it.

A moment later, the Mexican man came back, set a large tray on the table, then quickly began setting out plates and napkins. He set a tall glass of lemonade at each plate, then placed a large plate of tamales and tortillas, plus a bowl of red and green peppers, in the center. Stepping back, he nodded at Miguel, then left the room.

"Have all you want to eat, Chaps. There is plenty more," Miguel urged.

"Thank you," she replied, and began heaping her plate with food. When she was satisfied that she had more on her plate than she could possibly eat, she took a long drink of cool lemonade and smiled in pleasure.

"My people are preparing for siege and battle," Miguel said, taking a tortilla.

"You may not need to, *mi amigo,*" Cord replied, then ate a tamale and downed it with lemonade.

"What do you mean?" Miguel questioned. "Alicia said that—"

"I know," Cord responded. "I wanted you warned, just in case they don't follow the trail I'm going to lay for them."

"I do not understand," Miguel replied, looking confused.

"Red Duke wants me and Chaps bad, because we rescued Alicia, but he needs us dead and quick because we know where his hideout is. And that includes Alicia."

244

Miguel paled. "I will never let him get his hands on her again. Did you see what he did to her back?"

"Yes," Chaps agreed, "but it could have been worse. Much longer and—"

"Do not mention it," Miguel entreated.

"Red Duke didn't molest her," Cord stated.

"As glad as I am about that, I don't understand it," Miguel said.

"He may like to talk more than act," Chaps explained, pausing between mouthfuls.

Both men looked at her, then nodded in understanding.

"But what I'm trying to say, Miguel," Cord continued, "is that I want you warned and prepared here."

"I have already sent runners out to neighboring ranches and to my vaqueros all over the ranch. We will be getting reinforcements in here by nightfall. And with my family safely away, I won't worry for them. Now I must persuade Alicia, when she is feeling stronger, to join them."

"That sounds good," Cord agreed, "but I'm going to ride out of here as soon as I can get some supplies and three fresh horses."

Chaps looked at him in shock. "But, Cord, I thought we were going to stay here."

"No. It's too dangerous. Red Duke may get here before Miguel's got enough forces to hold off the Comancheros. I'm going to try and lead Red Duke away, make him think all three of us kept going after getting horses and supplies here. I'll pack the two horses I'm not riding, so the tracks will look like they're carrying women."

245

"You can't do this alone, *mi amigo,*" Miguel said. "It is too dangerous."

"I'm going up into the mountains. Red Duke is bound to follow me, and I plan to lead him a merry chase, maybe even pick off enough of his men to discourage the whole bunch. Anyway, whatever I do, it'll give you enough time to get prepared."

"You aren't going without me," Chaps said, surprising herself. She felt hurt that Cord could so easily plan to leave her behind, while he took all the danger on himself. "What if Red Duke catches you, what if you get hurt, what if you need to send a message? You need me. Besides, I've been in this from the start, and you're not going to leave me out now."

"More notes for your novel?" Cord asked, a cold edge to his voice, but real concern for her in his eyes.

"I want to see Red Duke stopped as much as you do," Chaps insisted, "and my books have nothing to do with this."

"Señorita, it is much too dangerous for a young woman in the mountains. You don't know what you ask of Cord."

"I've already been through a lot, and I can take care of myself . . . or almost," Chaps replied stubbornly.

"I want you to stay safely with Alicia," Cord insisted.

"She may not be any safer than me if I go with you," Chaps replied. "What if Red Duke arrives right after you leave, but doesn't follow you?"

Cord whitened. "Miguel, Chaps is right. You've

246

got to get Alicia out of here."

"I can't, *mi amigo*. She is as stubborn as your woman. What can we do but keep them near us and defend them with our lives?"

"All right, Chaps," Cord finally agreed. "You're coming with me. Finish eating, and let's get on our way as soon as we can."

Miguel stood up. "Go safely, my friends, and rest here a moment while I see to your horses and supplies." Then he quickly left the room.

Cord looked at Chaps. "I hope you know what you're getting into."

"I have no idea, but I don't want to be trapped here, either. I had enough of that in the hideout."

He nodded in understanding, then looked up as someone entered the courtyard. "Alicia!" he exclaimed, then strode over to his sister and gently hugged her. Setting her back, he looked her over and smiled. "You hardly look like the same woman we rescued from the hideout."

Alicia laughed gently and took her brother's hand, leading him back to the table. She was wearing a cool white dress of soft cotton, with green ribbon threaded around the waist, bodice and hem. Her thick, black hair had been pulled neatly back into a chignon. She had large dark brown eyes, a small straight nose, and smooth olive skin.

"You think I look better, brother?"

"Yes," Cord replied without hesitation.

"You're beautiful," Chaps added in admiration.

"Thank you, Chaps," Alicia said, sitting down stiffly beside her. "I ache all over, but that will go away. The cuts on my back will heal, but Miguel's mother told me she thinks they will leave scars."

"I'm sorry," Chaps replied. "That Duke—"

"Don't be sorry," Alicia interrupted, taking Chaps' hand. "I am alive and reunited with my beloved. We will be married soon and live together for many long years. My back? It will not show, except to my husband, and the scars will simply remind us of how we almost lost each other. That knowledge will strengthen our love through the years. So, do not be sorry for me. I am alive and happy."

Chaps blinked back tears, her respect for Alicia growing even more. She looked at Cord, and he was smiling in loving adoration at his sister.

"You're right, Alicia," Cord agreed. "But I wish you'd gone with everybody else. You're not safe here."

"I have been separated from Miguel too long as it is. We are going to fight this together, and win."

"That's what Cord and I are going to do, too," Chaps agreed, then blushed slightly as Alicia looked at her in sudden understanding. Looking away, she realized how much she had come to think of herself and Cord as a team, and she shouldn't be doing that, for wasn't that just another fantasy? She wasn't sure, for she and Cord had been through a lot together. But how could she trust her own thoughts and desires anymore when she had so misjudged him?

"She's right," Cord agreed, taking Chaps' other hand. "We're going to try and lead Red Duke away from here long enough to give Miguel time to get some men in and fortify this place."

"Chaps," Alicia said, her large, dark eyes serious, "you do not have to go. You have done enough. For the rest of our lives, I will think of you as my sister. You have a home with me and the Vincentes. Miguel can send you right now to safety, and no one will think the less of you, for you have already proved your courage and strength many times over."

"Thank you," Chaps replied, "but I'll go with Cord. He may need help, and I'm going to finish what I've started. After all, I've come to think of all of you as family, too."

Alicia quickly hugged her close. "Cord has told me that you have no family, but we are family now, and you will never, ever be alone again." Then she leaned back, patted Chaps' shoulder, and glanced at Cord. "But I understand your desire to go. Take care of her, brother, for I intend for her to bounce all of my babies on her knee."

Tears stung Chaps' eyes, and she looked away, embarrassed for feeling so much emotion at Alicia's words and realizing, too, how alone she had felt after her father's death. To suddenly be taken into the hearts and home of this family was almost overwhelming. She had expected to take from the West, but had never expected to receive such heartfelt gifts.

Cord stood up and pulled Chaps with him. Looking into her eyes, he said, "I'll take care of her, Alicia." Then he glanced at his sister. "Do you think she could mean more to you than me?"

Alicia stood, too, and smiled in understanding at her brother. "Go safely, and return soon."

Chapter 17

As Chaps and Cord rode away from the Vincente hacienda on fresh mustangs, Cord leading a third one with supplies, they stopped at the point where Miguel had originally met them, and looked around. To the northeast, a large cloud of dust was moving steadily toward them.

"Damn!" Cord exclaimed. "That's Red Duke and his Comancheros."

"How do you know?"

"That's a big group of riders, and they're headed this way. Who else is it going to be? We shouldn't have stayed so long with Miguel, but I thought we had more time."

"Cord, we weren't there any longer than it took to explain what was going on and get supplies and horses."

"Then, Red Duke must have had relay horses, or he'd never be this close."

"Should we ride back and tell Miguel and Alicia?"

"No. Miguel's got vaqueros watching, who'll warn him. Right now, we've got to get out of here, 'cause we won't be safe till we're in the mountains."

Chaps shuddered at the thought of riding

through mountains again, but said nothing.

"Let's get going. Red Duke has probably spotted our trail and they'll follow, if I know him."

"What if Duke splits up his Comancheros and leaves some to take the hacienda?"

"Red Duke's too smart for that. He'd never split his group this close to catching us. We're more important than the hacienda and the Vincentes, and he'll think Alicia's still with us when he sees tracks for three horses. He'll also figure we warned the Vincente family, so he can't take them by surprise, which means there'd be a fight, and he'd lose men and supplies. No, he won't want to take a chance on losing us, so he'll plan on getting us first, then taking care of the Vincentes."

"So, we'd better go, right?"

"Right."

They started forward at a walk, urged their horses to a trot, then finally into a gallop. Their horses were fresh, but still they knew they couldn't keep up the pace for long, or they would lose their mounts. However, for now they wanted to put as much distance as they could between themselves and Red Duke.

Riding across the valley, Chaps kept looking back, and there was soon no doubt that the cloud of dust was following them. On one hand, she was relieved, for it meant Miguel and Alicia would be safe, but on the other hand, she knew Red Duke was closing in again. She shivered, realizing she could have been riding to safety, and wondered why she had put herself into such danger again. Then she glanced at Cord and knew.

251

As the sun lowered in the west, and the cloud of dust dropped back somewhat, they slowed their horses as they neared the Peloncillo Mountains.

"Chaps, that dust cloud hasn't gotten any smaller, so I don't think you have to worry about Red Duke splitting up his Comancheros."

"Good. But how does he plan to capture us?"

"With that size group of men, I'd guess he figures to cut us off somewhere in the mountains, then take us dead or alive."

"But that didn't work in the Black Range."

"No, but those were a different kind of mountains. Here there won't be any hiding behind thick brush and trees, 'cause there aren't any. These mountains are dry and deadly to people who don't understand them, but good to those who know their secrets."

"And you do?"

"Yes. Apache lore. And that's where Red Duke is going to slip up. He doesn't realize it yet, but I'm the Joker in the deck. He's trying to anticipate my moves and he can't. But I know him. I studied his patterns and learned everything I could about him and his outlaws before going after Alicia. That's going to pay off now."

"I hope so."

"He's not going to win anymore, Chaps." Riding closer, he squeezed her hand. "Anyway, how can he? I've got you now, and you're the lucky charm in this battle."

She didn't know how lucky she was, but she had helped free Alicia, so maybe that qualified. She did know that Red Duke was a formidable and dangerous foe, but if anybody could deal with him, it was Cord. She just hoped she would be more help than hindrance in the coming days.

As they continued riding, Chaps kept checking behind them. The cloud of dust kept pace, and as the sun disappeared behind the Peloncillo Mountains, the air began to cool and the sky to darken. It would be time to camp soon, and she grew a little concerned, glancing at Cord.

"What's Red Duke going to do when it gets dark?" she asked.

"If he's smart, they'll find a stream and bed down by it. Nobody's going to bother a group that size."

"And what are we going to do?"

"We'll ride into the mountains. I know a place you'll like for the night."

"I don't know if I can sleep, knowing Red Duke is so close. What if he gets up early and finds us?"

"He may get up early and try to catch us asleep, but he won't find us. I know these mountains. He doesn't."

"Maybe he has an Apache guide."

"I'd know if he did, but he doesn't." Cord hesitated, then gave her a hard stare. "Chaps, do you have so little faith in me?"

"I'm sorry if I sound that way, because I do trust you. It's just that the longer I ride the more ways I can think of for Red Duke to catch up with us, capture us and torture us. That man has me spooked, and I admit it."

"You can't let him turn you against yourself, or me. Remember, against impossible odds you got

Alicia out of Duke's hideout. Have faith that you can get away from him again, and not just that, but stop him for good."

"How?"

"I don't know yet, but trust me, we'll get him."

"I do trust you, and you're right, I've got to start having some faith in us."

"That's right."

"I normally have more assurance, but everything has been so strange, so frightening, and so over-whelming, that I've felt out of control for too long."

"You mustn't feel that way. You've done damn well, especially for a greenhorn." He chuckled.

She joined his laughter, feeling her mood lighten. He was right. She had escaped Red Duke's hideout, and that was quite an accomplishment. If Cord could laugh about their situation, then she might as well, too. And she was also going to start having more faith in them, for it was almost as if Cord was leading Red Duke now instead of being chased.

"Chaps, look ahead, see where the dying sun is shining through that narrow crevice?"

"You mean that brilliant slash of light at the top?"

"Yes. If we somehow get separated, you're to look for that at sunset. You can read directions off it anywhere along this side of the Peloncillos and find your way back to the hacienda, can't you?"

"Well, yes, theoretically I suppose that would work. But we'd better not get separated."

"You've got food and water on your mount, and

254

if something happens to me, you'll be all right for a while."

"Something happens to you? Cord, you're starting to scare me."

"I don't mean to do that, but I don't want you going into this blind, either. After everything you've said, I'm starting to kick myself for letting you come."

"No, you did the right thing. I couldn't have stood just waiting somewhere. What if you'd never come back? I wouldn't have known what happened. I couldn't have helped. No, Cord, we're in this together, and we're going to finish it together. Red Duke is going to wish he'd never heard of either one of us."

Cord laughed. "Okay, that's the way I like to hear you talk. Come on, it's time to get into the mountains and settle down for the night."

Leading them around fallen rocks, past cacti in bloom and a few twisted piñons, Cord headed into the mountains, Chaps following, trusting her horse to pick its way through the rough terrain, just as her mount had taken her safely in and out of the Black Range.

After they had ridden upward for a while, the sky growing darker by the moment, Cord stopped and looked behind them at the valley. He pointed at a light with dark shapes around it near a clump of trees.

"That light is Red Duke's campfire," Cord explained. "They've bedded down now, but they'll be back at the chase tomorrow."

"I'm glad to know they're not still following us."

"It's the kind of thing you need to learn to watch for."

"Thanks, I'll remember."

"Good. Another thing, while we're riding or walking through this country, don't pick up anything that looks like a stick without first examining it closely, and don't reach back under any crevices where you can't see. There are a lot of rattlers out here, and they'll leave you alone most of the time, but if you disturb one, then it's most likely going to strike."

"Thanks for warning me. I'm sure I'll sleep real well knowing a snake could crawl up on me."

Cord laughed. "The only thing you have to worry about crawling up on you is me." Then he started forward again. "Come on. Now that we know Red Duke is bedded down, we can get some rest."

Cord lead them deep and high into the mountains, until they could no longer see the valley of Vincente Rancho, nor Red Duke's campfire. By the time they had wound their way to a box canyon, the sky was dark, and stars twinkled overhead around the rising moon.

Instead of leading them down into the canyon, Cord took several twists and turns along its side, then suddenly disappeared behind a piñon tree. Confused, Chaps followed and was surprised to see that Cord had stopped by the tree and dismounted.

"Wait here," he said, then hurried back out.

She was curious and got down, glad to stretch her legs a moment, and watched him from under the piñon tree. He picked up a dead branch and ran back to the entrance to the box canyon, then carefully began destroying their tracks behind him as he walked toward the piñon tree.

Having seen all she needed to, Chaps hurriedly remounted, just before Cord reappeared. Throwing away the branch, he got on his horse, and they started down a steep incline.

Not long after, they rode through a narrow break in a cliff and were suddenly in a small glade. Chaps glanced around in amazement, for once more Cord had brought her to a place of lush beauty in the middle of desertlike surroundings. A small waterfall poured into a deep pool of water. Trees, grass and flowers grew in abundance around it, and with the moonlight shining down, everything sparkled like a fairy tale. She gazed at Cord and smiled.

"Sometimes fantasy can be real, can't it?" she said.

"Yes. It's beautiful here." Then he grinned. "I remember the last time I asked if you wanted to bathe. As I recall, you thought it was an insult."

"That was a long time ago. I hardly remember it at all. Besides, you wanted me to take off all my clothes for a bath, and I hardly knew you."

"We knew each other a lot better afterward, didn't we?"

"Yes, we did, and I want a bath just as badly this time. And to sleep forever."

"The bath you can have, the sleep, well—"

"I'll take a few hours."

"Good enough. If you'll unpack some food, the blankets, whatever will make us comfortable, I'll

257

see to the horses."

"Okay, but don't expect me to slave like this forever, partner."

"You'd rather have the horses?"

"No!" She laughed, pulling off blanket rolls and saddlebags, then started looking for the most comfortable spot of grass she could find. It didn't take her long to lay out the blankets, then sit down and unwrap some food. The aroma made her stomach growl, and she smiled, amazed that she could feel so happy and relaxed.

It had been a long, harrowing ride from the Black Range, and this was the first time she had felt safe enough to relax. She stretched her hands high above her head and inhaled deeply, smelling piñon, sage and sweet grass. Yes, it felt good to rest for a little while, and she would just put Red Duke out of her mind until tomorrow.

Cord finished with the horses, hobbled them, then sat down by Chaps. He took her hand and squeezed it. "I'm glad you came with me. If I'd been here alone, I'd have been thinking about you and nothing else, anyway."

"And I'd have been thinking about you."

"What would you have been thinking?"

"That I was probably going to have to come and get your body out of these mountains before the buzzards got you."

"That's not much faith, Chaps."

"No, but that's what I'd have been worried about."

"And would you have cared?"

"Yes, of course."

258

"Good." He smiled. "Can I have something to eat now, or am I to die of starvation?"

"Oh, have something to eat. We've been through too much together for me to lose you now."

Cord chuckled and picked up a tamale. "You know, we do eat food besides tamales and tortillas down here."

"So you say. I have no proof yet, except Red Duke's peculiar cuisine."

"Okay. When we get out of this alive, I'll cook you the best meal of your life. Deal?"

"Agreed."

They both began eating hungrily, and she watched him, wondering how he could make her so happy with only a few words. Actually, just being with him made her feel good. He was nothing like the fantasy man she had always envisioned, the hero of her novels, but then how could she have imagined someone she didn't know existed?

Cord was a very real, solid, dependable, caring man, who had risked his life to save his sister. She smiled at him, and he grinned back, his eyes crinkling at the corners. She wished they had a fire so she could see him better, but maybe in the moonlight she could pretend he was her real fantasy man.

Suddenly her heart beat faster. What if Cord Cordova, rather than a one-dimensional fantasy man, was her true love? Their lives were completely different. They could never blend their two different worlds. She suddenly felt very sad. Maybe she loved him, and there was no chance at all for it to work.

"Chaps, what are you looking so sad about?" He grasped her chin with strong fingers, looked into her eyes a long moment, then gently brushed her lips with his. "It's been too damn long since I've held you, and if Duke had touched you again, I was going to cut off his hands."

She smiled, touched by his words. Maybe it wasn't love, just an intense physical involvement. And maybe that was enough, for when everything was settled, the feeling would probably go away. Then her life would return to normal, but she was no longer sure she wanted that.

"Chaps, I'm going to throw you in the pool with all your clothes on if you don't stop looking at me like that. You gave Duke happier looks than you're giving me."

She shook her head, throwing off the melancholy. She had been through horrible danger, she had had her illusions shattered, and at the moment all she wanted to be was happy. Cord made her happy, and she was going to enjoy him, no matter the future.

"If you took my clothes off, would you still throw me in the pool?" she asked mischievously.

"Yes," he said, pushing aside the leftover food and pulling her into his arms. "You have no idea how I've burned for you."

He pulled the pins from her hair, and as it fell free, he pushed his hands into it, pulling her head back so that her face was exposed to him. Kissing her from her chin to her eyes, he groaned, then pressed a hot kiss to her lips. When it deepened, she moaned, feeling him stab into her depths, exploring her, exciting her, demanding more and more until she responded, pushing deep into his mouth.

While he kissed her, he unbuttoned her shirt, then jerked it back, exposing her chemise-covered breasts. Cupping them, he massaged, growing more passionate by the moment. He lifted his head and looked down at her.

"Damn, I've missed you, Chaps. And I've been worried sick about you. I don't want to go through anything like that again."

Then he pulled her to her feet and began stripping the clothes from her body. When she stood nude in the moonlight, he stopped and simply stood still for a long moment, looking at her body as if he would memorize it for all time.

"If you were any more beautiful, I wouldn't think you were real." He touched the tip of each breast and watched the rosy nipple grow taut. "And if you were any more passionate, I'd have to think you were a dream. As it is, sometimes I think you're more fantasy than real, just suddenly coming into my life and turning it upside down."

"You affect me the same way, Cord." She unbuttoned his shirt, then pulled it open, exposing the dark hair on his chest. Running her fingers through it, she delighted in the feel of him. And when he inhaled sharply, she knew he felt the same about her.

"Enough of this," Cord said gruffly, then jerked off his boots and pulled off his denims. Picking her up in his arms, he walked to the pool. "I never forget a promise," he said, and dropped her in the water.

She burst to the top, water streaming down her face. She tossed back her hair, sputtering, "Not fair!" Treading water, she glared.

"I warned you." Cord chuckled.

"Come here, and we'll see who has the last word."

Cord dove in, cleanly cutting the water, then turned upward to grab her around the waist as he resurfaced. "Now, what were you saying?"

"Just this." She quickly put a hand on top of his head, pushed him under, then swam for the bank.

But he caught her before she had gone far, and pulled her close so that her breasts were against his chest and they could feel the heat of each other. Treading water with his feet, he held them up, and kissed her, running his hands through her long hair.

Finally, he raised his head. "You're like some sea nymph come to lure me to my doom. Do you have a siren's song?"

"Come here, cowboy," she said seductively, turning toward the bank and pulling him with her. When she had an arm on firm ground to support herself, she pulled him close, feeling the taut muscles down his back with her free hand until she reached his buttocks, then sighed as his long, hot hardness slipped between her legs. She moved against him and groaned.

"It's been too damn long, Chaps," he complained, stroking down her back, then pulling her hips toward him. "I need you bad."

"No more than I need you. Make love to me."

"You don't have to ask twice. I'll help you out

262

of the water."

"No. Here. Now. I can't wait."

She put both arms on the bank and leaned back, offering herself up to him. She felt his hands caress her body, beginning with her shoulders and working downward, gently massaging her breasts until she moaned. "This is my siren's song."

"Then, making love must be worshipping you, because I can hear and see and feel nothing but you, Chaps, and that's the way I want it to be."

"Love me, now."

She threw back her head as he grasped her hips, raising her slightly, then she felt him at her entrance. Her body tensed with desire, and heat poured through her, exciting, making her ready for him. As he pushed his hard length in deep, she moaned and looked upward, seeing the moon and the stars shining down on them, bathing them in silvery light. Then she looked at Cord, and his dark eyes shone with passion as he began to move inside her, so hot compared to the cool water surrounding them.

Then he lowered his head, touching his lips to hers, before plunging his tongue deeply into her mouth as he covered her hands with his, splaying their fingers together. She wound her legs around his hips and held on as his movements grew harder, faster, bringing them closer and closer to ecstasy.

They clung to each other, riding the waves of passion, melding their souls together as their bodies meshed closer and closer, drawing them together in a timeless dance of desire that neither wanted to ever end, and yet both desperately

263

fought to complete.

Then Chaps broke the kiss, moaning, "Cord, please, now."

"Yes," he groaned, and pushed harder, faster, reveling in the passion that was exploding through them.

Suddenly they shuddered, clinging together as they reached complete fulfillment, then hung a moment in total union before dropping back to reality.

Cord was breathing hard as he held her close, pressing soft kisses over her face, murmuring endearments in Spanish, and she snuggled against him, wanting never to be parted. If Cord Cordova wasn't her fantasy man, then she didn't know love when she found it.

Love? She froze. Could she really be in love with Cord? She had always thought of him as an Apache renegade, but after meeting Alicia and hearing him speak Spanish, she doubted he had told her the truth about his heritage.

She hugged him hard and felt tears sting her eyes. Did it matter what he was, who he was, Apache, half-Apache, half-Spanish, anything at all, except that they made each other happy?

But could she trust her feelings, because if she was wrong, she wouldn't be able to stand the pain. Then she carefully reminded herself that maybe she wasn't in love with Cord. It was simply a series of extraordinary events that had brought them together. They had nothing in common. She would simply have to remember that passion was one thing, fantasy was one thing, but hard, practical reality was quite another; and that was what she

264

must deal with from now on in her life.

"Chaps, did I hurt you or something?"

"No. It was wonderful. Truly. I was just thinking that I never want to leave here. Could we stay forever and forget all the ugly reality outside?"

He chuckled. "If I thought I could keep you happy here, I'd camp here forever."

"And you don't think I'd stay happy?"

"You're used to a lot more, Chaps. I know that. I wish I didn't, but I do." He paused. "But let's don't talk about that now. I'm starving. I want to eat, and then I want—"

"You'd better want to make me happy some more."

"I'm already hearing your siren's song again."

Chapter 18

"The chase is on," Cord announced the next morning, then gave Chaps a quick hug.

"You sound almost gleeful. I don't understand. We're being hunted by the dreaded Red Duke and his Comancheros, scourge of southern New Mexico and Arizona."

"Right," Cord agreed, and grinned. "By the time we get through running them around the desert and mountains, they'll wish they'd have stayed home."

"I wish I felt as confident as you sound."

"You will. It's just a matter of time." He finished saddling the last horse, then turned to watch Chaps fill the canteens. "Of course, as much as I'm going to enjoy leading Duke a merry chase until he's worn down and an easy target, I'd rather stay here and make love to you."

Standing, she looked at him, shaking her head. "I had no idea you had such a sense of humor, Cord."

"I haven't been in the best of moods since you met me."

"I guess not." She handed him three of the canteens and saved one for herself.

He hung two of the canteens on the pack horse,

266

made sure the saddle and packs were good and tight, then turned back. "I'm serious. When I'm with you, it's hard to care about anything else."

"I know what you mean, but Red Duke's probably already broken camp."

"You're right." He looked at the waterfall, then back at Chaps. "I can't take this place with me, but I'm taking my sea nymph."

She laughed, shaking her head. "And I've got you."

"All of me. Come on, let's hit the trail before I change my mind and we never leave."

They mounted, both smiling, thinking secrets spawned by the night before as they started back up to the top. They passed the piñon tree nestled near the mouth of the box canyon, then continued back the way they had come the night before. Cord led them to the original trail, then they stopped and looked down into the Vincente Rancho valley. A line of men on horseback was starting the trek into the Peloncillo Mountains.

"Right on time," Cord said with satisfaction.

"Is that Red Duke?"

"Got to be. Besides, it's hard to miss that big black stallion of his."

"Do you think they see us?"

"Maybe, but they're probably concentrating on the ground trail, instead of looking up."

"I bet they'd be surprised if they saw us. Don't you?"

"Yes." Cord chuckled. "You ready to ride?"

"Lead on, great scout."

Cord laughed, patted her knee, and settled his hat on tight.

Turning their horses around, they started down the other side of the Peloncillos, heading southwest. It was another beautiful day, and Chaps gazed up at the clear blue sky with no signs of clouds. Although it wasn't terribly warm yet, she knew that before the day was over the temperature would hover around one hundred, and she would be hot.

Tightening the drawstring on her hat, she was grateful for the protection against the sun, and also grateful her pale skin hadn't yet been burned. She was wearing her green plaid cotton shirt and the dark green, cotton split skirt, because it was cooler than her leather skirt. She was also wearing boots and a pair of pigskin gloves Alicia had given her to protect her hands. Her gun ring was tucked in her saddlebag, right near the top for easy reach.

Satisfied she had done all she could to protect herself from the elements, she glanced at Cord and nodded approval at his comfortable buckskin shirt, faded denims, scuffed cowboy boots, and red bandanna around his neck. As usual, he was wearing a Colt .45 in a holster low on his right hip. There was also a rifle tucked in a holster tied to his saddle.

As he rolled a smoke, his reins were momentarily wrapped around his saddle horn. Feeling her gaze, he glanced up. "Want a smoke?"

"No, thanks. I was just enjoying the view."

He looked at her and smiled. "Enjoy all you want, but I'll expect payment tonight."

She laughed, shaking her head, pleased with discovering his humor. He was a man of many talents, many sides, many loyalties, and so far she

268

liked them all.

They rode on silently for a while, their horses nimbly picking their way through rock and sand, around cacti and piñon trees. Cord kept checking behind them to make sure they were leaving a strong enough trail for Red Duke to follow as they angled downward, staying in the mountains as they turned south.

The sun rose higher in the sky, and the day heated up. Lizards scurried out of their path, and rattlesnakes sunned on nearby ledges. A buzzard circled overhead in the distance, and a slight breeze brought the scent of smoke.

Cord glanced back, his eyes narrowed. "Red Duke's men must have stopped to rest their horses and eat, and they've built a fire. Fools! Don't they know there're renegade Apache bands around here?"

"Maybe Red Duke thinks nobody can hurt him."

"That wouldn't surprise me."

"Cord, I didn't know about the Apaches. I thought they were all on reservations."

He gave her a hard stare. "Most of them are, but there're a few still fighting the army for their land and their way of life. That bother you?"

"Well, it might if you weren't with me. Do you, by any chance, know these people? I mean, they wouldn't just scalp us, and ask questions later, would they?"

Cord chuckled, shaking his head in amazement. "Sometimes I forget how most whites think about the native people of Turtle Island."

"Turtle Island?"

"That's what this continent was called before

white people came, conquered and renamed."

"I think that's called discovering, Cord."

"Chaps, I hope you'll try to write the truth about the West in your books, and not pump it up bigger than it is, or try to make it fit into some sacred white beliefs."

She stared at him in astonishment. "You keep surprising me, Cord. I think I know you, then you turn around and show me another side of you. You really care about the West, don't you?"

"Of course I do, and about its people, too. I've seen the horror of what has happened to the Apache and the other nations, I've seen land stolen from the old Spanish families, and all of it done quite legally . . . legal if you belong to the group in power."

"You sound bitter."

"I am, and disillusioned, but hopeful, too, that a difference can be made in the lives of those who are left, so that they don't have to live out their lives in starvation and fear."

"Getting Red Duke will help that, won't it?"

"Yes. He's just another white who came to live off the land and its people, thinking he could do anything he wanted. But his reign is about over. I'm going to see to that."

"I'm glad you are, Cord, and I'll help. But all whites aren't bad, you know."

He smiled at her. "I know, but we've had enough bad ones to last a lifetime."

"I'm sorry, but if it helps, I plan to write the truth."

He gave her a long hard look, as if seriously considering her words before he spoke again.

"Chaps, I'm going to take you to a renegade Apache band. You can meet them, talk to them, see how they live. It's the last chance you'll get to see Apaches living free, or as free as they can since they're hiding out in the mountains."

"I'd be honored. I mean, if they won't hurt me, or something." She hesitated and glanced at him. "Are you sure they won't mind?"

"If you're with me, then you're my woman and one of us. Also, it'll be a good way to lose Red Duke when we're ready."

"All right, I'd like to meet them. But I have a question. If you're Apache, then what is Alicia? I mean, she's Spanish, and I don't understand why."

Cord nodded. "It's a part of what Red Duke doesn't understand, too, and not knowing will wind up costing him everything, because he doesn't know I exist."

"How can you say that? He knows you. You've been in his hideout."

"He knows Cord, outlaw and gun-for-hire, since I stole Alicia from him."

"Then he doesn't realize you're Alicia's brother. He thinks you were hired to get her back."

"That's right." He began rolling another smoke.

"But how can he not know you and Alicia are related?"

"Alicia is Spanish, as pure blood as they come. But I'm half-Apache. We share the same father, but my mother was an Apache maiden, who raised me with the Apache since she was totally unacceptable to my father's family. Even so, he spent a lot of time with us. Later, when she died, he married Alicia's mother, from a very proper Spanish

271

family."

"Now I understand."

He lit his cigarette and took a long draw. "My ties with the Cordovas aren't well known outside of the Spanish grandee families, so Red Duke thought Alicia was an only child, heir to the vast Cordova holdings in southern New Mexico."

She frowned. "I remember Red Duke told me he wanted to take over all the ranches and build an empire."

"I'm not surprised. He tried again and again to marry Alicia, offering money, bribes, anything, but my father and his wife, as well as Alicia, of course, refused."

"So he kidnapped her to force the marriage?"

"Yes, but first he murdered my father and his wife and burned the hacienda."

"Cord! I didn't know. No wonder you've been so determined to get him."

"My family isn't the only one hurt by him; but he did the most damage to mine, and all the grandees are behind me, even though I'm half-Apache." He finished the cigarette and tossed the tobacco to the wind.

"But why did Red Duke want to marry Alicia? Couldn't he have just killed everybody, then taken over the land, maybe even made up a fake deed?"

"He wanted more than the land. He wanted the respectability that comes with marrying into one of the oldest families in the area. He wanted his children to have the proper legacy, and because he believed Alicia was an only child, he thought he could get away with it, finally by killing her parents and forcing her to marry him."

272

"But it didn't work."

"No. He doesn't understand the strength and pride of the Spanish and Apache. Miguel wanted to go after Alicia, but I persuaded him that I'd have a better chance of bringing her back alive, since I was unknown. But if I hadn't come back, he would have gone in, with an army of ranchers if necessary, even if it was too late to save her. He knew, as well as I did, that Alicia would have died before marrying Red Duke. And she almost did."

"Duke's even worse than I thought," Chaps said in disgust. "But how could he think he could get away with it?"

"He's been getting what he wanted for a long time, and who could question him if he had legally married Alicia? He could have kept her drugged, or in seclusion, and then eventually killed her if she caused him too much trouble."

"That's terrifying. Then what did he want with me?"

"By the time you arrived, I think he must have realized he wasn't going to break Alicia. He was probably planning on falsifying a marriage paper after she died, then marrying you and carrying on as he wanted. Besides, he hates the Spanish, so he wouldn't have wanted the blood of his children tainted."

"Duke mentioned my color of hair and skin over and over, as if it was more important than me." She touched her strawberry-blond hair, thinking of what a simple hair color had done to her life.

"It probably is, Chaps, because you were going to be—"

"A brood mare."

"I wasn't going to put it that way."

"But it's true, isn't it?"

"I'm afraid so." Cord hesitated, thinking. "Red Duke can't stop now. He's got to get us; he's got to prove his superiority, that there are no holes in his dreams of ruling this land. Otherwise, what has he got?"

"A lot of trouble."

"Yes, but also a realization that he's not the man he thinks he is, or has convinced his followers he is. That'd be a dangerous position to be in."

"What do you mean?"

"If he can't handle us, then he looks weak to his followers, and there's sure to be a power play for his position."

"I hadn't thought of that."

"It's one more reason Red Duke has for catching us, and he'll stop at nothing to do it."

Chaps shuddered and glanced behind them. "Are you sure we're safe?"

"We're never safe, but the odds are on our side."

"That's not what I wanted to hear, Cord."

He smiled at her, then leaned over and squeezed her hand. "We'll be okay, and we'll be in Apache country soon."

"I hope you're right."

"Trust me."

He dropped her hand and moved ahead, so they could ride single file on the narrow trail leading down the side of a cliff. As they moved closer to the valley below, Chaps yawned, watching Cord's broad back, thinking of the night ahead, of campfires, stars and moonlight skys. Yes, Cord had opened up a whole new world for her, and one she

274

was anxious to explore again.

Suddenly, a man leaped from above onto Cord's back, knocking him off his horse. They rolled to the side of the cliff, clutching at each other, trying to fight, and went over the edge. Cord's horse spooked and galloped down the trail. The lead to the pack horse was attached to its saddle horn, causing the other mustang to run behind.

Alone, Chaps' mind raced wildly. Red Duke! Comancheros! She expected to be attacked at any moment. Jerking off her right glove, she pulled the gun ring out of her saddlebag and pushed it onto the first finger of her right hand. Feeling a little better prepared, she looked over the side and could see Cord and the man struggling below.

Terrified for Cord, and not knowing what to expect next, she urged her mount forward, going after Cord and the other horses. It seemed to take forever, and by the time she got to the base of the cliff, the other horses were contentedly grazing. She galloped by them and rushed around a clump of piñon trees to rescue Cord.

To her surprise he was calmly sitting with the man who had attacked him, and they were leaning against a rock, talking, laughing and smoking. Cord glanced up, smiled and motioned her over.

Fury washed over her, and she got off her mount, dropped the reins and stormed over to him. Putting her hands on her hips, she spat, "I almost broke my neck getting down here as fast as I could, thinking you were being killed by Comancheros, not knowing when Red Duke was suddenly going to throw a rope around me and drag me to the top of the mountain and slowly boil me in oil, or roast me over a fire, or tie me to a horse and let it drag me all over the mountain." She paused for breath.

"Sorry if I worried you, Chaps," Cord said, not looking contrite at all. "I'd like you to meet—"

"And then," she interrupted, stepping closer as her anger boiled over, "I get down here, and you don't even get up, or act worried about me, or the horses, or the Comancheros, or anything. No, you're too busy discussing the weather, or the crops, or horses, or cattle, or who-knows-what with this man who almost killed you to ask how I am."

"How are you, Chaps?" Cord asked.

"I'm terrible, as you can plainly see. You scared me to death, and for all I care you can just go play follow the leader with those Comancheros by yourself. And you can go smoke pipes with those Apaches all you want, and you can even go riding with this person"—she pointed to the man sitting beside Cord—"for all I care. But I'm not having anything else to do with any of this, because it just doesn't make any sense."

"I'm sorry I frightened you," the stranger said, his voice accented.

"I wasn't frightened," she protested. "I was . . . was caught off guard, and I thought you were going to kill Cord."

"I could have. And you are right, that is exactly what I did. I caught you both off guard. On purpose."

"On purpose? Cord is he supposed to be a friend?"

"Yes," Cord replied, smiling.

"Some friend," Chaps sneered.

276

"I was acting as a friend," the man objected. "You would both be dead if I had been the enemy. Very foolish, Cord. Very foolish. I thought I trained you better."

"Trained?" Chaps finally calmed down enough to take a good look at the stranger. He was obviously Indian, although dressed as a cowboy. "I don't suppose," she hesitated, "you're Apache?"

"Yes," he replied, smiling only with his eyes.

"This is Chief Black Ears," Cord introduced. "And this wild woman is called Chaps. I'll tell you later how she got that name."

Chaps didn't reply or respond in any way; she was staring at Black Ears without even blinking.

"Chaps!" Cord exclaimed. "What's wrong with you?"

"I'm sorry I got mad, Mr. . . . Chief Black Eyes, I mean, Ears. It was an easy mistake, I assure you. I mean, it isn't often I see a man who hurls himself off a cliff onto the back of a man on a moving horse, then tries to strangle him as they roll down a cliff. Anyone could have made the same mistake. I mean, it was easy to take you for an enemy, since we'd never met before, and . . . you aren't going to scalp me over a little mistake like that, are you?"

"Chaps are you trying to insult him? Do you really think Black Ears would do that?"

But Chaps was completely focused on Black Ears, who sat cross-legged, his thick black hair cut off straight below his ears. A red cotton headband held back his hair, his prominent nose had been broken several times, his black eyes were sharp and narrowed, his cheekbones were high and his face

277

was weathered and bronzed. And he sat completely still, a bowie knife held easily in one hand.

Cord got up, put his arms around Chaps, and turned her around so that she couldn't see Black Ears. Blinking, she finally focused on Cord.

"Are you really all right?" she asked, her voice shaky. "I've never been so frightened in my life, not even when you kidnapped me. Are you sure he's not going to scalp me? My hair's an unusual color, and—"

"Chaps, Black Ears is an Apache warrior. He doesn't murder innocents. He has as much honor as any man you have ever met, probably more. What he did was important. He was teaching me a lesson, and one I needed to remember. I had gotten too sure of myself, back in my own territory, and instead of Black Ears, it could just as easily have been Red Duke or one of his Comancheros."

"But couldn't he have just ridden up and told you that you were behaving in a dangerous manner?"

"Would the message have been as clear?"

"No, I suppose not, but it wouldn't have been as frightening, either."

"But we needed to be frightened, so we would always remember never to take anything for granted. That's what he was reminding me of when you walked up."

"But why didn't you come back for me as soon as you could?"

"There wasn't much time, and you needed to learn a lesson, too."

"What lesson?"

"That if something happened to me, you could

278

take care of yourself."

"I only came down the mountain."

"And you didn't panic."

"I had to save you."

Cord laughed and hugged her close. "Black Ears was right. We had much to learn. Now come back and stop insulting him by acting like he's going to attack you. And, remember, Apaches hold bravery very highly."

They walked back to Black Ears, who stood and nodded, smiling slightly at Chaps.

"I'm sorry if I was rude," Chaps apologized, trying to see the Apache as simply a man, not a wild animal, and it made a difference, for he didn't seem quite so menacing now, although he was a formidable person, so self-contained, so powerful, so sure of himself.

"You reacted quickly, bravely," Black Ears responded. "You have no reason to apologize. But we should not remain long in one place. Go on, and I will get my horse and meet you." He nodded, then quickly walked back up the cliff and disappeared behind some boulders.

"Well, that was some experience," Chaps said, exhaling in relief.

"He's right. Let's go. We can talk on the way."

"All right," she agreed. "I'll be glad to get out of here."

They remounted and were soon on their way, crossing grasslands again, with cacti here and there, and a few scrub trees. The sun was beginning its descent in the west, and it had grown hot. Chaps packed her pigskin gloves into a saddlebag, deciding they were too hot, and not wanting to take a chance on not wearing her gun ring again.

"What did you think of Black Ears?" Cord asked.

"He is the scariest man I have ever met. Whatever he told me I would believe, and I would never, never cross him."

"What would you think of whole nations of men, women and children like him?"

"How could they possibly have lost their wars to whites?"

"Oh, that's simple. For one thing, they're terribly independent and rarely fought together in large groups, like the whites. For another, they didn't have advanced weapons, or the resources to keep what weapons they did have always working or equipped. And no matter how many whites died, they had more because of an endless amount of emigrants, and the nations had only their children to replace their dead."

"Simple? I don't know about that, but I'm sorry I wasn't here to see the Apache when they roamed their land free."

"Oh, they were fierce" — Cord chuckled — "and still are. But they aren't perfect, either. They made war, punished, hunted, stole, just like any other people, but their way of looking at the world is disappearing now, and may never return. That's why I hope you'll preserve some of it in your books."

"I'll try, Cord. I'll really try."

He smiled and rode closer. "You were really mad, weren't you?"

"Yes. I was terrified for you when I saw that man leap on your back, and I rushed down there only to find you calmly smoking with the man who had just tried to kill you and—"

"You're getting angry again."

"Well, it's all your fault."

"Why?"

"If you hadn't made me care what happened to you, then I wouldn't have been so worried."

He took her hand. "How much do you care?"

"Now, Cord, I don't know how to answer that. Anyway, it's not something a gentleman asks a lady."

"I want an answer."

Suddenly Black Ears rode up and tapped Cord on the shoulder. Cord jerked around, going for his gun.

Black Ears grinned. "Now I know what makes you eyeless and earless. A woman. Hah!"

Cord looked sheepish. "You've caught me twice."

"Was I that bad a teacher?"

"You were the best, and you know it."

"Can my best pupil have lost his cunning to white ways?"

"I'm sorry to say it may have happened."

"That's not true," Chaps defended. "We're tired. We just rode to the top of the Black Range, rescued his sister under terribly dangerous and difficult conditions, then raced across the country to the Vincente Rancho, left off Alicia and warned them about Red Duke and his Comancheros coming, then took off for the Peloncillos to lead Duke astray. I hardly think that would be called losing his cunning."

Black Ears threw back his head and laughed long and hard.

Insulted, Chaps sniffed and looked the other way.

"She's your woman, all right, Cord," Black Ears finally said when he stopped laughing. "Like a wolf with cubs. But does she always talk so much?"

Cord chuckled, squeezing Chaps' hand. "He's complimenting you, Chaps, for defending me so well."

"Really? It didn't sound like it."

"Where did you find your she-wolf, Cord?" Black Ears asked.

"Near El Paso when I was trying to find Red Duke's hideout. She led us there, and like she said, we're leading Red Duke."

"I came scouting the campfires. I saw the men, but I was surprised to find you. Why did you bring these men to our land?"

"Somebody's got to stop them, and we've got them smoked out. They were coming after the Vincentes, but I led them back here, hoping to tire them and then—"

"Finish them off," Black Ears completed.

"Or persuade them to give up their life of crime," Chaps added. "They could surrender."

Black Ears looked at her a long moment, then glanced back at Cord. "Where is she from?"

Cord chuckled. "New York City."

"But justice can be served everywhere," Chaps added.

"I agree," Black Ears said. "We know well of this Red Duke and his Comancheros. He has hurt our people, kidnapped and killed our women, stolen our people's government supplies. He has hurt many. The United States Army has not stopped

282

him. If it has come to the Apache to stop his crimes, to see justice done, then we stand ready."

"But—" Chaps began.

"We can give them the chance to surrender," Cord added, "if that'd make you feel better, Chaps."

"It would, if that's possible," Chaps agreed.

"The Apache always give a man the chance to live or die," Black Ears added solemnly, "but it is the Great Spirit who decides."

Chapter 19

Around dusk the next morning, Chaps, Cord, and Black Ears reached the San Simon River. They were tired, hot and dusty. Also, they were tense, for Black Ears had brought the news that Red Duke and his Comancheros were catching up with them. It seemed the outlaws had brought extra horses and were changing mounts so they could ride without rest.

It was what Cord had feared, but there was nothing he could do about it, nor would he have done anything differently. He had led the Comancheros away from the Vincente Rancho, and he would do it again. Now they would have to deal with the situation any way they could. The lighter mood of earlier in the day was gone, and they were silent as they rode along the riverbank, looking for a good place to camp for the night.

After selecting a campsite, they watered the horses, then hobbled them for the night. As they prepared camp, they listened and watched for any sign of Red Duke, for at the river they were caught between two valleys, and it was a vulnerable position. The next day they would travel on toward Cochise Head, the highest point in the area, but if they were caught in the valley getting there, they would be in serious trouble.

Not building a fire so they wouldn't give away their position, they settled into a thicket among huge cottonwood trees growing close to the bank. As Chaps set out tamales, tortillas and canteens of water, they all listened intently for any unusual sounds. But the night was quiet, and they began to relax.

"This is good food," Black Ears said, smiling. "We do not eat much but what we catch in the mountains."

"And that's not much, and scrawny at that," Cord added.

"You don't buy supplies?" Chaps asked, surprised.

"We have no money," Black Ears replied. "And we do not want to be anywhere near the U.S. Army. They will hunt us down if they can, and take us to the reservation."

"But surely hunting isn't enough," Chaps persisted, realizing Black Ears was much too thin. She pushed more food at him, and he took it.

"No, it is not enough, but we survive and get extra now and again from friends and family. But food is harder and harder to find. I do not know how much longer we can hold out. I see our ways dying, even though we have tried to remain true to them. I am finally coming to believe some of us will die as warriors, and those left must pass down our ways in stories so that the true Apache spirit lives on for our grandchildren."

Chaps felt like she should say or do something to make the situation better, but there was nothing she could do to make it all right. Money, food, beliefs, nothing would bring back what the Indian had lost, and that saddened her.

But then she realized there was a way to help. Words. Black Ears had said that tales of the Apache would be told to children, but they could also be put in books and last forever. She felt better, knowing that she could help, that she could make a difference, and she suddenly had a renewed purpose in life.

"Black Ears," she said, "I can't change what has happened with the Apache, but I can record, accurately, your way of life, your history. I'm working on a series of novels right now, but later I can write other things, maybe chronicle the Apache. Would you help me?"

"What do you think, Cord?" Black Ears asked.

"It sounds good. Instead of telling tales around a campfire, she could write the words down, and they would be published in a book and sent out to many, many people."

"Although words on paper will not last as long as words on the wind, it is good, then," Black Ears decided. "And if I get a vision from the Great Spirit, I will speak to this white woman of things past and things yet to come."

"Thank you," Chaps replied, "and I don't mean to disagree with your beliefs, but a book will last forever, while a tale told to a group will only last as long as those people remember it."

"And pass it on," Black Ears added. "We believe that what rides the wind goes to the Great Spirit where all exists forever, therefore it can return to us when we have great need of it again. But a book cannot ride the wind, and it can be destroyed."

"Not all the copies, surely."

"You are young yet. You have not seen the great changes that have come to the land, to my people. After seeing what I have seen, I believe nothing exists forever except that which rests within the Great Spirit."

"I would like to record your beliefs, so that everyone could know about them," Chaps said, beginning to understand that Black Ears had a very different view of the world, and one he believed in completely. She was fascinated and yet disturbed that there could be this much difference between the Apache and whites. It went much deeper than the color of skin or type of dress, and she wanted to explore it in her books.

"It's a good idea," Cord agreed, then finished eating a tamale and took a drink of water. "But, remember, while the Apache are different, they are still the same. We're all people."

"I'm beginning to realize that, too," Chaps replied. "Would it be possible for me to talk with some of the women and children?"

"They are on the reservation," Black Ears replied. "The renegade groups in the mountains are male war parties. We have to be to stay alive."

"Could I go to the reservation with you, then?" Chaps persisted.

"It will depend on my vision from the Great Spirit."

"Oh, yes," Chaps responded. "You'll let me know, won't you?"

"Yes," Black Ears agreed, smiling, then looked at Cord. "She is a woman who likes words, yes?"

287

Cord laughed. "That's true."

They all laughed at that, then grew quiet. Cord rolled a smoke, lit it, then shared the cigarette with Black Eagle. In the gathering darkness and stillness of the evening, their thoughts turned to Red Duke and his Comancheros. The chase had become very dangerous again, if it had ever been anything else. And it was possible they wouldn't live long enough to chronicle anything, much less give Chaps the opportunity to write a number of books.

"I'll take the first watch," Black Ears said when they had finished the cigarette, then got up and walked away without making a sound.

Cord moved close to Chaps and put an arm around her shoulders. She laid her head against his chest and sighed. He rubbed her shoulder thoughtfully, watching the water as it moved downstream.

"I'm beginning to think there is no normal life out here, Cord, for there are only battles, chases and furious action. I've found no time for quiet moments, or thinking, or reading, writing."

"You don't like a lot of excitement?"

"I've probably experienced more excitement since I met you than I have previously in my entire life."

Cord chuckled. "Is that a compliment?"

She laughed, too. "I'll tell you, if this keeps up much longer, I'm going to start sitting out the dances."

Cord laughed harder. "I know it's been bad, Chaps, but don't give up on the West yet. There are quiet times here, too, time for contemplating, reading, writing; but there's also a lot of action, and you seem to fit right in."

"If you say so, partner," she quipped, then snuggled closer to his warmth. "But I am getting tired, Cord, and scared again. Red Duke is vicious and determined."

"He's not going to win anymore, Chaps, and that's a fact. One way or another, his outlaw days are numbered."

"I truly hope so."

"Trust me."

They grew quiet again and snuggled, enjoying the pure pleasure of simply being close to each other. They listened to the night sounds, crickets in the bushes, frogs in the stream, and an owl high above in a tree. The moon had risen, casting soft light on the stream, turning the water to shimmering silver.

"This is what I meant, Cord," Chaps said sleepily. "Quiet times."

He pulled her closer and kissed her cheek. "I know what you mean, Chaps, but have you thought about it meaning more when you've got someone special to spend those quiet times with?"

"No, I hadn't thought of it that way."

"I want to be alone with you, to talk, to laugh, to make love. There's a lot I want to know about you that we haven't had time to discuss. And I want to share more of myself with you, and not just my body . . . my hopes and dreams." He kissed her again, inhaling her fragrance.

"Do you suppose there'll ever be time for that?"

"Yes." He hugged her tight. "But you'd better get some sleep. We've got another long day ahead of us tomorrow."

They laid down, snuggling on their blanket, and Chaps was asleep almost instantly, feeling safe and protected in Cord's strong arms. Later, she stirred when he got up for the second watch, and she saw Black Ears settle down across from her. Then she drifted back to sleep, burrowing into the blanket, comforted by Cord's scent.

Sometime later, she was suddenly shaken awake, and she jerked up, fighting off sleep. "What?"

Cord clamped a hand over her mouth. "Shhhh. Over here."

She followed him to the riverbank. An Indian she had never seen before was talking with Black Ears in sign language. By moonlight, she could see that he was young, perhaps only thirteen, but his eyes were old, filled already with the sights of violent life and death.

"What is going on?" Chaps whispered against Cord's ear.

He shook his head warning her not to speak again, and she took a deep breath, trying to calm her racing heart. She wasn't ready for some new horror. She wanted a few days of rest anyway. Glancing out over the San Simon, it was hard to believe there could be any danger nearby, for everything was so peaceful and calm. Then she noticed that she could no longer hear the frogs or crickets, and she grew cold. Something was wrong. But what?

She looked back at the two Apaches. Cord had joined their conversation, easily communicating with sign language. Should she start packing? What time was it? Dawn should be near. She hated not knowing what was going on, and not being able to understand the sign language. If she stayed long in the West, she should learn Indian sign language, and perhaps even Spanish.

But how long would she stay? She gazed at Cord. Could she trust her feelings for him? And what did she truly mean to him? She shook her head. Now was not the time to be thinking about Cord. Something was wrong, and she had to find out what it was; then she had to be ready to react quickly, no matter what they told her.

The conversation over, the two Apaches disappeared into the underbrush, and Cord came back to her. He looked at her a long moment, then gave her an encouraging grin and a big hug. Her heart beat faster, for it must be bad news, and bad news had to mean Red Duke.

"That Apache brought us word that Red Duke's got men downriver, not far away. Black Ears thinks they plan to attack at dawn."

"What can we do?"

Cord shook his head. "Not much. We're outnumbered. And we've got you."

"What's wrong with me?"

"You don't know the first thing about melting into your surroundings, and you couldn't walk quietly if your life depended on it."

"Well, I never needed to before."

"I know. I'm not blaming you."

"What are we going to do?"

"We're going to build a fire at dawn and send smoke signals for help."

"Smoke signals! Will that work?"

"Yes. But keep your voice down. We'll get help, but if we'll get it in time, I don't know."

"I'll give myself up, and the rest of your can get away."

"I'd never let Red Duke have you, Chaps." He pulled her hard against his chest and pressed his lips to hers. Then he pulled back. "And don't try to be a martyr. If you do just as we say, we may all come out of this alive."

"Whatever your plan is, I'm not going to like it."

"It's simple. We don't have much choice. We can't run with you, so we've got to make a stand and wait for help."

"I don't like it. I'd rather run."

"Chaps, we're not deep in the mountains anymore. We've got a little stretch of trees and bushes along the river, but there's no way to hide in that. And we're surrounded on both sides by valleys, where there's no place to hide at all. And here, by the stream, we can only go up or down, and Red Duke knows that. It's why he pushed so hard to catch us here."

"He's got lots of men, Cord, and lots of guns. We just don't have much to fight him with."

"We'd be in a lot worse shape if he had crept up on us and attacked during the night."

"Who is that Apache who warned us?"

"Shadow Chaser. He's the best there is at tracking. Black Ears left him to follow Red Duke and warn us if necessary."

"I'm glad of that, but he looks young, too young. Why don't we just let him slip away?"

"He's fourteen, and a man. He's been fighting for years. Don't insult him by suggesting he is merely a boy to be sent home when the fighting gets rough."

"I'm sorry, but I don't want him hurt."

"None of us do, but a lot of Apache have died,

292

and more will, too. That has become our way of life."

Chaps shivered at the harsh reality of Cord's words. "I want to run. I don't think I can stand to sit here and wait for Red Duke."

"This is our best chance, Chaps," Cord insisted, squeezing her hand. "Black Ears and Shadow Chaser are setting up some defenses out there that should slow down Red Duke. Meanwhile, we're going to build the best stronghold we can and take care of the horses."

"Cord, are you sure this is the right thing to do? I'd rather give myself up than have you killed."

He looked into her eyes, his own dark brown gaze shadowed. "And I would never give you over to him, Chaps. Never. Even if it means our lives. Now, let's hurry. Dawn isn't far away."

As she stepped away, a twig cracked under her boot, and she glanced at Cord, grimacing.

Shaking his head, he put a finger to his lips, indicating for her to be quiet, then walked silently away. She followed, trying to make as little noise as possible, but not succeeding very well.

Nearby, Cord had found a good place to hold off Red Duke, for it was a high place with access to the river. Tall trees and thickly growing bushes surrounded it. Chaps helped Cord carry their saddlebags, blankets and saddles over to the new area, then she refilled the canteens with water from the stream, all the time being as quiet as possible.

Cord gathered the horses and walked over to her. "Chaps, I'm going to lead the horses across the stream, and let them loose to graze in the valley. They won't go so far we can't get them later, but they'll be out of Red Duke's hands and away from his gunfire.

"Will they be all right?"

"Yes. There's food and water out there."

"But how can we get them back?"

"They're well trained. Don't worry."

"All right, but be careful."

He gave her a quick kiss, then led the horses toward the San Simon.

While he crossed the river with the horses, she gathered wood for the fire that was to summon help, then placed it near a clearing where nothing could interfere with the rise of the smoke. Hoping she had done what the Apaches needed, she stood back and waited, not knowing what else to do.

Soon Cord returned, then Black Ears and Shadow Chaser arrived a moment later. They looked pleased with the wood she had gathered and the place she had picked, and quickly built a fire, then began sending up smoke signals with a saddle blanket.

While they did that, Cord showed Chaps how to load and aim the rifle, then placed it and extra ammunition at the center of the rise they had chosen for their fortress. He made sure his gunbelt had a bullet in every slot, checked his Colt .45, then pulled out the slim dagger he wore in his boot. He handed it to her, hilt first.

"No, Cord. I can't take it. You might need it."

"Damn it, Chaps, take the knife. You've got to have some way to defend yourself if they get in this close."

She took it, closing her fingers around the horn handle. "Thanks." Not mentioning the gun ring she wore, she touched it, too, knowing she would kill the first Comanchero who tried to get her.

"If they come in fast and hard, Chaps, you're going to need to reload for all of us, especially if they circle around behind. Can you do that?"

"You showed me, and I'll do it one way or another. I'm just sorry I can't shoot straight."

"It's all right, but if we get out of this alive, I'm going to teach you."

"Thanks."

She walked over to the two Apaches and watched the thick white smoke billowing upward. The wood for the fire had been laid a certain way to create the thick smoke. Glancing upward, she wondered if anybody really would see it or be able to read its message.

Cord followed her and put an arm around her waist. "Duke'll be here soon, now that he's seen the smoke."

"But he doesn't know you're Apache."

"He'll know an Indian smoke signal when he sees it, so maybe he'll be more cautious when he attacks."

"I hope so."

When they had completed sending the message, the Apaches put out the fire and turned to Chaps and Cord.

"This is Shadow Chaser," Black Ears said formally. "He brought us warning of Red Duke."

"Thank you," Chaps replied, smiling at the young man, who was painfully thin, small, wiry and very determined. "You may make all the difference in our survival, and if so, I'll write about your bravery so all will know."

Shadow Chaser nodded, looking slightly embarrassed, then walked quickly away, gripping his rifle.

"He was pleased with your words," Black Ears said, "as am I."

"All we have to do is come out of this alive," Chaps responded, glancing at Cord.

"We'd better take our places," Cord said.

Black Ears nodded in agreement, then walked after Shadow Chaser.

Cord led Chaps to the center of the rise, gave her a hard hug, then stepped back. "No matter what happens, stay in the center with the ammunition, so you can load for all of us. You'll be safest there, too, and when the firing starts, lay down, so you're less of a target."

She sat down in the center, feeling slightly detached from it all, for the danger didn't seem quite real on such a beautiful, quiet day just beginning to dawn. She watched the men position themselves equidistance around the small area, then also sit down.

They began their wait, but it wasn't long before they heard the crash of men moving toward them, breaking limbs, stepping on fallen logs, snapping branches out of their way. It was obvious the Comancheros weren't trying to sneak up on them now that they were so close.

Suddenly there was a long, agonizing scream, then all was quiet. Chaps looked at Cord, her eyes wide. What had happened? He nodded in reassurance, and she remembered that Black Ears and Shadow Chaser had set some type of traps for Comancheros. One had obviously worked, and well.

Then the noise started again. Red Duke and his men were advancing on them, but from the sounds, more slowly, more cautiously this time. Suddenly, another man screamed, then silence again.

Waiting, Chaps glanced at the three men around her, but their eyes were focused on the distance, as if they could see what was going on behind the trees and undergrowth, hear what the Comancheros were thinking, and know Red Duke's next move. Maybe that was what it meant to be Apache.

Once more, the Comancheros started coming toward them, but even more slowly, cautiously this time. And then, very close, there was the sudden sound of a man caught by surprise, then a choking sound and a thud.

Red Duke called, "Enough of your Injun games, Cord. You're outnumbered. Give yourself up."

Chaps looked desperately toward Cord.

He shook his head, warning her to be quiet.

Then it was silent again, until suddenly there was movement behind them. Chaps jerked her head around in that direction. Red Duke was surrounding them! Once more Cord shook his head for her to be still and patient, but the rustling of men moving closer and closer front and back made her want to run into the river and try to swim away. But she knew she couldn't do that, knew that Red Duke was sure to catch her that way, and still she could hardly keep herself from doing it.

"I've got you surrounded, Cord," Red Duke shouted. "The river's on one side, the valley on the other. You can't hide. Give yourself up, and I'll take Victoria and Alicia."

Chaps smiled at Cord. Red Duke still thought Alicia was with them; so that trick had worked anyway.

"Alicia's not well," Red Duke continued. "You can't escape with her. You know that. Were those silly smoke signals to try and scare me? Don't be a fool, Cord, give yourself up and save the women."

Cord still remained silent, and Chaps clinched her hands, her fingernails digging into her palms. Did they have a chance? Would the Apaches arrive in time? Their ammunition was limited. And although Red Duke had already lost several men by the sounds of the dying, he probably had so many men it didn't matter.

"Okay, Cord! Your chance is over. We're coming in, and we're leaving nobody alive."

Suddenly the area exploded in gunfire, and Chaps, Cord, Black Ears, and Shadow Chaser fell to the ground. The noise was almost defening as bullets whizzed over their heads, thudding into the trees and brush around them. It seemed to last forever, then it was over and silence reined again.

"You hit, Cord?" Red Duke called.

Silence.

The Comancheros started forward again, noisily moving toward the rise. Lying on his stomach, Cord glanced at Black Ears and Shadow Chaser, then signaled to fire back. They quickly began peppering the area around them with rifle bullets, and several Comancheros cursed. Again, the place exploded in rapid gunfire, lasting so long Chaps covered her ears, wondering if they could possibly keep from being hit.

Once more, silence, and Red Duke called, "You

hit yet, Cord? We've got ammunition to last days. What've you got? Might as well give yourself up. Those women won't be any help, and you can't keep running around, firing in a circle all day, even if you had the bullets. Be smart, save the women."

All was quiet while Red Duke waited.

Cord gave a signal, and the three men slithered silently out into the brush. Chaps bit her lip in terror for them. What were they doing? Suddenly she heard them each fire several times rapidly, then answering thuds and groans from the Comancheros, followed by rapid gunfire.

Under heavy fire, Cord, Black Ears, and Shadow Chaser moved silently back into the clearing. Chaps nodded at them in relief, glancing over them to make sure they were all right. They didn't seem to have been hurt, but she hoped they wouldn't go out like that again, for she could hardly stand for them to be in so much extra danger.

Suddenly, the Comancheros stopped firing, and Red Duke called, "I'm beginning to think those women can shoot, Cord, so this may take longer than I thought. But you're a dead man, never doubt that."

There was another volley of fire, then the sound of the Comancheros withdrawing, but they didn't go far. Soon, there was the smell of a campfire, then coffee boiling.

Chaps looked at Cord in amazement. Red Duke was even more brazen than she had thought. He was so sure of himself that he was cooking food right in the middle of a battle. Was he trying to scare them into thinking they couldn't possibly win, or was it just more self glory? Whatever the case, it infuriated her, and she wanted to shoot him with her gun ring. But she could never get that close, and knew it.

Glancing at Cord, she saw that he was speaking to Black Ears and Shadow Chaser in sign language, and she wondered if they would take the battle to the Comancheros, or wait for help. They seemed to be doing pretty well on their own, and she was proud of their small group. Then she noticed that Shadow Chaser's arm was bleeding.

She grabbed her ointment and a cloth bandage and crawled over to him. He looked up in surprise and shook his head when she motioned that she wanted to bind his wound. Glancing in concern at Cord, he simply shrugged. She looked for support from Black Ears, but he wasn't any more help than Cord.

So she simply grabbed Shadow Chaser's arm, cleaned off the blood, spread ointment, wrapped a bandage around his wiry muscles, then nodded in satisfaction and crawled back to her central place. There, that would show them. She was the nurse and doctor, and that was that.

She glanced over at Cord, and he smiled. He was pleased, she could tell, even proud. She realized that these men appreciated spunk and cunning, and she had just passed a test. They also liked her taking care of them, even though, as warriors, they didn't want to admit it.

Encouraged, she got some food and the canteens. If they were going to fight, then they had to be strong, and she was going to see that they ate properly. She crawled to each man, handed him a tamale and a canteen, then returned to the middle.

When she saw that they were eating, she began reloading the rifles, realizing that she should have done that first.

From now on, she would remember her priorities: keep the rifles loaded, then keep the men on their feet with bandages and food. Narrowing her eyes, she glared in the direction Red Duke was having a hot meal. He wasn't going to win. She wouldn't let him, and neither would the Apaches.

It was just a matter of time now, and they could hold out that long. In fact, they were doing a good job of defending themselves. Red Duke was losing men, and they weren't. Of course, it all depended on the Apaches coming before they ran out of food and ammunition, but they would come. She was sure of that.

Chapter 20

Red Duke's pattern repeated itself all that day,
and by night Chaps was exhausted, tense and
scared. When she saw the Comancheros' campfires,
she thought longingly of hot food, and when the
smell of roasting meat came to her, she felt as if
she were starving, even though they were eating
tamales and tortillas. It was easy to see that their
food would run out in another day or so, and if
the Apaches hadn't come by then, they would have
to do something desperate.

Surrounded by Comancheros, there was nothing
to do but wait and watch and listen. They couldn't
light a fire, or talk, or sing, or tell stories, but they
also couldn't sleep because the tension was so
great. What they did do was check their weapons,
count the number of bullets left, and think a lot
about the Apaches coming soon. They had done
well the first day, but what about tomorrow?

Finally Chaps' tiredness overtook her, and she
leaned her head against Cord's chest and began to
doze. She slept fitfully, waking up from dreams of
Red Duke and Comancheros chasing her, Red Duke
whipping Alicia, Red Duke killing Cord, then Red
Duke coming for her, his face scarred and full of

302

hatred. She would wake suddenly, fighting to escape, and Cord would pull her close, comforting her until she fell asleep again. But nothing could take away the fact that Red Duke was out there, just waiting to get them.

Then it was Cord's turn to watch, and she reluctantly let him go. She lay down, and he kissed her softly before leaving to prowl silently around the camp. Black Ears and Shadow Chaser slept, too, but lightly, for Chaps noticed them moving around uneasily when she woke up, which was frequently, for she simply couldn't rest well at all.

The night progressed that way, with sounds of the Comancheros in the camps nearby reminding Chaps of when she had lived with them in the hideout. She shivered, and when Cord finally came back from his watch, she snuggled hard against him, then slept better the rest of the night. When early morning light began to filter down through the trees, she woke up with a start, glancing around, feeling as if Red Duke were sneaking up on her. And then she noticed that Cord was gone. Her heart started hammering in her chest.

She quickly sat up and looked around. The clearing was empty, and she had to stifle a cry of alarm. Then she saw the bushes nearby moving slightly, and she shuddered but made no sound, waiting to see if it was a Comanchero. When Cord stepped into view, she sighed in relief. Putting a finger to his lips, he smiled and was soon joined by Black Ears and Shadow Chaser.

Sitting down together, they began a breakfast of tamales and tortillas, and not far away they heard the Comancheros begin making campfires, cooking

food, talking, laughing and making jokes. The outlaws' attitude infuriated Chaps, and she wanted
desperately to defeat them. But glancing at the
three men around her, she didn't know how much
longer they could hold off Red Duke.

After they had eaten, Cord pulled her close and
whispered, "Chaps, you know we're running short
on everything. We can probably make it through
today, but that's it. If help doesn't show up by
tonight, we're going to try and get you out of
here."

"Cord!"

"Hear me out. We'll try to steal you two of Red
Duke's horses, give you two canteens of water, and
send you back to the Peloncillos. Can you find
your way from there?"

"I don't know."

"You must, because if you can get back to the
Vincente Rancho valley, you'll have help. Miguel's
men will be on guard. Once they see you, you'll be
protected. Remember, you only have to make it as
far as that valley and you're safe."

"But what about you and Black Ears and
Shadow Chaser?"

"We'll keep the Comancheros busy long enough
for you to get well into the valley toward the Peloncillos. If you can get far enough away, it'll take
them a while to figure out you're gone. And if you
can get into the mountains first, then you should
make it."

"But that depends on you three men sacrificing
your lives, doesn't it?"

"If the Apache don't come, we'll be dead anyway."

"No. You could get away if not for me, I bet. Three for one is too big a sacrifice, Cord. I won't do it. Either leave me, or let me fight by your side."

"I can't let you die." He pulled her hard against his chest and held her close.

"And I don't know how I could go on without you."

Cord hesitated. "Then we'll have to find a way to live."

"We will. The Apache will come. I know it."

Cord took a deep breath and released her. "All right. We're in this together. We'll hold Red Duke off as long as we can, then decide what to do."

"Your brothers will come," Black Ears said, "but they must have time."

"Then we'd better make time for them," Cord replied grimly.

Suddenly, Red Duke called, "Are you ready to give up, Cord? I'll still let the women live."

Silence followed.

Several Comancheros fired at close range, and Cord, Black Ears, and Shadow Chaser shot back, driving the outlaws backward, but using up precious ammunition to do it. That pattern continued until early in the afternoon when Shadow Chaser slipped from the camp to try and catch a few Comancheros off guard. But the outlaws were more prepared now, and fired at Shadow Chaser, driving him back to the safety of the camp.

"You've got to be more careful," Chaps said, trying to still her hammering heart.

"If we don't take some chances, we aren't going to make it," Cord responded. "Tonight we'll have to

305

steal some ammunition."

Chaps simply rolled her eyes, thinking the task impossible, but all three men seemed to believe one of them had to try it. Now she was really desperate for the Apaches to arrive, but by late afternoon she had almost given up. For there had been no sign of help, and ammunition was running low. There didn't seem to be much hope, but she was determined to keep her spirits as high as possible.

She struggled to think of something more she could do to help win the battle, but could think of nothing short of turning herself over to Red Duke. But then Cord and the Apaches would come after her, making the situation even more dangerous for them all.

Suddenly Red Duke and his Comancheros stormed their position, firing volley after volley into the bushes surrounding them. They all dived for cover, and the men began returning fire, hoping to hold off the Comancheros a little longer. But they were running out of bullets fast. And that was obviously Red Duke's intention, for he wanted to win the battle now.

They were hard pressed to keep the Comancheros back, the ammunition was almost gone, and soon they would have to start fighting hand to hand. With so many outlaws, that was a battle they knew they couldn't win. Chaps checked her gun ring, ready to kill any man who came for her. She reloaded with the last of the bullets, then looked at Cord, knowing she might never see him alive again.

But, no! She mustn't give up yet. Suddenly a Comanchero got through and headed straight for Cord. He clicked the trigger of his pistol several times, but he was out of ammunition. She caught her breath, watching, not knowing what to do, then remembered the knife Cord had given her.

"Cord," she called.

He glanced up, and she tossed him the knife. He caught it and grinned. Turning back just as the Comanchero pulled the trigger of his .45, Cord threw the knife, embedding it deep in the man's chest. Quickly stripping the dead man's pistol and ammunition belt from him, Cord looked back at Chaps and grinned in triumph.

She knew it wasn't much, but it bought them time to fight a little longer. The Comancheros were starting to swarm through the bushes toward them when, suddenly, there was the sound of voices whooping in unison, rifles being fired into the air, and across the plains came a group of Apaches on mustangs, their faces painted for war.

Cord gave an answering war whoop, along with Black Ears and Shadow Chaser, then he hit the Comanchero who had been sneaking up on him, knocking him back into the bushes. Chaps cried out along with the Apaches, thinking she had never heard such a beautiful sound. Suddenly, they had renewed vigor, and Chaps felt strong enough to fight off any Comanchero, even Red Duke himself.

Red Duke's men called to each in confusion as the Apaches galloped across the stream, leaped from their horses, and plunged into the fight. Soon there were cries, gunshots and sounds of fighting and death. Cord, Black Ears, and Shadow Chaser followed the Apaches into the fray, and Chaps found herself standing alone. No longer feeling needed, she didn't know quite what to do, but with everybody gone and concentrated on fighting, she began to feel a little vulnerable.

Suddenly Red Duke splashed out of the San Simon on his huge black stallion. Chaps screamed in shock and turned to run, but his horse was fast. He grabbed her, lifting her into midair. As he started to throw her across the saddle, she saw his face and was horrified, for it was now mottled with livid red patches. Knowing he blamed her for marring his handsome face, she struggled hard to get away, for he would surely torture her now.

"That's right," he hissed, gripping her hard and holding her away from him so he could look into her eyes. "You scarred me and you'll pay."

"No!"

She glanced around desperately. They were completely alone. She had only one chance, and she had to take it. Throwing up her hand, she aimed the gun ring at his face and fired.

He bellowed in sudden pain, dropping her to the ground as he threw a hand over his left eye. Then he wheeled his stallion around, galloped out of the clearing, across the stream, and headed south as fast as he could go.

Chaps simply sat in stunned horror, unable to believe what she had just done. The tiny bullet had gone directly into his eye. But it hadn't killed him. Would he die later? Or would he simply be blind in that eye? She shivered. It was the most horrible thing she had ever done, and she couldn't get it out of her mind. But he had deserved it. She'd had to save herself.

But somebody had to catch Red Duke before he escaped. She got up, dusted herself off, feeling bruised all over, then searched for Cord, or Black Ears, or Shadow Chaser. But she couldn't see them. Instead, there was a rolling, tumbling, fighting mass of bodies on the ground and in the bushes around the camp. She could hear more than she could see, and that was no way to find Cord. Yet, she desperately needed him.

Stepping into the brush, she was almost knocked over by two men fighting, then a stray bullet almost hit her. Finally, she stepped back into the clearing, knowing she wouldn't do any of them any good if she got hurt at this point.

So she waited, pacing, watching, listening, and finally the battle began to lessen; then Apaches began to stagger into the clearing, some pulling dead Comancheros, some dragging live ones. She kept looking for Cord, but he didn't appear, and finally she realized he could have been hurt or killed during the battle. He wasn't invulnerable, although she usually thought of him that way.

"Cord!" she called, beginning to panic. "Cord, are you all right?"

"Chaps," he replied tiredly as he walked from the bushes. He was dirty, bloody, and his clothes were torn, but he was alive and well.

"You're all right," she said in relief, throwing her arms around his neck and hugging him close. Then she stepped back. "You're bleeding!"

"A lot of us are, but we won. There won't be any more Comancheros raids in this part of the country. And if I don't miss my guess, there'll be a lot of reward money when we take in these men." Then he looked around. "Who's got Red Duke?"

"Nobody," Chaps said. "I've been waiting for

you. He got away, but he may be dying."

"Damn! What happened?"

"He came after me. I was all alone. He picked me up and was going to kidnap me; but I shot him with my gun ring, and he dropped me."

"You shot him with your what?" Cord looked around in confusion.

"My gun ring." She held up her hand, proudly displaying the ring.

Cord took it off her hand and started laughing as he examined it. "Does this really work?"

"I told you. I shot Red Duke in the eye with it, and he dropped me."

"Well, I'll be damned. I never saw one of these before. You got any more bullets for it?"

"Yes."

"Then, get it loaded. You think that bullet'll kill him?"

"I don't know, but it's bound to have put out an eye."

"What direction did he head?"

"South."

"Then he's headed for Mexico, but he won't get far with an eye like that—maybe just across the border, if he lives. Somebody'll have to get that bullet out, and he'll leave a trail a mile wide. I can get him later."

"Later?"

"I mean I've got to finish up here before I can go after Red Duke."

"But he's getting away."

"Not a chance. If he doesn't die, he'll be licking his wounds across the border, and I'll get him there." Cord hesitated and ran a hand through his hair in agitation. "But, damn, I wish we'd gotten him now."

"We almost did," Chaps replied, "but you can't go after Red Duke alone. He's wounded and even more dangerous."

"I know, but so am I."

"Oh, I forgot you were hurt. I'm sorry. I got to thinking about Red Duke and forgot about everything else. I'll bandage your wound right now."

"Thanks, but do it while I talk to Black Ears."

As they walked back to the center of the clearing, Chaps had a chance to look at the Apache band. They were all thin, but strong and determined. She was impressed by them, amazed at their fierceness, and still a little in awe that the smoke signal had actually worked. They were taking care of their own wounded and tying up the Comancheros who still lived.

"Black Ears," Cord said, slapping the older man's shoulder, "your Apache band did a good deed for whites and Apaches alike today."

"Yes, you are right," Black Ears agreed, watching as Chaps began cleaning the wound on Cord's chest.

"There's reward money for the Comancheros," Cord continued, "and if you and your men get it, then you can live better, maybe even move onto the reservation and have money enough to live right, perhaps raise and train horses, like you've always done for the tribe."

"You think it is time we gave up, my friend?" Black Ears asked.

"Not give up, but join your families and survive, keeping the nation alive through tales of glory."

"It will be hard to do, but you may be right. We will not last much longer here, but to give up our freedom to ride the land at will may kill us anyway."

Cord nodded. "I understand, but it may be for the best."

"That is true. But how do we get this reward money? We cannot go to the fort and claim it."

"We'll take the Comancheros to the Vincente Rancho and let Miguel handle it from there. What do you think?"

"I will discuss it with our brothers. You may be right that the time has come to accept our fate."

"But you won't starve."

"Not for food, but what about our spirits?" Black Ears asked, then sadly walked away.

Chaps finished binding Cord's wound. "Is this his last battle?"

"Maybe. I want him to live, although going to the reservation may kill him. I hope I did the right thing by suggesting he give up."

"It's not giving up, Cord. It's surviving, and with that reward money, it may not be so bad after all."

"We'll see. But for now, we need to round up the horses, then start back. I don't want to spend another night here."

"I guess we couldn't go after Red Duke?"

"I'd like to, but I can't let this band of Apaches and Comancheros go riding into Miguel's armed camp alone. Who knows what might happen."

"You've got a good point. So Red Duke waits."

"For now, if you haven't killed him already."

"Maybe I have."

"Don't worry. I'll find him, dead or alive. But

for now, we've got more work ahead of us."

He put an arm around her shoulders, and they started toward the horses. Soon they were mounted and headed toward the Peloncillo Mountains. Chaps glanced around. She was near the center of a large group of riders, and she was very glad they had the Apache band with them to control the Comancheros, who were looking more mutinous the longer they rode. But there were also a number of dead Comancheros tied to their saddles, who would never hurt anyone else again.

She just wished they had caught Red Duke. She looked south as they crossed the valley. Had he died from her bullet? she wondered. He had been in pain, half blind; but he was a big man and strong, and he had wheeled, seemingly in control.

Looking down at the gun ring on her hand, now reloaded, she decided not to depend on it to completely stop a foe in the future, but it obviously would work very well at distracting or hurting somebody.

She looked south again and noticed Cord was doing the same thing. They wanted to take after Red Duke right now, proving finally that the man would never harm anybody again, but they would have to be satisfied, for now, that Red Duke was wounded and hiding out in Mexico, with no men, no money, nothing . . . if he still lived.

Then she turned her thoughts away from Red Duke. He was broken, his men dead or captured, and she should think about more positive matters now. She glanced around at their group, wishing she could have spent more time with the Apache renegades. Of course, Cord had explained that the bands did not live like the tribes, with tepees and women and children, too. They were constantly on the move to keep from being found, and it had worked a long time.

Maybe she would go to the reservation; but that would mean being involved with Cord longer, and now that Alicia was safely back with Miguel, Red Duke wounded and hiding in Mexico, and the Comancheros about to be turned over to the military, was there any more reason for them to stay together?

She had plenty of material for several novels. Perhaps Black Ears' vision would urge him to talk to her, tell her exciting tales of the Apache when they roamed the land. Did she really need Cord anymore? And did he need her?

Feeling a strange pain in her heart, she looked at him, remembering how his body felt against hers, and glanced away. Rationally, it was a fact they no longer needed each other, then why did she feel so desolate at the thought of losing him forever?

Once she had thought she might love him, and now that they had been through even more together, she felt closer than ever. Yet he was Apache, and half Spanish, but he had been raised with the Apache. Would he go with them to the reservation, or would he continue traveling the land, living free, just one step ahead of death?

Shivering, she knew she couldn't live that way. As she had told him, being with him had been exciting, but she also needed peaceful times, when she could think and write and talk with others. She wanted a home, where she could entertain friends, And Cord? She was afraid he would forever want

314

to roam, and no matter how she felt about him, she didn't think she would be happy with that kind of life. Besides, he had never mentioned them staying together after this was all over.

Just when she should have been feeling good, triumphant, she felt sad, as if she were losing part of herself. When they were done at the Vincentes, it would be time for her to go on, to get back to where she was before Cord had kidnapped her. But she wasn't the same person anymore, and it was going to be very hard to go back to being an observer of the West, for she now felt very much a part of this country, not just somebody who had come to look through glass windows at the natives, then write amusing stories and take her money.

In fact, she felt a little embarrassed at the way she had been approaching her novels. There was so much to the West and its people than she could ever have imagined back in New York City, and she wanted to write the truth now, could write it, where before she couldn't have begun to understand the real depth of life in the West.

Her father would have been proud of the way she was going to write the novels they had conceived together, and she felt good about that, too. She glanced at Cord again. But she didn't feel good about Cord. Was there a chance he could change? No. She couldn't imagine him any way but like he was, and yet she knew he had many sides, for he kept surprising her. Maybe she should give him a chance, but that would mean he would have to give her one, too. And would he?

No. She didn't think she could take the chance on that kind of rejection. Cord had needed her to help him. Now the job was done, and it was time they went their separate ways. But she didn't have to deal with that yet. They still had a little time left, and she would enjoy it. She would also enjoy their victory. And that was that.

Smiling, she rode closer to Cord, and he looked over, taking her hand. Squeezing her fingers, he smiled. They shared a moment of triumph, of togetherness that nobody else saw, or would have understood, for they had rescued Alicia and conquered Red Duke and his Comancheros together, as a team, and it had made a bond between.

Then somebody called Cord, and he rode away, the moment broken; but Chaps knew the experience they had shared would last a lifetime, no mater what else happened in their lives, no matter if they were separated.

Chapter 21

Leading the Apaches and Comancheros, Chaps and Cord rode onto Vincente Rancho land two days later. They were hot, tired and dusty, but proud of what they had accomplished. As their group got closer to the hacienda, Vincente vaqueros began to join them, one after another, until, finally, a large group moved toward the house.

Alicia and Miguel rode out to greet them, smiles on their faces. Cord rode forward, hugged his sister, then clasped hands with Miguel. Alicia turned to Chaps and hugged her close, then together, they all started for the hacienda.

"Congratulations," Miguel said, riding beside Cord. "You did a good job."

"Thanks," Cord replied, "but we had a lot of help."

"The important thing is that you returned safely," Alicia added, glancing around. "But where is Red Duke?"

"I'm sorry," Cord responded, "but he got away."

"Escaped!" Alicia exclaimed.

"Chaps wounded him, so he can't get too far. I figure he's licking his wounds across the border in Mexico. As soon as we get this business settled,

I'm going after him."

"I will go with you," Miguel said, his eyes glinting fiercely. "But until we get him, I will keep a few extra guards on duty, just in case."

"Good idea," Cord agreed, "but I don't think there's anything to worry about."

"You were very brave, Chaps," Alicia added, "but how did you wound Red Duke?"

Cord laughed. "Go ahead. Tell them. Then show them that gun."

"All right," Chaps agreed, smiling. "I didn't know it was so unusual until I told Cord about it, but I bought a gun ring in Silver City."

"A what?" Miguel asked, a puzzled look on his face.

Chaps held out her hand, showing the ring on the first finger of her right hand. "This is a gun ring. It's called 'Little Stinger,' and I shot Red Duke in the eye with it."

"Really!" Alicia remarked, and reached over to lightly touch the ring.

"I would like to have seen that," Miguel added. "Then what happened?"

"Duke was holding me, and he dropped me fast. I don't know if the bullet will kill him, but it's got to have blinded him in one eye."

"I would think so," Alicia agreed, looking at the ring in amazement. "I have never heard of anything like that gun ring before, but you were wearing it at the hideout, weren't you?"

"Yes. I didn't want anybody to know what it was, just in case I needed it as a last defense. And it saved my life. Red Duke was going to carry me off, and I don't even want to think about what he

318

would have done to me."

"Nobody does," Cord agreed. "One thing about Chaps, she may be a greenhorn, but she catches on real fast. She's been saving us ever since I met her."

"Not all by myself," Chaps protested, "but I'm glad I could help."

Alicia squeezed her hand. "I will never forget what you did for me."

"None of us will," Miguel agreed, "and as soon as my Vaqueros rode in with the news you had captured the Comancheros, I gave the order to prepare a feast."

"And we sent out riders to let the other ranchers know all was safe, and to bring back the family," Alicia added.

"Good," Cord said, "but Chaps and I didn't do this single-handed. In fact, we wouldn't be alive right now except for Black Ears and his Apache band." He turned around and motioned for Black Ears to join them.

Black Ears moved up to their group.

"Black Ears, this is my sister, Alicia, and her fiancé, Miguel Vincente."

"It is good to meet Cord's family," Black Ears replied.

"Cord has spoken of you before," Alicia said, "and always in praise. Now I would like to add our thanks and praise for what you have done."

"Red Duke and his Comancheros have hurt the Apache, too," Black Ears replied. "We are all well rid of him."

"You have my thanks, too," Miguel added, "and if there is ever anything the Vincente family can do for you, please let us know."

"As a matter of fact, there is," Cord added.

"Name it," Miguel responded.

"There has to be dead or alive reward money for these Comancheros, and this Apache band deserves to get it. But you know as well as I do that renegade Apache bands can't be caught anywhere near the law."

"I understand perfectly," Miguel agreed. "I will gather a group of my best vaqueros, we will take in the Comancheros, get the money, and bring it back to Black Ears."

"Thanks," Cord replied. "That's just what I wanted to hear."

"You have the thanks of the Apache, too," Black Ears added.

"No thanks is necessary," Miguel replied. "What you did for us is beyond price. Now, you all have to be tired. Black Ears, why don't you and your friends stay in one of the bunkhouses until this is all said and done. And we can use a storeroom as a jail for the Comancheros until I take them into the law."

"Thank you," Black Ears replied, "but we do not need a bunkhouse."

"I want you to be comfortable," Miguel insisted.

Black Ears laughed. "We will be more comfortable under the stars, near a stream."

Miguel joined his laughter. "I hadn't thought of it that way. That is fine, then. The Gila is near here, but I want your men to count on eating up at the hacienda with the Vaqueros until we get back with your reward money."

"We will be glad to do that," Black Ears agreed.

"Good, then that is settled," Miguel replied,

looking pleased.

"One other thing," Cord added. "Black Ears and his group may be settling down on the reservation when they get the reward money, and I suggested they might want to raise and sell horses. You know, there's no better breeder and trainer than the Apache."

"I know that," Miguel agreed.

"So, I was wondering if you and some of the other ranchers might be interested in buying or trading ranch horses with his group."

"It is a good idea," Miguel agreed. "If Black Ears decides to do this, I will talk with the other ranchers, and we will work out a deal."

"I guess I should have helped catch those Comancheros sooner," Black Ears said, chuckling. "You are making this sound so easy, I may have to settle down on the reservation after all."

"It won't be easy, and you know it," Cord replied, smiling, "but if we can make it a little smoother, then that will help. Also, the ranchers always need good horses, and if they can get them from you, so much the better."

"We will see," Black Ears responded. "I will talk with my men and wait for a vision from the Great Spirit."

"Speaking of the Great Spirit," Chaps interrupted, "have you decided whether or not you can tell me about the Apache for my books?"

Black Ears nodded. "Yes, you will have help from me and my people."

"Oh, that's great."

"What is this?" Alicia asked.

"I'm going to chronicle some of the Apache leg-

321

end and history," Chaps replied.

"That is very good," Miguel added.

"If we keep her busy enough," Cord said, smiling, "maybe we'll be able to keep her in the West forever."

"Then we will keep her very busy," Alicia agreed.

They rode on, and when they got to the hacienda, Alicia and Chaps dismounted and went in the house, while Black Ears led the Apache down to the Gila River. Cord and Miguel and the vaqueros rode around to the back of the house to put the Comancheros under lock and key.

Upstairs in the hacienda, Alicia took Chaps to a bedroom overlooking the Gila River. It was a large, airy room, and cool because of high ceilings and thick walls. A breeze, with the scent of grass and wild flowers, came in through the open windows. Glancing around in delight, Chaps saw that the bedroom was decorated in shades of blue with a large canopy bed, an armoire, and a dressing table with mirror and matching stool occupying much of the room.

"I hope you will be comfortable here," Alicia said, gesturing around the area.

"After all we've been through, you know how much I'm going to like it."

Alicia smiled, nodding in understanding. "The moment I heard you were coming, I ordered a bath. It is behind that screen."

Laughing, Chaps looked behind the screen, and sure enough there was a tub of warm water. "You knew that'd be the first thing I'd want, didn't you?"

Alicia joined her laughter. "Yes. I knew it would

surely be what I wanted, so I knew you would like it, too."

"Thanks. I really appreciate this."

"Oh, Chaps, I would like to do so much more." Alicia walked quickly to Chaps and hugged her, holding her fiercely a moment before letting her go. "You will always be my sister."

Chaps smiled. "Thanks, but you helped me, too."

"But to shoot Red Duke in the eye. What courage!"

"It was more fear than courage. I didn't tell you, but that coffee I threw on him blistered or scarred his face, because it's all mottled now."

"What!"

"That's right, and since I did it, I hated to think what kind of revenge he had planned for me."

Alicia chuckled. "But he is so vain, and then you shot him in the eye." Suddenly she shuddered. "If he ever got his hands on you again, I don't even want to think—"

"Neither do I. So, let's just hope he's dead or south of the border."

"You don't think he might come after you, do you?" Alicia's dark eyes widened in dismay.

"No. He was wounded and heading south fast."

"You are safe, then. Let us forget about Red Duke. Miguel and Cord will take care of him later. In the meantime, you have to be exhausted. Take a long, hot bath, and I will bring your saddlebags up soon. If you want something else to wear, you can borrow something of mine." She glanced down at herself, then back at Chaps, and chuckled. "No, I am afraid we are not nearly the same size, nor is any other woman in the Vincente family as tall as you."

Chaps laughed, too. "That's all right. I'm sure to have something clean left."

"Don't worry. I will see that all your clothes are made ready. Leave everything to me." Then she hugged Chaps again. "I'm just so glad to have you safely here." She walked to the door, then looked back. "Now, take your time."

When Alicia left, shutting the door behind her, Chaps sagged against the bed, then lay down, throwing her arms out to the sides. Suddenly she felt exhausted, as if all her energy had been just enough to hold her together this far. At that moment, she didn't know if she could ever get up and move again. Was it all really, truly over?

Yes. Finally. She pushed herself up and began undressing, but feeling as if she might just simply curl up on the bed and go to sleep at any moment. Jerking off her boots required almost too much effort, and she lay back down before forcing herself up again. She had better stay away from the bed, or she might not get up again for a week.

Finally, she removed her clothes, leaving a trail behind her to the screen. Stepping into the bath, she decided the temperature was just right, then eased into the water until it came up to her shoulders. Sighing in relief, she leaned back her head and closed her eyes.

Then dozed.

Sometime later she awoke, and the water had cooled. Feeling better, more rested and refreshed, she quickly washed her hair and body with lavender soap, then rinsed off and dried. Alicia had left a pale pink satin robe near the tub, and she slipped into it, smiling at how short it was, for it left a great deal of her legs showing.

On the dressing table was a silver-backed comb and brush, and she began brushing the tangles from her long, strawberry-blond hair. Walking over to the window, she glanced outside. Down by the river, she could see the Apache making camp and tending their horses.

She sat down in a small rocker by the window and continued brushing her hair, letting the wind dry it. Soon she noticed a scent on the breeze and realized it was the smell of roasting meat. Suddenly, she felt very hungry, remembering that she hadn't eaten very much for days. Yes, she could certainly use a feast. And so could Cord and the Apache, she had no doubt.

How peaceful it was here, so quiet. She felt very content. True, it lacked the hustle and bustle of life in New York City, but maybe this pace was better for a writer anyway. She smiled, thinking that at the moment she could hardly call herself a writer, for she hadn't put pen to paper since she had been in the bordello in Juárez.

Mexico. That experience seemed a long time ago. So much had happened. So many dreams were dead. And yet there were new dreams to replace the old. Perhaps that was the way life worked. Maybe nothing remained constant very long. Except one thing. Cord. He had been the one constant in all she had experienced, infuriating her, tantalizing her, thrilling her, encouraging her. Yes, Cord.

Chaps felt a sudden catch in her heart. She had hoped her desire for him had gone only skin deep, but she had gradually come to realize it went much deeper, clear to her heart. And, finally, could she admit she loved him? Did she dare admit that? Would the pain be too great? Or would the joy be overwhelming?

Maybe she had already felt all the highs and lows she could stand, for at the moment all she felt was a deep fullness, a contentment, that she knew would give way to a terrible loneliness when she had to leave him. And leave him she must, for he had never mentioned love to her, never mentioned a future together.

Perhaps it was better that he hadn't, for then she would simply have had to say no. Their lives were too different. They were going in diverse directions. Cord was at ease living on the back of a horse, never knowing where he was going to bed down next, or staying with renegade Apaches, perhaps helping out on a battle now and then. Where would she fit into a life like that?

What of books, of learning, of writing, of sharing quiet moments and discussing ideas, of a place where children could grow up loved and protected and free?

If Cord was only more like his sister, then there might be a chance for them. But as it was, if she stayed with Alicia and had to frequently see Cord, knowing their lives would always be separate, she knew her heart would break. No, she couldn't hurt herself that way. It would be better if she went soon, getting on with her life, with her writing, but how she hated the idea of leaving him forever.

She stood up abruptly, walked across the room, and set the brush down with a snap. There was no point in feeling sorry for herself. She had dealt with the death of her father, and she could deal with this.

Glancing around the room, she saw that her saddlebags and her valise had been brought in and unpacked. Her boots had been cleaned and polished, but all her clothing had been taken for washing, except a set of underclothes and the Mexican fiesta outfit which had been pressed.

Laughing, she picked it up and twirled around with it in front of her, delighting in the idea of finally having a place to wear it. But thinking of Cord's face when he saw her wearing the fiesta outfit made her laugh most of all. And then she sobered, thinking of her loss when she could no longer share moments like that with Cord. She pushed the thoughts from her mind and began dressing.

When she was finally ready, the black and white Mexican fiesta outfit comfortably hugging her body, she grinned at herself in the mirror over the dressing table, for she had left her hair down, tying it back with a black velvet ribbon she had found on the dressing table. She looked carefree, happy and ready to celebrate.

And she felt that way, finally free of Red Duke and his Comancheros. If only it could have been a celebration of a future for her and Cord, the occasion would have been perfect. But she knew that couldn't be, and suddenly her face didn't look so happy anymore. But, no, she should enjoy all the time she had left with Cord and not think about the future, for it would come soon enough and she would be alone again.

Glancing out the window of her bedroom, she could see a long table covered with a red cloth had been set out on the lawn, and food was being carried to it. The smell of roasting meat was strong in the air. Vaqueros were gathering in groups near the table, talking, laughing, and one had brought a guitar and was strumming melancholy tunes. The Apache were riding up from the river, and Cord had just stepped out from the hacienda.

Her breath caught in her throat at the sight of him, for he was dressed as a Spanish grandee, like the time in the bordello in Juárez. Sometimes it was hard to think of him as an Apache renegade, for he was so multifaceted, like a precious jewel. But she had seen the way he lived, on the roam, his possessions on the back of a horse. Not that she disapproved of that, only that there wasn't a place for her in his life when he lived that way.

But here she was trying to turn reality into fantasy, so her dreams could come true. She had told herself she wouldn't do that anymore. She must live with the reality of Cord and herself and put her idea of a fantasy man away.

Clenching her fists, so that her nails bit into her palms, she turned away from the window. She would enjoy tonight, the reality, and not be upset because she couldn't have some fantasy tomorrow. Taking a deep breath, she left her bedroom, determined to have a good time.

She walked through the hacienda, thinking what a beautiful home it was, especially since it had the fine patina of age. She walked down the stairs, then glanced into the courtyard as she passed it. Alicia, looking cool and comfortable in a pale yellow gown of cotton with white lace trim, was just walking out and motioned for her to wait.

"Chaps," Alicia said, joining her, "you look wonderful in your fiesta clothes. Where did you get them?"

"Thank you. You look lovely, too. I got these in Juárez, when Cord and I were down there buying horses."

"How exciting," Alicia responded, linking her arm with Chaps' as they started walking toward the foyer. "I can't wait to hear everything about you and Cord . . . things like where and how you met, where all you have been, how you finally found me. I guess I was just too tired and scared to think to ask before."

"I'll be happy to tell you, and we were all too exhausted to talk much on that long ride. But we can talk later tonight, if you want." Although, secretly, Chaps wasn't sure just how much she could tell Cord's sister.

"That would be great," Alicia agreed enthusiastically, "but for now we had better join the party before Miguel and Cord come looking for us."

"You're right," Chaps agreed, and they stepped out of the hacienda.

The sun was low on the horizon, taking with it the heat of the day, and under the shade of the large cottonwoods in front of the house, it was very comfortable. Alicia and Chaps walked arm in arm to where Cord and Miguel were standing near the end of the table, directing the placement of a large side of beef, which had been cooked to perfection over an open pit.

The table was piled with food from one end to

329

the other, and Chaps immediately began looking it over, seeing what was familiar. There was corn-on-the-cob, beans, chile peppers, baked sweet potatoes, tortillas, tamales, cakes, pies, lemonade and stronger drinks, and several dishes Chaps didn't recognize but planned to try.

"It all looks delicious, Alicia," Chaps said, ready to begin eating.

"Thank you. It would probably look even better if Miguel's mother had been here to supervise, but I think I did a fairly good job."

"I don't know how it could be better."

Alicia laughed. "I am anxious for you to meet Miguel's family. They should be home in a few days."

"I'd like to meet them, too."

"What did you say about my family?" Miguel asked, placing an arm around Alicia's waist and smiling down at her.

"That they would be home soon, and I was anxious for Chaps to meet them."

"A good idea," Miguel agreed, "but a better one right now is to let all these hungry hombres eat their fill."

Chaps glanced around and noticed that vaqueros and Apaches alike looked like they could easily eat everything on the table and ask for more. She smiled, feeling good about being a part of the group. Then her gaze drifted to the end of the table, and her breath caught.

Cord was watching her, and his face mirrored exactly the thought that had just crossed her mind. He wanted her here with him, with his family and friends. She could see it in his eyes, in the way he stood, and then he walked toward her. She had never seen a more possessive man, as if he would never let another man near her, for she belonged to him, forever. And then she shook her head. No, a fantasy. She must remember to deal only in reality.

Then he was by her side, taking her hands and pulling her close enough for her to smell his scent of tobacco and leather. "Seems like I've seen that outfit before." He chuckled.

She smiled. "As I recall, you thought it was very funny."

"I should have known you'd find a perfect place to wear it. I'm just sorry you didn't get the chaps."

Laughing, she lightly punched his arm. "Chaps! That's something I'll never hear the last of." And then her throat tightened, for if she wasn't with Cord, nobody would ever call her Chaps again; and she felt sadder than she could ever have imagined.

"No, you won't," he agreed. "But if you're so hungry you have to look that sad, then it had better be women first right away. Anyway, if you don't get your food first, there won't be enough left to rub two bones together." He chuckled, showing even, white teeth.

She smiled back, feeling her heart pound, thinking that she could happily drown in his eyes, forgetting everything except the two of them. Then he looked away, picking up a plate for her, and the moment was broken. Reality set in, and she glanced at Alicia.

"Come on, Chaps," Alicia said, "our men are going to fill our plates and bring them to us. But let's get our lemonade and two napkins. I think that meat is going to be messy.

"I'm right behind you," Chaps agreed, laughing at Alicia's enthusiasm.

Picking up large glasses of lemonade, they walked over to a cottonwood tree and sat down. Soon, Cord and Miguel brought heaping plates of food, then went back for their own. From a comfortable distance, they watched the vaqueros and Apaches get in line and start piling food on their plates. Slowly the area grew quieter and quieter as men began eating instead of talking.

Cord and Miguel soon came back, balancing huge plates of food and glasses of whiskey. Cord sat down beside Chaps and Miguel beside Alicia, then they were all quiet for a while as they ate, except for Chaps, who frequently exclaimed in delight over one type of food or another which she had never tasted before. Finally, when they could eat no more, Chaps leaned back against Cord, while Miguel lay down and put his head in Alicia's lap.

A vaquero began strumming his guitar, then was joined by another who began a sad song in Spanish. It was beautiful music, and romantic, and Chaps wished the moment could last forever. But she knew she truly didn't fit into this world, or with these people, for she was from far away and she still had a job to do. Of course, she could write anywhere, and it would be a fantasy come true to write in a hacienda.

But for the moment, she enjoyed the blissful evening, watching the contentment of the men around them. She smiled at Black Ears and Shadow Chaser, who looked like they were full for the first time in years. She had made friends, and she wouldn't forsake them, no matter if she had to move on. She could always visit again, and she wanted to go to the Apache reservation. But that could all be done without Cord, even though everything in life would be better with him.

Finally, she sat up and, looking into the distance, forced herself to say, "This is a lovely place, and I've enjoyed being here a great deal, but now that Alicia is safe, I should be moving on. I've got the books to write, and there's the research to do."

Her words were met by stunned silence.

"But Chaps," Alicia objected, "I thought you were going to stay, at least for a little while. The Vincentes will be so disappointed if they don't get to meet you. And I had planned a lot of things for us to do. Oh, Cord, can't you get her to stay awhile. I thought you two—"

"Chaps is going with me to Cordova Rancho tomorrow," Cord said brusquely. "I want to check on it. And I want her to see it. Then we'll talk about where she's going to spend some time. Right, Chaps?"

There was a steely thread in his voice, and Chaps didn't look into his eyes, for she knew the anger she would see there. Strangely, she was glad of his anger, for it meant he cared if she left so soon. And she didn't want to be parted from him yet. If she went to the Cordova Rancho, it would be a good excuse to stay with him longer. She knew she should be stronger and just leave, but she couldn't, not when Cord had sounded like he really cared.

"You're going with me to the ranch, aren't you?" Cord pushed, and gently grasped her chin, turning

333

her head so she would have to look into his eyes.

They were as hard and dark as she had expected; but there was also a light in them, a promise, and she felt an answering response deep within herself. "Yes," she said softly, then louder, "I'd like to see the Cordova Rancho."

"Good," he replied, his eyes never leaving hers.

"Wonderful," Alicia said in relief. "And when you are done there, you can come back here and meet Miguel's family. And, Chaps, don't scare me like that again. You are part of the family now. You tell her it is so, Miguel."

"That is correct," Miguel said, smiling. "And as part of our family, you should not go around making decisions without first discussing it with us, otherwise you might make Alicia cry and nobody wants that."

"That is right," Alicia agreed, tapping Chaps on the arm. "If I cry, I might ruin your gorgeous fiesta outfit."

"And we sure wouldn't want that," Cord added, a touch of humor in his voice.

Everyone laughed, and suddenly Chaps felt light-hearted.

Part Four

Chapter 22

Cord and Chaps spent the next day riding Vincente and Cordova ranch land, for the two ranchos shared a long boundary, with most Vincente land in Arizona Territory and Cordova in New Mexico Territory. Cordova Rancho was south of Silver City, but also contained land on the Gila River and in the mountains to the north, where silver was mined.

Cord had pointed out familiar landmarks, herds of cattle, favorite campsites, and places where he had spent time with his mother, learning Apache ways and history. As Chaps began to see into his childhood, she realized he was more linked to the land and his family then she had understood before. And, once more, she realized she was seeing another side to him, one she liked equally as well as the others.

Around sunset, when the sky was streaked with brilliant rays of red and orange and magenta, they rode between two ancient stone gateposts, the wrought-iron fence gate twisted and listing open, with 'Rancho del Cordova' in wrought-iron grill overhead. Following a dirt road, they continued on toward the Cordova hacienda.

Cord was getting increasingly tense, and as they started up a slight incline, his jaw clenched. Suddenly, on a hill overlooking the land for miles around, appeared a large hacienda. The dying sun cast its light on the right side of the house, illuminating the blackened hulk with red-orange light.

"Damn!" Cord exclaimed. "It looks like it's still on fire."

"Don't look, Cord," Chaps replied, feeling his torment almost as if it were her own. She couldn't believe their timing was so bad, for the right side of the house did look on fire, but at least the majority of the hacienda still appeared intact.

"How can I not look? I've seen it that way in my dreams over and over, but always I arrive in time to save them. If only I hadn't been gone, if only I had been somewhere close by, if only—"

"Cord, there's no point in blaming yourself." Then she hesitated and glanced at him. He was intently watching the hacienda. "Did you find them yourself?"

"Yes. Several days later."

Her stomach churned. What shape had his father and Alicia's mother been in? Were they burned, or maybe wild animals—she refused to think about it. "Were others killed, too?"

"Yes. There had been a fight. Vaqueros near the house had tried to defend the hacienda, but Red Duke's Comancheros were too many and too well prepared. It was a slaughter, but a few escaped, too afraid to come back until I sought them out. Nobody's there now, though. I left it empty."

"It must have been awful, riding up to find the house burned liked that."

338

"This is the first time I've been back since the funeral. I thought it wouldn't be so bad, after time, but I was wrong. I still expect to walk in there and find them all over again. And I suppose I'll always blame myself for not being here to help."

"Cord, what could you have done if you had been here?"

"I would—"

"You would have been overpowered, too, and then who would have been left to save Alicia? Who else but you could have gotten into Red Duke's hideout? Now, you tell me!"

Cord hesitated, watching the hacienda get closer and closer, the sun's rays slowly dying down the blackened side of the house. "I suppose you've got a point, still—"

"You saved Alicia, and I'm sure your father would much rather you be alive right now, having rescued his daughter, than buried with him in the family graveyard."

Cord finally looked at her and smiled slightly. "You have no idea how much you sound like him. He would have said the exact same thing, in just that tone of voice. You're right. That's what he would have wanted. Come on. Let's lay some ghosts to rest."

They rode on up to the hacienda, similar in design to the Vincente house, but with more plants and shrubbery and flowers in front, now untended and many dead for lack of water. The house and lawn already had a wild look, as if nature was swiftly taking it back. Vines had begun to climb up the blackened, broken walls of the right side.

339

"It must have been beautiful once," Chaps said, wanting desperately to comfort Cord, yet not knowing what would really help. "And I'm sure this end of the house could be repaired."

Cord didn't reply. He simply stopped his horse and sat looking at the house. Long moments crept by, then he gazed at Chaps. "Well, the day's not getting any younger. I can't put this off any longer. Let's go inside."

She nodded and quickly swung off her horse before he changed his mind, knowing he needed to face his ghosts. She was so glad she had come with him, unable to imagine him riding back to face all this alone. But he would have done it and been strong enough. She was just glad they could share it, so that she could help to ease the burden.

Cord dismounted, then seemed to step into a dream, for he walked slowly toward the blackened end, seemingly unaware of Chaps. She quickly followed, worried for him. He stepped into the ruins, wood and stone crumbling under his feet, but he didn't seem to notice. Growing more concerned, she approached him, taking his arm. Still, he seemed unaware of her, concentrating entirely on the house around him.

She walked with him, saying nothing, not wanting to interfere, knowing he needed to lay his ghosts to rest. He had rescued his sister. He had stopped the Comancheros. He had stopped Red Duke, needing only to pick him up in Mexico. But there was nothing he could do for his father, or Alicia's mother. They were dead, at Red Duke's hands, and nothing could bring them back . . . no amount of wishing, dreaming, or fantasy. And he had to deal with that. Now.

Cord wandered around the ruins, sunlight turning the blackened walls and floors a bloody red, but he seemed to be seeing something else, something that had been there before, furniture, possessions, people Chaps would never know, because they were gone forever . . . destroyed by Red Duke and his Comancheros.

Then suddenly Cord turned and grasped her, pulling her tightly against him, as if she were his anchor in a shifting world, someone to pull him back to safety from the netherworld that was drawing him down into darkness, deeper and deeper to where his ghosts awaited him.

She held him close, stroking his back. "It's all right, Cord," she said soothingly. "It's all right. You have to let them go. You've done all you can. They know that now. You rescued your sister. You avenged your father and his wife. And you've returned home in triumph. There's nothing more you can do. Nothing."

Suddenly she felt a wetness against her cheek and realized he was crying, probably the first time he had allowed himself to do that since finding his family dead. She was touched by the depth of his emotions and by the fact that he would allow her to witness his vulnerability. She hugged him fiercely, ready to defend him against all odds until he regained his strength. Her heart swelled. How she loved him! She would do anything for him, anything, if only they could remain together always.

But she pushed that thought from her. It was Cord who mattered right now, not her. Cord needed her strength and reassurance. She held him slightly away from her and looked into his eyes wet with tears. Then she kissed his lips gently. "Let's go into another part of the house. We've seen enough here."

He nodded and let her lead him through the ruins, walking from blackened husk to elegant decor, smoke and water damaged, but indicative of what the hacienda must once have been like. It had the patina of age like the Vincente hacienda, and there were still beautiful pieces of furniture in the drawing room, deep blue velvet drapes, hanging askew from the windows, and a silver tea service rifled through, mostly stolen, but still testament to what had once been, and could be again.

She shivered and pulled him onward. It was like seeing old ghosts, and Cord didn't need to see any more of those. She walked into a hall and saw a beautiful curved, mahogany staircase leading upstairs. It was getting dark now, and soon they would need lights, food, and the horses would have to be tended. But Cord came first.

"I used to love coming here," he said softly.

She glanced at his face. There were no longer tears in his eyes, but he was obviously filled with a deep sadness. She needed to do something for him, but what?

"It's a beautiful home, Cord. Did you have a room here?"

"Upstairs."

"Why don't we go up there?"

He smiled and took her hand. Leading her up the stairs, he stopped at the top, looked down once, then turned left. They walked down a hall, past three doors, then he stopped outside the last door on the right. Again, he smiled at her, then opened the door.

They walked into a large room, and he shut the door behind him. Lighting a lamp on a bedside table, he turned to her. She smiled, then glanced around the room. It was very masculine in decor, with dark woods, leather, and burgundy for color. Near the double windows was a comfortable-looking rocking chair with a worn leather back and seat, and beside it a table piled with books.

"I like your room." She turned to him, gesturing toward the large canopy bed with a deep burgundy cover.

"I like having you here." Then he hesitated. "I don't cry often."

"You had every reason to cry."

"I don't want you to think I'm weak."

"How could I after all we've been through? Besides, only a man very sure of himself will cry."

Cord grinned. "I'd feel a lot more sure of myself if you'd make love to me."

She smiled back and gently touched her lips to his. "Are you sure you're up to it?"

"We'll see," he replied, hugging her fiercely. He held her tight for a long moment, as if to let her go meant losing her forever. "I need you," he said against her hair. "You don't know how badly." He captured her lips with his and pushed deep into her mouth with his tongue, ravaging as if he would conquer her through the kiss so that she would be his for always.

Moaning, she was ignited by his touch, his kiss, the smell and feel of him. Warmth flooded her, making her twine her hands around his neck, then run long fingers through his thick black hair, unable to get close enough to him, wanting to consume him, to be consumed by him, wanting to be united with him in the most complete way possible.

"Chaps, love me," he groaned, pulling the pins from her hair so that it fell free, cascading down her back in a fiery mass. He pushed his hands into it, savoring its softness, smelling its sweetness, then dug his fingers into the thickness, capturing her head so that he could plunder her face. He placed soft kisses on her eyes, her nose, her cheeks, then her lips, where he paused, nibbling her lower lip.

When he moved to her ears, teasing the sensitive lobes with his tongue, she shivered against him, running her hands up and down his back, harder and harder until her nails were digging into him, for she needed him more and more, wanted him more and more, loved him more and more.

Suddenly he ended the kiss so that he could look at her, his eyes blazing with passion and need, then he began to pull the clothing from her body. She helped him, anxious to be free of its constraints, wanting desperately to feel his body against hers. Finally, when she stood in nothing but her chemise and drawers, he pulled her hard against him again and massaged her breasts lightly, then roughly as his desire began to flame more brightly.

Moaning, she felt her body grow hot and languid, and she desperately wanted him to slake her desire, to give her the pleasure for which she burned. "Cord, I want you," she whispered, as he leaned down to kiss the tip of each breast, then suckle nipples through the sheer silk of her che-

344

mise.

He picked her up and walked to the bed. Tossing back the burgundy cover, he laid her down, gently, reverently, then kissed her tenderly on the lips. Then he removed the last of her clothes and started on his own. Quickly pulling off his own clothing, he tossed one piece after another until he stood naked before her, dark and bronzed like an ancient Apache chief come to vent his lust on his white conquest.

But she was the conquest of love, not war, and raised her arms up to him, drawing him down, thrilling at the touch of his hard body. Excited by his scent of leather and tobacco, Chaps shivered as he placed soft kisses from one breast to the other, lingering to make the nipples taut and sensitive, creating an ache deep in her center, an ache only he could satisfy.

She pulled him to her, feeling his chest hard and hot against her breasts, and dug her nails into his back, suddenly feeling fierce in her need for him. Drawing him harder against her, she nipped at his ears, then bit them harder, playfully hurting him in her sudden need to exert some control over him, somehow make him hers forever so that they could never be separated again.

They rolled across the bed, playfully fighting, biting, clawing in growing desire. Then he raised her above him, and she straddled him, leaning down so her breasts touched his face. He captured a nipple with his lips, then sucked hard. She moaned, thrusting her fingers into his thick dark hair, as her body began to writhe in an agony of passion.

345

Then he slowly lowered her hips until he was sheathed deep inside her. On the threshold of fulfillment, they hesitated, feeling the ache, the need, the desire to be fully joined, then they trembled as he began to move, thrusting deep into her, building the pace, drawing the passion faster and faster, until they were clinging to each other, riding their crest of desire higher and higher, their mouths clinging to each other, as they delved completely into one another.

Their bodies shuddered, reaching the peak of ecstasy, where they clung together, totally joined, before descending again, clutching each other in the aftermath of bliss.

Panting, Cord lay back and pulled her against his chest. She tasted him, salty, hot and wonderful. Her fantasy man. She sat up and looked at him hard. Yes, Cord was her real fantasy man. But was there any place for her in Cord's life, or any place for him in hers?

He pulled her back down, his breathing beginning to slow. "Don't go so far away," he murmured, stroking her damp hair back from her face. "And thanks."

"I should thank you," she replied, smiling at the sheer pleasure of being in his arms.

"No, I mean I needed you to draw me back, to be with me, to make me want to stay."

"But, Cord, how could you not want to stay here?"

"It's tainted, Chaps. Everywhere I look, I see Red Duke. He raped the place, killed my father here, and Alicia's mother. I don't know how I can go on."

"Cord, those are ghost memories. We'll get rid of them together."

"How?"

"I don't know. I mean. Yes, I know. We'll have a party."

"A party?"

"Alicia sent us plenty of food. We'll set out a picnic downstairs. We'll light all the lamps in the house. And then we'll laugh and sing and dance and make love. Then there won't be any more room in this house for death or unhappiness, only life and laughter."

Cord pulled her to him and kissed her fiercely. "I don't know how I ever got along without you."

She smiled. "We'll just make sure you never can again." Laughing, she stood up.

"Hey, come back. Where are you going?"

"I'm going to light some lamps and get the food. Come on, lazybones. Get up! There's a lot to do."

He grumbled, but kept smiling, and got up. Pulling on his denims, he tossed her his shirt. "That's enough clothes for you, if I let you keep that much on."

Smiling, she slipped into his shirt, loving the scent of him surrounding her.

He led her out of his bedroom, and they went from room to room, throwing open the doors and lighting all the lamps. She didn't know when she had seen such lovely decor or such fine furniture, and she was so glad not all of the house had been burned. The one end could be repaired, and the house would be completely beautiful again. Finally, the upper story of the hacienda glowed with light, pushing back the darkness of the night and laying

347

to rest the sadness of ghosts.

They descended the central staircase, feeling the cool night air coming in from the open, burned part of the hacienda, but when Cord would have entered that area again, she took his hand and pulled him back, leading him into the second drawing room, one that was still in its original condition.

They lit lamps, revealing a beautiful room decorated in shades of blue, with delicate Queen Anne furniture upholstered in deep blue velvet and blue rose tapestry. Chaps was enchanted with the exquisite decor of the room and smiled delightedly at Cord.

"My lord," she mimicked royalty, "would you care for tea?"

"My dear, I'm afraid the service has been stolen," he replied, just as seriously.

She burst out laughing and leaned against him for support.

"If you're so weak, I think we'd better feed you," Cord suggested, laughing.

"Oh, and the poor horses, just standing out there waiting, hungry, thirsty, while we've been inside . . . well, they really have been missing out, haven't they?" Chaps laughed harder than ever.

"I think you've been in my company too long. You'd never have said something like that when you first met me."

"Probably not. But then I hadn't lived till I met you."

"Do you mean that?" He was suddenly serious.

She smiled coquettishly at him, then tapped him on the arm. "See to the horses, sir, and I'll tell you

348

when you get back."

"Already giving orders," he accused, then kissed the tip of her nose. "But I'll give some, too. While I take care of the horses, I'd like you to bring in the saddlebags and set out dinner."

"Agreed."

She followed Cord outside into the darkness, then looked up at the house. She shook her head in amazement, for the hacienda appeared strange. A fourth of it, a black,hulking shape, reached upward into the night, while the other part was glowing with soft lantern light, as if a family was at home expecting guests.

Cord stopped, put an arm around her waist, and looked up at the house, too. "You were right, Chaps. That light makes a lot of difference. I'm glad we lit the lamps." Then he kissed her quickly and began piling saddlebags into her arms. "Now, hurry up and take those inside so we can get our party started."

"Yes, sir."

Laughing, she walked back toward the house as he led the horses around back to the stables. Inside, she returned to the blue parlor, glanced around, and decided to set out the food Alicia had sent with them on a low table between two velvet blue settees. Fortunately, Alicia had included a tablecloth and napkins, so it would be easy to protect the furniture while they were eating. As she opened containers of food from the feast the night before, she grew hungrier and hungrier, for the aroma was reminding her of all the delicious new foods she had discovered.

Taking a small bite of this and that, she waited

for Cord to return. But soon she grew anxious and stood up to walk around the parlor, for she had become a little nervous in the large house all by herself. Then she shook her head. If she wasn't careful she was going to let her imagination run away with her, and she would be seeing ghosts in all the corners and behind the doors. There was nothing to fear in the hacienda, and that was that.

Glancing around, she saw Cord walk in, and she shivered. He had been so quiet she hadn't heard him, but that was his Apache blood, for there was nothing ghostly about him—and nothing ghostly in the house, either.

He smiled, then walked over to a table and picked up a small, gilded box. He looked at it for a moment, then opened the lid, and a tinkling waltz began to play. Setting the music box back on the table, he held out his arms.

"Would you care to dance, Miss Victoria Malone?"

"That's Chaps to you, sir," she replied, laughing, then walked over to him.

He kicked back an expensive, imported rug, and she stepped close so he could take her in his arms. They began to dance slowly, sensuously, lovingly around the room. Chaps thrilled to be in his arms, so pleased that she could look directly into his dark eyes as they danced, and she knew without a doubt that they were perfect for each other.

Then she realized how well he was dancing and blinked in confusion. He danced like a Spanish grandee, not an Apache warrior. Who was this man really? And then she answered that herself. He was her fantasy man, so why should she be surprised that he could do everything, be anything, and do it all superbly. After all, could her fantasy man be anything less?

Smiling, she waltzed around the room with him, until the music box finished its tune, then stopped. Stillness filled the house, and Cord looked around, his eyes slightly haunted again.

"Cord, you must remember the good times. Think how much they would have wanted you to go on, to be happy. You know your father would have wanted that."

"There's something I want to show you, Chaps."

He took her hand and abruptly led her from the room and down a hall where they hadn't been before to the back of the house. He threw open the door to a dark room, then lit several lamps. Stepping back, he gestured around the room. "This is my favorite room in the house. My father and I spent a lot of time together here."

She walked into the room, glancing around and around in wonder. It was a large library, the walls completely lined with books from floor to ceiling. A heavy oak desk dominated the room, with a leather chair behind it. Papers and pen and ink littered the top of the desk, beside several books with open pages held down by paper weights. A large, leather couch occupied the wall across from the desk, and books were stacked on it, as if someone had been pursuing a subject when interrupted.

"Chaps, I've got to tell you that I'm not what you think I am. You probably won't want me after I tell you, but I've got to take the chance, for you're going to find out sooner or later. I know you wanted an exciting man, one who takes

351

chances . . . more like an Apache warrior. But, Chaps, I'm more than that. I like to read, to write, to spend time in here thinking, working. I can't always be on the warpath."

She looked at him and laughed.

"Damn! You don't have to be insulting about it. Okay, I might as well tell you the worst of it. I went to my father's university in Mexico City. I have a degree, and as my father got older, I traveled for him, handling his business in Mexico, wherever he didn't want to go. I was gone most of the time, and that's why Red Duke really didn't know I existed. Of course, I stayed out of the main family life, because of my birth, but that didn't mean I was any less a part of the family."

"But Cord—"

"And that's not all. Red Duke was really far off the mark. Alicia was never going to inherit the Cordova Rancho, because she and Miguel have been betrothed since they were children. I'm a Spanish grandee now, heir to all this, and it'll tie me down. I won't be able to roam much, or hunt with my Apache brothers, and I guess you'll hate that."

Chaps laughed again, utterly amazed that he could have so mistaken her desires, but then maybe she had given Cord cause to believe as he did.

"Would you stop that damn laughter. I feel like a big enough fool as it is. If you hadn't gotten so far under my skin, I wouldn't be standing here now, apologizing for inheriting land and money, or for being able to waltz, or—"

"Cord, please—"

"I even like art. There's so much I'd like to share

352

with you in Mexico City, but I suppose you'd always be looking for a handsome bandito."

"I don't want a bandito."

"You'd better not, because I have no intention of ever letting you look at another man."

"I don't want to look at another man."

"And if I hear you say Red Duke again, I'll—what did you say?"

"I want you. Only you."

"Chaps!" He stepped toward her, but suddenly the sound of a loud gunshot rang out. A look of pain crossed Cord's face, and he clutched his side. Looking confused, he took a step toward her, stumbled, then fell to his knees. Taking away his hands, he held them out, looked at them, then glanced up at her frowning, for his hands were covered in his own blood.

"Cord!" she screamed and ran toward him as he collapsed against the carpet, his blood staining the fabric red.

Chapter 23

"Stop, Victoria," Red Duke said, stepping into the room from the hallway. He cocked the Colt .45 he had trained on her chest.

She hesitated, trembling, her arms still outstretched toward Cord, who lay still against the carpet, his face pale. "Cord?" she whispered, feeling her whole body begin to shake. She dropped to her knees. "Cord!"

"Shut up!" Red Duke commanded. "And don't move again. Cord's dead, but that was a nice little story he told. If I'd known it sooner, he'd have been the one I killed first. But now he's dead, and I've got you."

Chaps inched toward Cord, unable to stop the trembling that had seized her whole body. Dead? Cord dead? It couldn't be; and yet he lay so still, so white, and there was so much blood on the carpet, on his chest. She shivered, drawing his shirt more closely around her. Dead? No!

"I said don't move. Pretty boy's dead. Now all you've got is me. And we're going for a ride."

Dead? It must be true. Cord wasn't moving. And there was so much blood. "Cord?"

"Shut up, and listen to me. We're getting out of

here, and I don't want you moaning all the way. Now get up."

"You . . . you can't just leave him like this. The place is open. Wild animals, or—"

"That's right. Wild animals, maybe buzzards, are going to tear his flesh clean from his bones. When we come back there won't be anything left to clean up."

She felt sick and clutched her stomach. "Go ahead, just kill me. It doesn't matter now."

"Sure it does. I've got what I want. You're going to give me the kids I need, and Alicia is going to get me the land. Maybe I'll even get Vincente Rancho, too."

"You can't get away with this, any of it."

"Nobody's going to stop me. Everybody thinks I'm dead or dying in Mexico. Right?"

"Yes," she replied weakly, still watching Cord for any sign of life. But he lay still, so very still.

"Just what I wanted you to think. But I'm not pleased about my eye, not pleased at all."

She looked at Red Duke for the first time. He was wearing a black patch over his left eye, his face was still mottled red, his hair was wild and unkempt, and a stubble of beard covered his face. His clothes were dirty, bloody and smelled. He was wearing two ammunition belts crossed over his chest, one holding bullets for his .45 and the other with bullets for his rifle. In his left hand he clutched a coiled whip.

"Don't like what you see, do you? No matter. No image to keep up now. Just you and me, and Alicia later. You owe me, Miss Victoria, and you're going to pay and pay good. But first we're going to get out of here. Wrap up that food you put on the table and get dressed."

"I'm not going anywhere with you."

"Sure you are, or how else are you going to revenge your lover?"

Chaps' eyes narrowed. He knew just how to make her obey, but she didn't care, for he was right. If she made him kill her, she couldn't warn Alicia, or avenge Cord, or anything. No, she would have to go along with him, until she could escape or kill him.

Looking down at Cord's still body, she wanted desperately to throw herself against him and cry and try to call him back. But Red Duke wouldn't let her near him, and there was no bringing him back anyway. He had joined his father now. For Alicia's sake, she must hold her grief inside, stay calm, and keep her mind clear. Somehow, she must beat Red Duke again.

"Good," he said. "I see you made the right choice, but don't move until you toss that thing on your finger over here. I'm not going to lose another eye to one of your tricks. Lucky for me I know a doctor who'll work for me any time, any place, and never say a word. He said it was a little bullet you shot me with."

Reluctantly, she took off the ring and tossed it to him. Keeping an eye on her and the .45 pointed, he reached down and picked up her gun ring, slipping it into a pocket. "I'll look at that later, when I've got you all nice and trussed up. Right now, you're going to dress for me and pack up some food, then we're going to get your horse and get out of here."

She took one last look at Cord. Tears stung her

356

eyes, and she bit her lower lip. No, she wouldn't cry in front of Red Duke. She wouldn't give him that satisfaction. In fact, she wouldn't cry at all, not until Cord was avenged and Alicia was safe. Then she would shed her tears and feel her loss. Resolutely she stood up and stepped toward Red Duke.

"Stop."

She obeyed.

"That's right, Miss Victoria. You better get used to doing what I say and nothing but what I say real quick, 'cause that's the way it's going to be. Any other way, and I may have to start cutting off little parts of you, parts that won't matter to you birthing babies."

Shuddering, she nodded in agreement.

He smiled, a cruel twist of his lips. "Another thing, as soon as we get clear of this place and back up in the mountains, I'm going to make use of that fine body of yours, and I'm going to make you regret ever having let a dirty Injun touch you."

"You're not ever going to touch me," she said, hatred in her voice.

He grinned. "You'll be begging me." He slapped the whip against his leg in warning. "Now, where're your clothes? I'm not going to cart you back into the mountains like that. You'd be torn to pieces, and if you get hurt, I want to do the hurting."

She shuddered, but let no expression cross her face. "Upstairs."

"Let's go. You lead the way, but no funny stuff."

Taking one last look at Cord, she felt her heart catch at the sight of his still body, then she led the way out of the library. Red Duke followed her,

357

cautious, alert and quiet. She walked back to the foyer, then turned toward the stairs.

"Wait."

She stopped.

"The food's in there."

"But we left our clothes upstairs."

"I see, in the bedroom." His face darkened. "Dirty Injun lover. I'll make you pay for that." He slapped the whip against his thigh again.

She started up the stairs, and he followed. When they reached the top, she hesitated, hating to lead Red Duke into Cord's bedroom, hating to take Red Duke to where she and Cord had last made love, but what else could she do? Revenge was what counted now. Later she could mourn her memories.

"Down here," she said, pointing in the direction of Cord's room.

"Okay, but don't try to get away, 'cause I'll shoot you if I have to."

"I believe you."

She walked quickly down the hall, wanting it over with, but when she came to the open door to Cord's room and started to step inside, she hesitated and felt tears sting her eyes. No. How could she take Red Duke in there to spoil what she had shared with Cord? She couldn't. She just couldn't.

"What are you waiting for?" He pushed the nose of the pistol against her back.

She took a deep breath. "I just wanted to make sure you were behind me."

"If I ain't behind you, I'll be in front of you, that's how close I'm sticking to you."

She entered the bedroom and almost cried, for it was filled with memories of Cord, with his love,

358

his laughter, so much of him here, so much of him lost. But she mustn't think about the loss, or she would never be able to go on. She glanced around for her clothes. They were scattered everywhere. She quickly began scooping them up, touching Cord's briefly whenever she came to them.

"You two were in a hurry, weren't you?" Red Duke remarked, sitting down on the bed and stroking the soft burgundy cover with his leather whip.

She didn't respond, but was keenly aware of his eyes watching her, looking at the room, imagining how it had been between her and Cord. She hated it, hated Red Duke for thinking about them, wondering about them. She wanted to scream, to cry, anything to release the emotions that were threatening to overcome her.

Instead, she coldly, calmly finished picking up her clothes, then realized he would expect her to dress in front of him. She couldn't do it. She simply could not let Red Duke see her naked again. It was an impossibility.

"Would you please leave while I dress," she said between gritted teeth.

He threw back his head and laughed, a great guffawing sound. "Get dressed, or I'll be over to help you."

She knew he meant what he said. She would just have to do it, but she would put him out of her mind. He didn't exist. He wasn't in the room. She turned her back and pulled her drawers on under Cord's big shirt.

"No fair," Red Duke complained. "Turn around and get that big shirt off."

She ignored him.

359

"That's an order." He slammed the whip down on the bed.

Turning around, she slowly unbuttoned the shirt then pulled it off. His eyes turned greedy as they studied her breasts, and she felt like a slave at auction. Quickly, she pulled on her chemise, then donned her red cotton shirt. Finally, she slipped on her leather skirt and felt a little more protected. Then she began pulling on her boots.

"You're going to have fine little brats, Victoria. We'll have beautiful daughters and handsome sons, and they'll have brains, too. They'll need them to run the empire I'm going to build. So just put that Injun from your mind and plan on keeping me happy. Now, come on over here."

She felt sick and couldn't move toward him . . . simply could not move a muscle.

"Come here, Miss Victoria, or I'm going to have to punish you, and you don't want that right before a long ride."

Clenching her fists, she drove her nails into her palms, the pain helping her to move. She had to obey him if she had any hope of avenging Cord and saving Alicia. She took one step, then another, until finally she stood before Red Duke, desperately trying to control her fury.

"He took you right here on this bed, didn't he?"

She didn't reply.

"Didn't he?!"

"Yes."

"Then, I'll punish you every night until you prove he didn't plant his seed in you. If he did, I'll have to kill you off, or the baby."

She shuddered.

360

"That's only right, isn't it?" He stroked her thigh with the handle of the whip. "Right?"

"Yes, if that's what you say."

"That's what I say, but there's not time tonight. We've got to get going."

She backed away, relieved he hadn't touched her.

Getting up, he suddenly snapped the whip full length, then viciously beat the bedcovers with it over and over, until they were sliced to ribbons. Then he looked at her. "There. That's what I'd do to your Injun if he were still alive."

Her eyes widened, and she backed up another step.

"Let's go."

She turned and hurried out of the bedroom, chills running up and down her spine. In the hall, she desperately turned her mind to something else and thought of all the lamps burning in the house. The safest thing to do was turn them out, but she knew Red Duke wouldn't let them take the time. Besides, she didn't want to leave Cord in the dark. He had wanted light to chase away the ghosts, he had wanted a party, and at least they had had a dance.

Again, the tears started to come, but she blinked them back and started down the staircase. No, she wouldn't cry now, not until Red Duke had gotten what he deserved. At the bottom of the stairs, she turned toward the blue parlor. Then stopped. Somehow, she hated to take the food from Cord. Even though he wouldn't need it again, it had still been his party and his food.

"Get going. I want that food." Red Duke poked her in the back with his Colt.

She moved toward the parlor as if in a dream. She would have to do as he said, but maybe she could leave a little food anyway. She hesitated at the open door. "I'll be right back."

"Okay, but hurry." Red Duke stopped, and started looking around, listening, obviously anxious to be away.

She could hardly believe her luck, but realized that Red Duke had wanted to stay out there to keep a better watch on the place. She quickly began gathering the food, but she left some of it on a napkin, which she put on the floor so Red Duke wouldn't see it. She even left a canteen of water there, too, thinking she was being foolish, but somehow comforted that Cord had light and food and water for his trip to the other side, and that suited his Apache heritage.

Joining Red Duke, she held out the food for him to inspect. He nodded in approval, then motioned for her to precede him out the front door. She stepped outside, but was immediately struck by how drastically things had changed since she and Cord had come out earlier. Now there was no happiness, no joy, no anticipation except revenge.

Red Duke's huge black stallion waited patiently, snorting at their appearance. He patted the animal's neck. "Okay, Victoria, get up on his back. I'll take you around to the stables, and we'll get you saddled. Then nobody can catch us."

"I can walk." She didn't want to be close to him, and certainly not with him holding her on the back of his horse.

"I won't tell you again. You obey or else."

"All right," she agreed, trying to sound meek,

but feeling more angry all the time.

While he pushed the food into a saddlebag, she mounted, glad of her height, for the horse was huge. He mounted behind her, then pulled her against his hard body, jabbing the nose of the .45 into her ribs. As he guided the stallion behind the house, she could hardly stand the stench of him, shuddering at his touch and hardly daring to breathe for fear the .45 would go off.

When they came to the stables, he got down and waited for her. She joined him, and they went inside. He motioned toward the saddles, but made no move to help her. Instead, he kept the Colt trained on her while she put a bridle, then a saddle on her mount.

The horse was still tired from the long day's trip, and she hated to ride it again so soon, but she had no choice. Perhaps Red Duke's stallion was tired, too, and they wouldn't go far without resting. But she didn't really believe that. Red Duke was merciless on animals as well as people.

For the next three days he proved that, driving them relentlessly onward, first across the grasslands of the Cordova Rancho, then past the outskirts of Silver City, on into the Mimbres Mountains, then finally back into the Black Range.

For entertainment on the long trail, he teased her, tormenting her, goading her, trying to force her into giving him an excuse to punish her with his whip. Not that he needed an excuse, but he liked to make a game of it, a game only he could win. Finally she decided he wouldn't hurt her because he feared slowing them down. It was only after they arrived at wherever he was pushing them

363

that she would really have to fear for her safety, for then he would have no reason not to hurt her.

She desperately tried to find a way to escape during the long, hard three days of travel, but he was careful, keeping her tied at night, and her wrists tied during the day. He was taking no chances, and she was unable to escape. By the time they were back in the Black Range, she was beginning to fear she might not be able to help herself, much less Alicia. And yet, somehow she must.

It was at dusk on the third day when they arrived back at the old hideout. She shivered as she was assailed with poignant memories, and thought of throwing coffee in Red Duke's face and of Alicia with rags in her boots. Those memories should have made her smile, but with Cord gone and Red Duke in control, she could think of no reason to ever smile again.

"You remember this place, don't you, Victoria?" Red Duke asked, motioning for her to precede him into the cavern.

She hesitated, for it was dark in there, really black, the cavern's dark depths hidden from the light of the stars and the moon.

"Get in there. I'll light a lantern inside."

Urging her horse forward, it stopped just inside the entrance. Red Duke rode around her, got off his stallion, then lit a lantern he must have had hidden near the opening. Glancing up at her, he said, "I could take you back in the cave and leave you tied up, Victoria. You could scream until you died, and nobody would ever hear you."

"Why don't you do it, then? What would I care?"

His eyes narrowed. "Don't tempt me. You aren't that brave. Besides, it would be a waste. Get down. I've got to pick up something, and I don't want you running off."

With her hands tied together, she had difficulty getting off her mount, but finally managed. As soon as she set foot on the hard stone floor, he grabbed her arm and, with the lantern in his other hand, hurried her into the cavern.

With only one tiny lantern lighting the huge cavern, the place was eerie. As they continued to walk, she realized that everything seemed to be much like she had last seen it. So, Red Duke had planned to come back. He had never intended to abandon his hideout, never dreamed they could actually get away. She was surprised he hadn't left a guard. But now, with his Comancheros dead or in custody, he had returned. But for what? Money? Gold? Food?

He hurried her, seeming almost to know his way without needing the lantern's light. He must have used the place for many years, he knew it so well. Still, it was almost as if he was a creature of the dark rather than of the day.

Finally, he came to his royal blue tent and thrust her inside, following. Pushing her down to the pillows, he lit two other lamps in the tent. She glanced around, resting while she could, and felt the strangeness of the place now that it was empty. How long would it take before all of this crumbled away, leaving Red Duke's legacy nothing more than dust?

She shook her head, realizing that she was allowing herself too many flights into fantasy. She had to stay grounded in reality if she had any chance of escape and revenge. Yet, it was all so strange, so unreal that she had trouble believing it was happening, no matter that her mind kept telling her it was real.

Still, she couldn't help expecting to see Cord suddenly come striding up, ready to help her escape as he had before.

Stopping her thoughts cold, she knew she couldn't let herself believe that. The pain of his death was bad enough that to keep conjuring him into the living would only make her situation worse. She had to think of Alicia and of herself. Cord had to become a memory, no matter that he seemed more alive now than ever before, especially here where they had braved Red Duke in his own den and stolen Alicia from him.

Looking at Red Duke, she saw him bent over the trunk, rummaging around in it. He frequently stopped and looked at her in warning. But she knew better than to run at this point. He was too much bigger, too much faster, and he knew the cavern too well. The last thing she wanted was to be left here alone and bound.

Finally, he pulled out a small piece of red silk wrapped around something small. Then he slammed the lid of the trunk and actually smiled at her. He knelt by her side and slowly unrolled the silk until lying in his palm was a single military medal.

"That belonged to my grandfather. My mother gave it to me. It proves I have royal blood. This was only worn by royalty, and someday I'll have that proved legally. But for now, it's the most precious thing I own. And the only thing of importance in this cavern." He reverently rewrapped the medal, then put it deep into his trouser pocket. "You should feel honored I showed it to you. I wouldn't have if you weren't going to bear my children."

He stood up, and she did, too, almost feeling sorry for him. Then she shook her head. No, she couldn't let him make her feel that way. She had to have no pity, no matter his past, no matter that he had a mother, or a grandfather, or a military medal of some sort. Red Duke was still Red Duke, a vicious murderer. And she was still going to get revenge.

Turning out the two lamps, they walked out of the royal blue tent and wound their way around the smaller tents. She noticed that items of clothing were scattered here and there: a hat, a boot, a sock. The Comancheros had obviously left in a hurry, but with the intention of coming back, and soon.

Red Duke led them back to their horses, where he stopped and looked at her. "You didn't ruin this for me. It was time to move on. It had served its purpose. Still, I didn't like the way it ended, and you're going to pay for that, too."

"Seems I have a lot to pay for, Duke. Why don't you just go ahead and kill me?"

"That'd be too easy. I want to see you suffer." He gave her a long look from his right eye, and she had no doubt he meant what he said. "Mount up."

She didn't wait for him to ask twice, for she wanted to be as far away from the cavern hideout

367

as she could get. It was filled with bad memories, and she was afraid he might leave her there forever, just as Alicia was almost left, in the dark, hurt and alone.

They rode out, and Red Duke turned north, heading higher into the mountains. Chaps looked back the way they had come. Would there be anybody to rescue her now that Cord was dead? Would Miguel and Alicia stop by the Cordova Rancho to check on them when they didn't show up in a few days? How long would it take for anybody to notice they were missing and come and check? And then what would they decide had happened? Like Red Duke had said, everybody thought he was in Mexico.

Except Alicia. Somehow Alicia would know, and she would be able to lead them back to the hideout. They could bring a force of vaqueros, maybe the military. Red Duke couldn't stand against all of that. But how would they find her now that he was taking her into unknown land? Then she thought of Black Ears. The Apache would help, and they could track better than anyone. They could find her. But would they find her in time?

She shivered. It was dark now. They should have stopped to rest the horses and wait for day when they could see better. It was treacherous trying to climb the narrow trail at night, and they could go careening over the side at any moment, but somehow she didn't fear it this time like she had before. Then she had been worried about Cord, and now she no longer had that worry. Besides, Red Duke seemed to be charmed, and she didn't have much doubt they would arrive at wherever he was taking them, no matter the danger.

But sometime Red Duke's luck had to run out, and when it did, she planned to be there . . . not that she had much choice of leaving yet. But she would get him someway, somehow, and soon, whether or not anybody came to rescue her. And she had better depend on herself, for it would be a while before anybody realized she was missing, and then it was a long way back into the Black Range.

They continued on, following a trail that became less visible all the time, until finally Red Duke's stallion was pushing past bushes and piñon trees that clung tenaciously to the edge of a cliff. She could hear rocks rattling over the edge, but she never heard them hit bottom.

If it had been dangerous before, it was getting increasingly so with each passing moment, and even with the moon shedding light on them, the path was still not lit nearly enough. Besides, the horses were exhausted and were beginning to stumble. With her hands tied, if she went over the side, she would have little chance of catching herself and stopping the fall.

She shivered, then suddenly smiled. Maybe it would be Red Duke who fell, then she would be free to find her way back down the mountain. At one time she wouldn't have thought she was capable of that, but now she knew different. She would get down one way or another, and then she would . . . what? With Cord gone, nothing seemed to matter much anymore. But she would go to Alicia and tell her what had happened. Then perhaps she would stay awhile, for being near Cord's sister would be the closest she could ever come to him again.

How she hated that thought, not of Alicia, but of Cord being lost to her forever. And it still seemed impossible to believe. If she hadn't seen him lying so white and still on the library floor, she wouldn't have believed it possible. But she had seen him, and just after she had discovered that if ever her fantasy man lived and breathed, he was Cord Cordova, for Cord was everything she could want in a man, a man to share all her dreams, all her visions, all her life.

She felt the tears come again and fought them down. She would not let herself cry, not here, not now, not until Red Duke had paid for his crimes and Alicia was safe. Then she would cry, then she would mourn, but not yet, not when she had to be strong and tears would only weaken her.

They rode farther into the Black Range, and she began to fear nobody could ever find her, or that she could ever find her way out. She quickly put a halt to those thoughts. She had to depend on herself; she had to have the confidence she could win, even against Red Duke. She had done it before, and she would do it again.

Suddenly Red Duke turned his stallion off the path, then pushed through some bushes and came out on another trail, this one wider but rough, as if it hadn't been used in a long time. He glanced back to make sure she followed, then continued onward.

She looked back and saw the bushes close behind them. Her heart sank. She should be able to find her way out if she watched closely enough; but unless someone was a very good tracker, this place would be harder to find than the cavern hideout, and that had been almost impossible to locate without help. Shaking her head, she tried to dispel her growing concern in her ability to save herself and Alicia, for Red Duke seemed to have an endless number of ways to protect himself.

Winding her way behind Red Duke, she passed bushes, trees, cacti and discarded mining equipment, and kept following, winding downward, then upward, but moving steadily. She began to recognize the area as an old mining outfit that looked abandoned. It would be dangerous if one didn't know their way around, and there could be any number of hiding places. She shivered, trying to memorize her way in, but knowing it would look quite different by daylight than by moonlight.

Finally, he stopped and motioned her forward. Pulling out his Colt .45, he pointed it at her.

She moved up beside him, wondering what new game he was playing.

"This is an abandoned mine. We're going down into an empty shaft now. I want you to stay right behind me. Don't let your horse step anywhere except right after mine. And don't try to get away. I don't want you hurt or killed just yet." Then he started forward.

She hated to follow him, but she did, taking one last look at the moonlight before following him into the dark, dank tunnel.

Chapter 24

A few hours later, Chaps was lying on her side, hogtied, her arms pulled behind her, her feet drawn up and tied to her hands. She was hurting from the strained position and was cold, lying against the damp, slick earth of the mine shaft. She also knew that if Red Duke kept her like this long, she would be sick from the damp and cold, and her body would be so stiff and sore from her position that it would be nearly impossible to escape. But maybe that was what he had in mind.

He had taken care of the horses after he had tied her up, taking off the saddles, blankets and saddlebags, and leaving them inside while he took the horses above to rub them down, then feed and water them. He had brought the animals back inside and stabled them nearby in another part of the mine, so from the outside it would be impossible to tell that they were all down there in the dangerous, abandoned mine shaft.

She called the place dangerous, because in the time it had taken them to ride down into the area he had chosen to use as a camp, there had been several small earth slides. She had never felt the kind of nervousness in the huge cavern that she had known since entering the mine shaft. Even though the shaft was stabilized with wooden beams, the wood was obviously old and rotting, for the mine looked like it had been abandoned for some time.

She had to admit it was a good place for a hideout, for who would come looking here? She shivered, as another chill raced through her, then a small spattering of earth fell loose and rattled down the wall, splattering her. She shook her head, tossing it away, but still the taste of dirt and the feel of grit in her mouth remained.

From somewhere she could hear the dripping of water, a constant, annoying sound that set her nerves even more on edge. But, at the moment, what angered her most was the fact that Red Duke was eating with great gusto the food Alicia had sent with them, and if he kept it up, there wasn't going to be any left for her or for the next day. But maybe he wasn't planning on having to feed her the next day.

No, she wasn't going to think that. He kept insisting he was going to use her to found a dynasty. She had never met a person so obsessed with building an empire before, but she supposed there were plenty of people around with that ambition. Red Duke had simply tried to do it the quick and relatively easy way, despite the cost to others. She shivered, knowing she had to get away from him soon.

But how? She couldn't be in a worse position. At least he hadn't gagged her, and she would use her voice if it was all she had. He surely wouldn't want to damage the future mother of his children. Anyway, he should take as good care of her as he had the horses.

"Duke," she began, coughing.

He glanced up, wiping the back of his hand across his mouth, smearing the grease into the stubble of beard. "What?"

"I'm cold and hungry and in pain."

"I'm glad."

"You're treating the horses better than me."

"They deserve it. You hurt me."

"I was just trying to get away."

"And you let that Injun use your body."

"You didn't want me."

He looked up, eyed her thoughtfully, then set down a piece of beef. "I wanted to do the right thing by you. I thought that's the kind of woman you were."

"No, you wanted to torment me."

He grinned. "Yes, and I did."

"That's right. You did."

"But it won't be that way now. I'll just use you, because your body is still good."

"But I don't understand why you're so insistent on having me as the mother of your children, or of having the Cordova lands."

"And the Vincente lands, and more if I can get them. Then they won't call me Duke for nothing."

"But how can you get that land?"

"I thought I told you. I'll marry Alicia, one way or another, then get rid of her. Remember, now that her brother is dead, she'll inherit it all. As her husband, I would inherit it all. And, don't forget I'll be marrying into that old name. That's important out here. It's the only way to get in with the old families."

"But why do you need that?"

"I want my children to have the best, to be the best, but I want them to have my heritage, and yours too. I've given it a lot of thought. It's the only way to get the land. Those Spanish don't sell. And it's the only way to be one of the landed gentry."

"But couldn't you buy land somewhere else?"

"I've got gold, so I could. But I want this land, and I want it now."

"Look, what if Alicia just signed the Cordova land over to you?"

"I still wouldn't have married into one of the families. I want that for my children. And I'll have it, too."

"But what about Miguel Vincente?"

"Oh, I'll kill him, or maybe I'll let Alicia marry him first, get his land, then marry her and get it all."

"What about his family?"

"Apaches or banditos can get them."

"You seem to have an answer for everything."

"Yes, I do, and it was all going just right till you showed up. I can't decide if you're here to test me or to help me. But if you don't help me more soon, I'm going to give up on you, no matter how you look."

"Could I see the medal again?"

"No."

"Do you know what it's for?"

"My mother told me it's to remind me that I'm not like anybody else, that I'm special, that my people have always been special, and that I should do something with my life, not just grub around till I'm old and broke."

"I see," she replied quietly, trying not to feel any sympathy for him. Maybe his mother had tried to help him better his life, but he had chosen to become an outlaw; he had chosen to hurt others and to try and take what they had. She couldn't feel any sympathy for him. She had to escape any way she could, or he might kill her at any moment.

"No, you don't. You've always had it good, just like those Cordovas and Vincentes. Well, I'm going to have it good, too."

Then he pulled up several planks in the floor and lifted out a large bag. By the way he handled it, Chaps could tell it was heavy. He untied the cord holding it shut, then pulled open the bag. Digging both his hands into it, he lifted them up, then let the contents, gleaming gold coins, spill downward.

"That's gold!"

"Yes." He grinned. "You could do a lot worse than me, Miss Victoria. A whole lot worse. Maybe now you'll start trying to be good to me, instead of hurting me all the time."

"I'd like to try. Would you untie me and let me eat? I can't go anywhere. It's dark outside. I don't have a lantern, and you're staying by that one. I'd get lost without you. Besides, if I get sick, I won't be able to have children."

He considered her words, slowly sifting gold coins through his large hands, the action seeming to soothe him. Finally, he smiled and glanced up. "All right, I wouldn't want the mother of my dynasty to get sick, would I?"

She didn't know if he was mocking her, or was

serious. She didn't care, either, as long as she could get loose and get some circulation and warmth back in her body. Also, she was hungry and needed to eat if she was going to keep up her strength to escape.

Walking over to her, he knelt and quickly untied her, tossing the rope to one side. He returned to the money, tied it up, then hid it again. "You never saw that gold, did you, Victoria?"

"No. I just want some food."

"Go ahead and eat."

Starting to eat the leftovers, she watched him, realizing that he was slipping more and more into his fantasies. Whatever his original plans and goals, he wasn't changing or adapting to what was happening in his life. He was determined to bind reality to his dreams, and it wasn't working, although he didn't seem to realize it, or simply wouldn't acknowledge it, or couldn't. Whatever the case, he wasn't adapting to the changing world around him.

If he had all that money, why hadn't he secretly come here, picked it up, then taken it across the border? He could have lived like a king, or duke, in Mexico the rest of his life. But that hadn't been in his plans, and to do that would have required building new dreams. He didn't want that. He wanted his original fantasy, or none at all.

His attitude was scary and made her realize that she hadn't gone nearly as far in her desire for a fantasy man as he had in his fantasy of life. No, she hadn't gone nearly as far as him, and she had known the difference when confronted with facts that simply didn't fit the fantasy. But he was determined to force his dreams on the world, and it was not going to work. It couldn't.

In the future she was determined to spin her fantasy into her novels, knowing that maybe once in a lifetime a true fantasy man came along, a man who fulfilled all one's dreams, making them real forever. Cord Cordova had been her fantasy man, and always would be. He might not live in her life, but he would live in her books as her hero.

Tears stung her eyes, and for a moment she couldn't swallow. Then she stopped herself. She had to remember to be strong. She had to escape Red Duke. She had to stop him, stop his fantasy, or many more people were going to be hurt or dead.

She finished eating, hardly tasting it, then glanced at Red Duke. He was looking at her, and there was a heat in his eyes that hadn't been there before. She moved away slightly, but he continued to watch her.

"If the baby had dark hair, we could kill it," he said thoughtfully.

Horrified, she backed farther away from him. "You said you would wait."

"I've already waited a long time. Why should I wait any longer? You're mine. I've got plenty of gold. My plan will get me the Cordova and Vincente ranchos, and a fine family heritage. I've got everything I want. I'm going to reward myself with you."

"Wait. You need to wait." Her mind was whirling, but she could think of no argument that would change the growing lust in his eyes. "No. It's not right."

He no longer seemed to hear her. He reached for her, grabbing her arms and pulling her toward him. She screamed, and then, aware of how futile that gesture was, she stopped to save her strength. Instead, she tried to fight him, but suddenly realized just how big and powerful he was, for she remembered seeing him in his blue tent, wearing very little.

"You want me." He nodded his head, smiling.

"No. This isn't right."

"I'll show you my medal."

"No."

He laughed. "I didn't say which medal."

"Red Duke, you don't want to do this."

"Yes, I do." He lunged for her.

They struggled, and she kicked out, hitting him with her boots and striking him with her fists as they rolled over and over, until suddenly she saw a shadow and glanced up.

"Cord!" A wild joy rushed through her, and she wanted desperately to run to him.

Red Duke ignored her words and pinned her down. With Chaps at his mercy, he jerked up her skirt, exposing her legs, then fondled her breasts. Breathing hard, he leaned down to kiss her lips.

There was a gleam of silver as Cord pulled out his Apache dagger, then sent it spinning through the air. Red Duke gave a groan of pain, looked confused a moment, then let go of Chaps as he looked around. He saw Cord and bellowed in rage. He tried to jerk the knife from his back, but couldn't reach it. Standing, he charged Cord, and they went down together, fighting, each desperate to get the upper hand.

But they were both wounded and bleeding more and more the longer they fought, each struggling to gain control, for they were both growing weaker by the moment. They were fairly equal opponents, and neither could seem to win over the other.

Chaps watched them, desperately wanting to help Cord, but not knowing what to do. Surely Red Duke would collapse at any moment from the knife wound; but he struggled on, and she began to fear for Cord, since Red Duke was the bigger man. Besides, Cord had to have lost a lot of blood in getting to her. She had to do something quick, but what?

Then she noticed Cord was wearing his Colt .45 and wondered why he hadn't tried to use it. Perhaps he couldn't get to it, or had forgotten it in the intensity of the fight. Feeling secure in the mine shaft, Red Duke had put his Colt and rifle on a beam above their heads, high enough that she couldn't reach them while he slept. She could see him angling for his guns now, and if he got one, Cord would be a dead man.

Lunging toward them, she grabbed Cord's .45 and jerked it out of the holster, then fell back, cocked the pistol and waited for her chance. But the men were constantly in motion, and she was afraid of hitting Cord. Still, she had to do something, for Cord was weakening fast, but Red Duke was too, his shirt now wet with his own blood.

Red Duke suddenly reached upward for his guns, and Chaps knew she couldn't wait any longer. She aimed carefully, then pulled the trigger. She hit Red Duke square in the middle of his chest. He grabbed the wound, looked at her in surprise, staggered toward her, then collapsed.

Cord checked the pulse in Red Duke's neck, then glanced at Chaps. "He's dead. We've got to get out of here. The sound of that .45 is going to—"

Suddenly there was a loud rumbling sound, and the whole shaft shook. The horses neighed in alarm.

"That's why I didn't use my pistol," Cord hurriedly explained. "This whole place is going to collapse."

"The horses!" Chaps exclaimed.

"I'll get them. You get out of here fast."

"No. You don't know where they are."

She ran toward the horses, while the mine shook and dirt began to fall. She tried to keep it out of her eyes, but the rain of dirt seemed to get steadily worse. Cord followed her, and as they reached the horses, a beam fell, striking her. She almost fell, but he caught her, steadying her; then he took the stallion's reins, while she caught the mustang's.

Leading the horses, they hurried back, but another beam fell, hitting the floor and filling the area with a cloud of dust. They choked, coughing. Frightened, the horses tried to bolt, but they held them steady. Cord grabbed the lantern and began leading the way outside.

"Hurry, Chaps!" he called over his shoulder.

"But, Cord, there's gold."

"Forget it. Let Red Duke take it with him to his grave."

She followed him, holding her hand up to ward off the falling dirt and debris, trying to keep her mustang from panic. She inhaled more dust and coughed. Her eyes burned, she could hardly see, but still she kept going, feeling the mine shaft shake and begin to give way beneath her. Afraid they might not make it, she hurried as fast as she could, only able to see a dim light up ahead where Cord was leading.

Then the whole shaft shook violently. She lost her footing and fell. The mustang neighed and shied, but she held on. Just as she started to get to her feet again, the shaft shook violently once more. This time, strong arms lifted her to her feet and pulled her and the mustang quickly from the mine shaft.

Outside, she inhaled deeply, then coughed, choking on the dust and dirt in her lungs. Suddenly there was a loud crash, the mine shuddered, and it collapsed in on itself, spewing out dust and debris.

Cord pulled her back, holding her tightly as they watched the mine completely cave in. Then they looked at each other, both covered in dirt, bleeding from numerous cuts, and smiled.

"I thought I'd never see you again," Chaps said, her eyes misting with tears of joy as she gently touched his face. "What happened? I thought you were dead."

"No. The bullet grazed my side, but bled enough to look worse than it was. I pretended to be dead, because I knew if I moved I would be and you'd be worse off. I hated to let you think I was dead, Chaps, but it was the only way to save you."

"It's all right now, but at the time . . . oh, I don't want to think about it. All I care is that you're here, we're together, and—"

"Red Duke's dead and buried."

"Along with his gold," she added.

"Too bad we couldn't have returned it to the people he stole it from."

"Yes, but it's all gone now."

"That's right." He hesitated, then gently kissed her lips. "Thanks for leaving the food and water. How did you know I'd need it?"

"I didn't. It just seemed right, an Apache thing to do."

"It was right in a lot of ways. Chaps, I don't want to be separated from you again. If you'll write your books at the ranch, I'll get you anything you need. Pens, paper, ink, special books, Apaches."

She laughed. "Would that be Black Ears?"

"Yes. But I'm very serious. I love you. I'll help you any way I can, even do research for you. I just want you to marry me and live on the Cordova Rancho with me, at least when Alicia hasn't got you at the Vincente Rancho. Will you say yes?"

"Oh, Cord, yes. I can't think of anything I'd like better than to spend my life with my fantasy man."

"That's a tall order for me to live up to, isn't it?"

"No taller than a sea nymph."

They laughed together, then kissed.

Smiling, they clasped hands, then leading their horses, started walking toward the sunrise, knowing their future was built on dreams but planted in the reality of their love.

LOVE'S BRIGHTEST STARS SHINE
WITH ZEBRA BOOKS!

CATALINA'S CARESS   (2202, $3.95)
by Sylvie F. Sommerfield

Catalina Carrington was determined to buy her riverboat back from the handsome gambler who'd beaten her brother at cards. But when dashing Marc Copeland named his price—three days as his mistress—Catalina swore she'd never meet his terms . . . even as she imagined the rapture a night in his arms would bring!

BELOVED EMBRACE   (2135, $3.95)
by Cassie Edwards

Leana Rutherford was terrified when the ship carrying her family from New York to Texas was attacked by savage pirates. But when she gazed upon the bold sea-bandit Brandon Seton, Leana longed to share the ecstasy she was sure sure his passionate caress would ignite!

ELUSIVE SWAN   (2061, $3.95)
by Sylvie F. Sommerfield

Just one glance from the handsome stranger in the dockside tavern in boisterous St. Augustine made Arianne tremble with excitement. But the innocent young woman was already running from one man . . . and no matter how fiercely the flames of desire burned within her, Arianne dared not submit to another!

SAVAGE PARADISE   (1985, $3.95)
by Cassie Edwards

Marianna Fowler detested the desolate wilderness of the unsettled Montana Territory. But once the hot-blooded Chippewa brave Lone Hawk saved her life, the spirited young beauty wished never to leave, longing to experience the fire of the handsome warrior's passionate embrace!

MOONLIT MAGIC   (1941, $3.95)
by Sylvie F. Sommerfield

When she found the slick railroad negotiator Trace Cord trespassing on her property and bathing in her river, innocent Jenny Graham could barely contain her rage. But when she saw how the setting sun gilded Trace's magnificent physique, Jenny's seething fury was transformed into burning desire!

Available wherever paperbacks are sold, or order direct from the Publisher. Send cover price plus 50¢ per copy for mailing and handling to Zebra Books, Dept. 2612, 475 Park Avenue South, New York, N.Y. 10016. Residents of New York, New Jersey and Pennsylvania must include sales tax. DO NOT SEND CASH.